I0536712

FATTY PATTY

A James Bay Novel

KATHLEEN IRENE PATERKA

DEDICATION

For my husband Steve, the love of my life. My biggest supporter and champion, Steve has been there with me through it all: the good and the bad, the fat and the thin. Every woman should be so blessed to have such a man beside her. He has always encouraged me to go for my dreams.

Steve tells me every day that I am the most beautiful woman in the world. Some days, I actually believe him.

.

ACKNOWLEDGMENTS

So many people helped in the creation of this book. Heartfelt thanks to them all.

Jenna Mindel and Christine Elizabeth Johnson, simply the best critique partners and friends an author could hope to have. Thank you both for holding my hand and never letting go. I have been so blessed by your friendship and support. The Queen of Hearts Club rocks!

Catherine Chant, with her fine eye for detail and love for the written word that expresses itself in truly amazing ways. Many thanks for pointing out so many inconsistencies in the storyline.

The Writing Buddies Group... Christine, Connie, Jenna and Karen, for providing such wonderful insight, pointing out redundancies and continually asking *"Why would she do that?"*

Edie Ramer, Amy Atwell and Dale Meyer for their tremendous support, consistent encouragement and excellent advice about the world of indie-publication. Ladies, you are the best!

Roxanne St. Claire, a forever friend continually cheering me on from the sidelines and ever reminding me to be tough, brave, persistent...and to never, never quit.

The ladies of GIAMx1. An author could never find a better group of cheerleaders.

Anne Victory, who graciously took on the task of editing a tasteless manuscript and helped refine it into a scrumptious story; Rae Monet, for providing such a sweet tempting cover; and Amy Eye, the Queen of

Formatting! The Kanine brothers: Jim and Bill. Jim was so accommodating and helpful in sharing his passion for coaching and basketball. Bill provided valuable assistance with answers for an author who is totally clueless when it comes to the world of accounting and finance.

My beta readers, Virginia Conlon, Martha Gasparovich, Natalie Weber, and Peggy Kusina. Their feedback of the original manuscript was invaluable and I am most grateful.

Abigail Paterka Carter: daughter, friend and my favorite teacher in the whole wide world.

And last, but not least, to all the *FATTY PATTYs* out there—women and men alike—who deal with the daily struggle of being overweight. This book is for you. I tipped the scales at over 9 lbs when I was born. A chubby baby, a chunky little girl, I eventually exploded into a fat teenager who never had a date, never went to her high school prom, and never thought a boy would ever want to kiss her, let alone marry her. No one but another overweight person understands the pain of what it is like to live in a society which worships the concept of *thin is beautiful*. If I can leave you with one truth, it is this: remember you are not alone. Surround yourself with people who care and let them be your mirror. Believe in yourself and go forward to live your dreams because **YOU ARE WORTH IT!**

CHAPTER ONE

Brand new school year. Brand new body. Brand new me.

That's what I love about starting a new diet. The world seems bright and shiny, and I'm filled with happy hope. Anything is possible.

Like swimming twenty laps in James Bay's community pool. Losing thirty pounds before Christmas. Finally winning that contest.

Patty Perreault, Teacher of the Year.

I've got the smarts, I just don't have the body. And I never will—especially if I don't let go of the smooth tiled railing and start swimming soon. So long, contest. Hello, loser. Not to mention, that new mantra of mine will need some revising.

Brand new school year. Same old body. Same old me.

"Brrr." Priscilla dips one foot in the water, then quickly pulls it out. "Sorry, Patty, I just can't do it. You know I love you dearly, but the water is so cold, and—"

"Don't worry about it." I sidle alongside her, hugging the pool edge. God bless Priscilla. My fraternal twin would probably jump in the deep end if she thought it would help, but I'm not going to force her to endure this torture, too. Tiny and frail since the day we were born, she could stand to put on a few pounds. Plus, Priscilla's a worse swimmer than me. If she jumps in, the pimply-faced teenage lifeguard will probably end up having to rescue us both.

"But I feel so bad, just sitting here like this. After all, I promised to keep you company and give you moral support, remember?" Goose bumps pop up on her thin arms as she reaches for her towel, then she suddenly brightens. "I've got an idea. How about you swim and I count off your laps? That way you won't have to keep track in your head."

"Sounds good." I yank at the too-tight bathing suit creeping up my rear end. If I plan to keep up this swimming-laps routine, I might have to break down and buy a new one. This ugly pink suit has seen too many summers and too many cookies. I'm pretty sure the James Bay School Board of Education would not approve of one of their teachers being arrested for indecent exposure.

Plus, I doubt a criminal record would be helpful in winning that contest. I'm a good teacher; my evaluations plus the fact my fellow teachers keep nominating me prove it. So why haven't I won yet? I'm a quick learner, but this one has had me stymied. Four years worth of stymied. But not anymore, because I've finally figured it out: if I change the way I look, I know I'll win the contest.

And I am *determined* to win that contest.

"Okay, I'm ready." Priscilla's blue eyes shimmer like the pool water. "Whenever you are."

I grip the edge tighter, suddenly finding it hard to let go. There's twelve feet of water swirling below me. What if I sink? Is that lifeguard properly trained? I taught him in fifth grade, and he never was very good in school. How did he do in Phys Ed? Is he any good at saving people's lives? I don't want it to be my life that puts him to the test.

"Patty? What's wrong?"

"Nothing. I'm thinking."

"Well, quit thinking and start swimming. How do you expect to finish if you never start?"

Easy for her to say, perched warm and dry, draped in a thick terry towel at the edge of the pool. I love my sister to death, but when it comes to dieting, exercise and food, she doesn't get it and she never will. They say twins have a psychic connection, and Priscilla and I have always been a team. We had our own secret language when we were small, and to this day still have this weird, uncanny ability to sense each other's thoughts. But when it comes to the way we look, we might as well be strangers, because the only thing that ties us together identically is our height. We are both short enough that we always ended up together in the front row during school musicals when we were little kids. But we're all grown up now and Priscilla, a thin delicate beauty, wears *short* well. On me, these extra thirty pounds make it look like I'm wearing an inner tube.

"Patty?"

"Okay, okay, I heard you. I'll do it." There's no use arguing with her. She's got my best interest at heart... plus a fiercely determined if-Patty-doesn't-start-swimming-soon-I'm-going-to-jump-in-that-water-myself look in her eyes. I finally let go of the slippery rail, sink below the surface, and start paddling toward the shallow end.

"One!" The faint shout of my twin's voice echoes through the water.

Great, just what I need. Priscilla keeping score, just like she measures and tracks our food, courtesy of that little diet scale she recently bought for our kitchen counter. Whatever possessed me to tell her I'd started another diet?

Because I know she loves me. Priscilla's always been my champion and she only wants to help. And at this point, I'll take all the help I can get. I don't think

I've got it in me to sit through another year of being nominated, endure another round of interviews, only to eventually lose out as Bay County Teacher of The Year. With the grand prize only one thousand dollars, it's not even like I'm in it for the money—though I've got to admit I wouldn't mind having my hands on that kind of cash. But after four years as a semifinalist-ultimate-loser, it's now a matter of personal pride—especially after last year's fiasco when I lost out to the ditzy third grade teacher everyone thought was so cute. So while it's not officially a popularity contest, who you know and what you look like are definitely part of the deal.

And if that's the case, I'll do whatever it takes. Schmooze whoever I can through the nomination process. Starve myself eating carrot sticks. Exercise by swimming laps.

And listen to whatever Priscilla tells me. She's not a teacher and doesn't need to lose weight. But when it comes to the looks department, there's no contest. Priscilla wins.

"I'm so proud of you," she says as I finally make it back into the deep end. "How many laps are you planning to swim today?"

"Twenty." I swipe the water stinging my eyes, gulp deep breaths, and hang on for dear life. Twenty laps? Dear God, what was I thinking? I'll drown before the day is done.

"You can do it, Patty." Her voice is as warm and bubbly as the nearby hot tub. "That's only eighteen more."

Only? I block out an overwhelming urge to yank my twin into the pool. No doubt some of her perkiness will dissolve in twelve feet of water. "I don't think I can do it."

"Oh, yes, you can. If anyone can, Patty, it's you." There's not an ounce of fat on Priscilla's body or smugness in her voice. "Why, look at that man over there. I'll bet he could do eighteen laps in no time. Just look at him go."

I follow her nod across the room. The pool is empty, save for us and the lifeguard, plus the guy two lanes over. He's big and bulky, with strong even strokes despite how heavy he is. He cuts through the water like a fish, taking the lane in easy rhythm, then—flip! With a furious splash, he slips under the water, turns, and races back down the length of the pool.

Damn. Why can't I swim like that?

Priscilla cocks her head, eyes him for a moment. "He's wearing goggles. Maybe you should buy yourself a pair."

"I don't need goggles."

"But—"

"No goggles," I say firmly. "They're just one more thing I can't afford. Besides, they won't help me swim any faster."

Still, I can't help wondering. Could goggles help? I slip another peek at the swimmer. The guy is fast. Really fast, despite his size. A flash of neon whips through the water as he nears the end of the lane.

"They can't cost that much. Look, he's headed our way. Let's ask him." Priscilla lifts an arm.

"No, don't!" I make a grab to stop her, but, as usual, I'm too late.

"Hello!" She waves him down as he comes up for air.

"Are you nuts? Stop that," I hiss. "What do you think you're doing?"

Priscilla blinks. "Trying to help. I thought you wanted advice."

"Well, I don't. And even if I did, I certainly wouldn't ask some guy wearing..." I squint, sneak a better look as he grabs the pool edge. Gaudy neon plastic covers his eyes. "From some guy wearing purple goggles."

"What's wrong with purple? I think they're cute."

"Maybe on a five-year-old," I mutter.

He steadies himself with a beefy hand. "Something wrong, ladies?" His voice hangs cool in the humid air and the look he shoots me isn't much warmer.

Oh, God, did he hear what I said?

"We were admiring your goggles." Priscilla flashes him a smile that lights up the pool. "Patty's not much of a swimmer and I was telling her maybe she should get herself a pair. What do you think? Would goggles help?"

"I suppose that would depend on the color." He yanks the goggles from his face and splashes them through the water. "Then again, your friend looks a little older than five."

Me and my big mouth. When will I learn to keep it shut? I cling to the edge when suddenly my hand slips and I sink like a stone, ending up with a mouth full of water.

A burly hand grabs me. "Whoa."

I sputter and cling tight, gasping and coughing as he thumps my back a few times. His arms around me feel like a big safety net.

"You okay?"

"I'm fine," I choke, though my self-esteem is plenty soggy.

Priscilla kneels at pool side. "Patty, for God's sake, what are you doing?"

I have no clue. I finally quit coughing, but it's hard to catch my breath. Brawny shoulders keep me upright, and his arms hold me close. His face is round and ruddy, and he's older than me, maybe mid-thirties. Neatly trimmed moustache. Nice eyes, especially without all that purple plastic hiding them. Soft brown eyes. Eyes that smile.

Not that he's smiling. And I don't blame him. I'd be mad at me, too.

One corner of his mouth turns up. "A five-year-old, hmm?"

"Sorry," I say quietly. "Sometimes I talk way too much."

"No problem." His smile widens. "Goggles might not be a bad idea. They add lots of chemicals to this water. My eyes get irritated if I swim without them."

I nod toward his lane. "We were watching. You're good." Especially for someone so big. It's hard to tell since we're both in deep water, but I'd bet a week's paycheck he could stand to lose at least fifty or maybe even seventy pounds.

"Swimming's a great workout." He swishes his goggles through the water, snaps them in place, covering up those soft brown eyes. "Sorry, ladies, I don't want to lose my stride."

He ducks under the lane dividers, then heads down the length of the pool, picking up his former rhythm in merely a few strokes.

"You should move into the next lane," Priscilla urges. "The two of you could race."

"Get real," I mutter, watching him. "I'll never be able to swim like that." He's already reached the far end of the lane while here I am still languishing at poolside like a beached whale. This whole losing-weight-by-swimming isn't going to be as easy as I thought. I felt so righteous yesterday, plunking down money to buy a pass at our little town's community pool. Money I can't afford. Money swirling down the drain if I don't get moving.

Brand new school year. Brand new body. Brand new me.

"Come on, Patty, I know you can do it."

Good thing Priscilla has faith in me because suddenly I'm not so sure. Is there something wrong with me? I'm lousy when it comes to money and math. Maybe the other teachers have it all wrong, nominating me year after year. Maybe the final panel of judges knows something I don't. Maybe I don't deserve that award.

Do I really look that bad?

"Patty, you've got to stay focused. You're so good at everything you do. Just keep your mind on that, and I know you can do this. You can't quit now."

Priscilla's right. If I quit now, I'll be nursing another heartache at this year's award ceremony.

Maybe, if I concentrate on the three P's—Professional, Polished, Perfect—and never let my eyes slip from the prize, maybe, *just maybe*, I'll come out the winner.

"Okay, start counting." With one last yank at the bottom of my suit, I slip back under the water.

# # #

Four laps later, my body refuses to go another inch, and I call it quits for the day. Every muscle—muscles I didn't realize I had—ache as I wade up the gentle incline of the handicap ramp. Thank God school doesn't start for another two weeks. That gives me fourteen days to get myself in gear.

Priscilla halts at the door to the shower area. "I don't think I need to bother. I never even got in the pool."

I reek of chlorine. "Meet you outside. Promise I won't be long."

"That's what you always say. I'll wait in the car." Priscilla starts for the women's locker room and I head for the shower. Our small northern Michigan summer resort community of James Bay is renowned for its beautiful beaches, but personally I've always thought Lake Michigan way too chilly for my tastes. And while the upper stratosphere of elite residents are wealthy enough to indulge their up-north style with vacation homes, private pools, and facilities at the James Bay Yacht Club, locals like me are lucky to have this community pool. I fling my towel on a hook, flick on the water, and soap up, welcoming the feel of the hot stinging needles hitting my body. Despite my time in the pool, I still feel grubby. I spent the afternoon at school on my knees, unpacking textbooks. Last I heard, they still haven't hired a replacement for the other fifth-grade teacher and I've been doing all the prep work by myself. Hopefully the school board will get their act together and hire someone soon. I might be gunning for the grand prize, but there's no way even Teacher of the Year can be expected to handle a class of fifty kids all by herself.

The shower room is big and wide. Cool blue tiles line the walls and there's room enough for ten women. But whoever designed the place forgot the shower curtains. I lather bubbles on my arms and legs, and swish them across my bathing suit. I'm alone now, but that doesn't mean some skinny little thing who wears a size four won't waltz in here at any moment. I'm not taking a chance and showering in the nude. Bad enough being forced to share a dressing room with women like that. Showering naked in front of them with no curtain to hide behind would be the ultimate in humiliation.

It's hard enough facing myself in the mirror every day.

If only Priscilla and I were identical twins. Either God has quite the sense of humor or our guardian angels took a vacation the day we were born. Priscilla weighed in at barely two pounds and was whisked off to the neonatal unit to be coddled by nurses who cooed over the precious baby with raven black hair and delicate features. Meanwhile, I came squalling into the world, tipping the scales at a healthy seven pounds with a hearty set of lungs and orangey-red curls. The hospital sprung me after four days while Priscilla didn't come home for another two months. Except for the time I spent away at college, we've been together all these years.

Thirty years, to be exact. You'd think the two of us would be settled down by now, happily married, with families of our own. We're settled down, all right… just me and Priscilla, rambling around together in the big old pink Victorian Mama left us—a shabby house with rotting windows, ancient plumbing and a habit of draining our joint checking account. If life's supposed to be a journey, I'd much rather be zooming down a freshly paved highway than bumping through potholes like we've been doing the past couple years. Maybe I need to buy us a GPS. If I could convince Priscilla to sell the house, that GPS could steer us straight down the road to a brand new condo.

Then again, who am I kidding? Priscilla refuses to consider selling… and she's not exactly the condo type.

Take care of your sister, Patty. She'll never be healthy and strong like you. Mama's voice dances in my head.

Poor Priscilla. Allergic to everything, she's always been a homebody. She swears she's content working from home at her job transcribing medical reports, but I'm not buying. Being cooped up like she is with only the occasional trip to the mall or weekly visit to the grocery store would drive me nuts. Plus, with her looks, Priscilla could have her pick of any man. But how's he supposed to find her if she stays home all the time?

And if he doesn't find her, I'll be doomed to living out my life in that pink monstrosity of a house we call home. I'll never convince her to sell.

I wiggle out of my wet bathing suit and into my favorite t-shirt. It's loose and comfortable, unlike the snug blue shorts pinching around my waist. Another summer gone, another few pounds found. Whatever possessed Priscilla to bake all those cookies? She knows better than to listen when I beg.

I jam my gear in an old school bag and head out into the empty lobby. The unmanned counter has a display of swimming goggles under glass. I crouch closer for a better look. Maybe Priscilla is right. If I plan on getting serious about this exercise routine, I should plan on getting serious about the equipment, too. Besides, how much can goggles cost? Five dollars? Ten?

"Decide to buy a pair?"

I glance up and see goggle-guy himself strolling up to the counter, gym bag in hand.

"I'm debating." My knees creak and I try not to wince as I struggle to stand. People my age shouldn't be this out of shape. "Payday isn't until next week."

He's taller than I expected but the extra inches around his middle are no surprise. Doesn't he realize he'd be seriously attractive if he lost some weight? Crisp white shirt and tailored pants. Brown hair, still wet from the pool, tending to curls. Dark brown moustache framing his mouth. And those warm brown eyes. A woman could get lost in those eyes.

He drops his locker key in a plastic tub on the counter. "If you're worried about money, you could probably pick up a cheap pair at the sporting goods store downtown."

"I'll think about it."

"Just thought I'd mention it." His gaze sweeps slowly across my body, then finally returns to meet my eyes. "I don't remember seeing you around here before."

Good God, did he just give me the once-over? I feel the hot flush shoot up my face as I struggle not to tug at my waistband. Whatever possessed me to go out in public wearing these shorts?

"I just started swimming laps," I stammer. "Today's my first day."

"Sam Curtis." He sticks out a hand. "And you're Patty, right?"

"Patty Perreault." The firm, smooth touch of his hand is a surprise. Do men use hand lotion? I sneak a peek at his left hand. No wedding ring. "How did you know my name?"

"Your friend." He glances around the lobby. "Did she already leave?"

I'm not surprised he noticed. Priscilla's looks attract men the same way hot fudge sundaes make dieters drool. Why should Sam Curtis be any different? Overweight or not, he's still a man.

"Priscilla is my sister and she's waiting in the car." I tug my hand out of his. "I have to go."

Sam grins. "Worried she'll get mad and drive away without you?"

The thought of Priscilla leaving in a huff makes me laugh out loud. "I don't think so. Besides, it's my car, and I've got the keys." I jingle them with a smile.

He leans one elbow against the counter. "So... you're going to start swimming laps. Coming back tomorrow?"

Tomorrow? Ouch. Climbing out of bed is going to be torture. Every part of my body already aches, down to and including my toes. "I don't know," I hedge. "Maybe."

"I'm usually here every afternoon at five. Early mornings tend to be pretty crowded. I like having a lane to myself."

"Are you in training?" I eye him carefully. Sam doesn't look like an Olympian, but you never know.

"Me? I'm no health nut." He gives an easy laugh. "I just like to swim. How about you?"

"I'm not sure."

"About what? The training part or the swimming part?"

"Both, I guess," I surrender with a grin. "Mind if I ask you a question?"

"Shoot." He shifts his weight against the counter.

"How many laps did you swim today?"

"Fifty."

My heart skips a few beats. I barely managed six; I can't imagine doing fifty.

"I've got a dinner meeting tonight, so I cut my workout short. Normally I average about one mile."

"You swim a mile every day?" I think about the informational sign posted near the pool's edge and quickly do the math. "That's eighty laps."

"Don't let it scare you. It sounds harder than it is."

"If you say so." I hear the doubt creep in my voice. Eighty laps is a lot of swimming back and forth. Maybe I should save myself the grief and give up right now.

He studies me for a moment, like he's weighing whether I'm serious or not. "I'll let you in on a little secret. Don't think about the bigger picture. Try taking it one lap at a time."

One lap at a time? Who does he think he's kidding?

Sam grabs his gym bag. "I've got to get going or I'll be late. Maybe I'll see you tomorrow. And by the way, in case you do decide to buy a pair…" He nods at the goggles in the display case as he starts for the door. "The pink ones get my vote. They match your bathing suit."

I stand there with my mouth open, watching as he strides out the door. Someone—a man!—noticed this ugly pink suit? No doubt about it. I'm definitely shopping for a new one tomorrow. Damn the cost.

A pretty blond teenager strolls out of the office. "Need some help?"

"No thanks, I'm just looking."

She shrugs, and turns back toward the office. I take in her clinging t-shirt and tight shorts. With that kind of body, she probably swims one hundred laps a day. I could never look like that.

And I never will, if I don't try.

"Wait. I've changed my mind." I point through the glass. "I need some goggles."

"Which color?" Her hand hovers over the array.

"The blue ones, please." I count out the money and hand it over. Forget that crazy idea of Sam's. Whoever heard of color-coordinating goggles with a bathing suit? At least the blue ones match my eyes. And as for that ugly old pink suit? Headed straight into the trash, as soon as I get home.

Two minutes later I bounce out the door with swimming gear in one hand and a small plastic bag containing a twenty-dollar pair of goggles in the other.

Priscilla eyes me as I open the door. "I was beginning to wonder if you fell in the pool."

"Sorry. I didn't mean to take so long." I throw my gear in the backseat, snap my seatbelt, and start the car. Fading sunlight in my rearview mirror glints against a steel-blue Jeep as it backs out of a narrow parking space. Talk about inspiration. A big sturdy car for a big sturdy guy. I return Sam's wave as he drives past us.

Priscilla stares. "Was that the man with the goggles?"

"His name is Sam." I shoot her a fast smile as we head down the driveway. "Sam Curtis. I bumped into him in the lobby and we started talking about goggles. And guess what? I bought myself a pair."

This time Priscilla is the one who smiles. "And they're purple, right?"

"You'll have to wait and see."

"I thought you said they were too expensive," she teases.

"A girl's got a right to change her mind."

"I don't think it was the girl who changed her mind. Sounds like the man did it for her." She settles back in her seat with a curious smile. "I like him, Patty. He seems nice."

I swing into traffic, my mind spinning along with the wheels of my tires. Sam Curtis *is* nice. What more could you ask for? He's attractive, easy to talk to. He's even the right age. The more I think about it, Sam might just be perfect.

Perfect for Priscilla.

Well, maybe *perfect* isn't the right word. He'd be perfect if only he wasn't...

The F-word eludes me. How can I call him that? I know how much it hurts when I notice people noticing my own extra pounds. I refuse to use the F-word about myself and I won't use it about him.

If only Sam wasn't so... hefty.

"Are you coming back tomorrow?" Priscilla asks.

"You bet I am."

"Good for you, Patty. I'm proud of you."

I'm proud of me, too. I can do this. Sam can spout off all he wants about swimming being fun, but this is serious business as far as I'm concerned. The contest nominations open up in November and I'm determined to lose this extra weight. Two pounds a week? I can do that. Maybe even three. Four, if I'm lucky. And who knows? I might even give Sam's crazy theory about *one lap at a time* a try. A good teacher is open to different methods and uses what works. Plus, I'm nowhere near as overweight as Sam. He might be able to swim laps around me today, but give me a few months and I'll blow him out of the water. I've got a goal: thirty pounds, eighty laps, and a grand prize waiting at the end of the lane.

Patty Perreault. Teacher of the Year.

Brand new school year. Brand new body. Brand new me.

CHAPTER TWO

James Bay is an up-north dream. Sprawled along the shore of Lake Michigan, the bay curves inward to provide yachts, sailboats and swimmers a natural shelter from the storms. Its pristine beaches are perfect for swimming and summertime picnics. The town itself boasts a year-round population of three thousand, which easily swells to nearly twenty thousand on any given day during the ten weeks of summer. With the auto factories shut down for their annual two-week retooling for new car lines, downstaters flood our little town, anxious to escape the heat of the city. They fill our hotels, shop the upscale stores the locals can't afford and dine at restaurants offering gourmet cuisine. Gourmet cuisine? Not at our house. Especially not tonight.

Tuna salad? *Yechh.*

Priscilla's dinner concoction—tuna, celery and dill pickle chunks on a bed of lettuce with tomatoes circling the plate—is meant as a dieter's delight. But tuna is tuna, no matter how you dress it up. I'd much rather be eating something tasty, like a grilled Reuben sandwich stacked high with corned beef, smothered in melting cheese, dripping with sauce…

"I know tuna isn't one of your favorites." Priscilla's voice wafts across the kitchen table. "But I made it with a yogurt dressing, so there's hardly any fat. And the best part is, it's only three hundred and fifty calories per serving."

"Really." I stare at the tuna and then at my sister. Poor Priscilla. She's much too excited about this fishy subject. I definitely need to figure out a way to get her out of the house more often.

"And you don't have to worry about the calories, either, because I weighed both our portions. Aren't you glad I bought that little diet scale?"

Her face glows and suddenly I'm ashamed. If memory serves correctly, Priscilla doesn't care much for tuna, either, but she's not complaining. Not to mention she doesn't need to measure her food—or lose weight, either. She's so thin, she could use a few Reuben sandwiches.

I poke my fork through the cold salad, force down another bite, and wash it down with a swig of ice tea. "It's good."

She beams. "I'm glad you like it. It was on sale, so I bought a whole case. I read somewhere that tuna is a great source of protein. Plus, we're saving money on our food budget. It's a win-win, all around."

"Wonderful," I mutter. Win-win? I think about the contest and choke down more tuna.

"I'll go online tomorrow and find some tasty tuna recipes."

For a minute I think about telling her not to bother, for she'll only be looking for something that doesn't exist. And I'm in big trouble if Priscilla plans on adding tuna as a regular staple to our dinner menu. Even diet Jello tastes better than this.

"How did things go at school today? Have they hired another fifth-grade teacher yet?"

"If they did, nobody bothered to tell me." I drain my ice tea in a long gulp. "Maybe I'll hear something at the staff meeting tomorrow."

"They'll find someone soon."

"They'd better. I can't have fifty kids crammed in my classroom."

"Patty, you are such a worry wart. Every one of those kids would be lucky to have you as a teacher."

"I won't feel lucky until the James Bay School Board has someone's signature on a contract." I push away my plate.

Priscilla stares. "You hardly ate anything."

"I'm not hungry." I hate lying to her, but it's safer than admitting the truth. She's trying so hard and I don't want to crush her spirits. Although I'd love to crush that case of tuna stored in the pantry.

But I am not going to sabotage myself this time. Today is the second day of my new diet and exercise plan. *Brand new school year. Brand new body. Brand new me.* And brand new goggles, too. I tried them out today after school, as well as Sam's theory. *One lap at a time.* Who would have thought it would actually work? I managed ten laps before I finally gave up and quit.

I prop my elbows on the worn kitchen table, watching as Priscilla stacks the plates and silverware and squirts pink dish soap into the sink. Doing dishes is a tiresome chore and one I'm sick of. "I wonder how much a dishwasher costs?"

"More than we can afford."

"They can't be that expensive." I wrap my toes around the thin rungs of the chair that's been my seat since childhood. The wood is smooth under my feet, worn from years of constant use and Priscilla's dust rag. But the chair legs wobble if I push too hard and the back rung is loose. I need to get some super glue. Or maybe a new chair.

Better yet, a new life.

The chair squeaks in protest as I shove it aside and join her at the sink.

"What's wrong, Patty?" Her hands swish efficiently through the hot, soapy water as she washes the glasses, then moves on to the plates. "You don't seem yourself tonight."

"I'm okay." I grab a dish towel and start drying. No use moping about it, and Priscilla doesn't deserve to get stuck doing all the work herself. "Just a little moody, I guess."

But moody isn't the word for it. I'm sick of doing dishes by hand, of living paycheck to paycheck, of scrimping to get by. If things don't improve in the next few months, I might even have to suck it up and take on a second job during summer vacation.

I grab another glass, swipe it dry. "Sometimes it doesn't seem fair. Why us? I mean, other people can afford dishwashers. They don't have to live this way."

Her hands stop midstream in soap suds. "What's wrong with the way we live?"

"For God's sake, Priscilla, do you have to ask? Open your eyes and take a look." I snap my dishtowel at the high-ceilinged kitchen. The cupboards, so old they're back in vogue, could probably get by with a new coat of paint… but the rest of the room, with worn linoleum floors and old countertops with permanent stains, is in desperate need of a make-over.

Just like the rest of the house.

Just like me.

"This place is falling apart," I mutter.

"That's not true," she shoots back. "Don't forget the new roof we put on last year."

"Don't remind me. I feel sick whenever I think about how much it cost." I never should have touched the home equity loan line of credit we took out after Mama got sick. Priscilla and the bank talked me into it, assuring me it would take care of Mama's mounting medical bills… and eventually, the funeral expenses, too. Then, after that nearly-a-tornado-storm blew through last summer, Priscilla convinced me to use it again. I didn't want to, but with the roof full of leaks and minus lots of shingles, I didn't see where we had a choice. Now we're deep in debt. The monthly sum we owe the bank is higher than a mortgage payment.

"It still needs a new furnace, plus some paint, inside and out—"

"So, we'll buy some paint." Priscilla goes back to washing dishes, and for a moment the muffled clink of submerged knives and forks is the only sound between us. "Paint's not that expensive. Although we might have a problem trying to match the color."

God help us, if that's what she's thinking. There is no way in hell I'm letting Priscilla re-paint the house in that hideous shade of Barbie-doll pink Mama picked out years ago. When it comes to house paint, pretty-in-pink does not apply.

"I'm not just talking about the paint." I grab some silverware, give it a hasty swipe. "We need new windows, too. That tiny one in my bathroom is almost rotted away. It needs to be replaced, just like every other window in this house."

"Then we'll buy new windows. We can go to Home Depot on Saturday."

But I don't want to go to Home Depot. I don't want to buy new windows. I don't want to paint the house.

I want something else. Something more. Something I can't put a name to, something no one else can give me… except myself.

Well, plus the people that vote for me.

I don't care what it takes. I have got to win that contest.

"Patty, pay attention to what you're doing, or don't do it at all." Priscilla plucks the silverware I shoved into the drawer back out and sticks them in the rack. "They're not even dry."

"Who cares?" I drop my rag and turn to face her. "Look, let's be realistic. The house needs an update, and that means money... money we don't have. We can't let things fall apart like this. It's not fair to the house and it's not fair to us."

Her eyes are wide and round. "But we've got the bank loan. You know we'll pay it back in time. Why not use the money when we need it? Let's just write a check."

"No," I say firmly. Priscilla's never been good when it comes to money matters, and I'll admit I'm not much better, but there's no way she's talking me into touching that home equity line again. I swallow hard, chewing on my thoughts. Is now the time to bring up the subject of a condo with top-of-the-line appliances? If only I could bring Priscilla to buy into my way of thinking, it would be an easy trade-off. With the right buyer, we could get a pretty penny for this old Victorian if—and that's a big *if*—I can convince her to sell. Up until now, she's stubbornly refused to consider the idea.

Well, I can be just as stubborn. Although I need to be careful how I do it. Priscilla isn't always strong enough to handle things. Hopefully this time she's ready to listen. I take a deep breath. "I think we should consider listing the house."

"I cannot believe you're bringing that up again." She throws me a wounded stare. "We grew up in this house, Patty. It's home. And it's all we've got left of Mama. Do you want to give her up, too?"

She leans over the sink, pulls the stopper. Water gurgles as it sucks down the drain. Too bad it can't suck away my guilt. Both of us loved Mama, and both of us grieved when she died two years ago, but Priscilla took it hardest. Maybe because she was the one who nursed Mama through her cancer. Long black hair swirls around her face, hiding her eyes. Is she crying? Priscilla often retreats to her bed, but she never cries in front of me. I don't think I can stand it if she starts to cry.

"I love this house, Patty." She turns to face me, eyes shimmering. "And I don't want to move."

Oh, God, she *is* going to cry, and it's all my fault.

"I'm sorry." She grips the counter. "You don't deserve this. It's all my fault."

I blink. "What?"

"It's my fault we don't have the money." Her voice is barely above a whisper. "I haven't worked much in the past month or so and I know I'm not doing my share. But I promise you, all that is going to change. There's no need for me to sit around, being lazy."

"Don't be silly," I scoff. "You are not lazy. You already do too much as it is. Besides, you just got over being sick, remember?"

"I'm not sick now."

"Let's keep it that way. I don't want you having a relapse."

Her chin tilts high. "I'm fine, Patty. When you are going to quit babying me?"

As soon as someone else steps up to take my place.

"Dr. Brown called from the clinic a few weeks ago and offered me more work, but I told him no. I let him think it was because I was still sick, but the truth is... well, the truth is, I didn't want to work." She bites her bottom lip. "You're going to think I'm horrible when I tell you this."

I try hard not to roll my eyes. Priscilla, always thinking up some new drama. "You are not horrible."

"I am," she insists. "And I'm ashamed. Only a horrible person would be so jealous."

I feel the frown pinch my face. "Jealous of what? Of who?

"You."

I stare bug-eyed at my twin, certain Priscilla has lost her mind. She's got things twisted around. She's the ravishing beauty: sweet, delicate, patient, and kind. While as for me…

"You have every summer off." Her eyes glisten blue and enormous. "You do so much for us and I know I shouldn't complain. You work hard, Patty, and you carry most of the load. That's not fair." She halts, her voice growing thinner by the minute. "Teaching isn't easy and you deserve a break. But you get Christmas vacation, plus a week at Easter… and then all summer, too. And having you home these past couple months, I started thinking it might be nice if I could take a little vacation myself every once in awhile, too."

Now I'm the one who feels horrible. Here I am, griping about what a horrible fiasco it would be to pick up a summer job, while Priscilla works all year round. Her job is a perfect fit for someone in poor health and she's comfortable in the cozy sterile niche she's created for herself. Medical summaries needing transcription are delivered daily by a runner from the clinic and a computer keeps her networked to the medical world, producing a small, steady income. But it isn't enough. It will never be enough. And while we're not on the edge of financial ruin, sometimes it feels like we're tottering dangerously close. It's a scary, lonely feeling.

"Starting tomorrow, things are going to change." Her eyes glow with a fierce determination. "I'll call Dr. Brown and ask him to send me more files. From now on, I'm going to work harder and smarter. I'll bring in more money and you won't need to worry so much. I can do it, Patty. I swear I can do it."

She grabs me in a fierce hug. Her shoulders feel painfully thin. "Things will all work out. We've lived in this house all our lives and I know you love it as much as I do. We can do this, Patty. We can save it."

My heart sinks. Priscilla would faint if she knew how I really felt. I've never dared admit the truth.

"I've got faith in you," she says. "You'll think of something so we don't have to sell."

Good thing she's got faith in me, because I'm totally without a clue. Mama left things in a tidy legal knot, putting the title to the house in both our names. Without Priscilla's signature, there will be no sale.

"You've always been the smart one, Patty. You'll figure out what we should do."

Smart one? I've got my doubts. But my twin is right about one thing. It's going to be up to me to figure out a way through this financial mess.

Problem is, I don't want to find a way through it.

I want out.

# # #

Ten years of humdrum staff meetings have taught me there's no need to hurry. I make it through the library door with minutes to spare. The room is crowded with familiar faces and loud chatter. I wave at a few teachers and head for the snack table where I pour myself a cup of lukewarm coffee and turn my back on the tray of assorted cookies. Those coconut macaroons can whisper sweet nothings all they want, but I'm done listening. Day Six of my brand new life. Cookies not included.

I scan the rows of chairs for Ruth Proctor, one of our school's fourth grade teachers, my former mentor, and now good friend. Ruth always saves me a seat. I finally spy her in the second row and start toward her—only to halt halfway up the aisle as I spot the man slouched comfortably next to Ruth... in what should be my chair.

Wavy hair, sparkling brown eyes. I peer at the stranger who's usurped my space. He looks flirty, fast and dangerous—the type of man Mama constantly warned Priscilla and me about. The kind of man you can't take your eyes off. The kind of man women dream about. The kind of man who would never spare me a second look except at the spare tire sitting around my waist. What's he doing in our stuffy school library, chatting with Ruth? He looks like he belongs on a billboard, or a beach somewhere, playing volleyball with bikini-clad girls.

I head toward the back of the library in search of an empty seat. Maybe he's a guest speaker at today's meeting. Strange, Ruth didn't mention anything about him earlier this morning when we were chatting. She knows everything that goes on at James Bay Elementary. Ruth's been here twenty years and she's an excellent teacher. Her Teacher of the Year Award she won years ago proves that. She's also one of the select few who serve as mentors to new teachers hired each year...

My heart skips a beat. New teacher? Fifth grade? Could it be? What if...

No. The gods of the Human Resource Department would never be so generous. I squeeze in between a kindergarten aide and the sour-faced library assistant I normally try to avoid. Who am I kidding? I must be suffering from a drop in blood sugar. The notion that Blond Adonis could be my new colleague is crazy thinking. Maybe I should have grabbed a couple cookies after all.

Five minutes later, Chuck Stevens' introduction reaffirms my faith in the heavenly powers.

"People, I'd like to introduce Nick Lamont. Nick's been hired to teach fifth grade at James Bay Elementary this year. Nick, glad to have you on board. Stand up so everybody can see you. People, let's give Nick a big James Bay welcome."

Blond Adonis has a name. My hands sting from furious clapping as Nick Lamont slowly comes to his feet with a modest grin and a quick wave for the room.

"How could you hold out on me like that?" I hiss in Ruth's ear an hour later when a break is finally called. I slip into the seat vacated by Nick moments earlier and give Ruth's arm a little shake. "You knew about him all this time, didn't you? And you never said a word."

"I'm sorry, Patty, but I had to wait until it was official. Nick only signed the contract this morning."

Brand new school year. Brand new body. Brand new CUTE male teacher in the classroom next to me!

"Quick, tell me everything you know." I shoot a glance at the door. Ruth needs to talk fast. Breaks never last long, and soon he'll be back to reclaim his seat. "Where's he from? How old is he? When did they decide to hire him?" I suck in a quick breath, feel the heat rush through my cheeks at the one question burning through my brain. I'd never dare ask anyone else, but this is Ruth. "Is he married?" I whisper.

She laughs and shakes her head. "No, Patty, no wife. I don't know much about him, but that much I do know. His application and résumé came in at the last minute. His credentials are perfect. They snapped him right up."

"I can see why." With eye candy like Nick Lamont behind the teacher's desk, any subject—even math—would be a pleasure studying. "I bet he's an excellent teacher."

Ruth clears her throat. "I'm sure he'll do fine."

I hear the catch in her voice. "What's that supposed to mean?"

She hesitates, one eye on the door. "He doesn't exactly have much experience."

I swing my head and catch a glimpse of him as he heads back into the room. Nick doesn't look like he's fresh out of college, but more around my own age. He must have at least eight to ten years experience in a classroom.

"How much is not much?" I ask, watching as he heads for the cookies. "Come on, Ruth, you owe me the truth."

She sighs. "He just finished his student teaching."

"They hired a first-year teacher?" I stare as Nick samples the coconut macaroons. How could the school board do this to me? I've been praying all summer that we'd luck out and snag someone with years of experience, brimming with energy, plus the knowledge and skills to put into team-teaching fifth grade with me. All those prayers and what do I get? A first-year teacher. I've never been so disgusted with our school board in my life.

And I don't care how gorgeous Nick Lamont is. I hope he chokes on those cookies.

"According to Mr. Stevens, Nick comes highly qualified," Ruth adds. "He has his certification plus a little something extra. Something they were looking for. Nick's a coach. He's been hired to coach the high school's varsity basketball team."

I slump back in the folding chair. No wonder the school board caved. James Bay is a sports-crazy town and Chuck Stevens' fanaticism with sports is legendary. Plus, he and the district's athletic director are chums. Who cares if Nick has no teaching experience? Obviously Mr. Stevens, the athletic department, and the school board are all on the same page and made their decision based on what matters most—the fact our basketball team hasn't won a district title in years.

"You worry too much, Patty." Ruth pats my hand. "Once Nick gets accustomed to being in a classroom and nailing down a routine, he'll be fine. And so will you. I had a nice little chat with him this morning after he signed the contract and I told him all about you."

Ruth's crazy if she thinks I'm letting her off so easy. "Exactly what did you say?"

"That you were an excellent teacher and could be a big help to him. Remember your first day teaching? How nervous you were and how I found you crying in the bathroom before the first bell rang? I'll bet Nick feels just the same."

Somehow I doubt I'll ever find Nick Lamont crying in the men's room—especially since I'm not about to go looking. Plus, Ruth needs glasses. Nick doesn't look nervous. More like damn sure of himself.

I give him the evil eye as he strolls to where we sit.

"Patty Perreault?" His face lights with interest and he grabs my hand as Ruth introduces us. "Just the person I've been wanting to meet."

I don't want to like him. I don't want to be impressed. But I'm fighting a losing battle. Half a room away, Nick was gorgeous. Up close and personal, he's perfect. Perfect hair, perfect smile. The warm press of his hand on mine sends a surge of adrenaline—pure feminine pleasure—shooting down my spine, straight into my toes. I wiggle them in my new pair of too-tight shoes and curse myself. Betrayed by my own body.

Is the word *scrumptious* on fifth-grade vocabulary tests?

"Nice to meet you. I'm sure we'll talk later." Standing, I suck in my stomach and start to brush past Nick.

"Where are you going?"

I nod toward the back of the room and my empty chair. The dour-faced library assistant blows her nose.

"Wait a minute." Nick grabs my arm. "Not so fast."

"But…"

His hand tightens on my elbow. "The fifth-grade team should sit together. Take my seat. I'll grab another chair."

Even if I wanted to argue, it's already too late. He places his hands on my shoulders and suddenly I find myself sitting again. I fight down a surge of desire at the touch of skin on skin, of male-female contact. Biology normally isn't a subject taught in fifth grade. Maybe our curriculum could use some revising. A few seconds later, Nick is back with another chair that he wedges in between us. "Now isn't that better?" His eyes sparkle.

"Fine," I whisper.

"Just so you know, I plan on sticking close," he confides in a low voice. "Ruth told me you'd teach me everything I need to know."

"She did?" I suck in a deep breath as his knee grazes mine and I try not to stare. God, when did it get so hot in here? Someone should turn on the air conditioner.

"I want things to work out between us."

"Of course." I breathe softly, catching a delicious whiff of the cologne he's wearing. It smells expensive, exotic, exciting. I close my eyes, thinking about being marooned with someone like Nick on a tropical island. You wouldn't care if you were ever rescued.

"This whole team-teaching thing? Just tell me what to do and you've got it. You're in charge," he whispers.

I suck in a gulp of air. Nick's breath is sugary-sweet, like coconut macaroons.

"You okay with that?"

I blink. Is he nuts? How could it not be okay?

"Yes. Absolutely. Whatever you want," I manage to sputter.

"Great. The two of us need to stick together. And now I've met you, I can see that won't be hard." He settles back in his chair with an easy smile. "I think the two of us are going to be great friends."

Chuck Stevens drones on from the podium. Something about lunch tickets and the new reading series. It's hard to hear over the pounding of my heart.

I chance a peek and catch Nick staring.

At me.

And then he winks.

At me.

God bless the James Bay School Board for hiring Nick Lamont. Maybe he doesn't have any teaching experience, but he looks like he can handle anything thrown his way… even by a group of rowdy ten-year-olds.

And who knows? Maybe if I'm lucky, Mr. Lamont will teach me a thing or two.

## CHAPTER THREE

My hand grazes the pool's rough surface as I reach the end of the lane. *Finally*. I tug off my swim cap and goggles, grab my towel, and head for the hot tub. A good long soak is just what I need to soothe my weary muscles and wash away the day's frustrations. Crummy doesn't even begin to describe it. I should have stayed in bed.

Thunder rumbling in the distance as I hit the alarm should have been my first clue. Breaking the zipper on my favorite pair of shorts was the second. Strike one, hoping to impress Nick. Rain pelted against the window as I finally settled on comfortable jeans, loose black t-shirt, and strappy sandals. Priscilla and I have started giving each other manicures and pedicures. At least my toes will look good if Nick finally showed up at school today.

Breakfast didn't improve my attitude. Dry toast is dry toast no matter how you slice it. Four ounces of juice chugged over the sink and out the door I went, my gloomy mood following me right down the driveway as I backed into the street. My car brakes have been acting up again. One more thing to add to the growing list of things that need fixing. By the time I finally made it to school, my depression was official—especially when I discovered the classroom next to mine still dark and empty. Exactly the way it's been all week.

Where is Nick? He's yet to put in an appearance. Doesn't he realize school starts in a few days? Cartons of textbooks, which I've opened for him, sit pushed against the wall near his door. The classroom is stark, walls bare, student desks still clumped together in a corner where they were pushed aside for summer cleaning. If Nick doesn't show up and get himself organized, he'll find himself a prisoner in his classroom before the first bell rings.

I drop my towel at the edge of the hot tub, hit the button starting the jets, and ease myself into the frothy water. Outside, the raindrops pound a steady rhythm against the windows. Days like this are meant to be spent cuddled up with a good book, not swimming laps. And so much for Sam Curtis and his stupid theory. Swimming laps isn't getting any easier. My patience is wearing thin and my appetite is growing. Ten days in and I've only lost three pounds. This dieting thing isn't going to be as easy as I thought. There's nothing more depressing than knowing you can't trust yourself when it comes to food... especially cookies.

I'd give anything for one of those pecan chocolate chip cookies Priscilla's got hidden behind the vegetables in the cupboard. Does she actually think a few cans of green beans can stop me? My food radar was finely tuned years ago and lately it's been operating on maximum power. Even now, I can hear those cookies calling my name. I swallow hard, close my eyes, imagine the sweet crunchy flavor melting against my tongue. Maybe when I get home, I should give myself a little reward. I've been so good up until now and everyone deserves a treat now and then. Besides, how many calories can there be in one little cookie?

Ha! I'll bet Priscilla knows.

Eighty calories in a slice of bread. Ninety calories in one ounce of meat. Priscilla's little diet scale reigns supreme. Who would have guessed that naked chicken breast I devoured at dinner last night contained a whopping three hundred calories? No skin, no bones, and no taste, either. Barbeque sauce would have helped, but as Priscilla so *thoughtfully* pointed out, just one dollop adds an extra fifty calories. My twin is worse than Old Mother Hubbard. She's swept the kitchen bare of anything remotely edible or delicious. No more moist chewy cookies, no more salty chips. No more pop or ice cream. All my favorites, banished by Priscilla to dieters' never-never-land.

Except for that bag of cookies stashed behind the green beans.

"Well, look who's here."

My eyes fly open and I peer up at Sam Curtis, poised on the hot tub steps. He snaps his towel in greeting.

"Want some company?"

"Be my guest." I don't even hesitate. Not only do I like the guy, but there's this little matter named Priscilla. Sam doesn't know it yet, but he could very well be the answer to my prayers. If I play things right, Priscilla's little diet scale will be sitting on his kitchen counter one day.

I scoot toward the middle of the bench. The hot tub is big, but so is he.

Sam eases into the bubbling water and makes himself comfortable directly across from me. "I've been wondering about you."

I eye him warily. "Good or bad?"

He grins. "That depends. I haven't seen you around here since the day we met. I thought maybe you gave up and quit."

Do I admit the truth? I *have* been thinking about quitting. Achy muscles and itchy dry skin are the only things I've gained from all this swimming back and forth. But if anyone has a right to complain, it's Sam. He submits himself to daily torture here at the pool.

"I haven't been coming as often as I should," I finally say. "I probably shouldn't have bought that pass. It's going to expire soon and I'll have wasted the money."

"Don't be so hard on yourself. Showing up is half the battle. Besides, you're here now, right?"

I feel the beginning of a smile tug at a corner of my mouth. "That's true."

He settles deeper in the swirling water. "Rough day?"

"Rough week. School starts soon and I'm still not ready."

"You're in school?" His voice carries a hint of interest. "What are you studying?"

I laugh out loud. How old does he think I am? "I'm a teacher, not a student. Fifth grade. I've spent all week prepping my classroom and I'm still not done. Twenty-five fifth graders will show up next week raring to go. Just thinking about it makes me tired. I don't know; maybe I'm getting old."

Good God, now I sound as bad as Ruth. I offer him a quick smile through the steaming bubbles. "Sorry, don't get me wrong. Normally I love my job."

"Today was just one of those days?" he suggests.

I nod. "The rain messed up my plans." More like, a certain fifth-grade teacher who continues to be a no-show.

"Plus my car has been giving me problems," I add.

So is my memory. I think it's playing tricks on me. There's no way Nick can be as fine as I remember.

"Everybody's entitled to do a little complaining now and then," Sam says. "Besides, I've got broad shoulders."

No kidding. His shoulders and arms are solid, like flesh-colored rocks. I slip further into the foaming water and try not to stare.

"Stress can get to you, if you let it. That's one reason I hit the pool every day. Swimming relaxes me. Once I'm finished, I reward myself with a ten-minute soak in the hot tub."

The irony isn't lost on me. Sam rewards himself by soaking in the hot tub, while I dream about cookies…

"What's wrong with your car?"

I blink. "Excuse me?"

"Your car. Didn't you say it was giving you problems?"

Why does he care about my car? Is he an auto mechanic? Seeing a person stripped down to their swim trunks doesn't exactly provide you with clues as to what they do for a living.

"I think it's the brakes." I know how to fill the windshield wiper fluid but I missed the chapter in Driver's Ed that dealt with brakes, transmissions, and all that greasy stuff lurking under the hood. "They're making this funny grinding noise."

"That doesn't sound good. You should get them checked out."

"How much would that cost?"

"No idea." He shrugs. "My friend Rod owns a repair shop. I could give him a call if you like. He'd give you a good deal."

"Thanks, I'll think about it." I sink back into the foaming bubbles. So much for Sam being an auto mechanic. And maybe that's a good thing. I'm not sure how much money they make. Priscilla needs someone financially secure who'll be able to take care of her. But there's good money in construction. And with those big beefy arms, Sam looks like he could spend all day swinging a hammer.

"By the way, I like your new bathing suit."

"You do?" I peer down at the one-piece suit I purchased last week, which now officially qualifies as the most expensive piece of clothing I own. I nearly fainted when I saw the price tag, but buying it was a no-brainer. It's a perfect fit: tight across the tummy, ample coverage in the rear.

"The blue matches your eyes."

"Thanks," I stammer. Sam might not be a heavyweight in the looks department but he's no lightweight when it comes to flattery. Suddenly the hot tub seems like it's shrunk. This isn't the way the conversation should be going. What am I supposed to say? Do I talk about Priscilla? I'm not used to chatting with men, except at parent-teacher conferences. Men speak a language all their own, with talk of sports, hardware stores, and how to land that really big fish.

My thoughts drift to a certain basketball coach with sparkling brown eyes and tousled blond hair. Would Nick be interested in teaching me his language?

"So, you're a teacher. Can't say I'm surprised. You seem like the perfect type to work with kids."

I check his left hand one more time. He's not wearing a wedding ring, but given the way things have worked today, that doesn't mean anything. Sam could have kids of his own—plus one or two ex-wives lurking in the background. And I don't care how nice he seems. If I'm going to play matchmaker and set him up with Priscilla, he needs to be single. The last thing she needs is someone with baggage.

"Do you have children?" I ask politely.

"Me, kids?" He looks startled, then breaks out in a grin. "Not unless you count my niece and two nephews. I spoil them rotten every chance I get." His smile broadens. "And just for the record, I've never been married."

Good God, did he notice me checking out his ring finger? Talk about embarrassing. Still, it seems odd that a nice guy like him isn't settled down by now. Maybe he's gay. But just as quickly as I come up with the thought, I toss it away. I'm not picking up any of those vibes. So, if Sam's not gay and he's never been married, what is there about him that scares women off?

Maybe the same thing about me that scares away men.

"Actually, when I started college, I planned on going into education," he says. "I'm good at math and I think I would have made a good math teacher. But being on my feet all day didn't sound particularly appealing, so eventually I switched majors and settled for a sit-down job. Can't say I regretted the decision, either." He chuckles. "I've grown pretty attached to my leather chair."

Sam doesn't look like someone who wears a suit and tie to work. I sneak a peek at his hands—beefy and broad. They're perfect for swinging a hammer or laying brick; yet the fingernails are neatly trimmed, with no sign of grease or dirt staining the edges.

"Guess you could say that leather chair of mine is one big reason I work out at the pool. My doctor was pretty blunt when I went in for my annual physical. He told me if I didn't lose some weight and start exercising, I'd be headed for a heart attack. I showed up here the next day and bought myself an annual pass."

Suddenly he points at me. "Hey, there's an idea. You should buy yourself an annual pass. It's only three hundred dollars."

Only three hundred dollars? He tosses off the figure like it's chump change. I can think of plenty of ways to spend three hundred dollars. Property taxes, insurance, the home equity loan. "Thanks. I'll think about it."

"It's the best deal they've got. Plus, with an annual pass, you don't have to worry about an expiration date."

"Hmmm." I close my eyes and try to shut him out. Hopefully he'll take the hint. And that part about him being a heart attack waiting to happen? Best thing I can do is write him off right now as potential husband material. Priscilla needs someone to take care of her, not the other way around. If they ended up together and then he got sick, I'd be stuck taking care of them both.

"If I were you, I'd buy that pass soon. They jack up the rates before the end of the year."

I've heard enough. If Sam Curtis thinks he has such a good handle on what and how I should spend my money, let him buy me the damn pass. Obviously he doesn't know much about money—or women, either, for that matter.

"Do me a favor?"

He eyes me with an easy smile. "Sure."

"Just stop with all the talk about that pass… because frankly, I don't want to hear it."

His eyebrows pinch together in a frown. "But—"

"Look, I should think it would be obvious. Do I have to spell it out? I'm broke, okay?" I feel the stony pride settle on my face. "I don't have thirty dollars, much less three hundred."

His face turns as bright red as his swim trunks, and I myself am mortified. How could I have embarrassed him like that? Good Lord, what if he has a heart attack right here? He was only trying to help. Maybe I should do us both a favor and drown myself right now. Quick and easy. Death by hot tub.

"I didn't mean to offend you. Sorry." He grabs the metal railing and stands. "Guess my sister is right. She's always telling me I need to learn to keep my mouth shut."

"Wait, please don't go." It's a miracle he hasn't already bolted, seeing I was screeching at him like a banshee just a few seconds ago. "I'm the one who owes you an apology. My money problems aren't your fault."

He shakes his head, starts up the steps. "People don't like talking about money. I know that. I had no business giving you advice."

Sam sounds as sincere as one of my fifth graders when they know they've messed up. "How about we agree we both were wrong and leave it at that?" I suggest. "Just... please. Don't go away mad." I hate it when people are mad at me. "Please? Sit back down."

He eyes me warily.

"Please?" I'm not proud. I know how to beg.

The hiss of bubbling water jets is the only sound between us for a few seconds as he stands there eyeing me. Finally he eases himself back onto the bench.

"Look, Patty, don't take this wrong—but if you've got financial problems, I think I might be able to help. I wasn't kidding when I told you I'm pretty good with money. Plus, you said you taught school, right? Teachers make a decent salary."

I blow out a long sigh. Men! Don't they ever listen? "Thanks, but I don't think so..."

His eyebrows rise as I sputter into silence. I don't want to talk about this. It's bad enough trying to hash things out with Priscilla. I don't need the grief. I came here to calm down, not get myself revved up. "It's a difficult situation," I add. "You wouldn't understand."

"Try me," he suggests.

I shake my head. "You can't help. No one can."

But Priscilla could, if she tried. If only I could get her to sign a realtor's agreement, we could list the house, find a buyer, and hopefully end up with a nice profit once the sale goes through. Enough profit for a brand new condo.

"It's our house. I hate the place. It's old and needs lots of work."

"Why not sell it and move?"

"It's not that simple." The smile on my face feels snug as my bathing suit. "It's a huge old place with stained glass windows, gingerbread trim, and a furnace that should have been replaced years ago. The heating bills last winter were ridiculous. It needs new windows, plus a new paint job inside and out, and I just don't have the time or energy." Or the heart for it, either. Not anymore. "I'd give anything to sell."

"Sounds familiar. Is it one of those Victorians over on Mulberry?"

I nod.

"Nice area."

"Nice enough when you drive by," I grudgingly admit, "but you wouldn't want to live there."

"What's holding you back? Sounds like it's a great house, even if it does need work."

"Maybe you'd like to buy it?" I ask hopefully.

"Me?" He gives a big belly laugh and water sloshes round us. "No thanks. I'm happy in my condo."

Sam lives in a condo? Lucky him. Obviously he doesn't have a twin brother fighting him about where to live. I try and hold back the flood of resentment threatening to suck me down.

"There are always plenty of people with money looking to find a deal."

He's got to be a realtor. He's good with money, he knows the neighborhood, as well as the ins and outs of the real estate market.

"If you're serious about selling, you shouldn't have a problem."

I've got a problem, all right. One delicate beauty with a mind of her own and a stubborn streak that might as well be forged of steel. "It's Priscilla," I confess. "We've lived in the house since we were born. She refuses to even consider selling."

"Priscilla." His brows furrow. "That's your sister?"

I nod. "You met her once, remember? She was here with me that first day at the pool. We're twins."

"Twins?" Surprise spreads across his face. "I wouldn't have guessed. She's…"

I push down the flash of annoyance. For once in my life, it would be nice if people didn't act so shocked when they learned the truth. It gets irritating after awhile. Thirty years worth of irritating.

"Obviously, we're not identical." Better to admit it myself, than wait for him to point it out. "Priscilla is thin and gorgeous and I'm… well, I'm stuck with these stupid red curls."

"What's wrong with your hair?" he asks with an indulgent smile. "I like it. It suits your personality."

I grimace. With all the humidity in the air, my curls at this point probably resemble a frizzy wet mop.

"They make you look a little wild," he adds. "Saucy and sweet. I think it's cute." He settles back in the foaming bubbles. "So, you've got me intrigued with this talk about your sister and the house. Let's hear the rest of the story."

"It's much too complicated." We've been sitting in this hot tub far too long. If Sam thinks I'm cute, the heat has definitely warped his thinking.

"Sounds like you could use some help. Professional help."

"And I suppose you're a realtor, right?" Everybody has an angle.

"No, I'm talking about an accountant."

"Thanks, but I don't think so. Accountants cost money... way more money than I have to spend."

He chuckles. "If you're so bad at math, what makes you such an expert at what you can or can't afford?"

I roll my eyes. "I can't even afford to fix my car. How do you expect me to pay an accountant?"

"There are always ways to work things out."

"And I suppose you're going to recommend someone, right? Like the guy who does your taxes?"

"Actually, I do them myself," he volunteers.

"Some advice guru you turn out to be. You tell me to hire someone but you don't even follow your own advice. Why should I listen to you?"

"You might say I have a professional interest in the matter."

I right myself on the slippery bench. Sam's got an office job with a leather chair. He knows people don't like talking about money. Suddenly things are beginning to make sense. "You're an accountant," I accuse.

"Guilty as charged." A slow grin spreads across his face. "I'm a CPA and CFP."

"Okay, I get the CPA part, but what's a CFP?"

"Certified Financial Planner. Someone who can help put your financial affairs in order and plan for the future. I'd be glad to take a look at your portfolio and offer some suggestions."

My portfolio? I nearly laugh out loud. I doubt my checking account qualifies for such a fancy term. It rarely carries a balance of more than a few hundred dollars, except on payday. "Thanks, but I don't think so."

"I'm serious, Patty," he urges. "I'd be glad to help. You should think about it."

"I should think about a lot of things." While Sam seems like a nice guy, I know his services won't come cheap. And I can't afford to waste one penny. Besides, what do I really know about him except that he likes to swim and he thinks I'm cute?

That last fact alone has me questioning his judgment.

"Maybe you could give me your business card."

He hesitates.

"You do have one, don't you?" I press. What kind of businessman doesn't have a card handy to offer potential clients?

"Not on me," he finally admits. His brown eyes twinkle. "Business cards aren't something I normally carry when I'm wearing swimming trunks."

"I guess they would get pretty soggy." I slump deeper in the swirling foam. Death by hot tub is sounding better by the minute.

"I started my own firm about five years ago. I've got four people working for me now. We're small and I intend to keep it that way."

It sounds legit. He seems nice. How can I go wrong? Still, it's a lot of money. But what if hiring him ends up saving me money? It might all work out, just like he's said.

"If—and this is a big if—I did decide to go with your firm, who would I work with? One of your associates?"

"I would handle your account personally. Being the boss has its advantages. I get first pick of clients." He eyes me with a confident smile. "I've always had a thing for redheads."

Good God, he's flirting with me! What am I supposed to do now? Flirt back? Other women would know what to do, but not me. This is not what I bargained for.

"Look, Sam, you're sweet to offer, but I think I'll pass. I don't have the money."

Or the courage. I close my eyes so I won't have to look at him. I'm not sure what's going on, but he scares me in a way I don't understand. But why should I be scared? Sam is just a guy. Still, there's something about him…

"We could barter for it. I help you out and you give me lessons."

I open an eye and squint at him. "What kind of lessons?"

One corner of his mouth lifts. "I suppose swimming lessons are out, since we both know you're clueless about that."

"Don't be so sure. Give me a few months and I might surprise you."

"You're on." He matches my grin with a steady one of his own. "Meanwhile, how about dinner?"

"Did you just ask me out?" I blurt.

"No, you're asking me out," he counters. "I do your financial work-up and you buy me dinner. Sound fair?"

How can I refuse? "I guess you've got yourself a client," I stammer.

His eyes light up. "I'll get you one of my business cards before we leave. Give me a call and we'll set up an appointment."

Much as I hate to admit it, just talking with him makes me feel better. Being with Sam is like sinking into an overstuffed couch with plump cushy pillows. He's like a neighbor who's lived next door all his life but doesn't know the details. Someone who can help. Someone guaranteed not to poke fun when he learns all the financial horrors I've hidden from everyone, including myself.

Maybe, with Sam's help, there's hope after all.

Never lose faith, Mama always said. Sooner or later, an answer will be provided.

But who would have thought I'd find it sitting in a hot tub?

CHAPTER FOUR

"Mind some company?"

I glance up from the catalogues scattered across my desk. I haven't seen Nick since the day of the staff meeting. Tousled blond hair, burnished summer tan, muscles rippling under his shirt. Every inch of him looks sculpted by a master, like some classic Greek god who's been suddenly transformed into a living, breathing male in a crisp white polo shirt and creased khaki pants. All the schools in this district and he walks into mine. How did I get so lucky?

Nick glances around the room, gives a low whistle. "You've been busy. The place looks great."

"Thanks." I shrink behind my desk, try to hide the wrinkled shirt and pair of too-tight shorts I'm wearing. I've dressed nice all week in hope of seeing him but it's just my luck that he finally shows up today, the one morning I oversleep and end up running late. I give a discreet yank at my shirt, pulling it lower to hide the waistband cutting around my belly bulge. This is ridiculous. I am definitely shopping for new clothes… just as soon as I find some extra cash and lose a few pounds.

"I like what you've done with the bulletin boards." He strolls between the desks and does a slow circle around the room. "Where'd you get the idea?"

"Instructional magazines." I stand, point out the stacks piled around my desk. One compliment from him and my heart is soaring. At this rate I'll be halfway to the moon before the semester ends. I concentrate on slowing my breathing. "You can borrow them if you like."

"Thanks." He ambles back to the front and perches atop the desk directly across from me. "I've been over at the high school all week getting up to speed with the coaching staff. Looks like I should have been here instead. I've got some serious work ahead of me if I intend to catch up with you." He flashes me a quick grin that makes my insides melt like hot butter sizzling on the stove.

"I feel better when I've got a head start on things," I say. "*Be prepared.* That's my motto. Just like the Girl Scouts." Not that I ever joined a troop. It's hard making meetings when one of you is always sick and I wasn't about to go without Priscilla. Being a twin means you're part of a team. Going it alone isn't an option.

"Seen your class list yet?" Nick swings one leg casually against the desk. "I've got twenty-four kids. Mostly boys."

"Ten boys and fifteen girls." I try not to grimace. The final class rosters were posted this morning and I'm not too happy with some of the names on mine. The Home and School Association would throw a fit if they learned how much teachers talk among themselves about their students. For years I've heard horror stories about the little group of girls heading up my class list: Becky, Katie, Amanda, Jamie, the *In-Group*, with their leader Lauren, a horrid little girl with a pretty face and a mean tongue. Their reputation has preceded them since kindergarten and teachers give them a wide berth each successive year. This year it's my turn to deal with them.

"Hey, check it out." Nick scoots off the desk and heads for the bulletin board behind my desk. Construction paper cutouts and students' names float in neon clouds of reds, blues, and greens. He studies it intently, hands clasped behind his back. "What's this?"

"Our class picture board." I resist the urge to yank at my shorts. Why does he have to stand so close? Why does he have to smell so good?

"What's with all the empty spaces?"

Beads of moisture trickle down my back as I join him at the picture board. Great timing. Nick finally shows up and so does my sweat. I back up a step or two, just in case I smell.

"I take the kids' photos on the first day of school and post them on the board. The pictures get updated every month. At the end of the year, we put together a class book for everyone to take home."

His eyes shine. "You're full of great ideas, aren't you?"

"Sorry, but I can't the credit." I tug at the collar of my shirt and gently fan the clinging fabric. Maybe if I get the air circulating down there, he won't notice my damp armpits. "I got the idea from one of my own teachers when I was in grade school. I remember it was lots of fun watching the pictures change during the year. When I started teaching, I decided to do the same."

"And I'll bet you've still got yours," he says.

"What?" I feel the frown pinch above my eyes.

"Your picture book. You've got it tucked away somewhere safe. Probably under the bed, or maybe in your closet. Am I right?"

I haven't thought about that little picture book in years. It's buried deep in a box somewhere high on one of my closet shelves.

"But how did you —"

"I've got five sisters," he informs me with a slow grin. "I know a lot about women, trust me."

Is that an invitation? I shiver, despite damp armpits. I'd like to do a lot more than trust him.

"Mind if I borrow it?" Nick points at the board. "Your idea, I mean. That way both fifth grades will look alike."

My heart is racing. He likes my idea. He thinks it's great. But what does he think about me?

"I've got a camera, too. You can borrow it." I scoot around the side of my desk, yank open the bottom drawer, show him my camera. "I keep it here if you need it."

"Thanks, Patty."

"No problem." I force deep breaths. It's hard to think straight with him standing so close. The smell of his aftershave (or is it cologne?) drifts between us. Something expensive, exotic, delicious. I lean in closer and close my eyes, imagining Nick fresh from the shower, shaving in front of the mirror. Bare chest, a thick white towel draped around his waist…

"Oops. Am I interrupting something?"

The sound of an all-too-familiar voice from the doorway catches me off guard. I whirl and bang my thigh against the corner of my desk.

"Ouch." The petite blonde waltzes across the room. Delicate gold bracelets jingle from her wrist. "That looks like it hurt."

I wince at the sight of her. Amy has always had a rotten sense of timing.

She scans Nick with interest. "I don't believe we've met. I'm Amy Lynn."

"Amy teaches kindergarten." I rub the raised bruise already forming on my thigh. It hurts like hell but not as much as my heart and self-esteem. In her flouncy yellow skirt and matching silk blouse, Amy looks like she waltzed right off the pages of a fashion magazine. Leave it to her to show me up again. She's been doing it since we were in grade school and not much has changed. Next to her, I still feel like a big old cow.

And from the scuttlebutt I'm hearing in the teacher's lounge, Amy's made it clear that she's interested in being nominated for Teacher of the Year. Thank God she's in Lower Elementary and I'm in Upper. At least we won't be competing in the same category. I'd never make it through the preliminary round of contest nominations if I had to go up against Amy.

Nick sticks out his hand. "Nick Lamont. Nice to meet you."

His voice caresses the words—a bit too tenderly if you ask me. But then, no one has. It suddenly feels like the world has shrunk to just the two of them, with me the lonely outsider. Maybe I should leave the room.

Wait a minute. This is my classroom.

I clear my throat, edge closer to Nick. *Solidarity.* If he can't help himself, I'll stand up for him. "Nick is our new fifth-grade teacher."

"I know. Everyone is talking about the new hire. I had to come see for myself." Amy's gaze settles on Nick with a calculating air. "Silly me, missing that staff meeting. Guaranteed I won't miss the next one."

I'd like to slap that smile right off her face. Why doesn't she leave him alone? She's already got a husband plus plenty of admirers trailing her around. Granted, most of them are only five years old and can barely recite the alphabet, let alone guess what color lipstick their teacher wears. But that never stops Amy. Little or big boys, they're all the same to her. It's absolutely nauseating.

And I'll bet she never dreams about cookies. More like devouring men, one by one.

"The two of you looked very cozy," Amy says. "What's so interesting?"

"We were talking about bulletin boards." I can't fault Nick for falling for that wide-eyed schoolgirl charm, but I've been around Amy all my life and I know what she's up to. I fight down the impulse to give Amy a well-deserved kick.

"Bulletin boards? I swear, Patty, you're hopeless. Don't you know better than to waste your time talking about boring things like that when you're with a good-looking man?" She throws me a how-stupid-can-you-be-smile. "No wonder you're not married."

I open my mouth, then shut it just as quick. The contest's preliminary round of voting takes place around Thanksgiving. I can't afford to make any enemies. Then again, Amy would never vote for me. We've been sworn enemies since we were five years old.

"Nick, are you married?"

"Nope."

Her eyebrows lift. "No wonder you're the talk of the school."

"Is that so?" He shoots her a grin that makes me want to cry.

Damn it, why doesn't she go away? She's not supposed to be the one he's looking at.

"She's really something." Nick turns to me a few moments later when Amy finally saunters out the door. "I bet she keeps those five-year-olds hopping. She's got plenty of energy for someone so tiny."

"You're right about that." Amy is petite but not when it comes to confidence. She knows exactly who she is. She's polished and perfect.

Perfectly sour.

"Guess I'd better get back to my own room and start working on that bulletin board."

I swallow down my disappointment as he heads for the door. Nick and I barely had a chance to talk before she showed up. Damn Amy and her silly chatter, wasting our precious time.

"Call if you need help," I call out behind him. "I'm right next door."

"I won't forget." He halts in the doorway. "By the way, which way to the kindergarten room?"

My heart drops. I should have known. Why did I assume Nick would be different? When it comes to men, Amy always wins. I just didn't expect him to be such an easy conquest.

"Down the hall and to your left."

"Thanks. Just want to make sure I know my way around." He throws me a wink. "That's one room I want to avoid."

"Excuse me?"

"Women like her scare me. The last thing I need is drama in my life."

I stand there bug-eyed as Nick strolls out the door. Is he kidding? Amy's ruled this school since we were in kindergarten—first on the playground and now behind a teacher's desk. Everyone knows the rules. No one challenges her authority.

Or maybe not. Maybe this year, things will be different.

Suddenly I can't wait for school to begin. Nick and I will make a great team. Together we can handle whatever the school year brings. Fifty fifth graders? No problem. That saucy little *In-Group*? A done deal.

Even Amy Lynn.

A feeling surges through me that suddenly makes me feel like anything is possible. I can do this. Make it through the preliminary voting round for Teacher of the Year. Conquer my lifelong fear of Amy by standing up for myself. Win the respect of my peers by finally winning that contest. And with Nick as my personal coach, who knows what can happen? I might even be tempted to try on one of those skimpy cheerleading outfits like Amy wore in high school. Back then, the mere thought of trying to stuff myself into one of those trim little skirts scared me silly. But I'm all grown up now. I can do it.

Especially if I lose another ten pounds.

I settle behind my desk, grab a catalog and start dreaming.

Brand new school year. Brand new body. Brand new me.

CHAPTER FIVE

Where do ten-year-olds get so much energy? I keep watch from my usual spot near the playground fence, eyeing my crop of fifth graders as they hit the playground for morning recess. Nick's class beat us outside and most of the boys—including mine—have lost no time joining Mr. Lamont beneath the basketball hoop. Their shouts of laughter are sucked up in the hot dry wind, scattering over the asphalt court. Some of the girls pair up in clumps of twos and threes, giggling as they scamper for the monkey bars, slide, and swings.

Only two hours into the new school year, but every September it's the same. Time and hormones dog them, especially the girls. They start fifth grade fighting over swings and finish the school year fighting over boys.

Brand new school year. Brand new students. Brand new faces. Most of them I already know by name. By the end of this month, I'll know their smiles and personalities, too.

Eric tops my list of kids-to-keep-your-eye-on. Painfully thin, dark smudges under his eyes, shabby clothes. A classic case. Problems at home.

Andrea, a diabetic whirlwind. No sugar. No snacks. Hopefully no seizures.

Billy and Joseph, big and brawny. Special attention for those two. They could turn into major troublemakers.

Matt and Mark, new to our district, identical twins. School policy mandates the brothers be separated; Matt's in my class and Mark is in Nick's. The twins haven't been separated since they started school. I spent extra time reassuring their mother that her boys would be fine. They look fine now, laughing and shouting, part of Nick's crowd under the basketball hoop.

The girls are another matter. Jenna and Sarah on the swings, twirling and whispering with their heads together. Tiffany is off by herself, knobby knees pulled tight, dirty sneakers squeaking in protest as she inches down the metal slide. The school year's barely started but Lauren, Becky, Katie, Amanda, and Jamie are already holding court. Head high, arms locked tight, they rule the playground.

I keep an eye on them as they make another loop, then head in Tiffany's direction. She sees them coming, tumbles down the slide and lands in a cloud of sand at the bottom. Loud hoots of laughter erupt from Lauren and her cohorts, making me cringe. Twenty years have passed since I was in fifth grade, subjected to daily torture on this very playground by the pretty girls. It wasn't called *bullying* in those days, but I've never forgotten how much it hurt.

"*They're mean girls, Patty*," Priscilla whispered on a daily basis. "*Just ignore them.*" Poor Tiffany has to go it alone, while at least I had Priscilla at my side. The silent code of twins trumped being part of the in-crowd and Priscilla gave it all up for me. She could have joined them, but both of us knew I'd never get an invitation. Amy had made sure of that. I'll bet she was the one who thought up that nickname that followed me through grade school.

Fatty Patty. If I listen hard enough, I can still hear the voices of my playground torturers chanting in my head.

"Hey, Miss P. Want a cookie?"

Tyler, one of the smallest boys in my class, stands before me with a half-eaten cookie in one hand and an open baggie filled with cookies in the other. Huge homemade chocolate chip cookies. The best kind. A promise of pure pleasure sitting on your tongue.

"They're pretty good." He grins, showing off gaping holes from two missing front teeth. "My mom made them." Sugary crumbs stain his lips as he spits out the words and holds out the sack.

Grab it quick, before he gets away.

"Thanks, Tyler, but I had a big breakfast." I swallow down a surge of desire. That dry piece of toast didn't go far. I suck in a deep breath, count to ten. "Why don't you share them with your friends?"

"Okay." He crams the rest of the cookie into his mouth and wanders off.

Ruth Proctor strolls over to join me. "Pretty outfit. Is it new?"

"I bought it Saturday." I glance down at the blue and white blouse with matching skirt. Last weekend's excursion to the mall for a pair of new shoes ended up a full-blown shopping spree. I cringe, thinking how much I spent. Sooner or later I'll have to admit it to Sam. But everyone deserves a little splurge now and then, right? Besides, the blue blouse matches my eyes. And I know Nick noticed.

At least I think he did. I hope he did.

"Can you believe it's another year already? Where does the time go?" Ruth shakes her head. "And these kids—where do they get so much energy? They're like wild monkeys."

"Better out here on the playground than during math class." I watch Tyler as he heads for the swings with his snack sack. Poor kid. He's got no clue how close he came to losing those cookies.

"The boys seem happy with Mr. Lamont." Ruth nods toward the basketball court. Nick has the boys split into two teams. They scrimmage and shoot hoops on the hot asphalt.

"They do seem to like him." I give myself a mental hug. It's not just the fifth-grade boys who think Nick is something special.

"What about you, Patty? What do you think of our new fifth-grade team?"

I stand there as the flush creeps up my face. What does she expect me to say? That at thirty years old, I'm nursing a schoolgirl crush on the fifth-grade teacher? That I think he's the cutest thing strolling the halls of James Bay Elementary? That I check him out every chance I get?

"Why do you ask?"

"No particular reason." She tucks a few gray hairs back into place. "Well, I suppose that's not entirely true. I will admit I do have a few concerns about Nick."

I shoot her a fast glance. "Anything I should know?"

"Nothing specific." Her eyes trail him around the basketball court, bouncing back and forth as he controls the ball. "He just seems a little... wild. Sometimes I wonder if he has those kids under control."

I watch Nick whooping it up under the hoop with the ten-year-olds. I'm not sure what Ruth's talking about. As far as I'm concerned, there's no mistaking who's in charge—the man in chinos, white shirt, and tie, dribbling the basketball. He darts, jumps, and scores the perfect shot, then takes an elaborate bow—much to the delight of his young fans.

"I think he knows exactly what he's doing."

She hesitates, like she's about to say something more, then changes her mind. "I suppose you're right. Forget I said anything. I'm sure it will all work out fine."

I watch Nick score another shot. How can Ruth have any doubts? Nick is perfect with the kids and just what they need. A masculine presence, steady and reliable. A man in charge who makes them feel important by getting down on their own level while still managing to control the action and keep everyone in line. When was the last time one of our staff was out there playing with the kids? I used to do it myself when I first started teaching, challenging the girls to a game of jump rope. It was exhausting but fun. When and why did I quit? Now recess means me patrolling the playground and checking my watch to make sure we don't exceed our fifteen minutes of freedom.

Exactly how and when did I become the warden?

"I just want to make sure he fits in here," Ruth adds.

"That's what I want, too." More than she can guess.

"Help me keep an eye on him, would you, Patty? We don't want our boy getting into trouble."

I glance at Nick, busy directing a crucial play. *Our boy?* Ruth has it all wrong. Nick's no boy. He's definitely all man. And he's *my man*. At least from the hours of 9 to 3. As for the rest of the time…

I block out the thought. Better not to go there or think that. Things are great between us and I don't want to mess it up. Nick is totally out of my league.

Still, there's nothing wrong with a girl dreaming.

"You can count on me, Ruth. I'm glad to help."

She pats my arm. "I was hoping you'd say that. Now, there's one more thing you can do."

"What's that?"

"Ring the bell." She nods at the brass bell in my hand. "We're five minutes late coming in from recess."

# # #

"Does everyone understand the assignment?" The chalk squeaks in my hand as I list the page numbers. When will this school modernize and buy some whiteboards with the dry erase?

Loud titters erupt behind me. I whirl around and scan a sea of way-too-innocent faces. "Is there a problem? Did I miss something?"

"Eric called you *Mom*," Joseph shouts from the back row.

"What a dork," Lauren sniggers. Four other little girls scattered around the room quickly follow suit and the class laughs even louder.

"All right, that's enough," I say. "Everybody settle down."

It's hard to keep my temper in check. Lauren is proving to be even nastier than her reputation. First rule of teaching: let them know who's in charge. Better they learn up front that I mean business, rather than me making the mistake of starting out soft.

Then again, it is the first day of school.

I glance at Eric, seated near my desk. Suddenly I'm glad I put him there. Something about the little boy brings out my protective instincts. Kids can be cruel and sooner or later he'll have to learn to speak up for himself. An adult stepping in often makes things worse and that's the last thing I want to do. I went into teaching to make a difference. To make things better.

I glance around the classroom with my dreaded-teacher look, as Priscilla likes to call it. My eyes settle first on Joseph, then Lauren, then the rest of the class. One after another until they get the message. "I'm sure Eric didn't mean to call me *Mom*, did you, Eric?"

His eyes fill with silent gratitude. "No, Miss P."

"Okay. And as long as none of you call me *Grandma*, we'll get along just fine."

I wait till the laughter dies down. "Let's take out our science books. Who wants to read?"

Four hands shoot up, but I ignore the wiggling fingers and waving arms. I've got plenty of instruction manuals lining my desk, but how do I teach these little ones what they need to learn most—life lessons on reading the language of the heart.

Lesson One: Patience, tolerance and kindness to your fellow man. And fellow students.

One student in particular has a big lesson to learn.

"Lauren, you've got a nice clear voice. Why don't you start us off?" I suffer through her eye-rolling and indifferent shrug. She's got a nice little attitude going but finally she picks up her book.

"All right, everyone," I say, "turn to page three. Let's listen as Lauren begins."

# # #

"You're quiet tonight."

"I guess I don't have much to say." I wiggle around on the couch, toss a pillow over my head, try to find a comfortable spot. How low can I sink? Not much lower, especially now I'm reduced to lying to Priscilla.

"Patty, I know there's something wrong. You hardly ate anything at dinner and you've barely said a word since you got home. That's not like you. Usually you're full of stories about your kids… especially on the first day of school."

"No more stories," I mumble. "Privacy laws."

"But we always talk about your kids. Why should privacy laws suddenly stop you?"

I hold back the sigh gathering momentum at the back of my throat. Tonight, of all nights, why does she want to chat? She always goes to bed after the credits roll on that silly cable TV wedding show she watches every week. I peek around the pillow but she's still there, knitting needles in hand.

"You're not getting sick?" she asks.

"I'm fine." Twins are supposed to have a psychic connection. Maybe if I concentrate hard enough, I can *think* her upstairs. *Go to bed, Priscilla.*

"You've been lying around on the couch all night."

"I'm tired."

Go to bed, Priscilla. Go to bed now!

"Maybe you should get your blood sugar checked."

I stuff the pillow over my ears, muffle out the sound of her voice. Low blood sugar isn't my problem. More like those three candy bars I wolfed down earlier this afternoon.

And the other three hidden in the bottom of my bag, waiting until she disappears upstairs.

"Maybe you should see the doctor. Your sugar could be all out of whack from this diet you're on. Would you like me to make you an appointment to see Dr. Brown?"

"For God's sake, forget the doctor business, would you? I'm not sick, I'm just tired." I fix her with a furious glare. "And I think I'm entitled. I work hard and those kids take it out of me. But some of us don't have the luxury of staying home."

I hate myself the minute the words slide out of my mouth. I hate myself a thousand times more after just one glimpse of her wounded, drawn face. How could I have said it? It's not Priscilla's fault I feel like this, all jazzed up and nursing a sugar buzz. Feeling like I'm about to crash if I don't get a fix.

Damn candy bars. I never should have bought them.

"Priscilla, I'm sorry." God, now I feel even worse. Living with the guilt will be horrible. "I didn't mean to—"

She tucks her knitting needles into a soft puff of yarn. "You don't have to explain and there's no need to apologize. I know how upset you are about this money thing. But you can quit worrying. I called Dr. Brown today and he's promised to send me more work."

I prop myself up on the overstuffed cushions, think about those three candy bars waiting for me. Damn chocolate, anyway. Priscilla thinks this is all about money. I should tell her the truth. I think of Sam Curtis's business card tucked in my wallet. I still haven't phoned him since we talked. Next week, I promise myself. Meanwhile, I need to deal with Priscilla. None of this is her fault. "Please don't overdo it. We can't have you getting sick again."

"You always think you have to carry the load by yourself." Her voice is firm. "But there's no need."

"You'll get sick…"

"No, I won't." She stands. "You can't stop me, Patty. Mama always thought she knew best and maybe she did. But you're not Mama. There's nothing wrong with me. I can do this."

Fine. Let her get sick. There's no use arguing with her when she's like this. I slump back in the cushions and eyeball the television. Looks like we'll both be starting new projects tomorrow. Priscilla, more work. Me, another diet.

"Quit worrying, will you?" She brushes a soft kiss on my head as she slips by the couch and heads for the hall. "Things will work out. They always do."

I sink deeper in the cushions, feeling like a crumb for letting Priscilla take the blame. Letting her think we were fighting about money. Letting her think this is all about her failures.

Let the guilt trip begin.

She hesitates at the doorway. "Sweet dreams, Patty."

"Sweet dreams to you, too," I mumble in return. It's our nightly ritual, traded back and forth since we were little girls.

Sweet dreams, all right. *Sweet dreams of chocolate.*

I stay on the couch, not daring to move until I finally hear the creak of her footsteps on the second floor and the firm click of her bedroom door closing. Finally I creep from the couch, unable to stop myself. Every step brings me closer to the hallway closet where I stashed my school bag and the sweet forbidden treasure. Chocolate-covered caramels with crunchy cookie underneath. A six-pack assortment, minus the three I devoured after school.

I don't drink, I don't smoke, I don't do drugs. If chocolate is like a drug, I probably qualify for Chocoholics Anonymous. But first, I'd have to be willing to give it up. Which I'm not. I'm not an addict. Besides, everyone deserves a treat now and then. And

I've been good for so long—how many days now?—and I've only lost four pounds.

Tyler offering me that cookie on the playground earlier this morning started the ball rolling. All day long, I couldn't let go of the thought of chocolate. And instead of hitting the pool on my way home from school, I detoured to an out-of-the-way party store on the other side of town where I grabbed a six-pack of my favorite candy bars. Why? There's got to be a reason. But at the time, I didn't want to think about the *why*. I didn't want to think, period.

I just wanted the chocolate.

The first candy bar was gone as soon as I hit the car, before I even fastened my seatbelt. I barely tasted it as it slid down my throat and it only whetted my appetite for more. I ripped into the lush caramel and rich dark chocolate of the second one as I nosed the car out of the parking lot. I gnawed through the third wrapper with my teeth as I pulled into traffic.

And now that Priscilla's finally off to bed, the other three are waiting.

I creep up the stairs, school bag in hand, and slip through my bedroom door. I throw the lock, then flop on the bed in the darkness. Moonlight filtering through the window is my only witness as I peel the wrapper off the fourth candy bar, settle back in the pillows and savor the lush sweetness filling my mouth. I've deprived myself far too long. The second gooey bite is even better than the first. *Chocolate bliss. I've died and gone to heaven.*

Polishing off the fifth candy bar takes a little longer. The craving is gone and I force myself to finish. I'm in no rush to unwrap the sixth candy bar. My stomach feels queasy. Maybe it would be better to stash it somewhere and save it for later. But if I don't eat it now, that one last candy bar will be staring me in the face tomorrow morning... a big gooey reminder of what I've done. I rip off the wrapper and stare at the chocolate. Tomorrow, I promise myself. Starting tomorrow, I'll put myself on a brand new diet. Starting with breakfast.

Food. Ugh. My stomach lurches and I drop the candy bar. My breath reeks of chocolate and I stumble into the tiny bathroom off my bedroom. I use my toothbrush like a weapon, attacking the enemy sugar on my teeth, scrubbing away the contraband. I swish water back and forth under my tongue, around my teeth, spit it in the sink. Somehow I find the courage to face myself in the mirror. It's not a pretty picture. Hollow, bloodshot eyes; mascara staining my face. I don't recognize this person.

What is wrong with me? Why in God's name did I do this? What happened to my resolve? What happened to my dreams of being thin?

What would Nick think if he saw me like this?

No more chocolate. Never again.

I pull off my clothes, drop them in a heap on top of the bathroom scales. Pulling a cotton nightgown over my head, I shuffle back into the bedroom, flop on my bed, and set the alarm. School again tomorrow. If only I didn't have to go.

If only...

If only I hadn't given in. Why did I crack? Now I have to start all over again.

What a horrible feeling.

But not as horrible as knowing when tomorrow dawns, there'll still be that one leftover candy bar taunting me from the bedside table. Suddenly I grab it, crinkle the wrapper around the candy so I won't smell the chocolate, then toss it in the trash, burying it under some used Kleenex and an old magazine.

I hit the light and try to settle down. Nick's face dances in the darkness. What is it with him? Why is he being so nice to me? I don't know anything about men. The three guys I dated in college turned out to be losers. So what do I do now? I've never chased a guy in my life. And Nick isn't just any guy. He's gorgeous and available—the type who attracts women wherever he goes. Nick is in the big leagues and way beyond my reach.

Isn't he?

I punch the pillow and flop on my side. If only I looked like Priscilla. If only I could lose ten pounds. If only I had the courage to try.

But I'll never find it if I don't get myself back on track.

And back on a diet.

Brand new diet. Brand new beginning. Brand new me.

Starting tomorrow.

I sit up straight in bed. Damned if I want to wake up tomorrow, knowing that last candy bar is hanging around to haunt me.

I fumble through the wastebasket in the darkness. My fingers snag the wrapper, then curl around the candy. I take one bite, force down another. The craving is gone. I've already brushed my teeth and the chocolate tastes like chalk. I choke down the last bite, throw away the wrapper, and head back into the bathroom for one more bout with my toothbrush.

This hasn't been the best day. I've broken my diet, upset Priscilla, shamed myself… and all for what? Why did I buy that chocolate in the first place? It's not like I even wanted it.

What I really wanted was cookies…

CHAPTER SIX

"Do I need a permission slip to talk with the teacher?"

I glance up from the pile of science quizzes I'm grading and see Sam standing in the doorway. He was unavailable when I phoned his office yesterday and I left a voicemail asking him to return my call. I never expected him to make a personal visit. He looks quite dashing—handsome, actually, in his suit and tie. I've only seen him at the pool in his swim trunks. Funny how people look so different with their clothes on.

I drop my red pen and throw him a smile. "Come on in."

He doesn't move from the doorway. "Sure I'm not bothering you?"

"Not at all. The bell rang half hour ago and the kids are gone. Welcome to fifth grade."

"Thanks." He strolls into the room. "They gave me your message. I was in the neighborhood finishing up an audit and thought I'd stop by."

"I'm glad you did." I like how his brown eyes crinkle with little fine lines around the edges. He's one of the nice guys. They're easy to spot. The laugh lines are a dead giveaway.

"I'm glad you called." He halts in front of my desk. "I miss seeing you at the pool."

"It's been hard to find the time. Things have been hectic around here since school started." But that's not the only reason. After my chocolate-bar binge the other night, the last thing I feel like doing is parading around in my bathing suit displaying my rolls of fat. "Maybe I'll be back when things settle down."

His eyebrows lift. "Maybe?"

The blush burns my cheeks. "Definitely. I'll definitely be back."

Then again, maybe not right away. Not until I lose a few pounds.

"Just don't wait too long." He perches against Tyler's desk. "I miss having you in the lane next to me."

He misses me? What exactly is that supposed to mean?

"So, this is your classroom." He glances around. "Things sure have changed since I was in school."

I scan the room, try to see it through his eyes, but I don't see much that's different. I grew up attending this school and the only thing that's really changed is my view. Now I'm the one who sits behind the teacher's desk.

"I like how you've got the desks facing each other in circles. When I was in school, all our desks were lined up in neat little rows. Six rows across, six rows back."

"That's thirty-six kids," I say, quickly doing the math. "No way a teacher can control a classroom with that many students. The union would never go for it."

"I doubt our nuns belonged to a teachers' union," he says with a wide grin. "But the good sisters never seemed to have a problem controlling us. We were too scared of them to get too far out of line."

"You went to a Catholic school?"

He nods. "Those nuns ran their classrooms with rosaries and rulers. When we got out of control— whack! Out came the ruler, right over our knuckles."

"Unbelievable," I mutter. Teachers today—even nuns— wouldn't dare chance something like that.

"That's not to say we didn't deserve it," he adds. "You learned the rules fast in Catholic school."

"Well, I don't know anything about nuns, but I do know that hitting a student doesn't build trust or respect. I think kids learn better when they know what you expect from them. And I expect them to do their best. Respect works both ways. Treat them with respect and they won't disappoint you."

One corner of Sam's mouth lifts. "Is that so?"

"And I don't believe having desks lined up in rigid little lines is necessarily conducive to learning. Granted, it gets a little noisy at times, but having things arranged this way seems to work. Plus the kids like it. It's easier for them to team up, share…"

"As in… sharing answers to tests?" He grins.

"I hope not." I grin back. "They've got more important things to learn. Like how to get along with others. How to work out their problems."

"Mini lessons in life?" he suggests.

"I suppose you could call it that." I didn't mean to spout off, but Sam doesn't look like he minds. In fact, he looks impressed. His eyes gleam like he thinks I'm something special. But I'm only trying to do my job, to help those kids learn when they need to know about math, geography, and language arts. It doesn't hurt to throw in a life lesson or two.

I eye him carefully. What's he doing here, anyway? I didn't expect him to show up at school. Why didn't he return my call like a normal accountant?

Or maybe he's interested in providing personal services because he's interested in something else. Like dating the teacher?

I throw him a flustered smile. Sam's a nice guy but no way is he interested in me. And I am definitely not interested in him. I have someone else in mind, thank you very much.

"Kids have no idea how lucky they've got it." He points toward the bank of computers stationed in a corner of the room. "Personal computers didn't come along until I was already out of college but today's kids are growing up right along with technology. My niece and nephews each have their own computers and they can type circles around me. I'm part of the lost generation."

"I know how you feel." I've taken three college computer courses in the past five years trying to keep up with the latest technology, but sometimes it feels as if I'm losing the battle. The world of gigabytes moves at cyber speed. My students could teach me a thing or two.

"My niece and nephews could probably teach me a thing or two."

I smother a giggle. He has no idea that he's reading my mind.

"At least you've still got a blackboard. Looks like some things will never change." He cocks his head. "But what's with all the names up there? Billy, Andrea, Tiffany, Eric…"

"…and Christine, Joseph and David," I finish. "They all have science homework due tomorrow."

"Billy? His name is up there all alone."

"A personal reminder." Detention tomorrow for Billy the Kid Connolly. One hundred years ago, even at the tender age of ten, that little boy would already have been an outlaw. But this is my classroom and I'm not playing sheriff all year long.

"Lauren, Becky, Katie, Amanda, and Jamie are listed under *Lunch*. What's that mean? They get more to eat?"

"Not exactly," I hedge. I've had quite enough of Lauren and her little clique. They've been relentless in their teasing of Tiffany and Christine on the playground every day. Today I finally cracked and handed out a punishment.

"Don't any of these kids have last names?"

"We don't list them. State and federal privacy laws require us to protect their anonymity."

He blinks. "You're kidding."

"I'm afraid not. The law was changed a few years ago. I suppose someone saw something they weren't meant to see and all hell exploded." I shrug. "We're only allowed to list their first names."

He shifts his bulk, rolls his eyes. "I can't imagine any of my teachers putting up with rules like privacy laws and things. Those nuns didn't budge an inch. It was their way or the highway—the Catholic road of guilt. If I didn't turn in my homework, they'd list my name in big capital letters for everyone to see: SAM CURTIS, ASSIGNMENT PAST DUE."

I swallow a laugh. Somehow I can't picture Sam as the type who gave his teachers much grief. He was probably one of those good kids who kept his nose clean and stayed out of trouble.

"I'll tell you something else's that's changed."

I cup my chin in my hand, throw him a smile. "What's that?"

"The teacher behind the desk. You're much prettier than any of the nuns that taught me."

I feel the fire leap in my cheeks. He's flirting with me. I squirm in my seat. Can't he tell I'm romantically challenged? Girls like Amy were straight-A students when it came to studying men and figuring out how to make a boy hold their hand. I was much too busy and my hands were never empty. There was usually a book in one and a fistful of cookies in the other.

I suck in a deep breath. What's he doing here, anyway? My afternoon was going just fine until Sam decided to drop by and chat. Or flirt. Or whatever he thinks he's doing.

And as for calling me *pretty*?

Then again, maybe I am, compared to a nun.

Sam looks neat and handsome in his crisp blue business suit. His yellow polka-dot tie looks like real silk and he's had a fresh haircut in the last day or so. And that little moustache of his looks so soft and lush.

What would it feel like to kiss someone with a moustache? Would it tickle?

Good God. I shrink back in my chair and fight the rising panic. Me, kiss Sam Curtis? Where did that come from? I drop my head and grab my day planner. "I think it would be better if we met in your office to go over my finances." I thumb through the pages, keep my head down. I can feel him looking at me. The heat of his gaze sears every curl on my head. "When's a good time for you?"

"How about over dinner tonight?"

"Dinner?" My head shoots up. Like, on a date?

"Why not? We both have to eat and it would definitely be more relaxing than meeting in my office. Brownwood isn't too far from here."

"I don't know…" The restaurant is casually elegant and I've been there a few times. Christmas parties, catered affairs. Always when someone else pays.

"My treat," he adds.

Slowly I shake my head. "Sorry, but I can't." I don't want him getting the wrong idea. Sam is nice…

maybe a little too nice. And no matter how nice he is, I have no intention of dating him.

No matter how tempting I find his little moustache.

"It's a write-off," he adds. "Client entertainment."

I can't help laughing. Sam's persistent, I'll give him that. "Is this how you treat all your clients?"

He comes to his feet and leans across my desk. "Only the pretty ones."

His face is merely inches from mine. Ohmigod, he's going to kiss me. I know he's going to kiss me.

I'm about to find out if moustaches really do tickle...

"Whoa. Am I interrupting?"

The familiar voice drags me back to the land of chalkboards and textbooks. "Oh. Hi." I throw a weak smile at Nick standing in the doorway. "Come on in. We were just... chatting."

Sam straightens to a stiff stand as Nick strolls in the room and sticks out his hand. "How you doing? Nick Lamont."

"Sam Curtis." The two men pump hands. "Nice to meet you."

I fan myself with one hand. When did the room get so hot? I push up some loose curls from the back of my neck and stand to join them. "Nick is the other fifth-grade teacher. He's new to our school this year."

"Brand new and inexperienced. Patty's been great helping me out." He gives Sam a fast once-over. "Sorry about breaking up your conference. You one of the dads?"

God, if Nick only knew. "Sam isn't a parent."

"Oh." He eyes Sam again, longer this time. "Right. I get it." Then he turns back to me. "Look, I won't keep you any longer. I just wondered if you had a couple minutes to give me some pointers about that field trip we talked about at lunch."

"Sure." I throw Sam a hesitant glance. "I mean, I guess so."

"Great. It won't take long. Just stop by my classroom before you leave." He shoots Sam a quick grin. "Sorry about busting in on the two of you like that. Usually our girl is over here all alone."

Our girl? Does Nick think Sam is my boyfriend? The last thing I want is anyone—especially Nick—thinking that Sam and I are dating. Granted, Sam's a nice guy. He's thoughtful and generous, but he's also…

"You weren't interrupting anything. Sam is just my accountant. He stopped by to set up a meeting." I grab my day planner and flip to an open page, feeling the scarlet flush rising on my face. God, how could I say that about Sam? He didn't deserve it. "How about next Wednesday?" I ask Sam. "I'm free after four. We can meet at your office."

A safety zone. No chance of running into Nick Lamont.

"So, I take it this means dinner tonight is off?"

The disappointment in Sam's voice makes me want to cringe. The soft look of surprise in his eyes makes me want to turn away. I haven't fooled him.

And I haven't fooled myself, either.

Nick cocks an eyebrow. "Why don't I leave the two of you alone so you can figure things out."

How do I get myself into these messes? I close my eyes and whisper a heartfelt prayer. *Dear God, please let the floor open and swallow me whole here and now.*

"You said that guy is a brand new teacher?" Sam asks as Nick heads out the door.

"Yes, he is. Plus he's coaching basketball at the high school." I toss the day planner on my desk and force myself to face him. I hate myself for what I just did, belittling Sam in front of Nick. I cut Sam off, acted like he didn't matter, that he meant nothing to me. I'm no better than Lauren and her groupies out on the playground.

But those little girls have an excuse. They're only ten years old and I'm an adult. I should know better. I wouldn't blame Sam if he told me to find myself another accountant. He's a nice guy and doesn't deserve to be treated like this. And he's not stupid, either. I'm sure he knows exactly what happened and why I said the things I did. I've been through it myself. I know what it's like to be put down, to be ignored and dismissed by people who don't want to be seen with you.

Simply because you're fat.

Fatty Patty. If I listen hard enough, I can still hear the cruel taunt ringing in my ears.

My heart is torn but my head wins the contest. *Fatty Patty* and *Big Sam* together? That combination will never work, no matter how nice a guy he is.

And to think I almost let him kiss me.

"Sounds like Nick is one busy guy… coaching basketball, teaching, planning all those field trips." He glances at his watch. "Guess I'd better get going. I've still got another stop to make."

I trail him to the door. That's it? No explosion? No chewing me out? No telling me what a worm I am? If he stomped out of my classroom and slammed the door in my face, I wouldn't blame him. Nothing Sam can say will make me feel worse than I already do.

He reaches the doorway, halts, and turns to face me. "By the way, you never gave me an answer."

"About...?"

"Tonight. Dinner? Remember?"

After everything I said and did, he still wants to have dinner with me? Sam has to be a glutton for punishment.

"A man's got to eat, right?" A rueful smile flits across his face. "And I guess it's pretty obvious that I like to eat. Everybody knows that. All they need is one look at me."

Guilt churns in my stomach. I need to apologize. "Sam, I—"

He holds up one hand to stop me. "Look, Patty, you know where to find me if you're interested in dinner tonight. No strings attached. Strictly dinner with... your accountant. If you show up, great. If not? Well..." He shrugs. "Guess I'll assume you got a better offer."

I swallow over the sudden lump forming in the back of my throat. How can he be so nice? Five minutes ago in front of Nick, I treated Sam like he was nothing. I know what that feels like, and I hate it when people act like that with me, like I don't count. But Sam *does* count. He counts way too much. If he didn't, I wouldn't feel so bad. Maybe I should have dinner with him. We can discuss my finances... and other things, too.

Like the apology I owe him.

"I'll be there, I promise." It might sound like I'm acting, but I've never been more serious in my life. I force a bright smile. "And Sam, I want to... I mean..."

Say it. Tell him you're sorry. Don't wait until later. Tell him right now.

"Yes?" He hangs back.

"I just want to say... well, to tell you that I didn't..." I break off, suddenly unable to meet his eyes. Somehow I have to get out the words and he knows I'm trying. This would be so much easier if he wasn't so kind.

His eyes soften. "How about we talk about it over dinner? Say, six o'clock?" He nods toward the hallway. "Don't forget, you've still got a meeting."

I'm stumped, but only for a moment. "Nick's field trip."

"Right." His smile disappears. "See you at six."

# # #

The doorway of Nick's classroom is slightly ajar. Loud voices, laughter, and rock music drift into the hallway. It sounds like a party is in progress. I halt, my hand on the door knob. I wasn't exactly invited. Then again, Nick did ask me to drop by. I wait a full minute, counting off the seconds to the beat of the music before I work up enough courage to push open the door.

"Hey, look who's here." He waves me in from behind his desk. "I thought you weren't going to show."

Nick's classroom is empty. I glance around, more confused by the minute. "I thought there were people in here with you. I heard voices…"

"Must have been the movie." He points to a sleek laptop centered on his desk. "I muted it when you walked in."

I take in the seventeen-inch screen and state-of-the-art wireless equipment and try not to drool. My home desktop computer, long past its expiration date, just keeps going and going and going, and much as I'd like to, I can't justify the expense of a new one. With a laptop like Nick's, I could work from home in the comfort of my bedroom.

Dream on, girl. You can't afford the type of equipment Nick's got. Not now, not ever.

"Nice computer," I choke out.

"Thanks. Gotta keep on the cutting edge. I bought it a couple weeks ago. Check out the monitor—this high definition screen is great for watching movies." He grabs the laptop and turns it at a ninety-degree angle, giving me a better view. "Ever seen this?" He points to the screen. "It's one of my favorites."

The movie is still on mute, but it doesn't look familiar. I spend a few minutes watching the actors stroll across velvet green lawns. Once the golf carts appear, I know why I've never seen it. A golfing movie? Talk about boring.

"I own the DVD. You can borrow it if you want." His eyes light up underneath a tousled thatch of burnished blond hair. "Do you play?"

Me, golf? He's got to be kidding. Golf is a rich man's sport. Not to mention it requires the right kind of clothes. Cute little white skirts, showing lots of leg. Plus, the right kind of body. A trim, athletic body. The kind of body I'll never have.

I skip the question and run one finger slowly across the laptop. If I had something like this, life would be so easy. "I suppose you've got all your lesson plans saved on it."

He stretches in his chair, shoots me a lazy grin. "Say again?"

"Your classroom files," I explain. Surely he knows what I'm talking about. "The forms we use every week."

Nick shrugs. "I don't bother with stuff like that."

I stare at him with an uncertain smile. "But it's so simple. All you have to do is create a form. Once you've got that, it's merely a matter of updating it each week."

"I'm not much of a computer geek. I bought it mainly for DVDs and poking around on the internet. Keep in touch with my sisters, Facebook, Twitter, that kind of thing."

Nick bought a laptop with all the bells and whistles and barely knows how to use it? What is his problem? He went to college, just like me.

"Hey, maybe you could teach me." He brightens. "Show me which programs you use and how they work."

"It's super easy once you get the forms set up."

"That would be great." He sounds impressed.

I can't believe it. He really has no clue. Maybe I *can* teach him a thing or two. "Nick, trust me, this computer is going to make your life so much simpler. You'll be able to update your schedules, prepare all your lesson plans, prep for classes—"

"Plan a field trip?" he interrupts with a sly grin.

I grin right back. "Exactly."

His face softens as he watches me and I feel myself start to melt.

"How'd I get so lucky, having you next door?" he asks softly.

Nick's got it all wrong. I'm the lucky one.

"Tell you what," he says. "You teach me this computer stuff and I'll give you golf lessons. You'll be swinging a club in no time, just like the pros. What do you say? Have we got a deal?"

I'm no golfer. Then again, on second thought, a golf course might not be so bad. Lush green lawns, rolling hills, and sitting close to Nick in one of those little golf carts. Warm sunshine brushing across my face and his arms around me, cradling me close as I practice my swing. Guaranteed I'll need lots of practice. And Nick is just the man to teach me.

"It's a deal." Another ten pounds and I might actually look halfway decent in one of those cute little golf skirts.

Except for my knees. I'll always have fat knees.

He leans over the desk and flicks the mouse, shuts down the screen. "What about your friend? Sure he won't mind? I don't want any problems with him."

"My friend?" None of my friends play golf.

"Your boyfriend. That guy in your classroom today."

I suck in a deep breath, sink down on top of the nearest desk. Nick thinks I'm dating Sam? I could just cry. "Sam and I aren't together."

His eyebrows shoot up. "The two of you looked pretty chummy when I walked in. And he's a big guy. I don't want him coming after me."

"It's strictly a business relationship. Sam's my accountant. He's helping me get my finances in order."

Nick grins. "No need to explain. Everyone's entitled to their private life."

"But it's true." I hear the panic in my voice. Nick doesn't believe me. Somehow I've got to make him understand. "Sam and I aren't friends. Well, I mean, we're friends but we're not friends like... well, friendly. You know?"

I realize I'm blathering and shut my mouth. If I keep talking, Nick will think I'm a fool. He probably already thinks I'm a fool.

A fat fool. With a fat boyfriend.

Nick grabs a tablet off his desk. "Let's get working on that field trip. I don't want Sam mad at me. Plus, the two of you have dinner plans, right?"

Sam. I glance at the clock mounted on the wall. He'll be at the restaurant soon and I promised to meet him. What if I don't show? How long will he sit there, nursing a drink, before he realizes I'm not coming? Before he gives up and finally goes home?

But I promised Nick I'd help with the field trip, and we haven't even started organizing things. From the clutter scattered around his desk, this could take awhile.

"We don't exactly have dinner plans. At least, nothing that can't be changed."

Because I just changed them.

"Great. At least we got that settled. Do you like pizza?"

My stomach drops. Pizza isn't on my diet. "Doesn't everybody?" I answer weakly.

Nick flips open his cell phone "I'll call and have one delivered. My treat. We'll plan the field trip over dinner."

I think of Sam, sitting across from an empty chair, waiting for me to show up. He's a professional. He'll understand some things take precedence. Things like helping out a colleague. Planning a field trip.

Sharing a pizza? That doesn't qualify. I force away the thought of Sam's face as he finally grabs the check and leaves... alone.

It's not fair. I shouldn't do it. I promised Sam.

But I promised Nick, too. How can I say no to Nick Lamont and pizza? I take a deep breath and attempt a smile. "Make it double pepperoni and you've got yourself a deal."

#

I touch the brakes, slow the car to a crawl. The restaurant's parking lot is crowded, but the autumn twilight provides just enough light to recognize the steel-blue Jeep parked near the front door. My heart pounds against my chest. I'm two hours late and Sam is still inside waiting for me.

I never should have stayed so long at school. Why did I insist on planning the whole damn field trip? What I should have done is show Nick how to get things started, then let him take over. But he hadn't the slightest clue. And once the pizza arrived, we ended up talking, eating, papers and pepperoni spread out across his desk. Granted, I ended up organizing most of everything, but at least next time Nick will know how. As for me, I'm exhausted and want to go home, collapse on the couch. But not yet. There's one promise I need to keep.

Circling the parking lot, I spy an empty spot in the last row. I'll go in, have a drink with Sam. A glass of wine will help me relax, loosen my tongue. But I'm in no mood to discuss finances. This conversation is going to be personal, starting with the apology I owe Sam.

The two of you looked pretty chummy. Nick's words echo in my head as I inch my car toward the narrow spot. Nick's got it all wrong. I'm not interested in getting chummy with Sam. He's sweet, sensible, and smart but he's not exactly Mr. Debonair.

And he's not Nick.

I tap the brakes, sit there a moment, eye the parking spot. Stay or go? Sam's been in the restaurant for over two hours. He's probably nursed his way through a few drinks, eaten a big dinner, indulged in dessert. What happens if I show up now? That will definitely give him the wrong idea about where things are headed between us.

Because there is no *us*.

There will never be an *us*.

Did I really promise to join him? Or did I merely promise to try?

He'll never miss me. He'll never know I was here.

A car horn blares from behind. "Come on, lady, move it!"

On second thought, that narrow parking space probably isn't big enough for my car.

I wheel out of the parking lot and head for home.

CHAPTER SEVEN

"Patty, you're being silly. They don't look that bad."

"Forget it. These jeans are too tight. I don't care if they are on sale."

I turn my back on Priscilla and the three-way mirror magnifying every inch of my chunky legs and thighs and storm back inside the tiny dressing room, slamming the slatted door behind me. Time's running out. I've got exactly one week left to find the perfect pair of jeans for our fifth-grade field trip. Nick's planned an excursion to an outdoor YMCA that doubles as a nature preserve. We'll be tromping through woods, fields, and open meadows... and tromping means jeans. New jeans. Jeans not too snug in the rear. Jeans that show off my figure to its best advantage.

Is it too much to ask to find something comfortable and remotely in my price range? Obviously it is because I haven't found it yet. I barely managed to fasten the zipper on that last pair I tried on. And no way I'm buying jeans with an elastic waist.

I hurl the jeans over the door and storm past Priscilla. "This shopping trip is over. I'm going home."

And no use blaming my problems on our old dryer in the basement. My clothes aren't shrinking. I'm expanding.

"I don't understand." Priscilla struggles to keep pace as we head for the exit. "I thought surely you'd find something here at Fordham's. They stock designer labels. Designer clothes are supposed to be cut generously to size."

It's not the designer labels that are to blame. More like those coconut macaroon cookies I stashed in my sock drawer. And it's not just cookies that are causing the problem. It's this damn diet. Ever since I started it, I've been surrounded by food. Fancy food, finger food, forbidden food. Every minute of every hour is a constant challenge. Every morning in the teacher's lounge, the table groans with fresh pastries stacked high beside the coffee urn. I never can decide which are my favorite: the sweet gooey cinnamon rolls or the glazed chocolate donuts. Things aren't any better in the classroom. The kids mean well, but they have no idea how difficult it is to refuse their daily invitations to share cookies and candy at recess. Plus every week brings another birthday celebration. Cupcakes swirled high with sugary frosting and elaborate sprinkles. How can I say no? My students would think I'm punishing them for being polite.

A horrible message to send children, I decided after the most recent party as I finished off the last remaining cupcake. How can I resist?

But obviously, I need to start. My only other option is to buy bigger jeans. And with Teacher of the Year nominations opening soon, time is running out. If I don't lose some weight, no one will vote for me. When you're a regular shopper in the plus-size department, it takes guts to dress yourself in self-esteem and parade it in public.

"I still don't understand." Priscilla frowns as we head out of the store and merge into the flow of pedestrian traffic inside the mall. "You've been so good on your diet."

I window shop as we walk. Better that than to face her and the guilt. Priscilla always believes the best of me. If she only knew…

"Don't let this get you discouraged, Patty. Maybe you should try weighing yourself when you get home. I bet you'll be surprised."

Weigh myself? I did it three times last night, shoving the scales around to a different spot on the bathroom floor each time. *Location, location, location*—ha! It didn't change a thing. Thank God Priscilla hasn't suggested we participate in weekly weigh-ins. She'd have been shocked last night to see that little needle move. Two pounds... in the wrong direction.

Damn cookies. Damn candy. Damn diet.

"Ohmigod, I don't believe it." Priscilla yanks my arm and pulls me flat against the store window. "He's here."

"Who?" I glance around the open space before us. The mall looks like it always does on a Saturday afternoon. Hip young mothers pushing baby strollers, giggling teenagers owning the aisles as they chat on cell phones, elderly couples arm in arm cautiously fielding their way through a fast-flowing sea of people. "Who? Where?"

"Right over there." Priscilla points across the aisle with a wobbly finger.

I focus on a short, slim man ambling through the mall. "Who's that?"

"Dr. Brown." Her voice trembles.

I crane my neck for a better look at Priscilla's boss, a busy internist with a thriving practice. She's talked about him non-stop for months.

Priscilla tugs me back into the store and takes up surveillance behind a rack of trench coats. "I wonder what he's doing here?"

"Probably the same thing as us... shopping. What else is there to do in this town on a rainy Saturday afternoon?" I grab her by the arm and pull her out of the coats. "Let's go say hello. You can introduce me."

"No!" Priscilla heads for a nearby clearance rack of summer sweaters and frantically paws her way through them, eyes darting back and forth between the hangers and her boss. "We can't interrupt him."

I venture a peek in his direction. "Interrupt him from checking out the latest releases in the window of that music store? I don't think he'll mind." I coax her with a firm tug. "Come on, quit being silly. I want to meet him."

"Patty? Is that you?"

I groan at the silky voice floating from close behind me. Bad enough I'm forced to co-exist with Amy during school hours. Do I have to endure her on weekends, too?

"And is that Priscilla? Whatever is she doing… playing hide and seek in the clothes?"

Priscilla peers out from behind the clothes rack. "I'm helping Patty find a pair of jeans."

"They don't stock jeans with sweaters." Amy shifts her shopping bags from one hand to another.

I bite my tongue and throw Amy a polite smile. The preliminary voting round for Teacher of The Year starts next month and I can't afford to alienate any potential voters. Not that I think she'll vote for me, but I don't need her bad-mouthing me all over school. "We're looking for matching sweaters and jeans."

"You ought to try Clarice's. I bought these last week. Aren't they cute?" Amy twirls before us in a pair of tight jeans molded to her hips. "Of course, they're on sale now so there might not be any left. I never wait for sales. I'd rather pay full price and get exactly what I want."

I conjure up my best evil eye. I'd like to see Amy get exactly what she deserves—reserved seating in the clearance bin.

"We've already been to Clarice's," Priscilla tells her.

Amy turns to me, smiles, and shrugs sympathetically. "Nothing in your size?"

Fifth-grade teacher kills kindergarten colleague with bare hands… news at eleven. I grit my teeth and clench my hands behind my back. They'd put me away for years and yank my teaching license. Not that I would need one. No fifth graders to teach in prison.

"Actually, Clarice's did have some jeans just like yours," Priscilla continues. "Patty put them back."

"Too expensive?"

My ears prickle at the thinly veiled smirk in Amy's voice. Maybe a jury would rule it justifiable homicide.

"It wasn't the price that stopped her."

Ohmigod. If she tells Amy those jeans were too tight, I'll be facing murder charges for sure… because I will kill Priscilla with my bare hands.

"The jeans fit fine, but we thought they made her look cheap. That's not Patty's style." Priscilla wrinkles her nose. "Although I suppose it doesn't matter what *you* wear. It's not like any of your kindergarten students would notice."

God bless Priscilla. I could just kiss her.

"Bravo, well done," I whisper as we turn our backs on Amy and fly down the corridor. "I owe you big time."

"What are sisters for? Besides, she deserved it." Priscilla's eyes flash. "I hate the way she always makes fun of you. She hasn't changed a bit since we were in school. She's still the same mean girl she always was."

"Priscilla Perreault, I'm shocked." I take a playful poke at her ribs. "You, of all people, talking like that. What will people say?"

"I don't care. Besides, it's the truth and you know it as well as I do." The ghost of a smile flits across her face as she slows to a walk. "Do you think she's still watching?"

"Who cares? Just keep moving." I pull her along, resisting the urge to turn around and look. "I'll hear about it soon enough on Monday morning anyway."

Priscilla halts. "I never thought of that." A guilty look creeps across her face. "Do you think she'll make problems for you?"

Guaranteed, but Priscilla doesn't need to know that.

"I'm sorry. I never should have said what I did."

"Don't you dare apologize." I shake her arm. "Sticking up for me like you did took courage. Besides, I've got big shoulders. I can handle anything Amy dishes out."

"Sure you're not mad?"

"Don't be silly. Besides, I'm the one who owes you an apology."

She blinks. "Why?"

"We lost Dr. Brown." I scan the busy corridor, but Priscilla's boss is nowhere to be seen.

"Good." The relief in her voice is evident. "I can't imagine what he'd think, us chasing him like that."

"I think it's about time I met the man who's been the chief topic of your dinner conversation the last few months."

"Do I really talk about him that much?" A pretty blush stains her cheeks.

Priscilla's smitten. Good God. Who would have thunk it? My twin's never been the type to indulge in the pursuit of men. For years, her chosen companions have been a digital thermometer and inhaler—just in case— plus a box of Kleenex to ward off sniffles. Most of her childhood was spent inside the house, coddled by Mama. Once she hit high school and then when she enrolled at our community college the telephone never stopped ringing. But after a few practice forays into the world of dating, for reasons unknown, Priscilla turned up her nose and turned them all down. Nowadays her ventures outside consist mainly of visits to the clinic plus weekly excursions to the grocery store. Men trail her through the aisles, trying to play flirty peek-a-boo with a disinterested beauty amidst golden bunches of bananas, plump juicy strawberries, and mounds of sweet, lush peaches.

As for me? I'm the one they ask when they're looking for the kitty litter.

"I'll introduce you to him soon, I promise. You'll like Dr. Brown. Just the other day, he told me that I present some intriguing medical maladies. He's very interested in checking me out."

I hold my tongue. Sounds like I should check this Dr. Brown out for myself… the sooner, the better. Mama would never forgive me if I didn't make sure he's suitable for Priscilla. He's been in town less than a year and all we really know about him is that he's a physician in the clinic's practice group. That fact alone makes him suspect in my book. Doctors hold positions of authority and Priscilla's grown up in a sterile little universe. She doesn't know much about men and how cruel and conceited they can be. This Dr. Brown could be worse than most.

Take care of your sister, Patty. She's too good and trusting. Mama's voice rings in my ears.

I need to keep my eye on Dr. Brown. He could prove to be trouble. Big trouble.

"When are you going to see him again?"

"Monday morning." Priscilla's face brightens. "I have some files that need to be returned to the clinic. I thought I'd do it personally."

"Be sure and tell me what he says."

"I will. And that goes for you, too. I want to hear everything."

"About what?" We reach the revolving door of yet another department store. Whoosh! We're swept through the entrance into air-conditioned comfort.

"What Amy says. Don't forget."

As if I could. Guaranteed Monday will start off with a bang with Amy's verbal fireworks in the teacher's lounge. And after school, I've got an appointment with Sam in his office. I'm not looking forward to what will probably end up being a tedious discussion about the woeful state of my finances... just like I'm especially not looking forward to the beginning of our meeting. The one that starts off with an apology from me. I owe Sam that much after cutting him down in front of Nick, then standing him up over dinner.

Good thing tomorrow is Sunday and a day of rest. Because come Monday morning, I'm going to need every ounce of energy I have... and plenty of courage.

# # #

Sam's suite of offices are airy and attractive. I follow him down a plush, carpeted hallway; past glass and wood partitioned cubicles; and interested so-that's-the-girl-he's-been-talking-about smiles on the faces of his colleagues. He leads me into a spacious office and closes the door. Sleek modern bookshelves loaded with industrial-strength-looking tax manuals and IRS codes line the walls. Thank God for people like Sam with a penchant for math. I doubt I'd be able to lift one of those books, let alone make it past the first page.

"Make yourself comfortable." He waves me into one of the two upholstered leather chairs positioned in front of his massive desk. It looks like a natural extension of Sam—sturdy and dependable, capable of carrying a heavy burden.

Does he still think about me that way? Or has he cleared off his desk and shoved me in a drawer somewhere, to be filed away and forgotten?

I smooth down my skirt and take a seat. My stomach drops as I see my name affixed in one corner of the thick manila file centered squarely on his desk.

"I'm glad we finally got a chance to have this meeting." He settles back in the leather chair and taps one finger lightly against my file. "I've been going through your paperwork and I've come up with a few ideas we can toss around. Things might not be as bad as you think they are."

"If you don't mind, there's something I want to say first... before we get into all that." I swallow over the sudden lump in my throat. I'm not sure which will be worse—talking finances, or apologizing for standing him up for the chance to spend some time with Nick. The greasy pizza wasn't even that good. I ended up with a bad case of heartburn.

"It's... it's about the other night," I add.

His eyes narrow and suddenly it feels like I'm hovering on the shore of James Bay in January. The water's still open but ice crystals are already forming on the frigid waves lapping against the beach. If I take the plunge, there's no guarantee I'll survive the numb, chilling coldness. But if I don't do this, I'll never be able to live with the guilt.

"I'm sorry I kept you waiting at the restaurant. I had every intention of making it in time, but—"

He holds up a hand. "Don't worry about it."

I straighten in my chair. He's tossed off my apology like an empty, crumpled sack of chips. Obviously he doesn't want to hear it. Maybe it would be better to simply let it go. If it doesn't bother him, why should it bother me? Maybe it shouldn't.

Yes, it should. It does. I can't let myself off so easily and neither should Sam. My stomach still rolls when I remember that night, how he waited for me at the restaurant. He waited two hours and I drove away. The guilt has tugged at my heart all week. Ditching someone isn't my style. At least, it didn't used to be. When and how did things change?

Sometimes I don't like the new me.

"I should have called. I should have told you I was running late."

"It wasn't a big deal," he says. "I figured you got caught up with something."

With someone else, you mean.

"I felt terrible. And I meant to come in, but—"

"Forget about it." He shrugs. "I only waited about fifteen minutes. Once you didn't show up, I ordered take-out and went home."

But that's not true. I saw his car. Why is he lying? We both know the truth. "But…"

The sudden realization slaps me into silence. Sam doesn't realize I've caught him in a lie. He never saw me at the restaurant that night. He was inside while I cruised the parking lot. So why doesn't he admit it?

Why doesn't he tell me, *yes, I waited*. He's got every right to make me feel guilty. I'm the one who stood him up. Why doesn't he do it? He's smart. He's got the embossed diplomas, the accreditations, and framed certificates lining the wall behind his desk to prove it. He knows the way things work. He's got no reason to lie.

No reason except one.

I'd have done the same if I'd been waiting for Nick. I'd have stayed until the restaurant closed if I thought Nick might show.

Is that the way Sam feels about me? The way I feel about Nick? The question makes my gut tighten and my heart pound; especially since I know the answer. I've known the answer all along. That's why I drove away from the restaurant that night. Because I couldn't face the truth. I didn't want to face the truth.

The truth I saw in Sam's eyes when he visited my classroom. The truth that he's interested. The truth that he likes me. He was about to kiss me when Nick interrupted us.

And I like Sam, too. But he's not the one I want to kiss.

"Then I'm glad it all worked out and you didn't wait long." The lie slips easily from my lips. Why embarrass him with the truth? He's much too nice a guy. "You know how it is when you're working late. Sometimes things happen and you can't get away."

He nods. "And the other night was one of those times."

"Exactly." The huge dollop of relief is frosted with guilt and sticks in my throat. So much for a diet of honesty and truth. Sam's offered me an easy way out and it's better that I take it... for both our sakes.

"Suppose we get down to business." He flips open the manila file.

I wince at the mound of familiar paperwork. I hate looking at the stuff. Every foray into the financial quagmire leaves me more confused, and Priscilla isn't any help. When it comes to math, our brains are identical.

"Why don't you give me your take on things?" Sam grabs a yellow legal pad and an expensive-looking pen. "What do you see as the biggest problem facing you right now?"

Fitting into that new pair of jeans for tomorrow's field trip. I squirm in my seat and try to focus. "It would have to be the house. It's like an enormous bucket with a hole in the bottom. We spend money patching it up and it springs another leak. The house needs major repairs and we don't have the money."

"You've got a home equity loan. That should help."

"I don't want to touch that anymore. We're already in deep enough with the bank as it is. It's going to take forever to pay off the loan."

Sam plucks out a photograph I provided of the house from the file. "It would be a shame to let things slide. The place has nice curb appeal."

"Maybe someone will buy it—I'd rather have a condo like yours. Do you like it?"

"My condo? Sure, it's nice enough. A two-bedroom, with all the amenities." His face relaxes for the first time since our meeting started. "I bought it five years ago as an investment property and thought I'd live there awhile, let it appreciate in value. After the economy crashed, I decided to stay put, hang on to it awhile longer. When the market starts to swing, I'll sell."

"Our house will never sell," I predict. "Someone would have to be crazy to want it. The furnace alone must be fifty years old. Swear to God, someday it's going to explode and take everything with it, including me and Priscilla. We'll shoot straight through the roof and end up on the neighbor's front lawn."

His grin only encourages me.

"The house used to be beautiful, with real turn-of-the-century charm. Priscilla and I found some old pictures of when we were little girls playing dress-up in the attic. Remind me and I'll show them to you sometime."

Suddenly it's hard to swallow. No matter how much I might want to move, the house has always been home.

"Mama made a big mistake when she bought that house. She had the money, but not near enough for the kind of upkeep a place like that requires. Over the years, things started to slide. People used to come around, make her offers, but she always refused. One thing about Mama: when she made up her mind about something, she was one determined woman." I smile, thinking of Mama, how much Priscilla takes after her. "And when it came to the house, she was determined not to sell. She used to say that living there made it seem like we were still a family, even though my father was gone."

I shut my eyes and drift for a moment on a cloud of hazy memories... two little girls cuddled close to Mama, listening to a story of lazy Sunday afternoons spent on meandering drives through neighborhoods of spacious homes and happy families... a story of a man and the wife he loved playing their make-believe game called *let's pretend we live there*...

Sam studies the photo in his hand, then my face. "Your father left?"

"He died shortly before Priscilla and I were born." I bow my head, remembering the story Mama told. "He was on his way home from work when a drunk driver took a curb too fast and smashed head on into his car. My father was dead before the ambulance arrived."

His face grays. "I'm sorry, Patty. That's rough."

"The other driver had great insurance and the company offered a generous settlement. They didn't want the case going to trial. Obviously their client was at fault and Mama was pregnant with twins. The jurors' sympathy would have been with her. The attorney Mama hired advised her to take the offer but she couldn't make up her mind. All the stress and grief put her into premature labor. Priscilla and I were born five weeks early."

I stare at the carpet beneath my feet. I haven't thought about the past in so long, it's like picking at a wound that's barely scabbed over. If I keep picking, it will start to bleed.

"Priscilla barely weighed two pounds when she was born. She spent weeks in the hospital. Even after she came home, she was very frail and required lots of care. Mama needed money but she couldn't work, not with Priscilla sick. She accepted the settlement offer. She bought the house and we've lived there all our lives.

"About five years ago, Mama got sick. Breast cancer. Priscilla nursed her through it and for awhile it looked like she might make it. Then, two years ago, the cancer returned. Mama was determined to hang on. She'd beaten cancer once before and she said she could do it again. She didn't let go until the very end. Then one morning I guess she figured it was just too much and she simply gave up. She was only fifty-four. Much too young to die."

I feel the tears start to pop behind my eyes. Why did I start talking about Mama? I haven't let myself go down that road in a long time and the last thing I want is to break down in front of Sam. The last thing I need is him thinking I'm pathetic, whining about the house, about my mother, about the sorry state of affairs in the world of Patty…

Sam doesn't say a word, only shoves a box of Kleenex in my direction.

I swipe my eyes. "Sorry for the melodrama."

"Losing a parent isn't easy. My mom died when I was in high school." His quiet voice mingles with the dusty sunbeams dancing across the carpet. "It sounds like you and Priscilla did everything you could. I'm sorry you had it so rough."

I stare at the paperwork spread across his desk and try not to think about Priscilla's anguish, my own heartache. "We took out the home equity loan when Mama was sick. It helped with the outstanding medical bills and then her funeral expenses. It was a lot of money, but we needed it."

No regrets. If I had to do it all over again, I wouldn't change a thing. But it's time to face reality. Mama's purchase of the shabby Victorian served to recoup some of the leftover dreams from the make-believe world of long ago. But Mama's game of *let's pretend we live there* was her dream… not mine. We buried Mama two years ago. Now it's time to buy her dream.

"That's all there is to tell you." I sit up straighter in my chair. "Except I know that things have got to change. We can't go on like this. I want to sell but

Priscilla won't budge." I think of my sister, how her face draws tight just like Mama's. "I don't know what I'm going to do."

"That's why I'm here to help you."

Our eyes meet and I stare at him a long moment. Inside me, a sweet flash of lightness takes hold, a powerful feeling I haven't experienced in a very long time.

Maybe I'm not as alone as I think.

Sam clears his throat and nods at the paperwork in front of him. "Let's get back to the house. You mentioned the furnace." His pen scratches furiously on the legal pad. "How about the roof? What kind of shape is it in?"

"We replaced it last summer with money from the home equity loan. But that's the only thing we've fixed. Most of the windows need to be replaced and the ceiling in the kitchen is starting to sag…" I think for a minute. What else needs repair? Everything. One look and Sam would understand.

"You should come over and see for yourself," I suddenly blurt out. "I'll give you a guided tour. We'll even throw in dinner. It's only fair, seeing how I left you in the lurch the other night."

His eyes narrow and I kick myself for extending the invitation. Given my track record, he probably assumes I'll bail on him again.

"Never mind. Dinner probably isn't such a great idea. I'm sure you don't have the time."

"Whoa, not so fast. Do you hear me turning down the invitation?"

"No," I admit.

"Are you that bad of a cook?"

"Actually, I am." A tiny smile tugs at one corner of my mouth. With Priscilla around, there's no need for me to cook. "So you'll come?"

"Give me the grand tour and I'll stay for dinner," he promises.

"What works best for you?"

"Guess it doesn't matter. Things would be different if you asked during tax season. Come January first, it gets crazy around here. We operate in crisis mode through April fifteenth."

"What happens then?"

"Come five o'clock, we pop the cork on a bottle of champagne, toast our clients and the IRS." A slow grin spreads across his face. "Then we shut down the office for a two-week vacation."

The idea of Sam and his employees noisily celebrating suddenly makes me want to giggle. From what I saw on my quick stroll through his office, none of his staff look like party animals.

Then again, who am I to talk? My idea of a good time involves a bag of coconut macaroons, a cozy chair, and a brand new book.

"October, November, December…" He counts off the months on his fingertips. "Three months left until I start working fourteen-hour days."

"I doubt my checkbook or the furnace can wait that long."

"How about tomorrow night? I'm free."

I hesitate. Tomorrow is Tuesday and our fifth-grade field trip is scheduled for early afternoon. But Nick is in charge, which means I won't have to worry. I can still do the field trip plus give Sam a tour of the house. Priscilla will be thrilled at the thought of having company. And once she finds out I invited him for dinner, she'll end up fussing in the kitchen all day. No doubt we'll feast on something tasty and delicious.

But if Priscilla goes all out, Sam might get the idea that I encouraged her. He'll get the wrong idea about us.

And there is no us.

Suddenly my mind is made up. Not one word to Priscilla. When Sam shows up, he'll simply be an unexpected guest. I'll give him a tour of the house and he'll stay for dinner. And talk about perfect timing. Tomorrow is Tuesday, and that means tuna. No way I'll be accused of making romantic overtures… not with tuna casserole involved.

Suddenly for the first time in weeks, I'm looking forward to the prospect of Tuesday. First, Nick's field trip, then Sam over for dinner. One more person at the table means one more mouth to feed. And less of that nasty tuna on my own plate.

I can't believe how much lighter I feel as he walks me to the door. My feet feel like skipping over the carpet. Once Sam sees the house, he'll understand what I mean. I'll finally have an ally and hopefully he'll be able to help me convince Priscilla to sell. Inviting Sam to dinner was a stroke of genius. And depending on how things go—and how much he eats— maybe we should consider giving him a standing invitation for every Tuesday night.

At least until tax season starts.

## CHAPTER EIGHT

"I'm sorry about eating in the kitchen, Sam. And I'm mortified about the tuna casserole. If I'd known you were coming, I would have made something special." Priscilla throws Sam a sweet smile and flashes me an evil eye. "Patty should have given me a heads-up."

"No problem. I'm more a kitchen-table kind of guy anyway." He grins at Priscilla, who's hovering at his elbow with the casserole dish. "And the tuna is great. My compliments to the cook."

I lounge in my wobbly chair, nurse my iced tea, and rub my sore feet. No worries on the Sam-and-Priscilla front. They're getting along great. All part of my plan. Priscilla will eventually forget about Dr. Brown. She and Sam are made for each other. And he even likes tuna! Who needs more proof than that? Priscilla hasn't taken her eyes off him since he showed up and they haven't stopped chatting. Good thing, too. After today's field trip, I doubt I'm capable of carrying anything—including a simple dinner conversation.

Tramping around a nature co-op reserve with forty-five fifth graders isn't exactly my idea of fun, but Nick managed to carry off his first field trip with great success. He deserved every bit of credit from his kids and the chaperones. I didn't do much.

Except remember the snacks.

I spied the large open cardboard box packed high with juice boxes and cereal snack bars when I locked up my classroom. Why was it still sitting on the floor outside Nick's door? It should have been loaded on the bus. I give the box a worried glance. Did Nick forget the snacks?

I try the door of his classroom, find it unlocked, peek inside the empty room. Where's Nick? I head for the exit doors and see an empty playground. A large yellow school bus loaded with students and chaperones waits at the curb. Noisy chanting blends with the rumble and vibration of the engines as eager fifth graders stomp their feet and cheer to take off. A shrill piercing whistle catches my attention.

"Come on, Patty, you're late!" Nick, clipboard and whistle in hand, steps down from the bus and waves me out of the building. "What's the holdup? We're waiting for you."

"Give me one minute," I yell and head back toward his classroom. We'll be facing an angry mob of ten-year-olds in an hour or so if someone doesn't take charge. I squat down and wrap my arms around the hefty box, but it's too heavy to lift. Outside a horn blares and I give the box a furious stare. Not only did Nick forget the box, he overloaded it, too.

I tug and kick it down the corridor, mentally kicking myself as well. Why should I be the one stuck doing this? Nick and I talked about the snacks during our meeting. Wasn't he listening? Anyone smart enough to earn a teaching certificate should know enough to make sure the all-important treats are on board before a field trip begins.

Then again, Nick is a brand new teacher. He can't be expected to remember everything. That's my department. Being in charge of food will always be my department.

One look at me in my tight jeans and everyone will know that.

With a hefty boost of one hip, I shove open the outer door and drag the box across the playground toward the bus.

"Guess I forgot." Nick grasps an end as I near the curb and together we haul the box onto the bus. "I owe you one, Patty."

I bite my tongue as I plop down in the empty seat across from the driver. Nick should know better than to call me by my first name in front of the kids. But my resolve starts to soften as I watch him maneuver the box into a tight space behind the driver's seat. Who am I to criticize? I'm not perfect and neither is Nick.

Well, he's almost perfect. And he's obviously trying.

"Thanks again." He sinks down on the bench next to me as the bus lurches away from the curb. "I can't believe I forgot." He grabs my hand and gives my fingers a quick squeeze. "What would I do without you?"

I quickly pull my hand away. He's got to be crazy, holding my hand in front of everyone. What if someone notices? The bus bounces along uneven streets and every jolt throws us closer together. Thank God the highway department hasn't found the money to fix this section of road. Nick's arm grazes mine as the bus sways again and I shiver, delicious little goose bumps popping up. We take a tight corner and his blue-jean-covered thigh presses hard against my own. The bus lurches again and his body molds into mine.

Nick balances himself with one arm and pulls away slightly. "Sorry."

"No problem." *More potholes, please!*

I struggle for balance, keeping one hand on the rocking seat instead of making a grab for Nick. His aftershave (or is it cologne?) smells heavenly. We could be headed down the highway toward our own private Garden of Eden… except for all these kids. An afternoon traipsing through fields, woods, meadows, and creeks to study a thriving eco-system with a group of rowdy fifth graders isn't exactly my idea of paradise.

I hang back, watching Nick take charge as the bus unloads. His coaching experience serves him well and the field trip proves a great success. Mr. Lamont has everything under control. Until snack time.

"Okay, fifth graders, line up. Get 'em while they last."

"Thanks, Mr. Lamont." Eager hands grab drink boxes and snack bars as fast as Nick can pass them out.

"Cool! Chocolate chip oatmeal, my favorite."

"Are you crazy? She can't eat that!" I snatch the sugary juice and bar from Nick just before he hands them to Andrea.

An irritated look shoots across his face. "What's wrong with you?"

"Not one damn thing," I mutter under my breath, trying to keep my cool as I filch through supplies for the bottled water, box of raisins, and baggie of baby carrot sticks I had tucked away earlier just for her.

Andrea rolls her eyes as I hand them over. "Thanks, Miss P."

I hold my tongue till she's out of earshot, then whirl to face Nick. "Andrea is diabetic, remember? She can't have that stuff. You should have been more careful."

His face hardens. "It was no big deal. She wanted it, and I thought—"

"It doesn't matter what she wants. You're the teacher. You're in charge. God, Nick, what were you thinking?" My heartbeat races as I imagine Andrea suffering an insulin reaction in the middle of nowhere. "We would have had to call 911."

"But—"

"Just forget it." I turn my back on him, shivering as I watch Andrea nibbling her carrot sticks near the edge of Lauren's crowd. She's fine. Crisis averted. I scan the field of milling students. No one out of line, just kids munching their snacks, having fun, trading insults. Even Billy the Kid Connolly is behaving.

"Look, I'm sorry I blew up." Nick's voice drifts over my shoulder. "You saved my ass again. I owe you, Patty."

Damn right he does. He should have known better. He should have had things under control. I struggle not to give in, not to let him off so easily. But Mother Nature isn't helping. The breeze picks up and I catch a whiff of his cologne again. Why does he have to stand so close? Why does he have to smell so good?

"Don't be mad."

I feel my resolve start to crumble like a dry cookie. "I'm not. I'm just…"

"Frustrated?"

"You could say that." I rub my forehead with the heel of my hand. Maybe I'm making a big deal out of nothing. Nobody got hurt. Nick learned his lesson. Why not simply let it go?

"You make everything look so easy," he says as I turn to face him. Admiration flashes in his eyes. "The kids like you. They respect you. I hope someday they look at me that way."

How can I stay angry? Everyone makes mistakes. Especially new teachers.

"Don't worry about it."

He grins, my heart lifts, and suddenly everything between us is okay again. "Hey, what's up with the

Miss P. bit?" he asks. "I've heard your kids calling you that all morning."

Hearing the familiar nickname puts the smile back on my face. "It's something that started my first year of teaching. You know kids. It's hard enough for them to spell, let alone pronounce a name like Perreault. They dubbed me *Miss P.* the first day of school."

"Miss P. I like that."

He likes the name, but what about me? We come attached.

"Patty, are you finished eating?"

Priscilla's voice drifts across the memory of this afternoon's open meadows and yanks me back into the salty reality of tuna fish casserole. "I guess I'm not very hungry."

"Sam, what about you? Would you like dessert? We've got ice cream."

"Thanks, Priscilla, but no dessert for me."

I scoot back my chair and muster up a smile. "Ready for our little walk-around?"

He grins. "If the rest of the house looks anything like the outside, this should be some tour."

"I take it you're referring to the pink."

He chuckles. "Patty, your house isn't just pink. It's *pink.*"

I laugh and nod. "You can blame that one on my mother. It's all her fault."

Priscilla frowns as she stacks plates. "I happen to like it just the way it is. Besides, Mama always said it made the house stand out."

"It sure does," I mutter. "Come on, Priscilla, the dishes can wait. The two of us are going to give Sam a tour."

She wrinkles her nose. "Does this tour involve the basement?"

"It's part of the house." I don't like the basement any more than she does, but the furnace is down there and Sam needs to see it. Besides, I could use some moral support—her physical presence. My plan to throw them together is working nicely. This dinner couldn't have gone better. Even Mama would be impressed. Sam is exactly what Priscilla needs. A true gentleman, pleasant and polite. And as for Priscilla? I haven't seen such admiration in her eyes since... well, since that day we were at the mall and she pointed out Dr. Brown. But he's out of the picture as far as I'm concerned. I don't care if he is a doctor. Sam's much more manageable. Not to mention, he likes tuna. He and Priscilla make a good match. She's a great cook and Sam likes to eat.

"You two go ahead without me." Priscilla carries the dishes to the sink. "I'll stay here and clean up."

"But—"

"No," she answers firmly as she fills the sink with hot, soapy water.

Sam leans near me as I start down the hallway toward the main foyer. "You know what this house reminds me of? One gigantic Pepto-Bismol bottle decorated with gingerbread trim."

I giggle in spite of myself. "Better not let Priscilla hear you say that."

"I think your sister needs glasses."

The grin on my face widens. Not only did Sam finish off the last of that nasty tuna, he's also got an eye for bad taste in decorating. He could definitely teach Priscilla a thing or two.

I look at him brightly. "So, where do you want to start the tour?"

He eyes the ornate, winding staircase. "How about at the top and work our way down?"

"Fine by me." I lead him up the stairs. Maybe it's a good thing Priscilla isn't with us. At least I can talk freely. And knowing Sam, he'll see soon enough that this house is a one-hundred-year-old eyesore in need of more than just paint. It needs a loving touch and an open wallet... I've got neither.

We reach the second floor. I point to a trapdoor in the ceiling at one end of the hallway. "The attic's up there. I can show you, but there's not much to see." Except for mice. I stay out of the attic as much as possible.

Sam shrugs. "Don't bother. If you had a new roof put on last summer, it's probably in good shape."

I throw open the door to Priscilla's bedroom—an airy, spacious room done up in pretty pastel pinks and soft apple greens. Lacy white curtains hang at windows overlooking the front lawn. Underneath one of the windows is a shabby chaise lounge that Priscilla puts to good use on days when she doesn't have much strength.

We wander through the hallway, me opening bedroom doors, Sam peering inside. Finally we reach the far end of the hall and my own bedroom door. I've come to love the odd-shaped little room tucked under the eaves. I moved in shortly after I started college. With its own tiny, separate bathroom just off the bedroom it feels like my own private wing in the house.

His gaze lingers. "This is your bedroom? Nice."

"It's okay." I quickly tug the door shut behind us. Thank God I made my bed this morning.

"This is a big house." Sam trudges behind me through narrow corridors.

"Seven bedrooms and four bathrooms. It needs a family." A family with plenty of kids and plenty of money.

Sam is thorough. He takes his time eyeing cracks and stains in the walls, stomping his feet for loose floorboards, inspecting bathroom faucets and sinks. Finally we wind our way back down the stairs and end up in the foyer. I wave one hand toward the spacious living room. "The fireplace works fine."

He glances around. "Where's the furnace? I want to take a look at that."

I nod toward a door tucked under the staircase. "It's down there. But are you sure you want to see it? The basement is creepy even in the daytime."

He flashes me a wide grin. "I'm a big boy. I think I can handle it."

"Don't say I didn't warn you." I grasp the knob with both hands, but the door doesn't budge. I roll my eyes and sigh. "Sorry. Sometimes it sticks." I try again with no luck.

"Allow me." He nudges me aside and gives the door a hard yank. It groans and flies open.

"Nice job." I stand back, admiring him. "Can I hire you?"

"You can't afford me." He pauses, grins. "But I'll cut you a deal."

I laugh out loud. Sam makes being broke almost sound like fun.

"There's nothing wrong with this door that a little WD-40 won't cure. I'll bring a can with me next time I come over."

I stare down into the gloomy darkness, then flip the wall switch. The basement remains shrouded in murky black. I peer down the narrow steps, then turn to Sam. "The light bulbs are burned out again. I guess we might as well forget about the furnace tonight."

"Get me a flashlight and I'll change them for you."

"You don't have to do that." He's got better things to do than poke around in our basement.

"Do you hear me complaining?"

He's so close behind me I feel the warm breath of his words on my neck. Suddenly I'm grateful for the hallway's dim lighting. When did it get so hot? Why is he so close? His arm brushes mine, his face mere inches from my own.

That soft little moustache over his lips is intriguing. Did he just have it trimmed?

"All I need is a flashlight," he says softly.

And all I need is just one little kiss...

He reaches past me and grabs the industrial-sized flashlight atop the basement ledge. "Voila." He twists it in one hand. "This is one heavy-duty flashlight. You don't mess around, do you?"

I shake the dizziness out of my head, grab the railing. "Be prepared, that's my motto."

Especially when it comes to things that matter. Like a dark, damp basement.

And men.

"You must have been quite the Girl Scout," Sam says as he brushes past me and starts down the narrow basement steps.

"Not really." I think about those flashy sashes all the Girl Scouts wore as I slowly start down the stairs after him. Given the chance, I could have earned a few of those merit badges, too.

Just as the bouncing flashlight disappears into the gloomy darkness, a hand grabs me and yanks me backward.

"Good God, Priscilla!" I halt on the third step, stare into my sister's eyes. "You scared the crap out of me."

"Why didn't you tell me he was so nice?" she whispers from the landing. "He's adorable, Patty. I really like him. He's smart, funny, and just the right age. He's just… perfect."

"Do you really think so?" I climb a few steps and meet her at the top, hugging myself with a smile. Things are working out better than I expected. Priscilla likes him, and from what I saw at dinner, Sam seems to like her. too. Given a little encouragement, the two of them could be dating soon. Who knows what might happen? By Christmas they could even be engaged and we might be planning a Valentine's Day wedding. "I'm so glad you feel that way. I think Sam's perfect, too. Perfect for—"

"Oh, Patty, yes! And he obviously feels the same way about you."

"Me?" I blink.

Priscilla beams. "I watched the two of you over dinner. Sam was so cute. He couldn't take his eyes off you. He likes you, Patty. He likes you a lot."

"You don't know what you're talking about," I hiss, giving her arm a little shake.

"Really?" She tilts her head with a soft smile and lifts a finger to her lips. "Shhh, he's coming back."

I eye Sam as he gingerly picks his way up the rickety basement steps. *Cute* isn't exactly the word I'd use to describe him, especially with his flushed face and those cobwebs in his hair.

"You're going to have to fix these stairs if you're serious about selling the place." Sam puffs his way up the last few steps, wipes the sweat from his forehead. "They're a lawsuit waiting to happen."

Priscilla's smile dissolves into a steely frown. "Who said anything about selling? I'm not selling the house."

"Calm down, we're just changing a few light bulbs." I shoot Sam a warning look. Has he already forgotten how Priscilla feels about the house?

He catches my eye, nods slightly. "The bulbs down there are burned out. I'll change them for you if you've got some extras."

"They're in the pantry. I'll be right back." Priscilla disappears, but not before shooting me a stern warning look. Light bulbs? Yes. List the house? No!

"See what I mean?" I blow out a deep sigh. "She's adamant about not selling."

Sam leans against the uneven stone wall. "What do you plan to do?"

I shrug. "Talk to her again, I suppose."

"Should be quite the conversation. Remind me not to be anywhere close."

"Close for what?" Priscilla returns with two packs of light bulbs.

"For more repair jobs." I grab the light bulbs from her and flash him a quick smile. "Thanks again for helping."

He halts at the top of the stairs. "You coming?"

"Right behind you." I'm not stupid. I'll take my chances alone with Sam in the basement rather than upstairs with Priscilla and all the questions she's sure to ask. I grab the railing and trail him down the rickety steps. It's been months since I was in the basement and it's just as dismal and dank as I remember. The flashlight beam bounces off the walls as we reach the bottom.

"The furnace is over there... on your right." I shiver as the light settles on the hulking cast-iron monster, which looks just as threatening as always, and I shut my eyes tight. Plus, I dread the thought of spotting some furry little creature scampering away in the darkness. I back up slightly toward the stairs.

"Hey, where are you going?"

I blink in the sudden brightness as Sam forces the flashlight into my hand and grabs a light bulb from me. He strains to unscrew the dead bulb hanging near the furnace. "Hold that flashlight still, will you? It's hard to see what I'm doing."

"Sorry." I do my best to keep the light steady. "This basement gives me the creeps. Every time I'm down here, I end up having nightmares."

He reaches for the cord and I try to keep the flashlight from bouncing, but my nerves aren't cooperating. The circle of light jumps in jerky movements, illuminating Sam, the walls, the naked light cord hanging from the ceiling.

A soft scurrying sound comes from a dark corner.

Goose bumps pop up on the back of my neck, and I nearly drop the flashlight. "What was that?"

He strains to adjust the bulb. "Probably just a mouse."

"A mouse!" Two quick steps and I'm so close to Sam, I nearly knock him off his feet.

Light suddenly floods the basement and the naked glare of the sixty-watt bulb illuminates the surprised grin spreading across his face. "Don't tell me you're scared of a little mouse? What happened to that Girl Scout spirit?"

"That's not fair and you know it." Without thinking, I bonk him on the forearm with the flashlight.

"Hey, that hurt." He rubs his arm and eyes me with an uncertain smile. "That's all the thanks I get for doing you a favor? Some Girl Scout you turned out to be."

"I don't like mice and I don't like being teased. And for your information, I was never a Girl Scout."

"Can't say I'm surprised, the way you go around whacking people with flashlights. I doubt violence is something the Girl Scouts advocate."

I stomp my foot on the cement floor. What I wouldn't give to wipe that smirk off his face. He's purposely goading me, trying to make me mad, and he's doing a good job. The air between us snaps and I lunge into his space. We're close enough that I can reach out and touch him...

Slap him...

Kiss him...

Sam grabs my arm and tugs me close into his arms. "Forget what I said. You'd have made a great Girl Scout." The flashlight slips from my hand and hits the floor. His shirt is rough against my skin. His eyes hold a challenge, warm and inviting.

"In fact, I'll bet you would have been a troop leader," he says, his voice low and husky. "Or risen to the top of the organization."

I close my eyes, breathing hard. Every part of me urges me to push him away before things go further. This is all wrong. I'm supposed to be playing matchmaker. What about Priscilla?

"Patty Perreault, President of the Girl Scouts of America." His breath is soft and warm against my ear.

"I would have made a terrible Girl Scout," I whisper. "Afraid of the dark, afraid of the basement, afraid of the furnace, afraid of mice..."

"You need to get your mind off that mouse." His face nuzzles my own. "And I know just the thing to do it."

What makes Sam think he knows what I need? "I don't—"

"You need to be kissed."

The hard press of his mouth on my own pushes away any further thought. My body goes limp as I surrender to the sweet taste of his lips on mine, the softness of his tongue touching my own. I lean in closer, every instinct urging me on, relishing the headiness of being in his arms.

And suddenly I have the answer to the question that's been plaguing me for weeks.

Moustaches do tickle!

My giggles erupt right through his kiss.

"Sorry." He stiffens and drops his hold. "I didn't mean to get carried away."

I stagger backwards, knock into the furnace. I can barely breathe.

"Patty?" Priscilla's voice wavers from the top of the basement steps. "Sam? Is everything all right?"

Yes! No! How do I know? The world's tipped crazily out of control. One minute he's kissing me and the next he's not. Sam Curtis kissed me, and I kissed him right back. Even worse, I enjoyed every second! Where did he learn to kiss like that?

More important, why did he stop?

"Patty? Do you want me to come down there?"

"Everything's fine. We'll be right up." I hesitate, throw him a glance. He's crouched low before the furnace, on his hands and knees, his back to me. "Sam?"

No answer. What did I do? Why is he mad? Why did he pull away?

"Sam? Is something wrong?"

"Afraid so." He clears his throat and labors to a stand, still with his back to me. "The furnace definitely needs to be replaced. You'll want to get that done before winter."

I feel like I've just been doused with a bucket of cold water. Who gives a rip about a stupid old furnace? What about that kiss? Doesn't he want to talk about that?

Doesn't he want to kiss me again?

Sam stoops to retrieve the flashlight from the cold basement floor, then turns to face me. His face is flushed and his forehead dotted with beads of sweat. If I didn't know better, I'd think he looks exactly like one of my fifth-grade boys deep in the throes of a first crush. All the signs are there. But I must be crazy. Sam's not a kid. He is a man. A man who definitely knows how to kiss. For one wild moment, I dissolve into the memory of his mouth hard against mine. How could I think that kiss was a mistake?

Sam's a man with a big heart.

And an even bigger stomach.

How could I think that kiss *wasn't* a mistake?

He labors to catch his breath. "Look, Patty, about what just happened. I won't lie to you. I've been wanting to tell you—"

I turn away before he can say it. I hate myself for feeling so heartless and cruel. I know what he's going to say and I don't want to hear it. I know how it feels being judged on how you look. I'm overweight. I know what he's going through. And Sam is so sweet. He doesn't deserve this. But I can't put myself through it… I just can't…

"I think I hear Priscilla again."

He reaches out, his hand grazes my own. "Patty, I—"

I skitter away from his touch. "We're finished here, right? You saw everything you needed to see?"

"Yes, I think I got the picture. Loud and clear." His voice hangs low with disappointment.

I scoot up the narrow steps. Who cares if I break my neck? Better than breaking his heart. I always knew the basement was dangerous and now I have proof. My lips still tingle from the sweet taste of his mouth on mine and the soft prickle of his moustache nuzzling my neck. Sam might be interested in me, but I need to get that idea out of his head. Our relationship needs to remain purely professional. No matter how he feels.

No matter how I feel.

Priscilla waits at the top of the stairs. Sam hands her the flashlight.

"Thank you, Sam. You were so sweet to help. I know how much Patty hates the basement."

I swipe the dust from my clothes and hair, keep my gaze from straying near Sam. I can't stand to see the hurt on his face. Especially since I'm the one who put it there.

He clears his throat. "It's getting late. I should go."

"You will come back, won't you?" Priscilla hands him his coat. "Come for dinner. Next time, no tuna, I promise. What's your favorite dish?"

For God's sake, why doesn't she shut up? I'm sure Sam wants to get out of this house as much as I want him gone. How could I have embarrassed him like that?

"My favorite food? I guess that would be lasagna."

Priscilla beams. "How does next Friday sound?"

"Like an invitation I can't resist."

I glare at my twin. She has no business issuing invitations without asking me. This is my house, too. I clear my throat but Priscilla doesn't seem to notice. She's too busy hanging on Sam's every word.

I trail after Sam as he heads to the door. Priscilla says her good-byes and slips into the kitchen. Thinking to play matchmaker, no doubt. Eager to leave us alone. Some fine sister she turned out to be. Just wait till I get my hands on her. I'll wring that pretty little neck.

I lean against the door as he shrugs into his coat. "Looks like you impressed Priscilla."

He stares at me a long moment. "But not you, right?"

"What do you mean?" I eye him warily.

"I know her invitation for next Friday put you on the spot." He never looks away. "Just say the word and I'll make up some excuse and un-invite myself. There's no need for her to know the truth."

I feel the color shoot up my cheeks. Are my feelings that obvious? "No, of course you have to come. Priscilla invited you. She's probably in the kitchen right now, hunting up Mama's recipe for lasagna. If you don't show up, she'll be very disappointed."

"But what about you? I know when I'm not wanted." He shifts on his feet, stares up at the ceiling, then finally back at me. "Look, Patty, I thought we were friends. In fact, I hoped we were more than friends. Maybe I got my signals mixed up. Maybe I was wrong." His mouth twists in a grim line. "The last thing I want to do is make you uncomfortable. So, unless you tell me different, next Friday is out."

How can I not like this guy? He hasn't done anything wrong... he's done everything right. Including—especially including— the way he kisses.

But that kiss needs to stay in the past. Sam and I can never be more than friends.

Then again, what would it hurt, having him over for dinner again? Everyone needs to eat.

"You'd better show up next Friday," I threaten. "Do you want me to be stuck eating leftover lasagna for a week?"

His eyes narrow. "You sure?"

I nod before the quick glimmer of hope leaping in his eyes makes me change my mind. Sam's much too trusting. God help me, what am I going to do?

He steps out the door onto the porch, then turns. "Just one more thing."

I grip the door, clench my teeth. I'm doing my best to forget that kiss. Why can't he?

"About that guy—that new teacher you introduced me to... Nick?"

I feel the nerves bunch between my shoulder blades. "What about him?"

"You said this was his first year teaching?"

"That's right. Why?"

He shrugs. "Just seems odd. I mean, it's not like the guy's right out of college."

"Lots of people start different careers midstream." Not that it's any of Sam's business how old Nick is, or what he's done in the past.

"I don't know. There's just something about him…" He shakes his head. "I think I've seen him before."

"I doubt that." I feel a stony look settling on my face. "Nick just moved to town."

"It'll come to me eventually."

"Fine. Be sure and let me know when it does. Good night." I shut the door on him without another word. Who does he think he is, interrogating me about Nick, making insinuations? What gives him the right?

Jealousy, that's what. Well, too bad for Sam. He'll just have to deal with it.

I throw the lock and deadbolt and turn, only to find Priscilla waiting.

"Sam seems very nice." She stifles a yawn from her seat on the staircase and stands with a tired smile. "I'm so glad you invited him tonight."

"And I can't believe you invited him over again. Why didn't you ask me first?"

"But I thought you liked him. The two of you are perfect for each other."

"You can get that thought right out of your head, Priscilla Perreault. I have absolutely no romantic interest in Sam. Period. Do you hear me? Don't encourage him. If you keep inviting him to dinner, he'll get the wrong idea. And as for making lasagna? Do you realize how fattening Italian food is? The last thing he needs to be eating is lasagna. In case you haven't noticed, Sam has a weight problem."

Priscilla's face quiets. "Yes, I noticed, but that doesn't mean I can't help. And for your information, I've been researching fat-free recipes. I found one for lasagna just the other day and I hope he likes it. But even if he doesn't, I bet we'll never know. Sam doesn't strike me as the type to complain. In case you haven't noticed, Sam has beautiful manners."

She's right, I grudgingly admit to myself, remembering my conversation with him at the door moments earlier. He was only thinking of me when he volunteered to back out of Priscilla's offer. Maybe I should take him up on it. Call him in a day or two, tell him not to bother. No lasagna, no Sam Curtis.

The less I see of that man and his moustache, the better off we'll all be.

"I'm going to bed." Priscilla's yawn finally breaks through. "Will you turn off the lights?"

"Don't I always?"

"Sweet dreams, Patty."

"Sweet dreams to you, too." I watch as she disappears up the stairs. Priscilla doesn't fool me one bit. If she thinks she's going to play matchmaker, she's got another think coming. Sam Curtis means nothing to me. I've got enough problems. I can't afford a fat boyfriend. No matter how I feel, Sam can never be anything more than our accountant. *Never*.

I move through the house, switching off lights, checking doors. Eventually I end up in the kitchen. One dim light remains, over the stove. I reach for it, then hesitate.

All alone. No lights. No camera. No audience.

And ice cream in the freezer.

I snap off the stove light and seal myself off in the darkness. I yank open the freezer door and scan the shelves, bypass the frozen vegetables and carefully labeled meats. Priscilla offered Sam ice cream for dessert. It's in here somewhere and I'm going to find it. I haven't had ice cream in ages. Finally I spot a colorful cardboard container hidden behind the Brussels sprouts and say a silent prayer that it's butter pecan, one of my favorites. Or better yet, chocolate fudge ripple.

I haul out the frozen container. Vanilla? Priscilla bought vanilla? Not even a rich fancy French vanilla, but some cheap store-brand substitute. My stomach growls with disappointment, but it's not enough to wipe away the craving.

Or my determination to indulge in one final treat.

I juggle the carton in my hand. Should I? Shouldn't I? I haven't lost a pound in days but I haven't gained weight, either. Plus it's only ice cream. No big deal. Ice cream is just ice cream. Just like men. All alike, all the same.

But that's not true. Some men are plain vanilla, while others tempt your taste buds like chocolate fudge ripple. Rich, delectable, desirable…

I rip off the lid, grab a spoon, and dig in.

## CHAPTER NINE

"I hear Amy's chocolate cheesecake is to die for." Ruth sinks into the chair across from me, samples a tiny bite, closes her eyes and smiles. "Delicious. Have you tried it?"

"No thanks." I keep my head down, keep my mouth shut, try to focus on the stack of math tests I'm grading. Bad enough I've been forced out of my classroom and into the teacher's lounge instead of being at my desk while the music teacher and her traveling piano take over my room to teach my kids. It doesn't seem fair I have to suffer through tempting desserts, too.

Maybe I should just forget all about that stupid contest and trying to win votes. The contest hasn't even opened for nominations yet. And what makes me think I'm a shoo-in to be nominated again this year? Maybe I'm not.

And if not, the first thing I'm going to do is tell Amy exactly what I think… that she should keep her fattening leftovers at her own house where they belong.

Ruth scrapes her fork against the plate. "What's wrong, Patty? Bad day?"

"More like *bad teacher*." Even if by some miracle I do get nominated for the contest, I don't deserve the award. The Teacher of the Year would never mess up like this. I throw down my red pen, shake my head. "I don't get it, Ruth. I must have missed something when I was teaching the lesson. Not one of these kids earned a passing grade on this math test." I thought the class understood while I took them through the material.

How could I have done such a poor job? Maybe I should just give up right now... quit teaching, get myself a job at a fast food restaurant. No more responsibilities, no more being polite to Amy. No more answering to the school board, running defense against the parents, running offense for the kids. Just me and the deep fryer. Plus all the French fries I can eat.

"Everyone has bad days. Don't get discouraged." Ruth pushes her plate aside. "Tell me what I can do to help."

Stuff the ballot box?

"I'll get through it."

Her eyes soften. "Everything okay at home?"

"Sure. Never better." Ruth's a great friend, but my money problems aren't her concern.

"How's Priscilla?"

"Fine." But she won't be if my twin doesn't stop issuing Sam dinner invitations. He's been a regular at our kitchen table for the past four Friday nights and I'm still struggling with a guilty conscience. Though I've got to admit, having Sam around definitely makes life interesting. He's smart, well-read and keeps us entertained. I love hearing his stories about all the traveling he did while working for an international accounting firm. His tale last week about the London hotel with the faulty door lock on his ground-level basement bedroom and him climbing through the window only to end up stuck halfway in had the three of us in hysterics over the low-cal pasta dish Priscilla had served.

But I don't care how funny Sam is or how nice a guy he is. No more tours of the house for him. No more repeats of that incident in the basement. I've caught him watching me over the dinner table. Why doesn't he keep his eyes to himself? I'm doing my part. I'm trying not to think about him. Or his soft little moustache. Or the taste of his mouth hard on my own.

Well, I don't think about him much. Better that I sample Priscilla's lasagna than another of his kisses. He's not the man for me. Doesn't he know how tight his shirt collar is? Someone needs to help him pick out clothes that fit. And I hate, hate, HATE myself for noticing, but surely Sam must have noticed it, too. He has the beginning of a double chin.

The last thing I need is an overweight boyfriend. How am I supposed to help him when I can barely help myself?

I'm tired of nibbling on carrot sticks. I'm bored eating fruit instead of cookies. I gag over steamed broccoli. I miss it drenched in rich, buttery sauce. Being at school only makes things harder. It's already October and I'm dreading the thought of Halloween. My fifth graders will be on a sugar high for days.

Given my track record, so will I.

"I'm sorry, Ruth. I don't mean to be such a grouch. It's this stupid diet Priscilla has me on. It's not working."

"Give it some time," she says with a patient smile.

"Time. I wish," I mumble. Just like I wish this stupid skirt fit. I never should have worn it today. It pinches around the waist like it did when I bought it weeks ago. Another extravagance I couldn't afford, but something wacky in my brain urged me on, convincing me a too-tight skirt would be wonderful motivation for losing weight.

Wishful thinking... the story of my life. If a person could *think* themselves into being thin, my entire wardrobe would fit.

"You're being too hard on yourself, dear. You look fine."

Much as I admire and respect her, Ruth has no idea what she's talking about. She's tall, slim and has no clue what it's like to be sitting minding your own business, only to suddenly hear the refrigerator or a bag of cookies calling out your name.

"Ladies? Mind if I join you?"

I fight down the impulse to tug my skirt as Nick strolls over. How can one man be so attractive, attentive, and available at the same time? No calories when it comes to romance. Maybe I need to concentrate more on Nick and less on food.

"You've been a stranger lately." Ruth throws him a smile. "Where have you been keeping yourself all week? We've missed you at lunchtime."

More than during lunch. Nick's barely around except for school hours. Personally, I'd like to know where he's been hanging out but I don't have the guts to ask. I don't want him thinking I'm nosy. Plus I might not like the answer.

"Amy mentioned cheesecake." He glances at Ruth's empty plate, then at me. "Did you finish it off?"

"Who, me? I never even had one piece." The last thing I want him thinking is that I've got no control when it comes to food... even if it is true.

And since when has he started chatting with Amy? I thought he didn't like her.

"There's more in the refrigerator." Ruth nods. "Help yourself."

Nick grabs the chair next to me and attacks a generous wedge of cheesecake. "This is great. Guess I forgot to eat lunch."

How can anyone forget to eat? Food is on my mind twenty-four seven. I open my mouth, then think better of it. I pick up my pen and another test.

"You're quite the mystery man lately," Ruth says. "Are you getting tired of all the female chatter around the lunchroom table?"

"Bored with you ladies? Never." Nick shoots us a lazy smile that makes my toes curl. "I was up at the high school. Basketball starts soon. The coaches had a staff meeting today. Coaching will keep me busy from now on."

"But it's only the middle of October," I say.

"Our team starts practice November first. That gives us two weeks to get things in place."

"How hard can it be to get a team together?"

He shoots me a quick grin. "Obviously you never played basketball."

Me, with my body, play sports? He's kidding, right? Or maybe he isn't. I eye him carefully. Did he mean that as a personal slam to me? Maybe a slam dunk? No, Nick isn't like that. Sarcasm is more Amy's style. "I don't know much about basketball," I admit, "or coaching, either."

"It eats up lots of time." He licks a finger and dabs the last few crumbs of cheesecake off his plate. "Prepping for tryouts comes first. Then once the team is in place, you set up the position strategies involved. Chart the offense, figure out the defense."

"It sounds very complicated." And piled on top of a teaching schedule? This is Nick's first year teaching. How in the world is the poor guy going to find the time? I don't think he realizes how much is involved. First year is the worst. Lesson plans to figure out, tests to make up, learning what classroom methods work the best, maneuvering the ins and outs of the politics involved in teaching.

Kathleen Irene Paterka

"It's not that bad." He shoves his plate aside. "I hope you're a big basketball fan. I'm counting on you to make all our games."

Basketball? Just the word brings a bunch of bad memories bouncing around in my brain. A hot noisy gym, crowded bleachers, and me part of the school band, waiting for half time when our pathetic little clarinet section—me and one pimply faced boy half my size— squeaked out six measures of a feeble duet. But that wasn't the worst. That prize went to the itchy wool band uniform I was forced to wear. Talk about humiliation. I was too big to squeeze into any of the girls' uniforms, so the band director stuffed me into a men's extra-large. Too long in the legs, too tight in the hips. *Fatty Patty*. Unlike the band uniform, the name fit perfect.

"I don't know, Nick. Sports aren't exactly my—"

"I'm not taking *no* for an answer. I want you there, Patty."

He wants me? I fight down a thrill of pleasure and force myself to breathe. It's not like he asked me out on a date. We're talking basketball. I hate basketball.

"You don't know how it feels," he continues, "playing to an empty gym. We need someone in the crowd rooting for us."

"I thought that's what cheerleaders were for." I've never been the cheerleader type. That would qualify as one of Amy's specialties. She was captain of our cheerleading squad in high school. They pranced around at half time doing pyramids and splits in cute little outfits with short flouncy skirts. No itchy wool band uniform for Amy.

"Not anymore," he says. "Cheerleading is a competitive sport. Some games, the cheerleaders don't even show up. They're out on the road at their own

140

meets." Nick shoves his plate aside and looks at me like I'm the best thing that's come along since cheesecake was created. "Come on, Patty, I need you at those games cheering on our team."

He wants me? He needs me? If I wasn't sitting down, I'd leap in the air and try some practice splits right now. "I suppose I could make a few."

You bet I'll make those games. I might even volunteer as head cheerleader.

Nick stretches back in his chair, eyes the window. Sheets of rain beat against the glass. "Doesn't the sun ever shine around here? I should have stayed in Arizona."

"If you think this is bad, just wait till December," I say. Northern Michigan summers are paradise, but the winters can be hell.

"Why did you move to Michigan?" Ruth asks.

"One of my sisters has a friend who teaches at a high school not far from here. She knew I was looking for a job. When she heard about the coaching position, she called my sister and bingo—here I am." He shrugs, grins. "With the economy the way it is, I couldn't say no. Guess I'm lucky to have a job, right?"

"Pretty lucky." But Nick's got it all wrong. We're lucky to have him. I love having this guy around. I cup my chin in my hand, hope to God he doesn't catch me openly admiring him. "So you went into teaching and ended up coaching, too?"

He drums his fingers against the table, playing harmony with the rain pelting against the window. "Actually it was the other way around. I never planned on being a teacher. I grew up in Arizona next door to a golf course. I had big plans to play the pro circuit."

There's a gleam in his eyes that I've never seen before, even when he's talking basketball. Never would I have taken Nick to be a golf nut. He seems so normal.

"So why aren't you out on the golf course?" Ruth asks.

He nods at the window. "It's raining, in case you haven't noticed."

"That's not what I meant. Why teaching, instead of golf?"

"I blew out my knee senior year of high school skiing in Lake Tahoe." The rain clouds outside are no match for the instant scowl covering his face. "One wrong twist and there went my hopes of playing the pro circuit."

Poor Nick. One fall on an icy ski hill and a promising golf career ends up in a sand trap. I'd be bitter, too.

"Surely there must have been something the doctors could have done?" Ruth and I trade sympathetic glances. "Arthroscopic surgery?"

"I had the surgery," he says bitterly. "Lots of surgeries, lots of physical therapy. None of it helped. The knee is shot." He slumps back in his chair. "I could have made the big time but that dream is dead. Talk about a raw deal."

It *is* a raw deal. Anyone in his position has a right to feel like he does. My dreams came true. I always wanted to teach and now I've got a classroom filled with kids. Even if some hideous accident occurred and I ended up paralyzed, I'd still be able to teach. I'd do it sitting down.

"You don't even limp." I try and make it sound like a compliment. Nick's in a foul mood and not looking for sympathy.

"My knee's strong enough to get around, even shoot a round or two of golf. But it's not good enough to make the pros."

"Wasn't there a way you could have stayed with the game? Maybe given private golf lessons?" Ruth suggests.

"You mean, stick around taking hack shots at a country club? Be some lackey for a guy who never would have been as good as I could have been? No thanks. Not interested."

I wince at the icy stare he shoots Ruth. If Nick ever looked at me like that, I'd duck straight into that half-eaten bag of coconut macaroons hidden in my desk.

"If you'd told me five years ago I'd be stuck in Northern Michigan teaching fifth grade, I would have laughed in your face. But a guy's got to make a living, right?" He shrugs. "Being a teacher seemed the best option. It's easy work… best of all, I get the summers off."

Easy work? That's not true.

"I always wanted to be a teacher," I say. "When we were growing up, my sister and I had a big playroom with a blackboard on one wall and we loved playing school. Priscilla—that's my sister—was always the student and I was the teacher."

"That doesn't surprise me." A wry smile tugs at Nick's mouth and I feel a tiny glow of happiness inside, knowing I'm the one who put it there. He had a setback. Anyone would feel bitter, given his history. "I played a little basketball in high school. The knee surgeries kept me on the bench my senior year. Coach put me to work keeping score and tracking defense. That got me interested in strategy. I started coaching part time after college."

"Why aren't you teaching up at the high school?" Ruth asks.

"Good question. It would make sense, wouldn't it? But there weren't any openings." Nick shrugs. "It doesn't matter. At least I've got a job. Besides, kids are kids, no matter how old they are. High school, grade school, they're all the same."

Where did he come up with that idea? From my experience, every student is unique and should be treated that way or you don't get anywhere. I might not know much about golf or life, but I do know kids. And the other thing I know is that no matter how old they are, kids aren't stupid. They know when you're faking.

Does Nick fake it in the classroom?

Then again, maybe high school kids are different. Maybe teenage boys are different. How would I know? I didn't have any brothers, and very few boyfriends. Maybe that's why I ended up stuck in fifth grade. Maybe I'm not grown up enough or qualified enough to handle high school boys.

Or men, either.

"Funny how life turns out. I always wanted to be a lawyer and argue cases in a courtroom." Ruth smiles softly. "Instead, I ended up in front of a classroom trying to make a case for reading and math."

I stare at her over my tests. Ruth, a past honoree as Teacher of the Year, never planned to go into teaching? But she's the best teacher I've ever met.

"What stopped you?" Nick asks.

"Money," she says ruefully. "My parents helped out with my undergrad studies but there was no way they could afford to put me through law school. And since my grades weren't good enough to pull a full scholarship, I made the decision to go into education. Looking back, I can't say I'm sorry. I enjoy teaching and my students. Well, most of them, anyway." She throws us an easy smile. "And I'm a firm believer that things turn out the way they were meant to be. Hopefully I've been able to make a difference in some of their lives. A few of my students have even gone on to become lawyers."

"For heaven's sake, what are all of you doing sitting around in here?" Amy flounces into the teacher's lounge. "Don't you have class or something?"

"My fifth graders have music this hour." Not that it's any of her business. Amy probably couldn't sing a true note if she tried.

Ruth stands and pushes in her chair. "I suppose I should head back. I've got a few things to finish before my students come back from gym."

I glance at my watch. I haven't made much of a dent in the tests I'm scoring but the bell hasn't rung yet, which means the music teacher's metronome is still ticking off the minutes in my classroom. Plus there's no way in hell I am leaving Nick and Amy alone.

I wrap my feet around the legs of my chair and grab another math test.

"Amy, that cheesecake you made was great." Nick crumples his paper plate and makes a quick shot at the trash basket.

"Silly boy, you think I cook? My husband Hughie picked it up at the bakery."

Nick grins. "Hughie's a lucky guy."

"He is. And good thing for him, he knows it. But I don't want to talk about him." She sidles close to Nick and wags her finger at him. "You're the one I've been thinking about."

Nick blinks. "Me?"

My heart flutters. If she moves any closer, she'll end up in his lap.

Her blond hair brushes his shoulder. "I've been thinking about you for days."

"Is that right?" He laces his fingers together across his stomach and sprawls back in his chair with a lazy grin. "All good, I hope."

"Could it be anything but? It's all about you," she assures him with a pretty pout.

How can she blatantly flirt like that with him? I hate sitting here listening to this. I hate Amy. I've always hated Amy. And at the moment, I'm pretty damn close to hating Nick, too. I thought he said he didn't like her. I thought he said he didn't trust her. Why do men get so weird when it comes to women? Say things they don't mean? Make promises they don't keep?

If this is the way he's going to be, he can just forget about me showing up at those stupid basketball games.

"Anyway, I came up with the most brilliant idea." Amy's eyes gleam. "I'm going to throw a party for you. A cocktail party, just before the holidays. Doesn't that sound like fun?"

"Sounds great," he says doubtfully. "But I don't know many people. Who would come?"

"That's the reason for the party… so you can get to know people. The right kind of people," she adds.

"Are teachers invited?" I pipe up, even though I've already got a pretty good idea what her answer will be.

"I suppose I'll ask a few people from school… but certainly not everyone. And especially not her." Amy wrinkles her nose and nods at the door Ruth just left through. "Bad enough we're forced to sit here every day listening to her prattle on. It's my house, my party, and I'm not inviting her."

I slump further in my chair. If Ruth's not invited, it's a virtual guarantee I won't make the list.

Amy turns back to Nick. "This will be so much fun! All you have to do is pick the date and I'll plan the party. There's a new martini recipe I've been dying to try. I can't wait to show it to the bartender."

"You're hiring a bartender?" His eyebrows lift. "This sounds like quite the party."

"What's the point in doing something if you don't do it right?" Amy asks as the bell rings. She scoots from the table and heads for the door. Delicate gold bracelets jingle as she throws him a little wave. "Let me know about the date."

"Looks like I'm in for it now." Nick shoves his chair under the table. "You're coming, right?"

"Sure." It's only a quick walk down the hall, but I might as well make the most of my opportunities and spend time with him while I still have the chance. Once Nick meets all those prominent people at Amy's party, he'll forget about me. I shuffle my tests into a big messy stack and grab my pen.

"No, I mean the party." He opens the door, holds it for me. "You're coming, right?"

I halt, blink, frown. "Amy's party?"

"Bingo."

"I don't think so." Amy was pretty specific about who would and wouldn't make the cut on her list. Maybe he doesn't realize how much Amy hates me. And I hate her. Who wants to go to her stupid old party, anyway? Not me. Well, not much. After all, the party *is* in Nick's honor. "I doubt I'm invited," I finally admit. Saying the words out loud makes it hurt even worse. I scoot under his arm, head into the hallway.

"Sure you're invited," his voice floats behind me. "I just asked you."

My heart pounds as I whirl around to face him. "You mean… go with you to the party?"

A frown hovers on his forehead. "What's the problem? You don't want to go with me?"

Am I messing up here or did Nick just ask me out? I must be crazy thinking like that. Guys like Nick don't date women like me. And even if he did ask me out, it's a pity invitation thrown to a fellow teacher. The last thing I want is pity from Nick or to have him feeling sorry for me. What I really want is…

"I don't think—"

His eyes narrow. "You're turning me down?"

Noisy kids rush by us as I slump against the door. My knees feel spongy, like rubber bands. "You don't understand. Amy and I aren't exactly friends. I doubt she'll be thrilled if I show up."

"Who cares what she thinks? You and I are a team, remember? Besides, I'm the guest of honor. That means I get to take who I want. And I'm taking you."

I want to go. I'm scared to go. I've got to be crazy, facing Amy's wrath for a date with Nick.

A date with Nick… I'd be crazy *not* to go.

"Come on, Patty, quit playing around. We both know you're going to say *yes*."

"All right." I lift my arms in defeat. "Okay, okay. Yes, I'll go."

"That's my girl." He winks, gives me a thumbs-up, and disappears down the hall.

His girl? Nick's girl? Did he mean it?

Yes!

I lean against the door another minute, trying to find my breath. My very first cocktail party ever, and I'll be on Nick's arm. First thing Saturday morning,

Priscilla and I need to hit the mall. I've got to find a dress. *The Dress*. This calls for drastic measures. No more sneaking food, no more hidden six-packs of chocolate. And that half-eaten bag of coconut macaroons stashed in the bottom of my desk? Headed straight for the trash. Serious dieting is in order, starting right now. Who needs cookies at a time like this?

I've got a date with Nick Lamont!

CHAPTER TEN

"Well, look who's here." Sam yanks off his goggles. "I thought you gave up on the pool."

"It was this or liposuction." I ease into the cool water in the lane next to him. Nothing changes if nothing changes and nothing's changed since I've been here. Same shimmering water, same plastic lane dividers bobbing on the surface, same skinny lifeguard sporting a wispy beard. Same chunky girl I've always been.

Fatty Patty.

Déjà vu. Day One, all over again. I haven't been at the pool for weeks, well before Halloween. Desperation brought me back. I've got exactly one month to trim these ugly inches from my hips and thighs if I want to look smashing and sexy in that new dress I bought for Amy's party. So far, I've lost five pounds through grim determination and a diet of carrot sticks. Fifteen more pounds and Nick will be wowed.

But I want him more than wowed. I want Nick to look at me like… like the way Sam looks at me.

"Got any plans for after your workout?"

"Why?" I tread water, glance at Sam. Thanks to Priscilla, I've grown used to having him around. He's like a big old cuddly teddy bear, the brother I never had. I'm not even embarrassed at having him see me in this bathing suit. Sam knows I have chunky thighs. He doesn't care.

And I've got to give him credit. Sam's kept his word and kept his distance… though sometimes I still catch him staring when he thinks I'm not looking. But he's made no romantic overtures, made no further attempts to kiss me. It's just meatloaf, lasagna, and friendly dinner conversation, much to my relief... plus a little regret, too. The last thing I want is to lead Sam on, but the easy banter between us is gone and I miss it.

Just like I miss the tickle of his soft little moustache.

Kissing him was fun. *More than fun.*

Kissing him was exciting. *More than exciting.*

Kissing him was...

"I was going to call you later this week," he says. "I've been crunching some numbers on your house. I've got the file out in my car. If you're not busy, we could go over it tonight."

My gut tightens and I grab the edge of the pool. "I don't know if that's such a good idea." Even with Sam propping me up for moral support, the mere thought of confronting Priscilla about selling makes me feel like I could be sucked under at any minute. "Maybe we should wait a few days. Priscilla hasn't been feeling too great. Her allergies are giving her fits."

"I was thinking it might be better if we discussed some things without her. We could do it tonight. Maybe over dinner."

I bob in the water, eye him carefully. Is this some trick to get me alone? Lure me into some dark corner, throw a few financial figures my way and then make his move?

Just when I was starting to trust him...

"Nothing fancy," he adds. "We can grab some hamburgers, spread out the paperwork, and talk in private."

Hamburgers? That doesn't sound like a date, but exactly like what he mentioned—a casual business meeting over dinner. Sam must be serious. His moustache hasn't even twitched.

"Okay, but can we please forget about the greasy hamburger? I'm on a very strict diet." I think about the brand new dress hanging in my closet. That cocktail dress simply *has* to fit.

"I promise we'll go some place where you can get a nice salad."

"And separate checks," I warn. He's been good so far, but I don't want him getting the wrong idea. "Plus, I need to finish my workout."

"I've still got a few laps left myself." He snaps his goggles firmly in place and sinks under the water.

I fasten my own goggles, take a deep gulp, and kick off against the wall. Did I make a mistake, agreeing to have dinner with him tonight? I like Sam, but sometimes being around him dredges up feelings inside me I don't trust. Feelings I don't dare give into. I don't need to get tangled up with Sam. He's big and bold, not afraid to take on the world… or a triple bacon cheeseburger.

Bad enough I look the way I do. The last thing I need is a boyfriend who's fat.

# # #

Sam eyes me across the table. "You didn't even look at the menu. How do you know for sure what you want?"

I sip my water with the lemon slice floating amid the ice cubes and ignore the unopened menu in front of me. Why tempt myself by peeking inside? "I've been here before. They serve salads."

"Yes, but they've got other things besides—"

"I'm having a chef salad." Why is he making this so difficult? I'm already regretting my decision to come here. Chuck's Tavern and Grill is a local place known for its Friday night all-you-can-eat-fish-fries, relaxed homey atmosphere, and big comfortable booths where people spread out and relax. But who can relax with those tantalizing smells drifting from the nearby grill? French fries, onion rings, sizzling steaks.

Why does food that's supposedly so bad for you have to smell so good?

"They serve great steaks. Have you ever tried their ribs? They make the best barbecued ribs you'll ever taste."

I squeeze my eyes shut, try not to think about barbequed ribs slathered in sauce, tender meat falling off the bone. How many calories in barbecued ribs? How many pounds do I need to lose before I look good in that little black dress?

Forget eating ribs. The only ribs I want are my own ribs showing in that dress.

"I'll have a chef salad, please. No croutons. Vinegar dressing." The waitress scribbles as I rattle off my order. "And a plain dinner roll. No butter."

Too bad Priscilla isn't here. She'd be so proud of me.

"I'll take the steak." Sam slaps his menu shut. "And a baked potato, please, with butter and sour cream. I'll have a salad, too… and throw on some extra croutons, will you? I'll take the ones she didn't want." He leans across the table as the waitress disappears. "I don't get it, Patty. Why nibble on rabbit food when you could eat steak or ribs?"

I squirm against the cushy vinyl booth. "I'm on a diet, remember?"

"No butter, no croutons?" His eyebrows lift. "Sounds like a pretty drastic diet to me."

What makes him think he's got a right to grill me about the food I choose to eat? Next thing, he'll want to know my dress size, or how much I weigh. Men aren't supposed to talk about things like that with women. Are they? Then again, how would I know? Until this year, the only men in my life have been ten-year-old boys.

But now I've got Sam... and Nick Lamont.

"I still don't understand why you want to lose weight. You look great just the way you are."

Never mind telling him about Teacher of the Year. Sam would never understand. There's a huge voting population out there in the educational community just waiting for the nominations to open up next week so they can cast their ballot for the one teacher best able to represent us all. Am I that person? Sam might think so, but he's not allowed to vote. Meanwhile, there's no mistaking the admiration in his eyes. I grab my water glass and force myself to take long slow sips. Coming here tonight was a huge mistake. I should have known better. When am I going to learn to trust my better judgment?

Our food arrives. I drizzle vinegar over the generous platter of assorted greens, fresh vegetables, diced ham, shredded cheese, sliced eggs. Working out at the pool always makes me hungry. I could easily wolf down the whole thing without any trouble. But can I get away with eating all of it? The plate overflows with healthy abundance, but is it too much for one person? A normal person would know—a normal person with a normal appetite.

Sam eyes my plate as I set down the vinegar. "I admire your willpower. I'm supposed to be on a diet, too."

"What kind of diet?" I spear some lettuce, a sliver of ham, nibble around the edges.

"I'm not sure what you'd call it. It's some plan my cardiologist suggested I try."

"Low carbs? No sugar?" I cringe as he plops an entire dish of blue cheese dressing over his mixed greens. Doesn't he know that blue cheese dressing is loaded with fat? Sam's doctor must be a quack.

"The guy's a fanatic."

Exactly what I was thinking.

"You know the type," he continues.

I nod. I've met my share of wacko physicians, thanks to Priscilla.

"I ignore most of what he says... except on Wednesdays."

"You see your cardiologist every week?" He must be in worse shape than I thought.

Sam grins. "We play poker with a couple other guys every Wednesday night. He plays poker the same way he practices medicine—like it's a matter of life or death."

"What kind of diet has he got you on?"

"Some basic food plan. Fruits and vegetables. Portion control. Watch the fat content." He spears a cherry tomato smothered in blue cheese and pops it in his mouth. "Get more exercise, he said. Eliminate stress. Get eight hours of sleep every night. Drink a glass of red wine with dinner every night. That's the kind of advice I like." He lifts his glass and toasts me. "But as for the rest?" He shrugs. "I haven't got time to deal with stuff like that. I've got a business to run."

My own appetite disappears as I watch him eat. Sam has no clue what he's doing to himself—or his arteries. What he needs is a Priscilla in his life... someone to watch over him.

"What do you think your doctor would say if he knew you were eating that steak?"

Sam throws me an odd look. "What's wrong with steak? I happen to like it."

"And I like chocolate. But that doesn't mean it's good for me."

"We're talking about meat, remember?" His voice is low and guarded. "Who said anything about dessert?"

Poor Sam. The man is hopeless. "And as for that blue cheese dressing on your salad..."

His eyes narrow. "What about it?"

"You just told me your doctor said to limit the fats. But do you listen? No. Do you have any idea how many calories are in one tablespoon of blue cheese dressing?" I refuse to back down. Sam needs to hear this. If he won't listen to his doctor, maybe he'll listen to me. It's for his own good.

"I don't remember asking you to be my food police." He shoves his half-eaten salad aside. "Do us both a favor, Patty. Quit the talk about food and diets."

"But—"

"I said *no*." His face is stern as he holds up a hand in warning. "I don't want to hear it."

I tear off a chunk of dry dinner roll and stuff it in my mouth. My cheeks burn and I'm sure they're as bright red as the cherry tomatoes on my plate. Sam's right. It's none of my business what kind of dressing he puts on his salad, or if he orders steak, if he eats dessert. Who am I to criticize him? I know how much I hate it when Priscilla does the same thing to me.

We sit there in awkward silence and then his steak arrives—a thick slab of meat nearly covering his plate. Two thousand calories, guaranteed. That doesn't include the potato, dripping with butter and a huge dollop of sour cream.

I cram the rest of my dinner roll in my mouth.

Sam ignores his steak and snaps open his briefcase. "I've been working on some spreadsheets." He pulls out a thick file and rifles through the paperwork. "I've done a cost analysis and breakdown of your assets."

"Priscilla and I don't have any assets." Our joint savings account is nearly empty… especially after last week when Sam insisted we didn't dare wait any longer to replace the furnace. "We're broke."

"Actually, you're not."

"But we spent the money when we—"

"Forget about the money part, Patty. I'm talking about that house of yours. It's your major asset. They don't make places like that anymore. Wraparound porches and big front lawns. You're sitting on a treasure. That's the kind of house where people want to raise families. It might not be worth what it was a few years ago, but it's still worth quite a bit. Plus, there's no mortgage."

"Don't forget about the home equity loan. That needs to be paid once we sell."

"Trust me, you don't want to sell that house."

"What?" I stare at him, feeling like Mama died all over again. Doesn't he get it? I don't want the house. I don't want the grief. I don't want the life.

"You do not want to sell."

"Yes, I do." I jab my finger on his paperwork. "You've seen Priscilla's pay stubs. They add up to practically nothing. And my teaching salary isn't much better. You know what they say about working in Northern Michigan. *A view of the bay is half the pay.*" I slump back against the booth. "We don't have a choice. We have to sell."

"Listen to me, will you? With some creative financing in place, you and Priscilla will be able to—"

"No." I swallow over the growing lump in my throat. Talk about feeling betrayed. All this time I thought Sam was on my side. I thought he understood how I felt. I don't want to live in that big old drafty house. I want out. I want a place of my own. A husband. A family. There's got to be more to life than this.

Or maybe there isn't.

Maybe this is it.

And suddenly I wish I hadn't hired him. What does Sam know about anything, anyway? No wife, no Priscilla, no kids to distract him. He's all alone and can do as he pleases. Plus he lives in a condo, which—from what he's said—sounds like a little piece of heaven. All the modern conveniences, no rusty plumbing, no big backyard. No neighbors complaining if the lawn isn't mowed.

Who needs a lawn? Give me a second-floor condo with a private balcony and I'll manage just fine.

"You turned to me for financial advice, so at least listen to what I'm saying. If you hang on to the house—"

"No!"

"For at least another year... maybe two, tops. It won't be forever." Sam reaches across the table and gently covers my hand. "I know it's not what you want but it's in your best interests. Meanwhile, think of that home equity loan as a financial Band-Aid. It'll help you make improvements that have got to be done."

I stare at his hand atop my own. Do I shrug it off? I stare at the paperwork covering the tabletop. Do I sweep it on the floor? But what good would that do? I'm tired of fighting. Tired of being broke. Maybe Sam is right. After all, he is the expert. We're paying him good money—money we don't have—for sound financial advice. Maybe it's time I started listening.

"There's something else that home equity loan will buy you," he adds. "Probably the thing you need most of all."

"What?"

"Time." He squeezes my hand. "Using that money will buy you time to bring Priscilla around."

He's made a good point. Priscilla's become an expert when it comes to evading the issue of selling. Up until now, I haven't pushed hard enough. I haven't wanted to force her hand. But that doesn't mean I don't know how to do it. I could make her life a living hell. I could threaten to move out, to leave her behind in that big old house. Priscilla would freak. We've never been separated except for the years I went off to college. Even then, she wasn't alone. Mama was still alive.

The mere suggestion of me leaving would have poor Priscilla packing in a heartbeat. She'd lug every one of our suitcases from the dusty attic. And every step would break her heart.

I can't do that to Priscilla. I love her too much. It wouldn't be fair.

I tug my hand from his, slump back in the booth. "Do you really think waiting a year is best?"

"I do." His eyes soften. "I promise you, Patty… it won't be forever."

"All right. I'll wait. But I'm not happy about it." I feel like I've lost the battle—for now. Hopefully Sam knows what he's talking about and has some strategic plan in mind because I'm not so sure. Convincing Priscilla won't be easy. That much I know in my gut. But maybe I've been going about it all wrong. Maybe with Sam's help, I can bring her around. Maybe if she sees how other people live, that it doesn't have to be like this, things might go smoother.

Sam clips the paperwork together and carefully slides it in his briefcase. I watch as he finally cuts into his steak. We've been talking for some time and the meat has grown cold. White blobs of fat congeal around the edges.

Maybe he won't eat so much.

"Have you decided about Thanksgiving yet?" I ask. Priscilla invited him for holiday dinner more than two weeks ago. "Or are you visiting your sister in Arizona this year?"

"I decided to stay in town." He stabs a piece of meat, washes it down with a sip of wine. "Eileen's working during the holidays. I plan on flying out to see her at Christmas."

"So, you're coming for Thanksgiving?"

He smiles. "Looking forward to it."

Wait till I tell Priscilla that Sam will be our guest. She loves cooking big holiday dinners. And if I think hard enough, I'll dream up some more people who would appreciate an invitation for a turkey dinner with all the trimming. The more, the merrier… and the better my chances of getting a conversation flowing in the right direction. Topic to be discussed: the joys of condo ownership. Sam has one. And so do Ruth and her husband, Jack. They downsized a few years ago. Maybe I'll talk to Ruth at school tomorrow. Hopefully they don't have any plans for Thanksgiving. Priscilla knows them both and enjoys their company.

And Priscilla loves having Sam around. She trusts him.

So do I.

Especially now I know he's on my side.

One more year. A person can get through anything for one year. And when the year's up, no matter what Priscilla says, we're going to sell the house.

CHAPTER ELEVEN

He isn't coming. I reminded him twice that dinner starts promptly at two. I glance at the grandfather clock standing guard near the hallway, its spindly hands inching toward the hour. Soon there'll be two solemn bongs, followed by Priscilla's announcement of Dinner Served. The living room will empty out as everyone gathers in the dining room to share in the feast. The table will be full except for the seat I saved next to mine.

Nick's chair will be empty on this day meant for giving thanks.

Thank God he's not coming!

I've been dreading this holiday dinner since last week when Nick overheard me chatting about it with Ruth. Somehow he ended up with an invitation, too. I'm not sure how it happened; did I invite him or did he invite himself? I spent the entire weekend in a panic. What if he doesn't like the food? Our house? The company?

And what's going to happen when he sees Sam is one of our dinner guests, too?

Damn that Nick. All the worrying he put me through, only to be a no-show—especially on the one day I manage to look good. No, not just good. Today I look great and feel great in this black velvet pant set resurrected from the back of my closet. It finally fits now that I've lost a few pounds. Even my hair cooperated today. Wild curls are tucked high atop my head, save for a few stray tendrils trailing down the nape of my neck. Draped in black velvet, pearls at my ears and around my throat, I feel sleek and voluptuous, sweet and sexy. If Nick had bothered showing up, I'm sure he would have been impressed. Everyone else seems to be… especially Sam.

I shoot him a sweet smile. God bless Sam and his contribution of this marvelous cabernet. He brought along two bottles, and it's not the cheap grocery store variety Priscilla and I buy on those rare occasions when we splurge. Sam brought the good stuff. Normally I don't drink, but fear of witnessing a showdown between Nick and Sam inspired my first glass… and the second. But now Nick's a no-show, there's no need to worry about heated glances full of testosterone or barbed comments flying across the table. Just relax and celebrate.

"Would anyone like to join me?" I lift the bottle and wave it with a bright smile. I'm not sure if it's my third or fourth, but who's counting?

"We'll be eating soon." Priscilla's voice floats across the room. "Maybe you should wait for dinner."

And maybe my sister should mind her own business. I love her dearly, but today is a holiday and I intend to have a good time. I pour myself a generous glass and purposely ignore her. "Sam, what about you?"

He throws me a funny look and covers his glass with one hand. "All set, thanks."

"I'll take a refill." Jack Proctor leans toward me with his empty glass.

"My pleasure." I fill his glass with a liberal hand and a gracious smile. No wonder Ruth is always so content. Who wouldn't be, with a man like Jack waiting at home every night? Tall and rugged with silver hair and an easy smile, he's a born gentleman. Lucky Ruth.

And lucky Priscilla. Dr. Brown's tranquil gray eyes are as kind as his smile. No worries there. I settle back in my chair, toast her happiness with another sip of wine, and toast my own cleverness for inviting him to join us today. He's obviously enjoying himself, waxing forth on the marvels of modern medicine as he rocks in Priscilla's favorite chair. Normally that chair is off-limits to anyone but her. But she's the one who escorted him to his seat—once she recovered from the shock of seeing him standing at our front door.

Contacting his office, arranging the invitation, and managing to keep the surprise from my twin was definitely worth the effort. Never in a million years would I have guessed Dr. Brown would be the one to steal her heart away. Short and slim, bland and bald, this immaculately groomed man with the beeper on his belt seems totally clueless that he alone provides the cure for what ails my sister. Who needs a medical degree to diagnose Priscilla's malaise? I can sum it up in one word… *love*.

"Isn't this all so lovely?" I smile happily, glance around the room. It looks like it could be straight out of a Normal Rockwell painting. The logs in the hearth snap merrily, the men are in suits and ties, the women look so pretty. Best of all, there's no bickering. Only happy, smiling faces. Happy Thanksgiving, me!

I lift my glass and toast them all. "Isn't this fun? Thank you all for coming today."

"Thank you for inviting us." Ruth raises her own glass. "We have so much to celebrate. For one thing, your nomination as Teacher of the Year."

"Intermediate Elementary Teacher," I correct her with a modest smile. Though I've got to admit that every time I remember how it felt hearing my name announced at last week's staff meeting, I still want to leap to my feet, pump my fist in the air in my best Rocky imitation. Yes! It's official! I'm in! I made it! "Plus it's only the preliminary round."

"Don't sell yourself short, my dear," she says with a confident air. "Obviously you're very well liked or you wouldn't have been nominated five years in a row. And now that you're in this year's competition… well, I think you'll find things will be different this time."

"You really think so?" I ask. But in my gut, I know she's right. This year, unlike any other year, I think I've got a decent chance of winning. I'm taking care of myself. I'm losing weight.

"You've got my vote," Sam says.

"That's very sweet, Sam, but you don't count," I tell him. "School staffs pick their nominees and then things move on to the county level."

"That's where you're at now?"

I nod. "I have to fill out a questionnaire before Christmas, plus write a paper about myself. Then, sometime after the holidays, all the nominees are interviewed by the selection committee. It's made up of mayors from each town, some advertising reps from the local newspapers—plus the president of the service club presenting the award."

Failing to impress that committee—that's been my downfall, year after year. But I'm done playing the nice girl. Forget modesty and all that crap. It's gotten me nowhere in the past. I intend to schmooze with the best of them. I'll fill out that questionnaire in my very best handwriting. I'll write a paper glorifying my teaching efforts at providing our students with the best educational opportunities available. I've already volunteered for every single opportunity that would look good on my résumé. I'm running the spelling bees, heading up substitute teacher training, peer mentoring new teachers, coordinating the after-school program.

Although how the hell I'm going to find the time for all the commitments I made is beyond me. But I'm determined to do whatever it takes. This is my year and I am going to win that contest.

"I got such a kick watching Nick when they called his name." Ruth laughs softly. "He looked so surprised."

Nick Lamont, First-Year Teacher of the Year. But he's the only new teacher in our school. No surprise there. Who wouldn't vote for Nick? I certainly would.

I'd like to do more than vote for him.

"And Amy," Ruth adds. "We can't forget her."

"Oh, right. Let's not forget Amy." That smug little kindergarten teacher pulled off a coup with her nomination as Primary Teacher of the Year. I don't know how she did it; maybe she rounded up a voting block by promising teachers invitations to the cocktail party she's throwing for Nick. Thank God I'm not up against her. Amy's Primary, I'm Intermediate. Both of us could win our respective category.

Then again, we're both competing for the same grand prize. Teacher of the Year.

Not to mention, we're also competing with Nick.

What if it comes down to a vote between Nick and me?

No. I take another swig of wine. Not going there, not going to think about that. Best Win Scenario: Nick walks away with First-Year Teacher of the Year, I waltz away with the Grand Prize, and Amy sits alone with a big fat nothing.

And if she thinks I'm stupid enough to let her get away with buying votes, Amy's got another think coming. Our house is plenty big enough. Maybe

Priscilla and I will throw a cocktail party of our own. And I'll be sure to invite Ruth. The goodies she brought are going fast. I scan the large tray of assorted gourmet crackers, toasted baguettes, fresh cheeses, and yummy homemade avocado dip, ignoring the crudités provided personally for me by Priscilla. What's the point in celebrating the holidays if you can't enjoy them? This is life, not prison. I refuse to be sentenced to doing hard time munching carrot sticks.

And if I can't eat, I'll just have to make do with Sam's wine. The thick smile on my face feels like cake icing that's crusted with sugar crystals from sitting too long. Everyone laughs and I join in, even though I have no clue what we're laughing about. Something Dr. Brown said. No. What *Harold* said. He wants us to call him Harold. He's so cute. Well, not exactly cute. But Priscilla seems to think so and I'm not about to argue with her. Thanksgiving is meant as a day of giving thanks, and I certainly am… especially for this wine. I sink into the couch pillows, wiggle my toes, enjoy the warmth surging through my body. Who would have thought Sam would have such excellent taste in wine? He's quite the Renaissance man. And quite attractive, too… despite those extra pounds.

"That is such a nice tie." I mean to purr but the words slop out of my mouth. "Did you pick it out yourself? And I love your moustache. Promise me you'll never shave it off."

"I certainly have no plans to do so." Dr. Brown fingers his tie and his pencil-thin moustache. "But thank you very much."

"Actually, Harold, I was talking about Sam." I toast him with a playful smile. "Although if you asked, I'm sure Priscilla will admit that she thinks your moustache is quite becoming. Jack, maybe you should consider growing a moustache." Memories of a dusty basement put a crooked grin on my face. "You never know. Ruth might love it. I recently discovered that moustaches make for quite the kiss."

Priscilla jams a plate in front of me. "Try some of these cucumbers. I sliced them just for you."

"No thanks." Who need vegetables at a time like this? My glass is empty. I'll have some more gift of the grape.

Priscilla grabs the wine bottle before I can and moves it out of my reach. "Harold, why don't you tell us about your practice? Immunology is a fascinating subject."

Someone needs to set my sister straight. No one wants to hear about medical procedures.

"I specialize in immunology and infectious diseases. We assess the patient's needs, then determine the best method in which to proceed. Of course, blood work is the telling factor."

Blood? I stare at my glass and my stomach crawls to a stop. Blood is exactly the color of the wine we're drinking. "Could we please talk about something more pleasant? This is a holiday, remember? I don't want to spend it discussing bodily fluids."

Priscilla rises from her chair. "Patty, would you please help me in the kitchen?"

"Since when do you need my help? You know I'm a terrible cook."

"Patty."

Oh, God, how well I know that tone of voice. She's issuing a demand, not an invitation. I roll my eyes, sigh and wobble to a stand. What is Priscilla's problem? There's no reason for her to act so witchy… or bitchy. I giggle at my little poem as I stumble after her. This has turned out to be the most wonderful holiday, especially after all those days I spent worrying over Nick, the no-show. No worries now. And I love this pleasant relaxed feeling. It would be so wonderful to always feel this way and freely speak my mind.

"I don't see why you need my help," I grumble, trailing her into the kitchen. "I'm having a good time."

"Yes, I noticed." Priscilla yanks open the oven door. "And for your information, so has everyone else."

"What's that supposed to mean?" I lean against the refrigerator and watch as she bastes the turkey. "You sound mad. Are you mad?"

"I should think that would be obvious." She slams the oven shut and whirls to face me. "You ought to be ashamed of yourself. You're drunk, Patty. First you embarrass Harold, then you embarrass Sam, then me. You've embarrassed yourself."

"I have?" Suddenly the world doesn't seem so friendly. I sift through fuzzy thoughts, trying to remember exactly what I said. Unfortunately, my mind refuses to cooperate. Whatever I said, it must have been terrible to put Priscilla in such a snit. She looks like a modern day she-warrior ready to do battle, wielding that turkey baster. Good thing it's merely plastic.

"Everything okay in here?" Sam pokes his head through the door.

"Patty and I are having a little discussion." Pots and pans bang as Priscilla slams around the kitchen.

"Sounds like a pretty loud discussion." He ventures into the room with a wary look. "FYI, they can hear you in the living room."

"And they sent you in to check for survivors?" I ask. Mama always said it's not nice to tease but it's hard to resist. Sam is usually so full of confidence, but not at the moment. Maybe he's spotted Priscilla's turkey baster. "Which one of us do you plan on rescuing?"

He moves closer to me, chuckling softly. "You girls should behave."

Priscilla levels the turkey baster directly at Sam. "I don't see what you're laughing about. You are just as much to blame as she is."

"Me?" He blinks. "What did I do?"

I lean against the sink, giggling at the protest in his voice. At least I'm not alone in facing Priscilla's wrath.

"Don't play all innocent, Sam Curtis. This is all your fault. You're the one who brought that wine. Just look at her. She's drunk."

With her blue eyes flashing and that rosy blush staining her cheeks, Priscilla suddenly looks like she's never been sick a day in her life. What's prompted this sudden burst of good health? Something... or *someone*. I feel the thick smile plastered on my face stretch like silly putty. Maybe I should have a little talk with Dr. Brown. Hopefully he hasn't already made plans for Christmas.

Priscilla throws down the turkey baster. "Sam, I'm putting you in charge. Don't you dare let her back into that living room until she sobers up."

"Thank God she's gone," I whisper as she slams out the door. "And thank God you showed up. She scares me."

But he doesn't. He's so close, I could reach out and touch him. I lift one finger, softly trace the curve of his cheek. "My hero."

He flinches. "Hey, stop that." A quiver runs up his jaw as he jerks away.

"Sorry." My heartbeat takes off as I search his face. He refuses to meet my eyes. "Are you mad at me, too?"

"Not mad. Just... don't tease. Okay?"

"What makes you think I'm teasing?" My eyes zero in on his soft little moustache and I swallow hard. One step, and I could be in his arms. One step...

"Whoa!" He catches me as I stumble against the counter.

"Sorry." I fan myself with one hand, pluck the clinging black velvet away from my skin. When did the kitchen get so hot? "I guess Priscilla was right. Maybe I have had a little too much wine."

"You need something to eat. Let's find you some crackers."

"Don't bother," I say as I watch him hunt through cupboards and drawers. "I'm not allowed to eat them."

"Why not?" He halts and turns to eye me uncertainly. "Are you allergic to wheat?"

The thought of me being allergic to any kind of food suddenly has me in a fit of giggles. "Priscilla's the one with the allergies. I can't eat crackers because they're not on my diet."

"Well, guess what? They are now. You need something to soak up that alcohol."

"Don't tell Priscilla," I warn him. "If she finds out you fed me crackers, there'll be hell to pay."

"Don't worry, I can handle your sister." He searches through another cupboard. "Where does she keep them?"

"Check the pantry. Behind the canned vegetables. That's where she hides the goodies."

Sam disappears and I lean against the counter, listening as he rummages through the cupboards. The room spins slightly and I close my eyes. Whatever possessed me to drink all that wine? Maybe Sam is right. I need some food in my stomach. Crackers will soak up the wine. I'll only eat a few. No one will know. No one but Sam. And he doesn't count.

Well, not much.

Well, actually, he does. The truth sloshes in my stomach. Sam counts a lot.

I don't want crackers. I want…

"Victory." Sam emerges from the pantry with a small box. "Hold out your hand."

I lift a cracker to my mouth and nibble around the edges, eyeing him with a smile. "Thank you."

"You're welcome." He plants himself directly in front of me with the open box. "Come on, eat a few more. You'll feel better."

"I already do." Obediently I take another bite. "You're very sweet, Sam. Have I ever told you that?"

He shrugs.

"You don't believe me?"

He smiles, but his eyes are wary. "Keep eating the crackers, Patty. Priscilla was right. You've had too much wine."

"You think I don't know a nice guy when I see one?" I lean in closer, eyeing his moustache. Tempting, enticing, much too delicious to ignore. "What's that they say …*in vino, veritas*? The truth is found in wine."

"Eat your crackers like a good girl and don't be saying things you don't mean."

"Who says I don't mean it?" I mean every word. He's such a sweet man. Honest and loyal… the kind of man a woman can trust. He keeps his promises. He's there when you need him.

He even showed up for Thanksgiving.

I lean into him, rest my head on his shoulder. "We don't deserve you. I don't deserve you." He stiffens for a moment, then suddenly his arms tighten around me, and the sensation is heavenly, like a sanctuary closing its gates. There's no need to be afraid. Whatever I say or do, I'm safe. I look up and search Sam's face. "All those things I said earlier are true. I *do* like your tie. And as for your moustache…" I reach up, trace it lightly with one finger. "Promise you'll never shave it off?"

"I told you not to tease," he warns.

"Who says I'm teasing? I'm serious." I snuggle closer, close my eyes. Being in his arms feels so good. "This is nice."

"Nice? That's all you can say?" he growls.

"What's wrong with nice? Nice is good." I stroke my hand against the thin fabric of his shirt. Under that shirt is soft chest hair and bare skin. A man's skin. A man's heart. My pulse quickens. "Nice is very good. Besides, I'm drunk, remember? My vocabulary is shot."

"You're not drunk. Slightly inebriated, perhaps, but…"

I pull away slightly, search his face. "But what?"

For a long moment he won't meet my eyes. Finally he blows out a long sigh. "Drunk or sober, I wish you thought of me as more than nice."

"Give me a better word," I challenge.

Sam's eyes darken. "How about if I show you?"

The swiftness of his kiss takes my breath away. I close my eyes and surrender to his lips crushed upon my own and the hard feel of his body pressed against mine. This is what I've been waiting for. This is what I want. This is what I need.

This is even better than that kiss in the basement!

174

"What are you doing?"

Sam abruptly pulls away. I stuff a cracker in my mouth and glare as Priscilla ventures into the kitchen. Just wait till I get her alone tonight. The two of us are going to have a little talk about her rotten sense of timing.

"I'm sorry, Sam." Priscilla's face is as red as the cranberry sauce in Mama's fancy crystal serving bowl. "I'm really sorry."

"No problem." His face is redder than Priscilla's.

I munch my cracker in frustrated silence. Some sister she turned out to be. No concern about the fact that she's embarrassed me, too. No, it's all *Sam, Sam, Sam*. How would she like it if I walked in on her and Dr. Brown?

Priscilla shuffles past me, between the stove and counter. "It's two o'clock. I need to put dinner on the table."

I cram another cracker in my mouth. If she thinks I'm going to volunteer to help, she's got another think coming.

"Need some help?" Sam ventures.

I throw him a scowl. If he really wants to help, he should kick Priscilla out of the kitchen and start kissing me again.

"You're sweet to offer but I think we're all set." She stops suddenly, gives me a hard stare. "Patty, are you eating crackers?"

"Blame Sam. He made me eat them. He said they would soak up the wine." I pop the last bite in my mouth and lick the salt from my fingers. "You said I was drunk, remember?"

"You were."

"Well, maybe I was." I shrug. "Maybe I still am. Who cares?"

"You're right, Patty." Her voice carries a hard edge. "Who cares?"

Suddenly all my resentment sloshes together in one huge wave of guilt. What am I saying? What am I doing? This isn't the way Priscilla usually acts. I think hard, cringing as vague memories of my living room debacle return, how I blathered on. And then I remember Dr. Brown and his moustache.

Oh God. No wonder she's mad.

"Priscilla, I'm sorry. I didn't mean to embarrass you." My head drops. "Is Dr. Brown upset?"

Priscilla refuses to look at me as she steadily ladles gravy into a serving bowl. "He left."

Oh, God. Me and my big mouth. Now she'll never forgive me.

"I'm so sorry. I didn't mean it. Do you think if I call and apologize, maybe he'll come back—"

"Don't flatter yourself." Her eyes narrow and she shoots me a dark look. "He didn't leave because of you. The hospital paged him out for an emergency."

I take a deep breath. At least it wasn't anything I said. Still, I owe him an apology. I probably owe everybody an apology.

"I'm sorry he had to leave. I didn't hear his beeper."

She shrugs. "Obviously you didn't hear the doorbell, either. He's in the living room."

I snatch another cracker, nibble the edges. "Who?"

"Nick Lamont. He showed up five minutes ago."

The cracker sticks in my throat. "Nick came?" I choke out.

"That's right." Priscilla stares at the serving bowls heaped high with food and crowding the counter. "And I hope he brought his appetite. Mine is gone."

"I'm not too hungry myself," Sam says quietly. He stares at me. "I'll help Priscilla out here. You go play hostess to your friend."

I hesitate. Leave the kitchen? But I don't want to go. And it's not the tantalizing aroma of the roasted turkey, Priscilla's homemade stuffing, or her crusty dinner rolls urging me to stay.

More like the look of longing disappearing from Sam's eyes.

"Go on." He gives me a little push. "Nick's waiting."

I glance back and forth between the two of them. For once in my life, I could care less about food. "You're sure you don't need me?"

"He's your guest, not mine," Priscilla says. "You need to greet him. Sam can help me get dinner on the table."

I pull myself away and head down the hallway. The sound of easy laughter floats from the living room. I pause just beyond the doorway, sink against the wall, listening to Nick chatting with Jack and Ruth. My feet feel like lead but my heart feels even heavier. Something's definitely wrong. I'm the one who invited Nick. Shouldn't I be happy that he finally showed up? What's wrong with me? I should be able to figure this out. I'm smart. I'm a fifth-year-in-a-row Finalist for Teacher of The Year. And Teachers supposedly have all the answers, right? But this is beyond any instructor's manual. There's no magic answer key at the back of a book to explain the way I feel.

Torn at being kicked out of the kitchen.

Reluctant to greet Nick.

What's the problem, Patty?

Maybe the problem is something I'm not willing to admit.

Maybe deep down, I already know the answer.

Taking a deep breath, I screw up my nerve and step into the living room.

## CHAPTER TWELVE

I stare around the table at the remains of our Thanksgiving feast. I'm not sure if my attitude of gratitude was sucked away with all that wine or if it's the men responsible for my bad case of heartburn.

What in God's name was I thinking, sitting Nick and Sam across the table from each other?

"Having Patty next door in the other classroom is great. I don't know what I'd do without her." Nick's lazy smile makes my insides melt like the soft butter slathered on the flaky dinner roll Sam just crammed in his mouth.

"She deserves that nomination as Teacher of the Year," Ruth says. "And you, too, Nick. Being selected is quite an honor. Not every first-year teacher at our school makes it."

I catch his easy shrug, the modest look on his face—and across the table, the glower on Sam's. My stomach tightens as I remember that wild kiss we shared in the kitchen. Sam doesn't look so enamored now, shoveling in bite after bite of turkey and dressing.

What was I thinking? I'm putting myself on a self-induced diet starting right now.

No more men.

"Only four more weeks till Christmas," Ruth says. "This year is going fast."

Christmas. Celebrations. Cocktail parties. And that little black dress hanging in my closet. I force my eyes away from the dish of candied sweet potatoes. It's one of Priscilla's traditional holiday dishes and one of my favorites, but I don't dare indulge, not even one bite. I still have another five pounds to go. That dress *has* to fit.

"Do you have plans for Christmas, Sam?" Priscilla folds her napkin across her empty plate.

"I'm flying out to spend the holidays with my sister and her family." He helps himself to another slab of moist, dark meat from Mama's antique turkey platter. "But I'll be back before New Year's. Tax season starts January first."

"Taxes. Now there's a dry subject." Nick fingers his wine glass. "Don't you find it boring crunching numbers all day?"

"Got to admit, I'm with Nick on that one." Jack settles back in his chair. "I wouldn't want your job, Sam, no matter how much they paid me."

"I like accounting. Numbers don't lie." He spears a bite of turkey on his fork. "Besides, it's a good business, especially in this economy. You know what they say: two things in life are guaranteed—death and taxes."

"They ought to do something about the tax code," Ruth says. "It's much too complicated for normal people to understand."

"Thank God Patty and I have Sam," Priscilla says. "I don't know what we'd do without him. He's been a big help."

Big being the operative word. If Sam eats any more of those sweet potatoes, he'll pop.

"He's been helping us get our finances in order. And not only is he good with money, he's very good at fixing things. He comes over for dinner every Friday night and he helps around the house..." She breaks off and glances around the table with an uncertain smile. "I guess it's obvious how I feel about Sam. I think he's wonderful."

"The feeling's mutual, Priscilla." He chuckles, shoves his plate aside. "And you're a great cook. When I was a kid, I always thought my mom made the best sweet potatoes in the world, but yours are even better."

Priscilla beams while my own stomach growls. Steamed broccoli can't compare to the leftover sweet potatoes and homemade dressing in the crystal bowls. Not to mention the sideboard groaning with pies begging to be sliced. "Can we please talk about something besides food?" I eye Nick, next to me. "What about you? What are you doing for Christmas?"

"Why? You thinking of inviting me to Christmas dinner?" He refills his wine glass and winks at me. "Though I'll probably be going home," he concludes. "Not sure yet."

"Where exactly is home?" Sam presses.

He shrugs. "I've moved around some."

"East Coast? West Coast?"

I shoot Sam a warning look. What is his problem?

"I grew up in Arizona, but we're scattered across the country now. One of my sisters will give me a call once they get the holidays plans straightened out. Until then, I'm not going to sweat it."

"Nick has five sisters." The words slide out of my mouth. I'm not sure why I feel the sudden need to defend him or why the sudden anger toward Sam. He has no reason to grill Nick.

"And where exactly do you fit in the family hierarchy?" Sam eyes him over the cranberry relish. "Oldest? Youngest?"

Nick's eyebrows rise and for one brief moment I catch the glint of a scowl hovering on his face. But then he laughs. "Guess you could call me the baby, seeing as I'm the youngest."

Ruth touches Jack's hand. "Sound familiar, sweetheart?"

"You're lucky you've only got sisters, Nick," he says. "I'm the youngest of three boys. My older brothers never cut me any slack."

Nick drains his wine. "I can relate. I've got a couple of brothers, too."

I stare hard. Brothers? Nick never told me that.

"They're older than me and we're not close. I get along better with women." He sprawls back in his chair and shoots me a lazy grin. "Right, Patty?"

Suddenly I'm aware of all eyes on me. As God as my witness, I will never invite a man to dinner again. My stomach's upset and my heart is confused. This isn't worth it. Why doesn't everyone eat their pie and go home? This holiday dinner is giving me a headache.

"Would anyone like dessert?" I ask weakly.

Priscilla brings pies from the sideboard, places them in the center of the table. "I made pumpkin and mincemeat, too."

Sam leans forward. "Pumpkin sounds good."

"Ruth? Jack? Nick?" She glances around with an expectant air, hesitates, then finally looks at me. "Patty?"

I stare at the slice she's placed in front of Sam. It has an extra dollop of whipped crème. Would one little piece of pumpkin pie hurt? I've been so good. And it *is* Thanksgiving. Why do I have to deprive myself? Don't I deserve to celebrate?

Nick drapes his arm across the back of my chair. My stomach does a slow, lazy flip-flop as I feel his fingers trace my right shoulder, dancing lightly over the black velvet.

Priscilla's eyebrows lift. "Patty?"

"No pie for me, thanks." I shiver as his fingers trail the nape of my neck. My face is burning and my body feels like it's on fire. I press my knees together, fight back the surge of desire. What if it had been Nick, instead of Sam, with me in the kitchen? What if he'd been the one feeding me crackers and kissing away the crumbs? I close my eyes for a minute, visualizing that little black dress hanging in my closet. What will Nick think when he sees me wearing it?

What will he do once the party's over?

Priscilla lifts the serving knife. "Last call."

"Just another sliver." Sam holds out his plate. "And maybe a piece of the mincemeat, too."

"Nick? Sure you wouldn't like a piece?" Priscilla asks.

"No, thanks. I'm all set." He winks at me as forks scrape in unison against china.

And suddenly I'm very glad I held out. Who needs pie? Who needs the extra calories? Not me.

I've got Nick Lamont.

# # #

"Here's the rest of the stuff from the table." Nick's hands are stacked high with plates.

"Thanks for helping out." Ruth and I unload his arms and find space in the cluttered kitchen amid the aftermath of a holiday feast. "I thought you'd be in the living room with the guys."

He slouches against the counter. "I'm not much for football."

Unlike some people I could mention. Sam is currently camped out with Jack in front of the television, watching the game.

"I'm good at drying dishes if you need an extra hand." He watches as Priscilla squirts pink dish soap into the sink. "My sisters have me well trained."

"Have a towel." I toss it at him, laughing as he easily catches it. "You're scoring major points, Mr. Lamont."

"That's my goal in life. I aim to please."

"Where's Mama's turkey platter?" Priscilla's hands swish through the steamy soap suds. "I want to wash that next and put it away."

I glance around the counter littered with dirty plates, but no turkey platter. "It must still be in the dining room."

"And we're missing some serving bowls, too," she says. "Would you get them?"

Nick glances up from the wine glass cradled in his dishtowel. "Need some help?"

"Stay where you are, Nick. I'll help Patty." Ruth grabs my arm and hauls me toward the door.

"What was that all about?" I sputter as the door swings shut behind us.

"Why didn't you tell me what was going on?" Ruth demands.

"What are you talking about?"

"He likes you."

Is it that obvious? My tummy does a slow flip, remembering Nick's arm draped across my chair during dinner... his lazy grin, his soft flirty laugh, the secret wink he gave me. I've never been good at reading signals put out by men but if Ruth thinks it's true, maybe there's hope after all. Maybe I'm not simply chasing rainbows.

"Do you really think Nick and I could—"

"Nick?" She rolls her eyes. "For heaven's sake, Patty, where did you get that idea? No, I'm talking about Sam." She nods toward the living room. "Anyone with eyes in their head can see how he feels about you."

"Sam? But he isn't… I mean, he's not the one…" I stumble over the words as I reach for Mama's platter. Ruth has things all messed up. "Sam's only our accountant. He's simply helping us get our finances in order."

Ruth picks up a bowl sticky with cranberry sauce. "Patty, dear, perhaps that's what you think, but that's not what he thinks. I know men. And when it comes to that man, he's got something more than money on his mind—and that something is *you*."

My stomach swirls and I grab the table for support. Sam and me? It won't work. It's not what I want. Does everyone know? Does Nick know?

"I'm not interested in Sam."

Her eyebrows lift slightly.

"I'm not," I insist. "There's nothing going on between us. Nothing."

She tilts her head, eyes me for a moment, then shrugs. "If that's true, it might be a good idea if you let him know that," she says mildly. "Men are funny about that sort of thing. They like to know if they're wasting their time." She starts for the door.

"Ruth, wait…" I make a grab to stop her and Mama's turkey platter slips from my hands, crashing onto the hardwood floor.

"Ohmigod." I stare in horror at the shards of china littered around our feet. Hot tears pop behind my eyes. "Priscilla is going to kill me."

"It was an accident." Ruth comforts me with a hug. "She'll understand. I'll help you clean things up."

"No, you don't understand. It was one of the few things we have left that belonged to Mama. Priscilla

185

will be so upset." My tears drip, wetting the broken china. Priscilla will be more than upset. She'll be brokenhearted.

"We'll tell her I broke it," Ruth suggests. "I'll say it was my fault."

"No, I can't let you do that. It wouldn't be right." My hands tremble as we gingerly pick up the pieces and stack them on the one large piece that remains intact. "I might as well tell her the truth. She's bound to find out anyway. Besides, it's not the end of the world. It's just a turkey platter."

But it's not. It belonged to Mama and now it's gone. Just like so many other things in our lives.

It feels like my world is breaking apart, piece by piece.

# # #

I was prepared for screaming, ranting, raving. I deserved it. I'll take my punishment. But not this. It was bad enough when I admitted what happened and saw the sad, haunted look slip across Priscilla's face. But nothing prepared me for this horrible silence that's existed between us for the past six hours. It's chewing me up inside.

"Patty?"

Finally, she's talking to me. I flip over from my spot on the couch, see Priscilla hovering in the hallway.

"I'm going to bed." She turns and starts for the stairs.

"Priscilla, wait." I haul myself off the couch, start after her. "It's not even nine o'clock."

She keeps walking. "I'm tired. It's been a long day."

"Priscilla?" She's nearly at the stairs. I make a fast move and grab her arm. "Priscilla, wait. I'm sorry about Mama's platter," I tell her for the umpteenth time.

She stares down at my arm, refusing to meet my eyes. "It doesn't matter." She shakes away from my touch. "What's done is done."

But it does matter. I wrap my arms around myself, hug myself tight. I wish it was Priscilla I was hugging instead. I hate it when things aren't right between us. Will she ever forgive me? Even Sam, the last to leave, couldn't cheer her up with his glowing compliments about the holiday meal when he said his good-byes. She kissed his cheek with the thinnest of smiles, looking pallid and forlorn, wretched and worn out. Black circles smudged her eyes.

Why did I ever let her talk me into agreeing to host a holiday meal? It was too much for her. Mama was right. Priscilla doesn't know her own limitations. Now she'll take to her bed and get sick again. It will be all my fault.

Just like Mama's turkey platter, buried in the garbage can. All my fault.

"Good night," I call after her as she starts up the stairs. "Sweet dreams."

Priscilla doesn't answer, just keeps climbing without a backward glance. She's never gone to bed mad at me before. We have our tiffs but she's always the one who ends up the peacemaker. What's happening to us? Every step she takes moves her further from me. What have I done? Will she ever come back?

I wait below in the foyer until I hear the soft sound of her bedroom door click. Then I turn and head back into the living room, flop down on the couch, tuck my bare feet under my legs. A dull throb—probably the beginning of a hangover— knocks at the back of my head. I rub my neck, stare around the living room. How did everything go so wrong? Just hours ago this room was filled with friendly faces, easy conversation, laughter. Now I'm alone. Just me and my misery, plus this nagging headache.

As God as my witness, I will never drink again. That was the beginning of things going wrong. I made a royal fool of myself today... first with Sam in the kitchen, then showing off in front of everyone by flirting with Nick, and finally breaking a treasured family heirloom.

What else did I break today? Sam's trust. Nick's illusions. Priscilla's love.

Is it any surprise everyone left so fast? Nick was the first to go, slipping out the door with a fleeting goodbye. Ruth and Jack quickly followed. Sam was the only one who braved Priscilla's wrath, sticking around another half hour to help clean up before he finally said goodbye.

I let everyone down, including myself. No wonder they all left. Who would want to be with me?

Sometimes I don't even want to be with myself.

The hell with that little black dress. It's waited this long. It can wait until tomorrow. I slip off the couch and pad barefoot into the dark kitchen. I yank open the refrigerator door and search the shelves. Through good times and bad, loneliness and indifference, there's one thing that's always been loyal and seen me through. Food has never failed me in the past and it's here for me tonight.

Finally I spy the whipped crème tucked behind the sweet potatoes.

Now, to figure out where Priscilla stashed the leftover pumpkin pie.

CHAPTER THIRTEEN

The doorbell chimes as I totter down the stairs. Nick will just have to wait. My toes are numb in my brand-new, too tight, three-inch heels and I can't move any faster. It's a guarantee by midnight I'll have blisters on my feet. If Cinderella's glass slippers pinched, I'll bet her happily-ever-after was worth the pain.

But my Prince Charming has shown up when I didn't expect him. Did Nick see my disappointment when he mentioned his late afternoon basketball practice today? I agreed to meet him at Amy's party but now I won't have to. Obviously he's changed his mind and plans on driving me to the party after all.

The doorbell chimes once more.

"Coming," I mutter as I wobble through the foyer. Damn that saleswoman for talking me into buying these shoes because they matched this shimmering cocktail dress… something else I never should have bought. It's still too tight, even though I've lost another two pounds. And I've never gone strapless. With my shoulders exposed and my breasts pushed into tight little cups that strain and cut against my flesh, I feel like a plump little sausage about to burst its casing.

If only Priscilla had helped me dress. She'd tell me the truth, if I look decent enough to wear this out in public. And I so much want to look beautiful for Nick. Hopefully he won't think I look like a model for fat-girls-gone-bad. *Vanity, thy name is Patty*. I don't dare eat one thing at the party or I'll pop right out of this dress. I smooth down the froufrou skirt, take a deep breath, and yank open the front door.

"Wow." Sam stares at me, frozen on the porch.

"Oh, for God's sake, don't just stand there. You're letting all the cold air in." As if I need any reminder that I'm nearly naked. I grab his arm and haul him inside, slam the door against the icy December wind. "Heat costs money."

He struggles out of his overcoat, drapes it on a nearby chair. His face wears a look of awe as he ogles me. "Wow."

"I believe you already said that." I pluck his coat off the chair and hang it in the closet, a little miffed that it's Sam and not Nick at our front door. And what is Sam doing here anyway? I didn't invite him and the few times we've seen each other since Thanksgiving, he's acted exceeding polite. This tiptoeing around each other is driving me crazy. Bad enough he witnessed me staggering around in a drunken stupor. Sam, always the gentleman. Not once has he mentioned my indiscretion —or the kisses we shared.

He can't quit staring. "You look…"

"Go ahead and say it. The dress is too tight, right?" I'm sure my face is as red as one of the bulbs on the Christmas tree in our living room. I fight down the urge to yank at the bosom and rearrange myself. What if the boned cups fail and I fall out of this dress during Amy's party? I can imagine the headlines now. *Teacher exposes herself at Christmas party.* There go my hopes of winning Teacher of the Year.

Sam shakes his head. "You look—"

"Listen, there's still time for me to change. Tell me the truth, Sam. Should I or shouldn't I wear this dress tonight?" My heart pounds against my chest at the thought of what he'll say but I know I can trust him to tell me the truth. Sam's got an honest streak as thick as his middle. I bite my lower lip, take a deep breath. "Does this dress really look that bad?"

"No, it's perfect." He shifts on his feet. "You look beautiful, Patty."

"Really?" A tiny thrill surges inside me. "You're not teasing? You really like it?" But I already know he does. The ruddy flush on his face is proof enough.

He nods. "It looks great. Stunning. Like you're going to a party."

"Well, that's good. Because I am." Suddenly, wearing this dress doesn't feel that bad. Funny how knowing you have a man's admiration can change your whole attitude.

"From the look of that dress, I'd say it's going to be quite the party."

"I hope so," I say with a careful smile and let it go at that. I learned my lesson months ago. When it comes to Sam, certain things are better left unsaid... especially things involving Nick. "What brings you out on a night like this?"

He frowns. "It's Friday. I came for dinner."

"But I won't..." I halt, suddenly confused. This isn't the way things are supposed to work. I assumed Sam comes for dinner on Friday nights because of me. Doesn't he?

"I'm going to a party," I finish in a tiny voice. "I won't be here."

"I didn't realize your being here was a prerequisite for my being invited." His eyes narrow. "And Priscilla never mentioned it."

Priscilla invited Sam to dinner tonight? She never said boo to me.

Then again, why should that come as a surprise? She's barely talking to me.

"Well, I'm sure the two of you will enjoy yourselves so much you won't even miss me." I toss my head, suddenly glad for the wild curls bouncing across my face, hiding my pinched frown. The thought of the two of them having dinner together alone makes me want to squirm, but I'll be damned if I'll let him know it. It's not like I'm jealous. There's nothing to be jealous about. Priscilla is interested in Dr. Brown. And as for Sam? I thought he was interested in...

I don't have time to figure it out. I've got a party to go to. Nick's probably already on his way. I dig in the closet and grab my wool coat. Tonight's forecast calls for snow.

"Who's throwing this party?" Sam takes my coat, holds it for me as I wrap myself inside. "Anyone I know?"

"I doubt it. Just a few of the teachers from school, having a little get-together." It's not exactly a lie. There'll be other teachers there—I think, though I'm not sure how many. I burrow my face in the coat's fur collar. I've got to be nuts, thinking about going out on a night like this wearing a strapless dress. It's Northern Michigan. It's December.

It's Nick.

"Jack and Ruth going?" he asks casually.

"I'm not sure." I'm not privy to Amy's invitation list, but it's pretty much guaranteed their names aren't on it.

Or my own name, either, for that matter.

"I'll probably be home early," I add breezily. "A bunch of teachers getting together doesn't make for much excitement."

"Oh, there'll be plenty of excitement," he predicts with a half smile. "The minute you take off your coat and everyone sees that dress." He eyes me for a moment. "What about that guy? Is he going to be there?"

"What guy?"

"You know who I'm talking about."

"Nick?" My chin shoots forward as I pull on my gloves. "Why?"

"Just asking."

My face reddens. "I don't see where that's any of your business."

Something hardens in his eyes.

"Is that Sam?" Priscilla breezes through the hallway, wiping her hands on her apron. "Why didn't you tell me he was here?"

"Why didn't you tell him I wouldn't be here tonight?" I counter.

She shrugs. "Sam always comes over on Friday nights. I don't see that it makes any difference whether you're here or not. Unless…" She glances back and forth between the two of us. "You don't mind, do you, Sam? Having dinner alone with me?"

"Looking forward to it," he assures her. "You're great company, Priscilla."

A wreath of a smile nearly as big as the Christmas wreath adorning our front door spreads across her face. "I hope you like omelets."

"One of my favorites."

"Good. I'm chopping the vegetables right now." She throws me a distant wave as she heads down the hall. "Have fun at your party."

That's it? I watch my twin disappear without a backward glance. Priscilla helped me pick out this dress. She pointed out the matching shoes. She was so excited that I'd been invited to Amy's party, that I'd have a chance to impress the movers and shakers in this town who might be on the voting committee for

Teacher of the Year. Priscilla used to be my champion, and now she's barely speaking to me. What happened?

I broke Mama's stupid turkey platter. That's what happened.

Damn plate. How do I end up in these messes, anyway? I cinch the belt of my coat and fish through my purse for car keys.

Sam plants himself in front of me. "Drive carefully. There's a lot of snow out there and the roads are supposed to get worse."

"Don't worry about me. I'm a good driver."

"I never said you weren't."

I snap my gloves together. The last thing I need is Sam lecturing me on how to drive. I'm nervous enough as it is, terrified I'll make some stupendous gaffe, terrified I'll spill out of my dress, terrified I'll fail to impress Nick. He's the guest of honor and he invited me. I don't want him regretting it. And as for Sam, he's got no business making me feel like I'm doing something wrong.

Like I'm cheating on him.

It's not like we're dating.

Because we're not.

"Take it easy on the roads. Remember, it's Friday the thirteenth."

I come up with a short laugh and my car keys at the same time. "I didn't know you were superstitious."

He cracks open the front door, peers outside. "Just be careful, okay? It's getting nasty out there."

"Don't worry." I've got a plan. Tonight, I intend to break all the rules. Isn't that what everyone else does? Why should I always be the one who ends up playing it safe? Well, not tonight. Snow be damned. Maybe what I need is some danger in my life. Maybe what I need is to take charge, be more daunting, more fearless. And I've taken the first step. Tonight I've got a date with Nick.

Who knows what will happen?

Brand new dress, brand new shoes, brand new me.

I start for the door, but Sam grabs my arm.

"Whoa, are you crazy? You can't go out there without your boots."

"Boots?" I stare up at him. "You're the one who's crazy if you think I'm wearing boots."

He nods at my heels. "You want to fall and break your neck?"

Neck, be damned. I've got no intention of showing up at Amy's party flashing cleavage and those ugly boots. And who is Sam to tell me what to do? Obviously the man knows nothing about fashion or he never would have paired a red-checked shirt with that bright orange sweater. A woman would have to be desperate to take fashion advice from him.

"Don't worry about me," I breezily assure him as I open the door. "I'll be just fine."

An icy gust of wind catches the door, nearly snatching it out of my hand. Snow blows in the foyer, spilling over my rhinestone heels. I do a little dance to stamp them clean but my toes already feel frozen.

Maybe Sam is right. Maybe I should wear my boots.

And have everyone laugh at me?

I peer outside. It's nearly a virtual whiteout, with snow squalls blowing across our front lawn and the wind howling around the corners of our house. I wrap my coat tighter around me. Sam said the roads were getting bad and I'm starting to believe him.

Do I really want to go to this party? I could run upstairs, shuck this dress and heels for my favorite pair of jeans and scuffed moccasins and be back downstairs in five minutes flat. Instead of flaunting myself in front of Amy, Nick, and God knows how many other people over cocktails and hors d'oeuvres, I could be sitting in a cozy kitchen, laughing and chatting over omelets with Sam and Priscilla.

I could say I'm sorry again and again. Maybe this time, she'll finally listen.

What reason do I have to go out in the cold when I could stay home, warm?

None, except Nick.

Would he even miss me?

"Fine. You want to go in this mess, be my guest." Sam shrugs, opens the door wider. "But don't say I didn't warn you."

"Duly noted," I shoot back and slam the door behind me. I grab the railing and totter down the steps onto the sidewalk. A good two inches of snow has already accumulated and my feet are soaked. Damn Sam Curtis and his big mouth. Even if I did want to grab those boots, I'm not about to turn back now. I refuse to give him the satisfaction. He's probably watching from the window.

No, he's probably already in our warm, toasty kitchen with Priscilla, chatting and laughing as they make their stupid omelets.

I reach the garage and hit the switch to open the overhead door. The garage is unheated and the car is cold. I slide behind the driver's wheel, my fingers numb as I start the engine. I'll be an icicle by the time I get to Amy's. The car wheels spin as I back down the icy driveway. I take a deep breath. If I'm going to make it in one piece, I'm going to have to take the roads slow. Hopefully Nick won't be mad that I kept him waiting.

# # #

Not.

The street in front of Amy's house is lined with vehicles, but Nick's dark green sports coupe is nowhere in sight. Where is he? He promised he'd show up directly after practice, once he showered and changed. He's already fifteen minutes late. I rub my hands together, snuggle deeper in my coat. My breath hangs like mist, and lacy frost designs etch the windows inside and out. This is ridiculous. The car heater is running full blast, but I'm so cold, I no longer care about the stupid party. I don't care if Nick is the guest of honor. I'll give him five more minutes and then I'm going home. I grit my teeth, close my eyes, and block out the sight of snowflakes piling up on the windshield.

A rap on the driver's door brings me upright. Someone scrapes a little hole in the snow, peers through the window.

"Why are you sitting out here in the cold?" Nick twirls his car keys in a leather-gloved hand as he offers me a hand. "Are you crazy?"

I clutch my coat tighter and lock the door behind me. "I didn't want to go in—"

"Without me? Patty, girl, what am I going to do with you?" He laughs, takes my arm, tucks it in the crook of his elbow. "Seriously, I'm flattered you waited for me. You're really something, you know that?"

Stupid, that's what I am. Stupid and cold, with wet feet, frozen fingers and toes. For all I know, my brain is frozen, too. And it's all his fault. Where the hell was he? I fight down the urge to blast him with questions as we make our way up the walk. His hair is still damp, probably fresh from the shower, and the light woodsy scent of his cologne drifts through his heavy leather jacket. He smells so good, I almost forgive him for the wait he put me through.

Almost.

My teeth chatter as we near the porch and head up the steps. Nick hits the doorbell, then wraps his arm around me and hugs me close. "Cheer up. You'll warm up once we're inside."

That's an understatement. Amy's wrath could prove hotter than the fires of hell.

"Poor Patty." He lifts a hand, brushes away some stray curls from my face. His brown eyes gleam in the soft glow of the carriage lanterns illuminating the porch. "So cold, waiting for me when you could have gone inside." He leans over and kisses the tip of my nose.

He kissed me! My breath freezes as a warm thrill of desire surges through me. He kissed me! And suddenly it's all right. No worries about my wet feet, tight dress, pounding head, empty stomach. Who cares? He kissed me!

"Listen, stick close tonight, okay?" His breath is soft and warm against my hair. "Last thing I want is Amy buzzing around me. Hang close and don't let go."

"Sure."

"Promise?"

I nod. Right now I would promise him anything. "Absolutely," I say as the door opens.

"Well, finally, you decide to show up." Amy eyes Nick across the threshold. "I'd just about given up on you." Then she catches sight of me. "Patty. Hello. What a nice surprise." She turns to Nick, eyebrows raised.

"I brought along reinforcements," he says with a grin.

I throw him an uneasy stare as I stamp the snow from my feet. Reinforcements? I thought I was his date.

"Whatever. At least you're here." Amy links her arm through his and tugs him through the door. "Now we can get this party started."

I follow them inside the large foyer and peek around Nick. From the look of things, there's already a pretty good party in progress. A loud party, with plenty of people milling about, music and laughter spilling from all directions.

"I'll take your coat, miss." A girl dressed in black, obviously staff hired for the party, offers an outstretched hand, but suddenly I don't want to relinquish my coat. I clutch it tighter around me. Who am I trying to kid? Amy is sleek and elegant in a red silk jumpsuit that clings like a second skin. Sam's words from earlier this evening jump to mind. *"There'll be excitement… the minute you take off your coat and they see that dress."*

Nick shrugs out of his own coat, eyes me. "You coming?"

Time for the unveiling, whether I like it or not. Reluctantly I slip from my coat and surrender it to the girl. Amy's eyes widen for a moment, then her face suddenly melts into a smile.

"What a marvelous dress, Patty. You look…"

Like a tart? Tramp? Trollop? I've been in the room less than one minute but I already know coming here tonight was a horrible mistake. I don't belong here. This isn't my crowd. This is way out of my comfort zone, way out of my league.

I throw a weak glance in Nick's direction. Why did I let him talk me into this? Will he forgive me if I grab my coat and bolt?

He gives me a thumbs-up. "Great dress. Nice and sparkly. I like it."

Amy rolls her eyes and tugs him away from me. "Come on, Nick. Everyone's waiting to meet you."

He shoots me a backward glance as she pulls him toward a grand set of French doors opening into an even grander room. "You coming?"

"Right behind you," I mutter, trailing behind them into a cavernous living room. As usual, I'm bringing up the rear. Just me and my big rear end.

Piano music drifts from one end of the room. Hang on tight, Nick said, but somehow he and Amy have disappeared in a crush of bodies. I stand on tiptoe, try to catch a glimpse of him, but I'm too short. I'll never find him in this mess of people. I fight my way through the crowd, bypassing groups of people laughing and chatting. Everyone seems to know each other and they all seem to be having a wonderful time. I skirt the edges of the room and finally end up at the bar.

"Merry Christmas," the bartender greets me. He sweeps his hand over delicate stemware with a little flourish. All the drinks are the same, a clear liquid with peppermint stick swizzles floating against the rims. "Christmas martinis," he says. "Gin, dry vermouth, and peppermint Schnapps."

Memories of Thanksgiving and my wine-induced meltdown float to mind. *Stick close*, Nick told me. If I'm going to find him, I need a clear head. "Is this all you're serving?"

He nods. "Mrs. Lynn's orders."

"Why am I not surprised?" Leave it to Amy, putting her fashionable alcoholic beverages on holiday parade. "Thanks, but no thanks," I say with a sigh. "My drinking days are over."

He nods and leans closer. "I've got a bottle of club soda stashed under the counter. I could put it in a martini glass, add a peppermint stick and she'll never know the difference."

"You'd do that for me?"

"Sure thing." He winks. "I'm a friend of Bill myself."

"Excuse me?" I stare at him confusedly. Exactly who is this Bill he's talking about? Amy's been married to Hugh for years.

"Better to keep the cork in the bottle than test your sobriety at a party like this," he adds. "Have you been to a meeting lately?"

Good God, he thinks I'm an alcoholic. I grab a Christmas martini and whirl around just as someone in the crowd bumps me from behind. Suddenly half my drink is no longer in my glass, but dribbling down the front of my dress.

"Oh!" Crushed ice and vodka seep slowly between my breasts. My eyes widen as I peer down and see the peppermint stick poking out between my boobs.

The bartender's eyebrows lift, but he never says a word, just hands me some napkins. I turn my back, fish out the candy, then stagger away, dabbing at the liquor soaking my dress. I reek of peppermint and probably look like a gigantic candy stick. Not exactly the type of image I hoped to project as a semifinalist candidate for Teacher of the Year. Who am I kidding? No one here cares anything about me. I should have known better than to come here tonight. I should have known better than to listen to Nick. This isn't my kind of party. These aren't my kind of people.

Maybe he's not my kind of man.

Exactly where is he, anyway?

I wander the fringe of the crowd, dabbing at my dress while keeping an eye out for Nick. But pushing through the crush of people is exhausting, and my feet are killing me. Finally I give up and sink down on a sleek Italian white leather couch. If who you know and where you come from and what your house looks like is part of the criteria for the contest, I might as well drop out right now. Amy even has a designer Christmas tree. And while I hate to admit it, the elegant ornaments of red and gold shimmering against tiny twinkling lights are dazzling. If Teacher of the Year can earn votes based on a Christmas tree, I'd vote for Amy, too.

Amazing, the things money can buy, I think as I sip the leftover slosh of my Christmas martini. A cocktail party with hired staff. A house that must be over four thousand square feet. Obviously Amy's husband is doing well. Hugh started out with us in grade school, a good old boy with a hammer and broad shoulders, and he's built himself a solid reputation as a general contractor of custom-built homes. But I'll bet a week's paycheck Hugh doesn't pound a hammer anymore. He's probably got plenty of guys on his payroll to do that sort of thing.

Meanwhile, he's stuck with Amy. Idly I wonder if he has a workbench in his garage where he can hammer out his frustrations. Living in a grand house is no guarantee life will be beautiful. That depends on the person you share it with.

I'll bet Hugh spends a lot of time in his garage.

"Something funny?" A middle-aged man with thick, wavy hair and ruddy complexion sinks down on the couch beside me. His suit reeks of money, his breath reeks of booze and his gaze is centered directly on my chest. "Come on, sweetheart, I won't tell. I love secrets."

I scoot deeper into my side of the couch. "You wouldn't be interested."

The man moves in closer, drapes one arm against the back of the couch, grazing my shoulder. "It's a shame, a pretty girl like you sitting all alone."

Speak of the devil. Nick isn't racking up any brownie points. Where is he?

"You look familiar." He peers at me across the couch. "Have we met before?"

"I don't think so."

"You sure? I never forget a pretty face." He slouches across the leather cushion and practically into my lap.

"Believe me, I'd remember."

Except that I think he might be right. The memories are fuzzy but I'm sure I've seen him before. Not that I'm about to admit it. Bad enough he's got me trapped in this leather prison. Where's Nick when I need him? He promised not to leave me.

No, I promised not to leave him.

I struggle to unearth myself from the deep recesses of the couch.

"Hey, where you going?" The drunk grabs my arm, presses his thigh against my own. One hand finds my knee, gives it a little squeeze. "I bet a big girl like you knows just how to keep a man nice and warm."

"Charlie, for Christ's sake, what are you doing? Get your hands off her."

I peer up at the petite woman in the clinging, rhinestone-studded, jersey-knit dress with long black hair and flat dead eyes. Like the man, she looks vaguely familiar. And she's strong, too. Despite her tiny size, she grabs the man and hauls him to his feet.

"You disgust me," she hisses in his face. "What do you think you're doing? Don't you know who this is?" She jabs a finger in my direction.

I blink. Somebody tell me. Who am I?

"What kind of man goes around making a spectacle of himself with his daughter's teacher?"

The man staggers slightly as he throws me a woozy gaze. "She's Lauren's teacher?"

Phyllis Conard tosses her hair and throws him a furious scowl. "You make me sick."

I feel sick myself. No wonder they look familiar. I met them both at parent-teacher conferences last month.

"I didn't realize you were friends with Hugh and Amy," she says, unsmiling. "I suppose you know each other from school."

"Amy invited a few teachers to the party." I struggle to my feet, grateful that I managed not to expose too much cleavage or thigh. "In fact, I'm here tonight with another teacher… Nick Lamont. He's the guest of honor." I stand on my tiptoes, scan the room. Still no sign of Nick. "Have you seen him?"

"Actually, I have." The pinched look on her face softens. "We were just talking a few minutes ago. Lauren is in his reading group. Now I understand why she loves to read." Her smile fades into nothing. "Actually, I've been concerned about her math scores lately. Perhaps she'd do better if she had Mr. Lamont for that subject, too."

I grit my teeth and dredge up my most polite smile. "Where exactly is Mr. Lamont?"

"I think he's somewhere over there." She waves vaguely toward the front of the room, then turns to her husband. "You. Sit." She points at the couch. "At least I'll know where find you. Meanwhile, I'm going to get myself another drink."

Charlie grabs my arm as she wanders off. "I'm sorry about what happened." His words are still slurred but his face is red and he looks just like one of my ten-year-olds, embarrassed at being caught and mightily ashamed of what they've done. "Lauren's a good kid. You won't say anything, will you? You won't hold this against her?"

"Of course not." My anger and resentment are gone. All that's left inside is a strange sort of pity for Charlie Conard and Lauren, too. No wonder she's such a horrid little girl. Growing up with a mother like Phyllis and a father like him.

"I appreciate that, Miss Perreault…" He stumbles over the words and his feet, catching himself before he falls.

I grab his arm, help him maneuver to a seat on the couch. Lauren's father is hardly in any shape to stand up, let alone navigate the room. "Mr. Conard, I'm going to find you some coffee. Promise me you'll stay put."

Nodding, he slumps back against the buttery soft cushions.

"And no more Christmas martinis," I add.

"The hell with those stupid martinis." He points to an empty nearby shot glass. "I'm drinking straight vodka."

There has to be coffee somewhere. I struggle through the crowd, push my way to the food buffet, which is covered with an elegant silk brocade of red and gold that matches the Christmas tree. It's all about matching. Everything has to be perfect. Perfect décor, music, food.

Everything is perfect, except this party. And the company. And the way I feel.

Deserted. Hungry.

I was so worried about fitting into this stupid dress that I never ate before leaving home. Smoked fish, cold shrimp, toasted baguettes, cheeses and spreads are laid out on the buffet table. Everything perfectly arranged, but not what I want.

What I really want is an omelet. One of Priscilla's omelets, loaded with cheese, diced ham, green peppers.

And Sam at the table. If he'd been the one escorting me to this party, guaranteed he never would have left my side. Is he still at our house or has he gone home? He usually stays long after dinner is finished and the three of us sit around the kitchen table telling stories, playing cards, eating popcorn, having a good time. Just like a family.

Except Sam's not family. He's merely our accountant. Someone who keeps tally on the bills. Just wait till he sees my credit card statement and discovers how much I doled out for this little black dress. It reeks of peppermint and it's full of bad memories. I will never wear it again. Same goes for the shoes. They pinch my toes and hurt like hell. I had no business wearing them or being at this party, either. What am I doing here, anyway? Alone, embarrassed, hurting, and hungry.

The server behind the buffet offers me a plate.

"No, thanks." I spy the coffee urn near the end of the table. "Do me a favor?" I point through the crowd.

"There's a man over there sitting on a couch. He needs some coffee. Lots of coffee."

"Certainly." She nods. "I'll make sure he's taken care of. Would you like anything?"

"No, thank you. I'm leaving."

For the first time tonight, I'm grateful Nick and I came in separate cars. At least I can make a quick escape with a clear conscience and no explanation. I make a beeline for the foyer, retrieve my coat, pull it tight around me as I head out the door. The snow has stopped, but the clear sky and twinkling stars invite a bitter cold. A sheen of ice covers the sidewalk and I teeter on my heels as I maneuver the long walk. The road is slick. Just as I reach my car, I nearly take a nasty spill, saving myself by grabbing the door handle. I burrow behind the wheel, start the engine, swearing softly as I wait for the heater to warm up. My back hurts where I wrenched it, but my pride hurts even more. Will I ever learn? Why do I always try to be something I'm not? It's time to face facts. I'm thirty years old and I'll never be a beauty queen.

Sam was right. Next time, I'll wear the damn boots.

Sam. As if my spirits could sink any lower. I check the green digital glow of the car's clock. I can't go home yet. I don't dare. It's way too early. He's probably still there. I can't face him. Not after the way things ended tonight.

No boots. No date. No fun.

And even if he is gone, how can I face Priscilla? If by some miracle she's finally talking to me, she'll grill me about Amy's house. She's always wanted to see it. She'll press me for details about the party, the guests, the food…

Food.

I throw the car in gear and head down the icy street. My stomach's empty and a dull headache pounds at the back of my head. No wonder I feel sick. The last time I ate was breakfast this morning. I take the corner and steer away from the downtown area, opposite the direction of home. There's a small convenience store not far from here. I'll pick up something, enough to tide me over until Sam leaves. Until Priscilla goes to bed. Until it's safe to go home.

Just a sandwich. And maybe some potato chips. I'll bet they sell cookies, too.

I jam my foot on the gas.

Let the feast begin.

CHAPTER FOURTEEN

"Just think, Miss P. Only four more days until Christmas vacation." Tyler throws his math assignment on the corner of my desk with a toothy grin. "And eight more days until Christmas." He slaps his hands together and whistles through the crooked gaps in his teeth.

I try to keep a straight face. Sometimes I just want to laugh at these kids, they're so cute. "You sound pretty excited, Tyler."

"You bet! I hope I get that brand new snowboard for Christmas," he says as he darts back to his seat.

If the weatherman's forecast proves correct, Tyler will have lots of fun playing in the snow. God bless fifth-grade boys. They're so different from the girls and not much has changed in the years I've been teaching. By the time Christmas rolls around, most of the girls have put away their toys and are more interested in playing with real live boys—most of whom, just like Tyler, don't have a clue. Things will be different ten years from now. This goofy little kid who shuns girls and lives for recess will be a man. His buzz cut will be gone and Tyler will probably have more than his fair share of girlfriends. But not yet. For now, he and his buddies seem more interested in shooting hoops with Mr. Lamont.

"Finish your math papers and hand them in, please. It's nearly time for lunch."

Katie and Lauren saunter up to my desk. Katie tosses her paper on top of Tyler's. She's written the answers in red and green ink. "Christmas colors, Miss P. Aren't they pretty?"

Lauren flings down her own inked-up paper. "We thought you'd like them."

I stare at the gaudy papers. So much for using red ink to make my corrections. Swear to God, Lauren's little clique will test me to the very limits before this year is through. I bite back the retort sitting on my tongue. After all, it's Christmas. Why not cut them a little slack? They already think I'm a grinch.

Books slam shut as the lunch bell shrills and thirty seconds later I'm herding twenty-five noisy ten-year-olds to the cafeteria. Five minutes later I'm back at my desk. Tyler's words jingle in my mind as I stare at the stack of messy papers covered in Christmas colors.

Only four more days till Christmas vacation. I grab my lunch from the bottom drawer. Carrot sticks and half a cheese sandwich face off against the stack of math assignments. I'm tired of eating lunch at my desk but it happens every year. T'is the season. I'm jammed with work and not enough time to spare. Completing that contest questionnaire and writing that paper about myself was a royal pain, but it's finished and in the mail. I grab a bite of sandwich, a purple pen from my drawer, and dig into the math papers.

"Got a minute?" Nick strolls through the door and across the room. He lounges against a corner of Eric's desk.

"What's up?" Hopefully I sound cool and calm, because inside I feel jittery and upset, sick to my stomach at the mere sight of him. I haven't seen or talked to him since Amy's party last weekend. He never phoned, which really hurt, but in some odd way I was also glad. *Don't ask, don't tell.* The last thing I want to hear is some flimsy excuse about why he dumped me. Knowing Nick, he'll come up with some grand excuse and talk in circles until the whole thing sounds completely innocent and makes total sense. Knowing me, I'll end up feeling sorry for him, guilty that I left, and probably even apologize.

"Come on, Patty, I know you're upset."

"Me? Upset? What makes you think that?" Damn right I'm upset. Who wouldn't be? I never should have gone to that party. Big mistake on my part. It's obvious Nick and I are merely friends and we'll never be more than that, no matter how much I wish things were different. Women like me don't end up with men like him. It doesn't make sense. No matter what everyone says, the way you look counts. People like to put a pretty spin on things and say it doesn't matter, but it does. They just won't admit that looks are important.

If I wasn't fat, I would have won that contest two years ago.

And Nick will probably win—at least the award for First-Year Teacher. His good looks, confidence and easygoing style attract women—and men, too—just like a magnet. Except for Sam. He's never liked Nick.

"You've been avoiding me. Don't you think it's time we talked?"

"I don't think there's anything to talk about." If he thinks I'm going to let him suck me in again, then Nick's got another think coming. He ignored the fact that I was his date. He abandoned me at that party. Does he have the slightest clue how much that hurt? How much it still hurts, three days later?

"Look, Patty, I'm sorry. I don't know what else to say. And I don't blame you for the way you feel. If someone did that to me, I'd feel like hell."

"Can we just forget it, okay? I'm busy." I shuffle the math papers into a neat stack, avoiding his eyes as I feel my resolve starting to slip. My head says *go away*, but my heart hasn't quite caught up yet. I take a deep breath. He's got no idea what he put me through, deserting me… and for Amy, of all people. I spent the weekend hiding in my bedroom, reading diet magazines, eating cookies and potato chips, stuffing down my tears.

And to think I actually cried over him. What a waste of Kleenex.

"I figured you'd take it all wrong. That's why I wanted you to hear my side of the story. Believe me, I never expected her to put the moves on me."

I try not to roll my eyes. How stupid does he think I am?

"She's a real piece of work. How the hell you put up with her is beyond me."

"You do what you have to do," I say with a shrug. I learned long ago to stay far away from the kindergarten room.

"Phyllis has a one-track mind. That woman doesn't know how to take *no* for an answer."

"Excuse me?" I stumble over a name I never expected to hear.

"Phyllis Conard."

I stare at him hard. "Lauren's mother?"

He frowns. "Who did you think we were talking about?"

I force the image of Amy clinging to his arm out of my mind. "Never mind."

"You've got to give her credit for trying. She's one determined lady. No matter what I said, she was going to get her way."

"God, Nick, I can't believe you're telling me this." I think about last Friday night, the crush of people at Amy's party, Charlie Conard's hand creeping up my thigh, Phyllis staggering off to find herself another drink. And if I'm reading him right, the two of them ended up together. Nick broke every moral, ethical, and professional standard a teacher lives by.

"She phoned the school office yesterday. I knew she was going to complain. Sure enough, she insisted on meeting with Chuck Stevens and me."

A meeting? I feel myself go cold. A meeting about what? Their romantic involvement? His sexual performance? I stare at my half-eaten sandwich. The sight of it makes me want to gag. God, I shouldn't be hearing this. I don't want to hear this.

"That's why I came down to talk to you. I thought I should be the one to tell you about Lauren switching classrooms."

"Wait a minute." I shake my head, suck in a deep breath. Somehow our conversation has wandered into a whole new territory. "Do you mean that Phyllis Conard came here to complain about me?"

Why the hell wasn't I at that meeting? Lauren is my student.

"Exactly," he says. "I told them you had a right to be there. I said you deserved to present your side of things. I did my best to try and make them listen. We're a team, Patty. You and me, right?"

If that's the kind of team Nick's running, I want no part of it.

"No need to bother you with all the details." Nick swings one leg against the desk. "Phyllis was adamant about pulling Lauren out of your class and putting her in mine. She wanted to do it this week instead of waiting until after Christmas break but I managed to talk her out of it."

"How wonderful," I mutter.

"Phyllis didn't think so." He chuckles. "She was not a happy camper.'

Blood rushes through my head, pounds in my ears. What a weasel! He looks so smug and proud of himself, but I'll be damned if I'll give him the satisfaction of seeing how much this hurts. And as for Chuck Stevens? I might just file a grievance against our principal with the union. After all, I'm still Lauren's teacher—at least until Christmas break. They never should have gone behind my back. I had every right to be at that meeting. I should have had a chance to defend myself.

And it's not hard to imagine the horrible things Phyllis must have said about me. I close my eyes, remembering the disgust on her face as she caught her husband fondling my thigh. Who knows? Maybe she turned this whole thing against me and made it look like I'm the one who came on to him. A parent complaining about a child's teacher? I might as well kiss that nomination for Teacher of the Year good-bye.

As for Nick Lamont? He's still in the running.

"So, I assume the meeting went well. Mind telling me exactly what was decided?" I struggle to keep my voice steady.

Nick shrugs. "You've known Chuck Stevens longer than me. He wasn't about to argue with Phyllis… especially since her husband owns a good chunk of the real estate in town. Basically he told her whatever she wanted was all right by him. As long as you and I get things squared away."

"And that's why you're here." I level him with a narrow stare. "To get everything squared away. To get a leg up on how Lauren's doing. To find out what you can about her before you take over."

"Huh?" Nick scratches his head. "I don't know what you're talking about. I told them Lauren didn't belong in my class... not when she's already got the best teacher in school."

My heart pounds to a stop. "Excuse me?"

"I said they'd be stupid to pull Lauren out of your classroom."

I blink. "You told them that?"

"Damn right I did. And they listened, too. She's all yours, Patty."

"I... I don't know what to say." Suddenly my throat feels scratchy and dry, and I can't get the words out of my mouth. Somehow, *thank you* doesn't seem appropriate. If only I'd been asked, I would gladly have transferred Lauren into Nick's class. She's been nothing but trouble since the school year started and her attitude gets worse by the day. But no one ever gave me a choice. Chuck Stevens and Phyllis Conard took charge of the situation and handed control of it over to Nick... who handed it back to me.

She's already got the best teacher in school.

"Except for reading, that is," he adds. "I'd like Lauren to stay in my group. She's been with us all year. You don't mind, do you?"

"Of course not." Somehow I manage a weak smile. "Thanks, Nick." When it came to crunch time, he stood up for me to both Chuck Stevens and Phyllis Conard. Who would have guessed?

Merry Christmas, me!

"Great. Lauren's the best reader in my class and the other kids look up to her. Having her around makes it easier for me." He hoists himself off Eric's desk. "I've got to get going, but I wanted to get this straightened out first. Like I said, I figured you heard about the meeting and I wanted you to know exactly what happened. The last thing I want is problems between us." His eyes soften. "You and me, we're a team, Patty. So, we're okay again, right?"

Okay? We are definitely more than okay. I force a brilliant smile. "We're fine."

He grins, gives me a thumbs-up. "Great."

I owe him an apology. A big apology. "Nick, if you've got a minute, I'd really like to talk. I just want to—"

"Can it wait?" He points at his watch. "I was due up at the high school for practice fifteen minutes ago." He starts for the door, then halts and pulls a folded scrap of paper from his pocket. He hands it to me. "I almost forgot. This is for you."

I scan the one page grid sheet. "What is it?"

"Our basketball schedule. The team had a lousy record last year. Last thing I want is those kids playing to an empty gym." He points a finger at me and winks. "You promised, remember? I'm counting on you to cheer us on."

I fold the schedule in half and tuck it in my purse as he heads out the door. Who cares if I'm still too big to wriggle into a cheerleader's outfit? Nick and I are a team again. He cheered me on in front of Chuck Stevens and Phyllis Conard. The least I can do is show up at his games. Let the other people root for the team.

I'll be the one cheering for the coach.

# # #

"Buying yourself a Christmas present?"

I glance up from the gleaming diamond display case and flash Sam a guilty smile. "Just window-shopping."

Little fib or big lie? I've been waiting in this crowded jewelry store for over five minutes for someone to wait on me. I'm picking up Nick's gift which the store had engraved. I casually shove the receipt for his Christmas present back inside my coat pocket.

"See anything that looks good?" Sam noses around the counter, scanning the cases.

"Actually, I did." I point to the elaborate arrangement of fine dishes elegantly displayed on a nearby wall. "Priscilla's still mad at me about Mama's turkey platter. I was hoping I'd find one to replace it."

He scans the shelf, frowns. "That looks like a different pattern."

I nod. "They can special order the one I want, but three hundred dollars is way over my budget." I sigh, shrug. "Hopefully next year money won't be so tight."

His eyes soften. "Don't worry. We'll get your finances straightened out before then, Patty. I promise."

Why is he being so nice? The last time we talked was the night of Amy's party when I turned my back on him and marched out the front door in those stupid high heels. Today I'm wearing boots. I tug at my scarf, run a hand through my curls, lift them off my neck. The store is crowded and I'm getting hot, standing here wrapped up in my coat.

Sam peers down through the shiny display case. Diamond bracelets and necklaces glitter like expensive ice. "Got all your other shopping done?"

"Well, there's still Priscilla."

"What about me?"

I can't help laughing at the hopeful grin on his face. I ordered his Christmas present online weeks ago and the sleek purple swim fins are already wrapped and under our tree. They're a perfect match for the goggles he wears at the pool. "You'll have to wait until Friday night."

I'm looking forward to our little dinner party. Priscilla actually worked up the nerve to invite Dr. Brown, and Sam, naturally, is a regular every weekend. But since Dr. Brown is working through the holidays and Sam leaves for Arizona soon, our Christmas celebrations this year are starting early.

"What about you?" I lean against the counter, try not to think about the receipt for Nick's gift sitting in my pocket. "Have you finished your shopping?"

He glances around the crowded store. "I need to find something for my niece. She turns thirteen on Christmas Day. I thought something sparkly might be appropriate, seeing as how I'm her favorite uncle."

"Her favorite uncle? That's a bit presumptuous, don't you think?" I can't resist teasing. "You're giving yourself lots of credit, Uncle Sam."

"Seeing I'm the only uncle she's got, I'd say it's not much of a contest." His brown eyes sparkle with an invitation. "Help me find something she'd like."

"I'm not good at picking out jewelry. You should ask Priscilla."

"But she's not here. Come on, Patty, I trust your judgment. You were thirteen, once upon a time."

"That was a long time ago," I protest, laughing.

He grins. "But you're still a girl. I thought all girls liked things that sparkle." He points to a glittering necklace. "How about that one? Do you think Gwynnie would like it?"

"Gwynnie? That's your niece?"

Sam nods. "Her real name is Gwyneth, after our mom. The older Gwynnie gets, the more she looks like her." His face sobers. "Mom would be so proud, if she were still alive."

I know exactly how he feels. I still miss Mama. I chew my lip, study him carefully. Sam's never opened up much about his family life, despite all the dinners we've shared. "How long has it been?"

"Fourteen years this June," he says in a low voice. "I was a freshman in high school when she had her first stroke. It left her paralyzed. My dad wanted to put her in a nursing home, but Eileen wouldn't hear of it. She's an R.N., and insisted on taking care of Mom herself. Eileen did double duty four years straight, nursing Mom during the day, pulling the night shift at the hospital."

"Your sister sounds like a wonderful woman." More like a saint. Sam and his family must have gone through hell.

"Eileen's great. We've always been close."

"What about your dad? Will he be there at Christmas?"

"No." Sam's voice goes flat. He grips the counter, stares at the jewelry.

Did I say something wrong? "I'm sorry. I didn't mean to pry."

He shrugs. "No problem. I don't know where my dad is and frankly, I don't care. Eileen and I haven't talked to him in years." The tight look on his face makes the back of my neck bristle. "He deserted us after Mom had her stroke. The last thing he wanted was an invalid for a wife."

"I'm sorry, Sam." I reach out and squeeze his hand. "That had to be so hard for you." His face looks like it's carved from stone, and my stomach feels like I swallowed a rock. No wonder he doesn't like to talk about his background. Who would, with a father like that? Families stick together, especially in times of crisis.

"My dad paid the bills, but that was it. He found a girlfriend and moved in with her. Eileen and John were already engaged, but they put off their wedding plans and Eileen moved back home." He sucks in a deep breath. "I helped out as much as I could, but I was only fourteen. Eileen took on most of the burden. Mom died two days after I graduated from high school. Eileen and John finally got married and I went off to college. I had a scholarship that helped and I worked my way through school. Dad offered to pay but I wasn't going to take one penny of his money. Not after the way he treated Mom."

He meets my stare with a bitter smile. "Maybe now you can understand why my dad is the last person I want showing up in my life on Christmas morning."

The irony isn't lost on me. Sam deliberately turned his back on his father while I've spent my whole life yearning for the one thing I've never had— the chance to know mine. I'd have given anything to have held his hand, had him read me a story, kiss me good-night.

"Eileen, John, and their three kids are the only family I've got. She's quite the lady, my sister Eileen. You'll like her, Patty. In fact, I think the two of you will be very good friends."

His fingers tighten around my own and I suddenly realize we're holding hands. When did that happen? My pulse quickens and I shiver at the tingle racing up my back. Something's happened between us. Something I'm not sure of. Something I can't put a name to.

Something that scares the hell out of me.

Sam's eyes search mine and my heart pounds against my chest. If only I could let him know that he's not alone, that someone cares… that I care. But I know

Sam well enough now to know I don't dare. He'll take it all wrong, read more into it than I mean. The last thing I want to do is hurt Sam. Thanks to me, he's been hurt enough. Friends don't hurt friends.

But being friends isn't what Sam wants. I know he wants more. He wants me. And he wants me to want him.

Why do life and love have to be so complicated? Things are so much simpler at school. No guessing games about how things work. Study hard, follow the rules and you earn an A… maybe an A+. This year, it might actually be within my reach.

Maybe as close as the other fifth-grade classroom.

I tug my hand out of Sam's and turn my attention to the row of shimmering jewels displayed before us. "What are you thinking about getting for Gwynnie?"

"I don't know." His voice hangs low with disappointment. I know he's upset that I've pulled away and I don't dare meet his eyes. After a moment he points out a solitaire diamond pendant on a shimmering gold chain. "How about that?"

"That necklace costs three hundred dollars."

"Who else have I got to spend it on?" He shoots me a fast look that tears at my heart. "You don't think she'd like it?"

"Of course she would. Any woman would love it. It's gorgeous."

"Then what's the problem?" he demands.

"It's just that…" I stare at the necklace, searching for the right words. "It's not exactly the kind of jewelry an uncle buys for his niece."

His eyebrows lift. "Because…?"

"Because it's… it's what a man would buy for his girlfriend. Or his wife."

I move away from the necklaces to another display case, where I spy a pair of diamond stud earrings in the very back row. Simple and elegant, less than one hundred dollars. The perfect gift from the perfect uncle. I point them out. "Does Gwynnie have pierced ears?"

"Don't all girls?" He bends for a closer look. "You really think she'd like them?"

"I do."

"That settles that. I'll take them." He straightens, glances around the crowded, understaffed store busy with Christmas shoppers. "Once I find someone to help me."

I peek at my watch. The store has extended holiday hours and doesn't close until ten. I'll come back and pick up Nick's gift once Sam is gone.

"When do you leave for Arizona?"

"I fly out Sunday… unless that snowstorm they're predicting screws things up. But I'll be back before New Year's Eve." He gives me a sideways glance. "Do you have any plans?"

"Priscilla and I usually go to Midnight Mass, and—"

"No, I'm talking about New Year's Eve. I thought maybe if you weren't busy…" His tone quiets. "Or maybe you're going to another party."

"No plans," I say with a quick smile. I won't lie to him. Sam doesn't deserve it. "At least, not yet."

Do they play basketball games on New Year's Eve?

"How about I give you a call when I get back? If you're not busy, maybe we can do something."

"That sounds good." I can deal with that. Casual, comfortable. Just like Sam. Easy, friendly, safe. Maybe a little *too* safe. Safe can turn dangerous, fast. I learned that lesson in the basement.

As soon as I get home, I'm checking Nick's basketball schedule.

A thin salesman in a shiny suit finally breezes over from another counter. He slides behind the diamond display case and eyes the two of us with a speculative smile. "Shopping for that special occasion?"

Sam nods. "That's right."

"'Tis the season." The salesman beams. "We have some beautiful wedding sets I'd love to show you. They're right over here if you'll just step this way." He waves toward a nearby case.

Sam breaks out in a fit of coughing and I clutch my hands behind my back, hiding my ring finger.

"Actually, I'm buying a gift for my niece," Sam manages to sputter. His face is redder than his sweater.

There's never been a better time for a quick exit and I'm grabbing it now. I squeeze Sam's shoulder, jam my hand in my pocket, and wrap my fingers around Nick's receipt. "See you Friday night," I say and head out the door.

CHAPTER FIFTEEN

"But you can't leave now." I stare at Nick across the empty table in the staff lounge. "Christmas vacation doesn't start for another two days."

"No choice." He sprawls back in his chair. "My sister Jenny got on the phone last night to rally the troops. I head to the airport right after school."

"But you'll miss the party. The excitement. The kids. You'll miss everything." How can he do this to me? I try to keep the disappointment from creeping over my face. "Couldn't you put off leaving just two more days?"

God, am I really begging?

"Sorry, but I've got to go. I was lucky to snag a seat. That snowstorm headed this way has everybody rebooking their flights. I'm getting on that plane tonight and heading west." He stretches with a lazy yawn and throws me a wide smile. "Christmas in California. Sunshine and blue skies."

"It sounds wonderful," I mumble. Wonderful for him, not so wonderful for me. But why should his news come as a surprise? What else should I expect from a golden boy like Nick?

"What about you? Got special plans?"

"Nothing to speak of." If the bad weather they're predicting comes true, I'll probably spend my holiday shoveling snow. At least the exercise will do me good. It will help burn off the calories from the Christmas cookies I plan on eating, once I discover where Priscilla stashed them.

"Perk up, Patty. It's Christmas, remember? You're supposed to be happy."

"It might be Christmas, but it's also cold," I glumly remind him.

Nick grins. "Why not give yourself a little present and take a vacation yourself? Hop a plane and fly someplace warm."

California, maybe?

"Is that an invitation?" I dare a quick smile, even though I know I'm not going anywhere. I can't afford it, plus I can't leave Priscilla. Especially not at Christmas. Holidays mean family and home. And home for Priscilla means that big drafty house.

The shrill ring of the playground bell sounds in the hallway. Nick shoves his chair under the table. "Back to the grind. You coming?"

"Right behind you." I trail him into the hallway, crowded with rosy-cheeked kids fresh from noon recess. "Be sure and stop to say good-bye before you leave," I call through the hallway hubbub. Thank goodness I brought Nick's Christmas present to school. It's been tucked away in the bottom of my desk for days. "I've got something for you…"

Did he even hear me? Nick just keeps on walking, disappearing into the crowd.

# # #

The final bell rings and the classroom empties out. I keep one eye on the clock. Two minutes pass. Five minutes, then ten. I take deep breaths, tell myself it doesn't matter as the minute hand sweeps past fifteen. I knew Nick was in a rush to get going. Why should he stop and say good-bye? Why should it matter if he does or doesn't?

Twenty minutes later, he strolls in the door and perches on the corner of my desk.

My heart pounds. He came!

"I have something for you." I pull open my bottom drawer and draw out the small box adorned with a silver bow. For weeks I've been dreaming about the look on Nick's face when he sees his gift. My heart races and my fingers tremble as I slide the box across the desk.

"You got me a present?" He picks up the box, fingers the ribbon. My stomach sinks as I catch the fleeting guilt on his face and I suddenly realize there's no present for me. I shouldn't have bought him a gift. I shouldn't have spent the money. All I wanted to do was make him feel good and I've embarrassed him.

"It's nothing, really," I assure him. "No big deal."

He stares at it a long moment, turning the box over and over in his hands. Finally he looks up at me. "I guess in all the rush, I forgot your Christmas present." The tips of his ears are tinged a brilliant scarlet. "You probably hate me, right?"

"No, it's fine, really." How could I hate him? "I never expected anything." I feel the hot flush rush up my cheeks. Of course I expected something. Friends exchange gifts, right? And Nick and I are friends, right? I was starting to think we were more than friends.

Guess I thought wrong.

I take a deep breath. If he didn't get me a gift, then so be it. It's Christmas, the time of giving. It's better to give than to receive. And if you expect nothing, it's easier to handle disappointment.

"I did get you a present. I just forgot it at home. I'm a total jerk." Nick slowly starts to unwrap the ribbons, his face growing redder by the moment.

The knot in my stomach tightens. Why is he lying? He never bought me a gift. That part is bad enough, but hearing him lie hurts worse than knowing he never even gave me a thought. Why doesn't he hurry up, open his present and leave? Who is he trying to kid?

And who am I trying to kid? I've always known he was way out of my league. Nick's a golden boy, meant for sunshine and blue skies. Why should someone like him care about someone like me when I don't even care about myself?

I'm nothing but a big fat loser.

Nick slips the silver whistle from the velvet bag and stares at it for a long moment. "Patty, this is—"

"I thought it would come in handy when you were coaching." Stupid, stupid, stupid. Why did I go to so much trouble? Now he'll know how much I care. *Too much.* When will I ever learn?

"And you even had it engraved." He flips the cord over his head and adjusts the whistle so it hangs below his shirt collar. His eyes shine. "It's perfect. I'll think of you every time I wear it."

I force a smile to my face. "I'm glad you like it."

"Like it? I love it." He grabs my hand, squeezes my fingers. "I'm going to miss you, Patty. I'll think about you every day I'm gone."

Sure he will. Just like Santa really slides down the chimney and leaves gifts under the tree for all the good little boys and girls.

"Merry Christmas, Patty." Nick leans over the desk, grabs me by the shoulders and softly presses his lips against my own.

My heart hammers against my chest and there's a sudden lump in my throat. He does care, I tell myself, my lips tingling as Nick pulls away. He never would have kissed me if he didn't care.

Am I wrong? Is there something between us? I'm so bad at reading men. "Nick, I—"

"I've got to get going if I'm going to make that plane." He touches the tip of my nose and gives me a tender smile. "Sorry again about forgetting your present. I'll make it up to you when I get back." He leans over, plants one last soft, lingering kiss on my lips. "Merry Christmas, Patty."

"Merry Christmas, Nick," I whisper as he strolls out the door.

# # #

"Patty?"

The unexpected voice startles me, and I nearly drop my watering can. I turn from my task watering all the plants lined up in my classroom window and see Nick standing in the doorway. His red down jacket is zipped up tight. His hair is wet with snow.

"What are you doing here?" I sink against the counter. My legs feel like rubber bands and the watering can suddenly feels like it weighs fifty pounds. "Aren't you supposed to be at the airport?"

"Soon." Puddles of melting snow dodge his steps as Nick winds his way through the maze of desks. "I went home and grabbed my stuff and then I thought… well, I decided to make a quick detour. You looked so down when we said good-bye."

I gulp for air as he takes one last step and finally stands in front of me. No desks separate us. The scent of the fresh outdoors clings to him, even with his coat zipped. He stares at me a long moment. "I couldn't leave remembering you like that."

He came back because of me? I shove some of the flower pots aside and perch on the counter. If I don't sit, I'll fall on the floor.

"I wasn't sure you'd still be here," he adds. "Then I saw your car in the parking lot."

"I'm just finishing up. I always water the plants on Wednesday." *Shut up, shut up, let him do the talking*. But my heart is racing like crazy and so is my mouth. "The janitors are supposed to keep them watered, but I don't trust them."

One corner of his mouth lifts. "You didn't trust me, either, did you? You thought I forgot all about you."

"No, I—"

"Yes, you did. You thought I didn't get you a Christmas present." He reaches in his coat pocket and draws out a little box. "Merry Christmas."

I stare at the tiny box with a silvery bow he's tucked in my hand. Unless this came from a quick-stop convenience store, Nick's had my gift all along. It's been less than one hour since we said good-bye, since he kissed me. He hasn't had time to shop.

He didn't forget me after all.

"I hope you like it." His words spill out in a rush. "It took me awhile to figure out what to get you. I wanted it to be something special. You're not like other girls, Patty."

I blink back hot, sudden tears. He wouldn't have bothered to get me a present unless he cared. And he came back. That has to mean something. Doesn't it?

"Aren't you going to open it?"

My fingers tremble as I tear off the ribbon and paper. I hesitate at the sight of the familiar blue velveteen box. It's from a jewelry store. The same store where I had Nick's whistle engraved. My breath catches as I snap open the lid. A glittering apple brooch on a bed of crushed silk winks up at me. Gleaming garnets, polished with gold and a twinkling diamond stem.

"You like it?" His voice is filled with hope.

Like it? I love it! First he kisses me and now he gives me diamonds? How could I not love it? How could I not love him?

"It's an apple for my favorite teacher," he says softly. "I know it hasn't been easy for you putting up with me, but you've been great, Patty. You never complain. I've learned a lot from you."

"Same here," I whisper. Biology, cardiology... when it comes to Nick, all subjects apply. Except psychology. Just when I think I have him all figured out, he gives me something like this jeweled pin. I don't know much about jewelry but I know enough to know I'm holding the real thing. Real gold, real garnets, real diamonds. This piece had to set him back some serious cash. Lots more than that silly engraved whistle I gave him which he still has draped around his neck.

He shifts on his feet. "Sorry to cut this short, but if I don't get going, I'll miss my plane."

"I know." I finger the delicate brooch. Being around him makes me crazy. What is he trying to prove? What does this present mean? Why did he kiss me? Will he kiss me again?

"Hey, what happened to your smile? Remember what Santa says—*you better not pout, you better not cry*." He wags a finger in my face. "We'll celebrate when I get back. Got any plans for New Year's Eve?"

"No." Then I remember Sam. "Yes. Well, maybe, maybe not. I'm not sure." Sam and I didn't make specific plans. "Why? Are you coming back for New Year's?"

"Not sure. I've got a return ticket for December thirtieth, but you never know when it comes to the weather." He tugs on his leather gloves and grins. "So, no more being mad at me?"

My face flushes bright red. "I wasn't mad."

He laughs. "Patty, that's one thing I love about you. You're so easy to read. " He reaches over and brushes away some wisps of curls from my face. "Now I can leave with a clear conscience."

He leans toward me and I close my eyes, wait for the soft press of his lips on mine. He loves me? He loves me! It's not Christmas yet but I've already got the best present in the world—Nick Lamont.

Too bad he has a plane to catch. Too bad he won't be here for Christmas. Too bad there's no time to continue this delicious…

"Merry Christmas, Patty."

His lips lightly graze my cheek. My eyes fly open and I stare after him as he breezes out the door.

I stare long and hard at the glittering pin still gripped in my hand. And here I thought women were supposed to be the complicated sex. Nick could teach us a thing or two. He complicates life in good ways and bad.

And what exactly did he mean by that kiss?

# # #

Candy canes, games and gifts, a holiday extravaganza. The kids were excited about the start of Christmas vacation and the voices buzzed higher as the cookies and punch disappeared. Even Joseph and Billy behaved themselves. It was quite the party, but it's finally over and I'm looking forward to fourteen straight days of blissful quiet, being lazy, and sleeping in late. I give my classroom one last look before I head out the door for home.

But my small canvas tote will never hold all the gifts I received, stacked high on my desk. Tins of homemade cookies, bottles of perfume, the customary stationery—four boxes this year—and a paperback joke book from Tyler, my resident clown. A beautiful silk scarf from Lauren in a delicate Japanese print. A glitzy purple ruler and matching tape dispenser from Matt and his twin Mike. My eyes fall on my favorite gift of all: a small ceramic angel in gaudy hues of yellow, pink, and blue. It's dusty and a little dirty, but it's precious to me. There's not much money or parental involvement at Tiffany's house and I'll lay money this little angel came right off her bedroom shelf, straight from the little girl's heart.

I pick it up, polish it with a Kleenex and place it on the highest shelf in the bookcase behind my desk. Tiffany's angel will stand guard over our classroom for the rest of the school year. Maybe seeing it will remind some of the girls to be more kind, to treat others the way you'd like to be treated. There's enough bullying in the world. I don't need it happening in my class.

My cell phone buzzes. It's buried somewhere underneath the gifts. No doubt it's Priscilla. I'm already late, and with Sam and Dr. Brown expected for dinner, she's probably frantic.

"Patty?"

Sam's voice surprises me. He sounds tinny and far away.

"Sam? Is that you?" It's hard to tell. It sounds like he's in a tunnel.

"Sorry about the… I'm on my cell… got to the airport."

"You're at the airport?" My stomach drops. It's a scratchy connection. Maybe I misunderstood. But I already don't like what I'm hearing.

"I managed… Phoenix. My plane… an hour."

"But you're supposed to come for dinner tonight. We're celebrating Christmas."

"I'm sorry about this, Patty. The snowstorm's moving in fast."

"We're having prime rib." I swallow over the lump in my throat. "Priscilla has the house all decorated. She invited Dr. Brown."

"Tell her… sorry."

There's an empty buzz and I think I've lost him.

"Sam? Are you there?"

The phone crackles. "I'll be back on the thirtieth."

Ten whole days without him. "Sam, I wish you weren't…"

"Tell Priscilla I'm sorry about tonight."

"Don't worry about it," I mumble. "She'll understand."

But what I don't understand is why I suddenly feel so disappointed.

"I'll miss you, Patty."

"I'll miss you, too." Even as I speak, I realize I'm admitting the truth. I'll miss his company at dinner. Miss seeing how his face lights up when he opens his gift. I'll miss his laughter, stories, jokes.

I'll miss the man.

"Merry—"

The connection breaks and this time I know I've lost him for good. No chance to even say good-bye.

"Merry Christmas, Sam," I whisper, though I know he can't hear me.

Everyone is heading out before the storm hits and the only place I've got to go is home. Priscilla's baked up a store. Homemade goodies are stashed all over the house. Gifts for the clinic, for friends we know. I think of the rich, buttery toffee candy she planned on making today. My favorite treat, made only at Christmas. How can I say no?

But how can I say yes? My eating's been out of control since Amy's cocktail party. I wouldn't be surprised if I gain another two or three pounds before New Year's.

Count your blessings, Mama always said. Things could be worse.

Blessings? What blessings?

Then I spy one, smack in the center of my desk. I pluck Nick's gift out of the velvet bag, snap the lid open and eye the apple brooch. I tilt the box in the fading afternoon sun. Garnets flash, diamonds shimmer. *An apple for my favorite teacher*. An apple, the forbidden fruit.

Forbidden food.

Who needs food? I don't need cookies or Priscilla's butter crunch toffee. I can make it through the holidays without eggnog, rum balls, or mincemeat pie. I can do it without gaining a single pound.

Count your blessings? More like count your calories… and from now on, I'm going to count every single calorie I pop in my mouth.

God bless that snowstorm moving into town. Shoveling snow burns calories and I'll shovel every hour on the hour if that's what it takes. I won't touch cookies. I don't need sugar. I've found something better. I can make it through Christmas. I know I can do it, especially with a little help from Sam's method of swimming one lap at a time. I'll take the food one day at a time. Christmas is only one day out of the year. And after Christmas comes and goes, Sam will be back.

And so will Nick.

I snap the lid shut on the twinkling brooch, grab my bag, and head for the door. I'm already late and Priscilla is probably anxious—but that's nothing compared to how frantic she'll be when she finds out Dr. Brown will be our only guest tonight. Hopefully he shows up with a big appetite. That dapper little doctor with the polite smile is going to find himself surrounded by plenty of delicious food and a heaping candy dish that he'll have to polish off without any help from me.

Who needs sugar when you've got Nick Lamont?

CHAPTER SIXTEEN

The telephone's shrill ring comes in the middle of Priscilla's tears and just before the hero's kiss.

"I'll get it." I jump up from the couch and scoot for the hallway, grateful to make an escape. We survived Christmas but I'm not sure I'll survive the aftermath, especially since Priscilla seems hell-bent on watching every single holiday film ever made. I grab the phone. "Hello?"

"Happy New Year."

"Well, thank you very much, Mr. Curtis... except you're one day early." I sink down on the upholstered bench, glad to hear his voice. We've talked every day since he's been gone, more than we ever do when he's home. I didn't count on missing him so much. "Where are you? Did your plane leave yet? Are you still in Arizona?"

"Would that make any difference?"

"Of course it does." Is he kidding? Two miles or two thousand miles could separate us.

An easy laugh rolls across the line. "We landed around dinnertime. I just walked in the door."

Sam's home. Delicious news. I curl up on the bench and tuck the phone under my chin with a smile. I won't have to waste my time watching any more cheesy holiday movies.

"Got any plans for tomorrow night? It's New Year's Eve, remember?"

I draw in a small breath, finger the apple brooch pinned on my sweater. All quiet on the California front. No word from Nick, not even a phone call. Not even on Christmas. I assume he's been busy with his sisters. Maybe his older brothers showed up. That would be hard on him. Nick said they don't get along.

And I know exactly how he feels. Holidays are tough, especially when one of you is mad at the other. It's been over a month since the Thanksgiving fiasco, and Priscilla's finally talking to me again, but it's not the same. There's an edginess between us that I'd give anything to fix.

"No plans," I say, ignoring the small tug in my heart. "I'm all yours."

"I like the sound of that," Sam says, chuckling. "But what about Priscilla? I don't want her feeling left out. I was thinking the three of us could have dinner together. A beautiful woman on each arm? I'll be the envy of every guy in town."

"Sorry, you missed your chance. She already has a date."

"Our Priscilla? You're kidding. Who's the lucky guy?"

"Dr. Brown, of course." Who would have guessed? Those two make quite the pair. Priscilla is smitten and it's obvious the feeling is mutual. If he wasn't busy at the hospital tonight, no doubt he'd be in our living room watching holiday movies without a single complaint.

"I guess I never linked the two of them together. He's such a plain-looking guy and Priscilla... well, she's—"

"Gorgeous," I supply. "Go ahead, you might as well say it. Priscilla's beautiful." *And I'm not*. But the fact doesn't bother me. I've lived with it for years.

"What I meant to say was, Priscilla could have her pick of any guy in town and yet she goes for him. Go figure."

I nod into the phone. Funny, to think that I once questioned Dr. Brown's motives and now I can't think of anyone more perfect for Priscilla. The two of them seem made for each other. Both of them are homebodies, gentle souls wandering through life trying to make others happy.

Except she's not happy with me. I'm sure no one else has noticed the rift, but I have and it hurts my heart. It's like living with a stranger instead of my twin. The easiness between us is gone and I'm at a loss how to get it back. Why is it you never appreciate the things that matter most until they're suddenly gone? Priscilla can be stubborn, but she's never been like this. And all over a stupid piece of china. I've tried apologizing over and over, but whenever I start, she cuts me off, says it doesn't matter, that she doesn't want to talk about it.

But it does matter. And we do need to talk about it. I know how much it's hurting me. And I know Priscilla. She's keeping it all bottled up inside. It's got to be hurting her. It's hurting us.

What if we never talk about it? Someday there might be no more *us*.

Maybe I should say something to Dr. Brown. She won't listen to me. Maybe she'll listen to him.

"Isn't it funny, how people get together?" I muse. "I wonder what it is that attracts one person to another? One of life's great mysteries, I suppose."

"No mystery," he answers in a low voice. "It's those beautiful red curls… and your freckles."

"Ugh, don't mention those freckles." He's flirting with me and I shouldn't encourage him. But everyone's entitled to a little fun now and then, and chatting with Sam is so much better than being trapped in the living room with Priscilla. "And as for my hair?"

I twist some curls around a finger, give up as they bounce in my face. "Maybe I should shave my head and go bald, like Dr. Brown. What do you think?"

"Don't you dare," he warns. "You're a gorgeous redhead. Make sure you stay that way."

A quick rush of pleasure shoots up my cheeks. "Enough with the teasing."

"What makes you think I'm teasing? You're every bit as gorgeous as your sister."

"And you're a liar, Sam Curtis."

"I'd never tell you something that wasn't true. I'm a man of my word." His voice catches. "You're beautiful to me."

Priscilla wanders through the doorway. "Who's on the phone?"

I cover it with one hand. "It's Sam. He just got back into town."

She yawns, heads for the stairs. "Tell him I said hello. I'm going to bed."

"Priscilla says hi." I watch her disappear up the stairs. "What were we talking about?"

"An adorable redhead with lots of freckles."

"Her again?" I laugh. "I can think of better things to talk about."

"That redhead happens to be my favorite subject. I missed you, Patty."

"Arizona wasn't fun?" I try to ignore the hint of longing I hear in his voice.

"It would have been more fun if you'd been there."

"Excuse me but I don't remember being invited. And some of that Arizona sunshine sounds pretty nice right now. I've been shoveling snow for six days straight."

"Next year I'll make sure you're invited."

"You do that, Mr. Curtis," I say lightly. Our conversation is taking a serious turn, and we don't need to go there. "Meanwhile, what about tomorrow night?"

"Name the place and I'll make reservations. Dinner?"

"I'm on a diet." I lost another three pounds over the holidays and the last thing I want to do is end the old year focusing on food.

"Okay, forget dinner. What about dancing?"

"Too fancy." Memories of that little black dress are fresh in my mind. Besides, Dr. Brown and Priscilla have plans for dinner and dancing tomorrow. She's been obsessed for days, wandering around the house muttering to herself about how to do her hair and what she should wear. *Ghosts of cocktail parties past.*

"It's New Year's Eve, Patty. Don't you want to go somewhere special and celebrate?"

Not if I can't have what I want. And what I want is still in California... I think.

"Why do we have to get all dressed up? Can't we go somewhere and have some fun?"

"Anything to keep you happy. How about a movie?"

Suddenly this is starting to sound like a real date. So far I've been successful in evading a romantic dinner or being in Sam's arms on a crowded dance floor. But sitting in a darkened movie theater would give him plenty of opportunity to slip his arm around my shoulder and pull me close. Do I really want to put myself through two hours fighting him off?

"Like you said, it's New Year's Eve. We could do a movie anytime. Let's do something special and fun… but can we make it someplace where we can wear jeans?"

"That's not very festive." Sam sounds doubtful.

"Festive or not, at least we'll be comfortable." Ringing in the New Year in my favorite pair of jeans sounds like the perfect ending to the not-so-perfect year.

"I guess I can figure something out."

"I trust you, Sam. I'm sure whatever you come up with will be lots of fun."

# # #

"We're going bowling?" I shut the front door behind him and stare at the puddles of wet snow as Sam stomps his shoes on the mat. "But I don't know how to bowl."

"Then tonight's the night you learn." He hands me his jacket with an easy grin.

Maybe I should have planned the evening after all. The thought of spending New Year's Eve at a bowling alley conjures up images of loud laughter, ugly shoes, and men swigging beer. I peer at him. "Are you on a team?"

He shakes his head. "A couple of guys that work for me bowl in a league and I sponsor their team. But that's the extent of my expertise."

I hang his coat in the closet. I don't want to go bowling. I'll make a fool of myself. What if I trip? What if I fall? What if I end up doing something stupid and everyone laughs?

"I've never been bowling in my life…"

One look at the doubtful look on Sam's face and I give myself a mental kick in the butt. I promised I'd be happy with whatever he came up with.

"Bowling it is." I suck in a deep breath and give him a big smile. "At least I'm dressed for it." My best pair of jeans and the new silk blouse Priscilla gave me for Christmas… plus Nick's brooch, twinkling on the collar.

"You look great," he says, trailing me into the living room. "Then again, you always look great."

"Thanks." I perch on the couch. There's nothing better than a man paying you a compliment, especially when you know it's true. My new diet is paying off royally. "I've lost a few pounds."

He sinks down beside me, drops a large sack on the floor. "I don't understand why you're trying to lose weight. You look perfect to me."

"Flatterer," I say with a breezy laugh, though I do feel nearly perfect tonight. My jeans are looser around the waist than the last time I wore them. Another few weeks and I'll be shopping for something smaller.

Now, if only I could convince Sam to lose some of those extra pounds. He'd look better, he'd feel better, he'd…

No. Sam's weight is none of my business. I promised not to harp and as he so bluntly reminded me once, I am not his food police. Sam could care less how he looks, but sooner or later, it will catch up with him. He'll have jowls, a double chin, and a belly to match. If only he'd let me help him, things would be different. But there's nothing between us and there never will be. Not with his attitude. The last thing I need is an overweight boyfriend. I've got my own problems to deal with. The two of us are friends and that's the way it's going to stay. Sam and I will be friends. Very good friends.

"How was Arizona? Did you have a nice vacation?"

He stuffs a pillow behind his back. "It's always great spending time with Eileen and her family."

"Did Gwynnie like the earrings?"

"She loved them." A wide smile cuts across his face. "And so did her mother. Now I know what to get Eileen for her birthday next year. Thanks again for helping me pick them out."

"Glad to be of service." I eye the bulky sack at his feet. "Looks like Santa did some Christmas shopping."

"We didn't get a chance to exchange gifts before I left." He bends over and hauls out a large box adorned with a huge red bow. "This is for Priscilla. Is she home?"

"Dr. Brown picked her up about an hour ago." I eye the package. "What is it?"

"You'll have to wait and see." He slides her gift across the floor toward the Christmas tree. "She can open it tomorrow."

"Come on, Sam, that box is much too big to keep a secret. What's in it?"

"I think you should wait."

The odd look on his face definitely has my curiosity aroused. "Please?"

He wavers another moment, then sighs. "It's a turkey platter."

I suck in a deep breath. "You mean, like Mama's turkey platter? The one they didn't have in stock? The one I couldn't afford?"

He nods. "I had them special order it."

I sink into the pillows and stare at the box. That turkey platter cost three hundred dollars. Sam spent more on Priscilla than the entire amount I spent on my holiday shopping this year. It was hard, stretching the money, but Sam insisted I stick to a budget and somehow I managed. And this was the first year I didn't go into debt. Still, three hundred dollars is a lot of money. Two weeks worth of groceries. Two months of utility payments. One turkey platter.

Or a glittering apple brooch. How much did that cost?

"Guess I felt a little guilty, knowing you would have bought it if it not for that budget I put you on." His eyebrows bunch together in a tight line. "You're not mad I bought it for her, are you?"

"Why would I be mad?"

"I don't know. I didn't want you thinking I was trying to take over." He throws me an uneasy glance. "And I didn't want you thinking I was trying to replace a family heirloom. Because I wasn't. That kind of thing is beyond money. And... well, I'm not family."

How can I fault him? Somehow he knew how bad I felt not being able to make things right with Priscilla. He knew I couldn't afford to buy it, so he bought it instead. I swallow over the lump in my throat. Sam's a big guy... but when it comes to size, the biggest part of him is his heart.

"Priscilla will be thrilled. She already thinks you're the sweetest man in the world. Besides Dr. Brown, that is."

"But what about Patty? What does she think?"

Something about the husky tone in his voice sets off faint alarms in my head. "I think Dr. Brown is very sweet, too."

"That's not what I meant, and you know it." His gaze never wavers. The shimmering glow of the Christmas tree lights are reflected in the warmth of his soft brown eyes—searching, questioning, waiting for me to answer.

Waiting for something I can't give him.

The last thing I want to do is hurt him. But it can't be. It just can't. Somehow I manage to find a voice. "You don't want to hear what I think."

"Yes I do." He leans across the couch and catches my hand. "I thought about you the whole time I was in Arizona, Patty. Why wouldn't I want to hear what you think?"

"You want to know what I think?" My heart pounds and I tug my hand out of his. "I think you should open your Christmas present." I scramble off the couch, grab his gift from under the tree. "Merry Christmas, Sam."

He shakes the box with a questioning smile. "It doesn't feel like a turkey platter."

"Open it." I sink to the floor, sit cross-legged directly in front of him. It's a good spot. It's safe.

He rips through the ribbons and paper and pulls out the purple swim fins. His face lights up as he turns them over in his hands. "Just what I wanted. How did you know?"

"I have my sources." A girl has to have some secrets. That pimply faced lifeguard turned out to be good for something, at least.

"I have a present for you, too." He sets the fins aside and reaches for the shopping bag. His hand fumbles deep inside. Finally he draws out a not-too-small box. "Merry Christmas, Patty."

"Thank you." The odd little smile on his face has me puzzled and a little nervous. It doesn't take me long to unwrap the present. I find another box inside, distinctly smaller than the first. I put the second box in my lap and undo the paper, lift the lid and peer inside to see yet a third box. A small, familiar, blue velvet box—the kind that comes from a jewelry store.

"Aren't you going to open it?" he finally asks.

How can I say *no*? I've already got a pretty good idea what's inside. My fingers shake and my heart pounds as I snap open the lid and peek inside. Just as I suspected, nestled inside the velvet box is the necklace from the jewelry store. The necklace I talked Sam out of buying for Gwynnie. The necklace I told him was the type of thing a man bought for his girlfriend. Or his wife.

I stare at the diamond. It sparkles and gleams in the twinkling lights of the Christmas tree. I snap the lid shut.

"You don't like it?"

"Of course I do. It's beautiful. I love it." I close my eyes, but I can't close out the flat hurt in his voice. "Any woman would love it. But I can't keep it." I fumble with the box, the ribbons, force them into his hands. "Please take it back. It's much too expensive."

"That turkey platter I gave Priscilla didn't come cheap," he replies.

"That's different and you know it."

"Different how?" His low voice holds a challenge.

But we both know what's at stake. No matter what the price, there's a big difference between a piece of china and a diamond necklace. Priscilla's gift was a sweet sentimental gesture, but there's no mistaking Sam's intention in giving me this necklace.

"Just try it on." He snaps the lid open and pulls the shimmering rope from its mount. The diamond twirls and sparkles at the end of the glittering chain. "I'll do the clasp."

"What would be the point? I can't keep it."

His eyes narrow. "It's yours, Patty. I bought it for you and I'm not taking it back." He leans over and lifts my hair before I can stop him. His fingers graze the back of my neck and I catch my breath as he fastens the clasp on the thin gold chain. I shouldn't let him do this. It's wrong. I can't keep it. I shouldn't keep it. The weight of the chain sinks against my blouse and the diamond nestles between my breasts.

Too late. I should have stopped him before it was too late.

I finger the pendant. "I don't deserve this."

"You deserve the world, Patty, and I'd buy it for you, if I could. But for now, you'll have to settle for this necklace."

I should take it off and give it back to him right now. I'm crazy to keep it. I don't want to lead him on. It's not fair to Sam. It will only cause trouble.

"Listen, I know what you're thinking. And you're right." His voice drops even lower. "You're a gorgeous redhead with a knock 'em dead figure and a personality to match. You wow people everywhere you go. You've wowed me from day one. Don't you get it, Patty? I think you're perfect. Absolutely perfect."

I choke out a laugh. "Me, perfect? I think you need glasses."

"I'm not joking." His eyes are solemn, his voice sober. "I've never felt like this about a girl."

I finger the diamond resting lightly on my silk blouse. I'm afraid to meet his eyes, afraid of what I'll see. "I'm no girl, Sam. I'm thirty years old."

"And I'm older than you. Are you calling me an old man?"

"No," I say softly. Sam doesn't look any older than me. Men are lucky like that. Older men with grey hair and chiseled chins come off looking distinguished and handsome, while a woman gains wrinkles, varicose veins, and sags in all the wrong places. Weight is the great equalizer. Man or woman, when you're overweight, every inch, every pound, matters.

And someday, Sam won't look like me. He refuses to do anything about the way he looks.

He won't sag. He'll only get bigger.

I finger his necklace, stare at the Christmas tree. There were a few holes gaping through the branches when Priscilla and I first put it up. But once the lights were strung, the ornaments hung, and the tinsel added, the tree took on a life of its own. Why can't people be the same? A little ornamentation, a little cosmetic tinsel here and there, and anyone can light up like a Christmas tree.

Anyone but Sam. He'll never change.

I hate myself for thinking it. I hate that I've sunk so low, that I could be so shallow and cruel. I know the truth better than anyone. It shouldn't matter how Sam looks or how I look or how anyone looks. But I also know another truth: that while it shouldn't matter... it *does*. Just like that competition for Teacher of the Year. If I'd taken better care of myself, prided myself more on how I looked, I might have won last year or even the year before that. Like it or not, people do judge you on the way you look. And if that's the case, then I'm doing my best to take care of myself, to fix what's wrong inside. Doesn't Sam see that? Why can't he do the same? Doesn't he realize how important it is?

To him? To me?

"I'll be forty years old in a couple years," he says. "It's taken me a long time to learn some things about myself. Some of them, I've learned in just the past few months. And here's the most important thing of all."

He leans across the couch and catches my hand in his. "Everything makes sense when I'm with you. It's worth getting up every day, knowing there's a chance we'll talk on the phone. When I wake up Friday mornings, I always feel great. That's because I know I'll be with you at dinner. You've changed everything, Patty. You make it all worthwhile."

My face burns, the skin on the back of my neck prickles, and suddenly I want to snatch my hand away. What if he says the L-word? What will I do? I'll never forgive myself for hurting him. I want him and I hate it, and I hate him for putting us in this predicament...

"You're the one I've been waiting for, Patty. I knew it almost from the minute we met. And how I feel inside..." He beats his fist lightly against his chest "...this is where you've changed me. Don't ask me to hide the way I feel, because I can't. Not when it comes to you. I can't and I won't. I'm not that kind of guy."

"Sam, I—"

"Keep the necklace, Patty. No strings attached, I promise. It's a gift, a simple Christmas gift, from my heart to yours."

I suck in a deep breath. Who would have guessed such a big, bulky man could be such a hopeless romantic?

"Thank you, Sam." I brush his lips with a soft kiss. A mere thank-you kiss. His breath tastes like mint, fresh and cool as he kisses me back. I close my eyes and somehow I'm suddenly in his arms. His wool sweater is scratchy against my skin but it doesn't matter. *Pull away*, my head urges, but my heart keeps me in his arms. How can something that feels this good be so wrong? He pulls me closer. The living room is quiet, the darkness lit only by the twinkling lights of the Christmas tree. Nothing seems to matter. I feel myself let go. I could lose myself tonight here in his arms, exploring the silken folds of his mouth, the dart of his tongue playing against my own. His lips press against my neck and I tilt my head back against the pillows.

So much better than bowling.

"Wait. Stop." He sits up, abruptly pushes me aside.

"What's wrong?" My heart pounds against my chest as I stare at him. *Just when everything was going so right...*

Sam blows hard, stands, his face hidden in the shadows. "I think it's time we got going."

"But I thought..." I ignore the hand he offers, stare at him confusedly. Doesn't he want me? Because I want him. And I'm willing to throw everything aside, all caution to the wind. I'll do anything to quench this desire he's ignited. "I thought you wanted—"

"What I want and what I'm going to do are two different things," he says. "And right now, I think it's best if we go. Before either one of us gets carried away and does something we'll regret."

Is that what he thinks? That he'll regret it? That I'll regret it? I feel like he's flung me out of a lifeboat and into a raging river. Sam's the one with the map and I've got no clue where I'm headed. I don't want to navigate alone.

"Come on." He holds out his hand. "We're going bowling."

There's no use arguing. The flushed red look on his face tells me that. Reluctantly I let him pull me to my feet and trail him into the hallway. My mind is swirling, but by the time we reach the closet and he hands me my coat, I've regained some semblance of sanity.

Thank God he had the sense to stop us before we got carried away and ended up doing something crazy. Something I'd surely regret. Something we'd both regret. What was I thinking, allowing myself to get caught up in a whirlwind of emotions? I never should have let things to go so far. I knew better. Sam is right. We would have regretted it for the rest of our lives.

Wouldn't we?

## CHAPTER SEVENTEEN

I sink into the swivel chair, twirl to face Sam. "That was the last ball, right? How did I do? Did I win?"

"Yes and no." He points to the computerized scoring monitor hanging above the lane. "The game's over, but you didn't win."

"Next time I'll leave you in the dust."

He grins. "Is that a threat?"

"Take it for what it's worth." I hadn't expected the evening to turn out so well, especially after our little tryst on the couch. But bowling proved the perfect antidote. It requires concentration, plus it burns calories. And the way Sam is devouring that pizza, he needs all the exercise he can get.

"Let's order champagne," he suggests. "We should toast the New Year right."

"Diet pop is fine with me." Who needs alcohol to celebrate? Fitting into my size 14 jeans is celebration enough. Next year, I'm shooting for a size 10… which will never happen if I stuff myself like Sam. I try not to watch as he snatches the last slice of pizza from the serving tray. Doesn't he realize what he's doing to himself?

"Something wrong?" He halts, pizza halfway to his mouth, gives me an odd look. "Sorry, did you want the last piece?"

"No, go ahead." I turn away. The pizza he ordered came dripping with double cheese, greasy pepperoni, ham and sausage, and I only allowed myself one slice. One slice of pure heaven and at least eight hundred calories. I don't dare indulge. I've got a date tomorrow night with the bathroom scale.

"I'll reset the pins and we'll play another game." He crams another bite into his mouth.

"I'll be right back." I can't sit here and watch what he's doing to himself. I make a quick escape for the ladies room where I linger as long as I dare. How can Sam do that to himself? He's eating his way into an early grave. Women come and go as I stand at the mirror, touch up my lipstick, try to calm down my wild red curls. Finally I give up. There's no use trying. I'm a hopeless case. I head back into the bowling alley. The pizza tray is gone but Sam is not alone. He's chatting with a large man sporting a buzz cut and there's a gaggle of little girls surrounding him.

"Here she is." Sam waves me over. "Patty, this is Rod Kay, a good friend of mine. We play poker together every Wednesday night."

Rod pumps my hand, scrutinizes me with a curious smile. "So, finally we meet. Funny, I feel like I already know you. Sam talks about you all the time."

"He does?" I cock an eyebrow at Sam. "What exactly does he say?"

"Sorry, you won't get that out of me," Rod says with a grin. "But I'll say this much. Now that we've met, every word is true."

"Okay, that's enough." Sam comes heavily to his feet and ruffles the hair of one little girl hugging close at Rod's side. "This is Rod's little girl, Meghan."

She beams at me with a crooked smile that's missing some teeth. "We're having a slumber party at our house tonight."

"I promised Kelly I'd take the girls bowling and get them out of her hair." Rod wraps his arms around his daughter. "They've been at the house since early afternoon. I thought Kelly could use a little peace and quiet." He winces with a guilty smile. "Although she might not be talking to me when we get home."

Meghan nods solemnly. "Mama was mad when we left. We made too much noise and woke up the babies."

"Kelly and Rod have six-month-old triplets," Sam informs me. "Three little brothers for Meghan."

Maybe it's the weight of the bowling ball in my arms that causes the sudden ache inside. Or maybe it's the picture of the happy child dancing in front of me. Of a father who thinks nothing of sacrificing the last few hours of the old year to give his wife a few hours of peace.

Maybe it's the idea of a family in love with each other.

Will I ever have what other people do? People like Rod and his Kelly? Not that I'm ready to settle down. I'm not looking for a husband or a house filled with children. But something's wrong in my life. Something's missing. Maybe it's the idea of something that I can call my own. Or someone who loves me, as much as I love him.

I shoot a quick glance at Sam. Is that pizza sauce staining his moustache?

Rod nods at my neon-pink ball. "You bowling with that?"

"Yes. Why?"

He chuckles. "You win the last game?"

"Sam beat me," I confess.

Rod grins. "You might want to try a heavier ball. The one you're using looks a little light. Twelve pounds should be about right for you."

"Hey, whose side are you on, anyway?" Sam protests.

"None of your business." Rod searches through the rack, comes up with another ball. "Try this one."

I grip the ball, heavier than the pink one Sam chose for me.

"Don't hold it so tight. Treat it like it's an extension of your own arm. Like this." Rod demonstrates a full swing, imaginary ball in the air. "See those marks?" He gestures toward the painted black arrows pointing toward the pins. "Don't square off on the bowling pins. Aim for the center of the arrows instead. When you've got them in sight, bring the ball straight back and follow through when you release." He steps back from the floor, gestures me forward. "Go ahead, give it a shot."

Turning, I concentrate on the painted arrows lining the floor. I take a deep breath, three straight steps, bring my arm back and release with a prayer. Crack! The eight pins at the far end of the lane tumble to the floor.

"You got a spare," Meghan squeals with excitement. Five little girls bounce up and down, clapping as I do a little twirl. "My daddy knows all about bowling. He's on a team."

"Thanks for the pointers, Rod." I sink down in the swivel chair next to Sam and shoot him an evil eye.

"Right, thanks a lot, Rod," Sam mutters with a good-natured grin. "You probably should get going. I'll bet Kelly is wondering where you are."

"He seems very nice," I say as Rod and his troop of five-year-olds disappear into the crowd.

"Rod's a good friend. And a client." He reaches for his bowling ball. "I told you about him once, remember? He started his own business a few years ago. He's got an automotive repair shop, but he used to sell cars. I guess he got tired of working for someone…

"Hey, that's it!" Sam, halfway to the center arrows, whirls to face me. "That's what I've been wanting to tell you."

I frown. "Tell me what?"

"About your friend."

"What friend?" I straighten in my chair. Something in his voice sounds funny and I've got a sudden feeling I'm not going to like what I'm about to hear.

"That guy you teach with."

My eyes narrow. "Nick?"

"Exactly." He does a semiturn and shoots the ball, which goes spinning down the lane dead center. Ten pins crack as they hit the alley floor.

"What about him?"

"I told you once I thought he looked familiar? Well, that's because I've seen him before, and I finally remember where." Sam drops in the chair beside me, forehead glistening with sweat. He grabs a hand towel from his bag and pats his face dry.

I swallow down my impatience as he buries his face in his towel. "Go on," I demand.

He pulls the towel away from his face, eyes me carefully. "Sure you want to hear this?"

A sudden chill prickles the back of my neck. Maybe I don't want to hear what Sam has to say. Maybe it would be better if I didn't hear it.

"He's not from around here. I saw him in Arizona."

I toss off an uneasy laugh. "Nick grew up in Arizona. I already knew that."

"No, this was a couple years ago." He waves away my protest. "I was visiting Eileen and she wanted to get a quick oil change for her car. We stopped at one of those big dealerships, the kind of place they do a fast-track. That's where I saw your buddy Nick. He was out on the lot selling used cars."

Nick, a used-car salesman? *No way.* "I don't think so."

Sam shakes his head. "It was him all right. Once Eileen saw him, she pulled out of the lot and we went somewhere else. She can't stand the guy. She'd talked about him before, but I never had a face to put with the story until that day. Then when I saw Rod tonight, things started to click and—"

"Why are you lying?" A fiery knot burns in my stomach, and it's not from the pizza. "This is crazy. Nick's a teacher, not a car salesman. He would never sell cars, new or used."

"Really?" Sam drops his towel in his bag, gives me a hard fast look. "Why wouldn't he?"

"Why would he? He's already got a job, teaching—"

"How much do you really know about the guy, Patty?"

"Stop grilling me!" My stomach lurches, and suddenly I'm furious. Sam has no right to question me about Nick or make accusations that can't possibly be true. "I know lots about Nick. Lots more than you do. He lives to play golf. He was headed for the pro circuit but he blew out his knee. That's why he went into coaching." I think harder, but there's not much more there. Maybe I don't know as much about Nick as I think I do. "And he's a first-year teacher."

"Bingo," Sam says softly. "He's not."

I glare at him. "Yes, he is."

"No, Patty, you're wrong. He taught in Arizona," Sam says quietly. "He taught at Gwynnie's school."

My heart pounds in my ears and it's hard to keep a grip on my bowling ball. I feel like throwing it at Sam. "That's a horrible lie, Sam Curtis."

He lifts his hands in protest. "Why would I lie?"

"Because you don't like him. Because you're jealous." He's jealous of the way Nick looks, how he acts, how much people like him. He's jealous of how much I like him. "You've never liked him," I add. "Not since that first day at school when I introduced you."

"You're right. I don't like him, and I never will. He's exactly the type of guy I can't stand. All bluster, swagger, full of himself." Sam's voice hardens. "And to tell you the truth, I'm surprised at you, Patty. I never figured you to be stupid enough to be suckered in by somebody like Nick. You're smarter than that. And frankly, I'm getting a little tired waiting around for you to see through the guy."

He jumps to his feet without another word, snatches his bowling ball and stomps onto the wooden lane, but I'm on my feet in a flash. I lunge for his ball, which spins out of his hands and crashes to the floor, barely missing both our feet. Sam breathes heavily as he grabs for the ball, but I beat him to it.

"It's my turn to bowl." I hug the ball close and glare at him.

"Fine." He steps down, waves me toward the open lane. "Go ahead. Give it your best shot."

"No." I stand my ground. "You've made an unfair accusation against Nick and I don't believe you."

He slides back into his seat and eyes me for a long moment. The longer he stares, the more uncertain I am that I want to hear what Sam has to say. A few things about Nick over the past few months have left me puzzled. He's not like the other first-year teachers that have started at our school. He's comfortable in the classroom, at ease in front of the kids, like he's been doing it for years. I'd chalked up all that energy and enthusiasm to his coaching experience, plus testosterone. We're not used to having men in the classroom.

"He was a teacher at Gwynnie's school. She didn't have him for any subjects and Eileen was glad about that. The guy had a reputation. I remember her telling me that some of the parents had complained. They said he could be rough on the kids, that he didn't spend as much time with them as he should. Most of it got tossed off as minor gripes. But then an emergency situation came up and he took off, leaving his kids to fend for themselves. That's when things—"

"Wait a minute." I halt Sam midsentence. Suddenly it's difficult to breathe. I lick my lips, swirl my tongue around inside my dry mouth. "What are you talking about? What kind of emergency?"

"An air-conditioning unit caught fire and he left his kids alone in the classroom."

I gape at Sam. *Nick took off instead of staying with his kids?* No way that would have happened. Teachers are trained to stay calm and to remain in control in emergency situations.

"We've all been through fire drills at school," he continues. "You shut the windows, get in line, march out the door until they sound the all-clear. At least that's the way they did it when I was in school."

I nod fiercely. In the years I've been teaching, the routine hasn't varied. You stay calm, you keep order, and everyone stays safe. Children are expert at sensing fear.

"He was in the hallway when the fire alarm went off and he bailed out a door at the first alarm. One of the other teachers had to take his students out."

I feel like I've been sucker-punched. "This is all hearsay. Besides, how would your sister know what happened?"

"Because she was there." His eyes narrow. "Eileen was one of the room mothers and she was at school helping set up for a party. She ended up out on the playground with the staff and the kids. Nick tried to bluff his way through what happened, but there were too many witnesses."

"If what you're saying is true, he would have been fired."

"He was fired," Sam replies quietly.

"That's impossible. Things like that don't go undocumented," I argue. "If Nick was fired, he never could have gotten a job at our school."

He shrugs. "Maybe he lied on his résumé. I wouldn't put it past the guy."

Suddenly the room feels hot. When did the bowling alley get so noisy? Kids shriek, people laugh, bowling pins crash to the floor. My head pounds and the vein above my right eye throbs. I grind it hard with the heel of my hand.

"Patty? Are you okay?" Sam's words sound far away.

I sink into a chair, gulp deep breaths, fight the urge to vomit. Am I okay? Things will never be okay again. What if everything Sam said is true? What if Nick really did teach in Arizona? What if he was fired? What if he lied on his résumé?

How would I know?

But it can't be true. It simply can't be. Nick is good with the kids. He's good with me. He's been nominated for First-Year Teacher of the Year Award. Someone would have checked his credentials. They have rules about these sorts of things. Besides, how would Sam know? He's an accountant, he's not in education.

And he doesn't like Nick. I've known that from the start.

Lies, all lies. Sam fed himself pizza and he fed me lies.

"Look, Patty, I know it's rough, hearing it like this. I know how you feel about the guy. You've made it pretty clear. I know—"

"You don't know anything, Sam Curtis. And you certainly don't know how I feel about Nick." I fumble to untie the ugly bowling shoes, yank them off my feet, grab my boots. "I want to go home."

"Come on, Patty, please don't be like this. I know you're upset." He eyes me uncertainly. "It's New Year's Eve. It's not even midnight."

"I don't care what time it is." I jam my feet in my boots, grab my coat and purse. "I'm going home. Will you take me, or do I call a cab?"

He blows out a long sigh, shakes his head. "I'll drive you." He sinks into his chair and slowly begins unlacing his shoes.

"I'll be outside." I whirl and leave him sitting alone.

# # #

We make the drive home in silence, me huddled against the passenger door. The car heater works fine, but the chill that's settled in my heart feels colder than the three-foot snow banks piled along the side streets.

No matter what he says, no matter how hard Sam tries, things will never be the same between us again.

We pull into the empty driveway. "Can't we talk about this?" he asks as I fumble with my seatbelt.

"You've done enough talking for one night." I hate the way my voice sounds, icy like the sidewalk glistening under the street light, but I'm helpless to stop myself. What Sam said about Nick was hurtful, and cruel, and I want to hurt him back. I hate him. I've never hated anyone so much in my life.

Sam catches my arm as I reach for the door. "You're overreacting—"

I glare at him. "Take your hands off me."

"Please, Patty, just listen to me," he pleads.

My chin tilts higher. "I'm done listening."

"This changed things, didn't it?" His breath hangs in the frosty air between us. "What I said about him tonight."

"Of course it changed things. It changed everything. Did you think it wouldn't?"

"Then I'm sorry I told you. I should have kept my mouth shut."

"It's a little late for that," I spit back. "What kind of man are you, anyway? What kind of a man accuses someone of something like you did tonight? You said some terrible things about Nick... and he wasn't even there to defend himself."

"Sounds like you're doing a pretty good job." His eyes never leave me.

"Someone has to," I shoot back. "The things you said could destroy Nick's reputation. Is that what you want? Is that what you've been doing? Biding your time, waiting for the perfect opportunity?"

"Why would I do that?" His brow wrinkles in the green glow from the dashboard.

"Because you're jealous," I spit back. "You're jealous of Nick and you always have been."

The rattle from the fan's heater is the only sound between us, but the blast of hot air does nothing to ease the chill gathering in my heart. I refuse to back down. Let Sam deal with the pain. Let him see how it feels. Let him hurt, just like I hurt.

"You want the truth? Fine… here's the truth. I *am* jealous." His voice ices over with a hard edge. "I'm jealous of whatever kind of hold that guy has on you. I hate seeing how you light up when he's around. I want you to see him for the man he is. He's a liar, Patty. A liar. A cheat. A coward. That's the kind of man you've been dealing with all year. God knows I wish I'd made those things up. At least then, I could take them back. I would if I could. Because I never meant to hurt you. Not intentionally."

"I don't believe you." I bite out the words, raging against every instinct screaming at me to believe what he's saying. Sam is someone I've come to know and trust. A man who's kept me laughing during our Friday night dinners. A man who's steered me on a steady course through my financial mess. A man who made me melt with desire earlier tonight when we kissed.

A man who accused me of being stupid… of letting myself be sweet-talked and duped by a used-car salesman.

"I didn't say those things to hurt you," he quietly insists.

"Then why did you say them?"

"Why?" His voice twists in bewilderment. "Because I'm in love with you, that's why. Haven't you figured that out by now?"

Suddenly the car is too close, too hot. So hot I can't breathe. I have to get out now before everything explodes inside my head and my heart. I grab the door handle and push.

"Patty, wait!" He grabs my coat sleeve. "You had to know how I feel about you…"

Damn him! I swallow hard, blink back the hot tears. Damn him for making this so hard. If Sam thinks I'll give him the satisfaction of seeing me cry, then he's got another think coming. I refuse to cry in front of him. I will not cry. I won't.

"I've been in love with you since the day we met. Remember? You wore that pink bathing suit and were hanging on for dear life to the edge of the pool."

I fight against the memory of that afternoon I started swimming laps. Priscilla had been there, cheering me on from the sidelines. And Sam was in the next lane, a willing champion from day one.

What's happening to me? Am I losing them both?

His hand tightens on my coat. "I won't kid you, Patty. I'm the type of guy who's content to go with the flow and to let things be. Maybe that's how I ended up nearly forty years old with no wife, no kids. But being away from you at Christmas gave me time to think. Nothing seemed right when I was out in Arizona. Maybe it was being with Eileen, seeing how happy she is with John and the kids. It got me thinking about what's been missing in my life. And that something is you."

I shiver despite the warmth circulating in the Jeep. The heater is finally working great and Sam is generating heat himself. He reaches out, lightly touches my cheek. A shudder of sudden desire courses through my body.

"I want what Eileen's got," he says softly. "I want someone to share things with at the end of the day. Someone who cares about me. Isn't that what all of us are searching for in some way? Someone who loves us and someone we can love? That's what I want, Patty. And I want it with you."

How can he do it? Speak so eloquently to my heart's desire, yet crush my hopes in a single breath? I shiver as his finger slowly trails the curve of my cheek, ending under my chin. He tilts my head to meet his gaze.

"What makes you so sure that's what I want?" I whisper.

"I don't know." His voice lingers in the hush of the car's dark interior. "But I hope you do. You're all I want, Patty. The entire package. I love you."

"It can't work. It won't work. Don't you understand?" My words come out in little burst, hanging like frosty mist between us. "It's not right.

"Why not?" he presses.

"Because… because it can't. It just won't." I feel torn, confused. How can I give voice to something I myself barely understand?

"It's Nick, isn't it? The bitterness in his voice slices through the darkness. "Are you in love with him?"

"I don't know." And as I hear the words tumble out of my mouth, I realize it's the truth. I'm still furious with Sam about the accusations he's made against Nick, but I don't know how I feel about Nick… or Sam, either, for that matter. Other women make it look so easy, but what do I know about love? Is this the way love is supposed to feel? Breathless, aching with a want I can't name? My head feels like it might explode and I'm afraid it will take my heart along with it. Being with Sam is as easy as donning a pair of comfortable jeans with elastic around the waist.

There's never any worry that things won't fit. It works between us. It's worked from the start.

Sam and I fit. We've always fit.

But what about clinging pants and tops that don't allow for an extra inch? Some women dress like that every day, deliberately putting their bodies on view. They count calories and work out at the gym, ruthless and relentless in their determination to be the best and have the best. In life, and in men.

Women like Amy.

Men like Nick.

My heart yearns to see beyond the excess pounds, but my eyes won't let me.

Bad enough I look the way I do.

"You're a fine one to talk, Sam Curtis." The words are out of my mouth before I can stop them. "When was the last time you took a good look in the mirror? Everything you do revolves around food. You should have seen yourself an hour ago, shoveling in that pizza. Do you realize I only had one piece? You might as well have eaten the whole thing yourself."

The sudden stricken look on his face sickens me. I put it there. How can I be so cruel? Sam would never say these things to me. How did I end up so shallow and heartless? How low can I sink?

"So, the truth emerges." His voice is low and guarded. "This isn't about Nick at all. It's about me and you. It's always been about me and you. You don't want to be with someone who's fat. You don't want to be with someone who looks like I do. You're embarrassed about the way I look."

"I didn't say that," I shoot back.

"You didn't have to," he says quietly. "Well, I've got news for you, Patty. If you think I'm going to apologize, you're wrong. I'm happy with the way I am.

If you ask me, I think you're the one who's got some issues. So instead of pointing a finger at me, maybe you should take a good look at yourself."

"I know how I look... and I hate it." I blink hard, trying to stop my tears. "All these awful freckles and this stupid frizzy hair. Don't you dare get me started about being overweight. For months I've denied myself, watching people eat exactly what they want, indulging themselves in all the things I want and can't have. I've tried so hard, and what has it got me? Nothing, I guess. Thanks a lot, Sam. Thanks for reminding me I'll always be a lost cause. Thanks for reminding me how ugly I am."

I swipe away the hot tears streaming down my cheeks, smearing my makeup. What a hell of a way to end the old year and ring in the new.

"I never said you were ugly." His voice fills the darkness. "I think you're beautiful. You'll always be beautiful to me."

He lays one hand on my shoulder but I pull away. "No more lies."

"What makes you think I'm lying?"

"You've been doing it all night. Telling me I'm beautiful when we both know I'm not. And those things you said about Nick..." The icy rage filling me inside scares me in a way I've never felt before. My heart feels like it will never unthaw. "I'll never forgive you for those things you said about him, Sam. Never."

I yank off my gloves and fumble with the chain around my neck. Somehow I manage to undo the clasp. I shove the diamond pendant into his hand. "I don't want this. Take it back."

"Patty, please don't. You've got this all turned around..."

Sam's wrong. And no matter what he says, it won't make things better. It will never be better. He's not interested in changing. He'll always be the same old Sam... the same guy with the big stomach I met at the pool. The last thing I want is to live my life smothered in a thick overcoat of love and resentment weighing seventy pounds.

"You say you care about me? How can that be true when it's obvious you don't even care about yourself? You don't care what people think. You don't care that you're f—"

The F-word burns on my tongue and I catch myself in time, but the damage is done. It's the worst possible insult, the one that hurts the most. I've heard it all my life and I almost hurled it at Sam.

I turn away and stare through the frost-speckled window at our house's side yard. Everything seems tilted and crazy in a sickening, off-kilter sort of way. The snow-covered shrubbery looks like an alien moonscape rather than the hedges we prune every spring. I press my head against the window, relish the cold biting my forehead. I deserve it, every bit of it. I am cold and heartless. A bitch. An ice queen. I've done Sam a terrible wrong. "It's better we don't see each other any more."

He blows out a hard breath. "If that's what you want."

Is that what I want?

Tell him you're sorry. Say it now, quick, before it's too late.

"Tax season starts soon," he adds. "I'll be busy, anyway. I won't have time for you."

But that's not true. Sam isn't like that. No matter how busy he is, he'd make time for me. I know that in my gut, with every part of my being. Sam would do anything for me.

Correction. Sam *would* have done anything for me. That's all finished now.

"I think it's better if one of my associates handles your account." His voice fills the frigid vacuum between us. "Unless you'd prefer to hire another firm."

"You already have my paperwork." What does it matter who does our taxes? A cold bitter ache throbs inside me, like icicles curling themselves around my heart. I've ruined everything. Sam's saying good-bye, letting me go. And I can't say I blame him.

Right now, I hate me more than Sam ever could.

He reaches across me, opens the passenger door. "If you ever come to your senses about that guy, give me a call. You know where to find me."

I slip from my seat into the frosty night air, stumble up the porch steps, fumble with my house keys. Church bells chime in the distance as his car pulls away, ringing in the New Year, mocking any hopes I had for a year filled with blessings or love.

The house is dark and quiet. I fling my coat on the bench, the words I spit at Sam still fresh on my tongue as I stumble into the kitchen. How could I have said it? How could I have done it? I lean against the sink, massage the back of my neck. My temples throb and there's a stabbing ache behind one eye. Headaches are a luxury reserved for Priscilla, but I can't stand the pain. I snatch the aspirin bottle from the shelf near the sink, swallow two pills with a glass of water. I lean against the counter and my gaze falls on the refrigerator.

Have a little something to eat, Mama always said. Maybe eating will help. I only had one slice of pizza at the bowling alley. I yank open the refrigerator door and peer inside. Lettuce, orange juice, carrot sticks. I slam the door and head for the pantry, ransack the shelves and finally unearth a jar of peanut butter stashed behind two cans of tomato juice. Something else winks at me from behind an unopened box of macaroni. A small bag of gourmet cookies Priscilla keeps hidden.

Sam's favorites.

I head back into the kitchen with the peanut butter in one hand and the cookies in the other. Snatching a spoon from the drawer, I dig deep into the velvety peanut spread. It's thick and pasty and glues to the roof of my mouth, but it doesn't fill the void inside. I polish off my makeshift dinner with two glasses of milk quickly chugged over the kitchen sink. The hypocrisy isn't so easily swallowed. How could I have done it? I ruined everything tonight, screaming at Sam the way I did. And the things I said? I cringe, thinking about how cruel and spiteful I was… how petty and mean. I treated him exactly the way I hate to be treated. I know better. I know what it feels like.

I lost a friend tonight. A good friend, a dear friend. *I lost more than that. I lost myself.*

I stare at the cookies. Priscilla bought them for Sam but after tonight, it's a safe bet he won't be joining us for dinner on Friday nights anymore. Priscilla will be furious when she finds out what I've done. I grab the cookies and shuffle through darkness into the living room. The twinkling lights of the Christmas tree and Sam's gaily wrapped box containing Priscilla's turkey platter are a grim reminder of what I've done. How am I going to face her tomorrow morning? How will I answer all her questions that are sure to follow? I have to come up with some plausible excuse why Sam will no longer be coming around. I don't dare tell her the truth. Priscilla will kill me. She loves Sam. He's like the brother we never had.

But I never thought of him as a brother.

I sink on the couch and fumble for the TV remote. It's buried on the coffee table amidst crumpled wrapping paper and an empty velvet box. The television drones in the background as I think about what I've got left. An empty box, an empty neck, and empty arms. No one to hold me on New Year's Eve. And it's my own damn fault.

I rip open the cookie bag and dig deep, cram the cookies into my mouth one after another. Who cares about crumbs? I'm all alone. Priscilla and Dr. Brown won't be home for at least another hour. No one cares what I do, how much I eat. No one.

Including me.

Salt mingles with the sweet taste of chocolate as I turn up the volume to muffle the sound of my tears.

CHAPTER EIGHTEEN

"Sure I can't convince you to come with me to the basketball game?" I rinse my plate, focus on the steaming hot water swirling down the drain. It's already a given that she'll tell me *no*, but I have to try. This impasse between us is driving me crazy. "Please, Priscilla? I hate going alone."

"Looks like you'll have to." She marches to the sink. "I need to finish the medical transcript I started this afternoon."

"Since when did you start working in the evenings?"

"Since when did you start going out on school nights?" She shrugs. "Never mind, I know the answer. Basketball season starts tonight."

"Forget I even asked," I mumble.

"I've got a question for you." She throws me a hard stare. "Who is Bill Walters?"

"I don't know." I shift on my feet. The name is unfamiliar. "You tell me."

"He works for Sam." Priscilla pulls an envelope from her pocket and slaps it on the counter. "And from what I understand, he's taken over our account."

My heart rate jumps as I stare at the envelope. Emblazoned in the right-hand corner is the letterhead imprint of Samuel J. Curtis, P.C.

"Since when did you start opening my mail?" I stammer.

"If you take a good look, you'll notice that my name is on that envelope, too." Her voice quivers. "Sam was handling things personally. Why did he give our account to someone else?"

"Maybe he's busy. Maybe he doesn't have time." I snatch the envelope, stuff it in my pocket. Knowing Sam has written leaves me hot and flustered and I'm dying to see what's in his letter, but I don't dare read it. Not in front of Priscilla.

"What did you do, Patty? Why is he mad?"

"What makes you think I did something?" The hair prickles on the back of my neck. What exactly did he say in that letter? "You're looking at me like I'm guilty or something."

"Guilty? You said it, Patty, not me." Priscilla's eyes blaze as she loads the dishes at a furious clip. I can take the silence and tears, but her sudden anger scares me. With Sam at the dinner table, Friday nights quickly turned into family nights—something we haven't had since Mama died. He and Priscilla get along famously. She kowtowed to him and he teased her like she was his little sister. Priscilla loves Sam, and she'll never forgive me if she finds out what I did. I've got to win her back. The two of us have always been a team. She's stuck with me through thick and thin—though mostly through thick. The last few weeks haven't been kind and the scales don't lie. My weigh-in last night wasn't pretty. All this inner turmoil over cookies, candy, ice cream, potato chips... for one lousy pound.

"Please, Priscilla, can't we work this out? I hate what's happening between us. Tell me how I can make things right."

She whirls around, blue eyes flashing. "You can start by telling me why you broke up with Sam."

"But I didn't break up with him. You can't break up with someone if you were never dating."

"Quit playing word games," she snaps. "You know what I mean. You need to fix this, Patty. Sam is the best thing that ever happened to you. Probably the best thing that will *ever* happen to you. The two of you belong together."

"No, we don't." *Especially after what I said.*

"Call him," she urges. "Pick up the phone and call him right now."

"I can't."

"Yes, you can." Her eyes soften slightly. "It's not too late, Patty. It's never too late."

My heart catches. Is she right? Would he forgive me? Is it possible to fix things?

Never too late. Never too late. Never too late.

The hallway clock chimes the quarter hour. "It's too late." I toss the last few forks in the dishwasher. "I've got to go. Nick's game starts soon. I promised him I'd be there."

Priscilla's face goes flat. "So, that's the way it's going to be? Well, I can't say I'm surprised. Some things never change."

I fold the dishrag, drape it carefully over the sink. "What's that supposed to mean?"

"You wouldn't want to disappoint him by not showing up. How would Nick manage without you?"

I gape at my twin. Sarcasm has never been Priscilla's style, but blaming Nick is wrong. He's got nothing to do with any of this. "If you think it's him that's keeping me from Sam, you're wrong. This isn't about Nick."

Pots and pans bang as Priscilla jams them in the dishwasher and slams the door.

"Honestly, he has nothing to do with this." I can't tell her the truth about the fight Sam and I had about his weight problem. She'd never forgive me. Never. Especially since she's tried so hard to help me lose weight. Dear God, I nearly called him fat. "What have you got against Nick? Everyone else likes him."

Priscilla's face tightens as she punches the start button and the dishwasher jumps to noisy life. "Have fun at the game."

I stand there gaping as she storms out of the kitchen without another word. A few seconds later, I hear the slam of a bedroom door from above.

So much for any hope of a January thaw.

Cold day, cold night, cold heart. I bundle up in my coat, pull on my hat, slap my hands together in a pair of thick woolen mittens. The temperature's hovered in the single digits all day and the weatherman is predicting below-zero temps tonight. I brace myself for a long night as I head out the door. Nick had better appreciate this. I've got no business going out tonight. I'll still have papers to grade once I get home. And if I don't draft Thursday's math test tonight, I'll have to do it tomorrow during lunch hour. Plus I need to start prepping for my interview with the judging committee for Teacher of the Year. My time slot is scheduled three weeks from Saturday. Nick's up for the award, too. How does he manage to get it all done—coaching and teaching? And today is only Tuesday. There's another home game this Friday night. I'll be sitting in the stands on a hard vinyl bench instead of at the kitchen table, laughing over low-fat lasagna with Priscilla and Sam.

I can't face the thought of empty Friday nights.

I can't face Sam. I can't face myself.

Gusty winds hit me as I plod through snowdrifts building across the driveway. It takes a minute before the car finally groans to life. I pull Sam's letter out of my pocket as I wait for the engine to warm. How bad is it? My fingers and heart are numb as I flick on the overhead light and muster up the courage to scan the crinkled page.

Three short paragraphs cover the thick creamy stationery. I suck in a deep breath and start reading. I read through the whole thing twice, letting the impersonal words sink in. It's a letter of introduction from Bill Walters, an associate accountant who works at Sam's firm. No wonder Priscilla was furious. Sam didn't even bother to write the letter himself. We've been handed over to Bill Waters like we're merely customers in a grocery-store line. I skim the letter one last time. No matter how nice he is, I already don't like him. Bill Walters isn't even a C.P.A.

And he isn't Sam.

Icy snow pelts the window. I flick on the wipers and give the defroster a chance to work. I must be crazy, going out on a night like this. And I'll be sitting alone in the bleachers. I've always hated doing things by myself. So why am I doing it? Especially since I've always hated basketball.

Slamming the car in reverse, I skid out of the driveway.

# # #

"Sure you don't want some? I can't eat all this popcorn by myself." Ruth's bag brims with popcorn purchased during half time.

"No, thanks, I'm not hungry. I already ate." The lie sticks on my tongue. One look at Priscilla's Tuesday-night tuna casserole served on a Friday night was all it took for me to skip dinner. I know she did it just to spite me. She's mad, I'm starving, and the popcorn smells delicious. But I can't give in now. I'll never stop eating.

"Thanks again for inviting me." Ruth glances around the crowded gym. "Perfect timing. Jack's gone off to South Carolina on a golf weekend with his buddies and I was feeling rather lonely."

"I'm glad for the company." When it comes to loneliness, I can relate. I've hated sitting through these stupid basketball games all by myself the past couple weeks. I shouldn't even be here tonight. I have an interview tomorrow at ten a.m. with the Selection Committee, who will ultimately decide who wins the award Teacher of the Year. I should be home prepping, studying my résumé, doing my nails, conditioning my hair… anything and everything I can do to impress them.

"I was going to curl up with my recipe books tonight," Ruth said. "Some of the partners in Jack's law firm are having a progressive dinner party next weekend and we're hosting dessert." She picks at her popcorn. "I'm trying to come up with a new recipe that's tasty but not too rich. Something low-fat. Now the holidays are over, everyone seems to be on a diet."

Her bag of popcorn is merely inches away. I'll bet each fluffy kernel has at least thirty calories. I breathe through my mouth, try not to inhale the rich buttery scent. "You should call Priscilla. She has lots of low-fat recipes."

Ruth beams. "Why didn't I think of that? Priscilla loves to cook. By the way, why isn't she here with you tonight? Doesn't she like basketball?"

I'm the one she doesn't like. "She's out with Dr. Brown."

Ruth's eyebrows twitch in amusement. "This sounds like it has the makings of a serious romance."

"They went to a movie." I think about the two of them together in a darkened theater holding hands.

Somehow I can't imagine Dr. Brown trying to steal a kiss. He's much too staid and proper. What Priscilla sees in him is beyond me. Maybe she needs to get her eyes checked.

Maybe I need to get my own checked, too. I can't keep them off the coach.

Nick stands directly in front of us, hands on hips as he stalks behind the thick black line on the glossy wooden floor. The line is the only thing separating him from the five young boys courtside playing their hearts out... and losing the game.

"He's certainly passionate about this, isn't he?" Ruth says. "Not at all like when he's at school."

I nod thickly. Nick, so casual and laid-back at school, is a different man courtside. Deep, determined lines etch his forehead and he rarely smiles as he paces the line and shouts at his players. He rides his team hard and scowls at the three refs dressed in black-and-white stripes, working their whistles as they careen up and down the court.

"Go, Justin, go! Take it, take it! Shoot!" Nick balls his fist and slaps it against his hand as the boy goes for the shot. The ball hangs in the air, rolls around the rim, then finally skitters off the side. The crowd groans and Nick's glare deepens. The scoreboard doesn't provide much hope. Fourth quarter, down by ten points, two minutes left in the game.

"Jack loves basketball, any type of sports," Ruth says. "I don't dare let him have the remote. He flips back and forth between the channels, trying to catch the latest scores. It drives me crazy."

I muster up a smile as I watch one of the other team's players sink an easy lay-up. "At least I don't have that problem. Priscilla hates sports."

"What about Sam? Does he like basketball? You should bring him to one of the games."

I reach for the water bottle at my feet. How long before people finally quit referring to Sam and me as if we were a couple? Bad enough I think about him every day. Bad enough I keep reliving the moment I flung those cruel words in his face. Bad enough I can't forget the hurt in his eyes, his disbelief at what I said.

Bad enough I have to live with myself.

"It's tax season. He's working nights straight through April fifteenth." Such a convenient excuse.

"I like Sam. Jack does, too. We've been talking about giving him a call. Our own accountant retired last summer." Ruth pops a few more kernels in her mouth, offers out the bag. "Sure you don't want some?"

"Maybe I will." I take my eyes off the court and reach for the bag when suddenly the crowd is on their feet, erupting with shouts and boos. My eyes fly to the scoreboard and my heart sinks. We're still behind by four and now a foul has been called on one of our best players. The other team takes their stance at the free-throw line. The first shot sinks clean, straight through the basket. The second bounces against the rim, then drops through the ropes. A six-point lead for the other side.

"We're going to lose," I mutter, with one eye on the scoreboard and the other on Nick. The coach isn't happy and neither are his players. The young boys huddle with him in a tight circle. Even from our seats three rows up, the air reeks of sweat and desperation. I flick more popcorn in my mouth. "I hate basketball."

"Don't worry, Nick will pull them through," Ruth says. "The other team wants to let the clock wind down but I'll bet Nick won't let them. He'll come up with something. It happens on television all the time."

But this isn't television, this is real life. And it's torture listening to Nick bark at the team. These are kids I know. These boys were in my classroom a few short years ago. Back then they were ten-year-olds shooting hoops at recess. Now they're lanky high school students sporting wispy beards. All legs and limbs, knobby knees, and squeaky gym shoes, they've lobbed the ball back and forth these past few weeks on their way to a winning season.

But they're not winning tonight. And the look on their faces as Nick chews into them is no different than the ten-year-olds in his classroom today. I shove more popcorn in my mouth, chomp the inside of my bottom lip, wince in pain. Serves me right. Coaching can't be that different from teaching. And ranting at a student doesn't teach them anything but fear. That's no way to earn the players' respect. No way to coach a winning team.

The crowd erupts as the home team sinks another shot.

Ruth grins, high-fives me. "What did I tell you?"

"Work it, Jake, work it!" Nick paces the court, screaming from the sidelines. He jabs his finger toward center court. "Get the ball, guys! Move it, move it! What's your problem?" The clock ticks down, second by second. "Time out, time out!" His hands rise in furious protest and he gestures at the team in with an impatient nod.

I gobble popcorn as we watch the five boys gather in another quick huddle. Nick glowers and snaps orders as he slaps his clipboard against his knee. Their faces strain and tense as he pushes them back onto the court.

"This isn't good. Look at Nick. He knows we're going to lose." I want to bolt from the bleachers and straight out the side door.

Ruth pats my hand. "It's not over yet. We can still win."

But she's wrong. The team is doomed. There's only one minute left in the game and we're four points behind, but it might as well be forty. Our boys already wear the look of defeat.

Nick yanks a large boy with a mean sulky look to his feet. I recognize Billy Iverson immediately. Billy, big and tough, was a bully in my classroom as well as on the playground. Nick whispers something hurriedly in his ear and Billy nods with a lazy half smile. What are they up to? Nick slaps him on the butt, pushes him toward the official's bench. I hold my breath as the buzzer sounds and Billy lumbers onto the floor.

The crowd is on their feet, stamping and whistling as the clock ticks down the remaining seconds. The visiting team has control of the ball. "Defense, defense," people scream from all sides as eight players chase the visiting team's top scorer with the ball. He heads down the court. Billy Iverson stands directly beneath the hoop. Arms and legs connect as the boy slams into Billy, who head-butts him in the face. Bodies topple, whistles blow, hands and players squirm for control of the ball.

The floor is slick with blood.

"Foul! Foul on 44!" Nick is on his feet, his face nearly purple as he screams the words.

Foul on 44? But that's the other team's player, the one who had the ball. If anyone should be fouled, it should be Billy. Am I the only one who saw what happened? The whole thing was choreographed by Nick. He sent Billy in to take the other player out and buy them some time… buy them a shot at winning the game.

"Did you see that?" I grip Ruth's arm as the boy from the other team comes to his feet. Blood gushes from his nose as they help him off the court. His hand is pressed against the back of his head and his face is white. The thought of Billy head-butting the boy makes me want to vomit. "Did you see what he did?"

Ruth winces. "I'll bet his nose is broken."

"This isn't right," I mutter as Billy lines up at the foul line and aims the first shot. "He's the one who should be called on the foul. He deliberately hurt that boy."

"Billy didn't do anything wrong," Ruth replies. "It's called taking a charge and it's perfectly legal. Billy had every right to stand where he was. He had control of the floor."

"But…" My words are lost in the roar of the crowd as Billy sinks the second of two shots. We're still down by two, but suddenly the game is in our hands to win or lose.

And we got here by cheating.

"You must have seen it, Ruth. Billy deliberately hit that boy in the face. Nick ordered him to do it."

She looks at me like I'm crazy. "Nick wouldn't do something like that. That's cheating."

"But he did, Ruth, I swear," I insist. "I saw it."

She shrugs. "Well, the refs didn't see it and neither did I."

I crumple the empty popcorn bag in my hands. No matter what Ruth or anyone else thinks, the foul on 44 was a cheap shot and ordered by Nick. I stare at him as he calls in his players for one last huddle. What kind of a man teaches kids to win by cheating?

The buzzer sounds. The crowd chants, delirious with screaming. Eight seconds to go. Everyone is on their feet. The visiting team has control of the ball and rushes it down the court. A lay-up, an easy shot... missed. The crowd explodes as Nick's team takes the ball and races it back toward the basket.

Four seconds left. Three... two... one...

A hopeless shot worth three points flies from midcourt. The ball kisses the rim, dances around the edge, and slides through the net.

"We won!" Ruth jumps up and down, grabs me in a fierce hug as the home crowd explodes in a deafening roar. "What a fantastic game. Come on, let's go congratulate Nick."

The victory song blares as we climb down the bleachers, but my feet feel dead, like I'm wearing Frankenstein shoes. It would have been so much better to have played fair and lost than to witness the ending played out in front of us. Didn't Nick hear the loudspeaker announcement at the beginning of the game before the playing of the "Star Spangled Banner"? The announcement reminded the crowd of the three Rs of sportsmanship: *Respect, Responsibility, Restraint.*

Too bad we didn't see any of that from the coach.

Nick's face is flush as we step off the bleachers and onto the court. "Some game, huh?" He grins. "Had you a little nervous we might lose?"

Ruth wraps him in a big hug. "You pulled off the perfect ending."

He wipes the sweat from his face. "I didn't do much. My job is to keep the kids moving, knock a little sense into them."

"You really knocked some sense into them tonight." I barely manage a smile. If I don't get away soon, I'll throw up all over the glossy gym floor.

I fish for my keys. Thank God Ruth and I came in separate cars. At least nothing will stop me from leaving. "Thanks for coming, Ruth. We'll talk later." I whirl and start for the exit.

"But Patty, where are you—"

I ignore her protest and step up my pace. Better that than to whip up some lame excuse about why I'm leaving. Better that than to scream at Nick, to accuse him of being a cheat.

He grabs my arm as I bolt for the door. "What's wrong? Where are you going?"

"Home." I turn my head away at the mere sight of him. He might think he can get away with duping everyone else, but he can't fool me. I saw what happened. I saw what he did. Nick's not charming his way out of this one. "I… I feel sick," I stammer. "I guess I shouldn't have eaten all that popcorn."

"You should know better." He releases my arm. "Stay away from that stuff, Patty. Popcorn makes you fat."

Did he just call me fat?

My face burns as I push through the crowd and out the thick double doors into the bitter night. I suck in deep breaths of cold frosty air. The popcorn churns in my stomach, a big greasy mess. How did I let Nick make such a mess of my life? Even if Ruth didn't see what happened, even if the refs thought the charge perfectly legally, I know what I saw. Sam was right. Nick is a cheat. And maybe he's a liar, too.

As God as my witness, I will never, ever eat popcorn again. And I've definitely just been to my last basketball game.

Never again.
Never.

CHAPTER NINETEEN

"The credentials you've listed in your questionnaire are impressive." Mayor Davis taps his pen against a thick sheaf of papers that includes my Teacher of the Year nomination and supporting documentation. "You're involved in training substitute teachers..." He glances at the paperwork, begins to read aloud "...*plus I'm responsible for coordinating our school's spelling bee. I run the after-school program, and also serve as peer mentor to other teachers.*" He leans back in his chair, eyes me with a how-much-of-this-is-true-and-how-much-are-you-padding-your-questionnaire smile. "You sound like a very busy woman."

"No busier than anyone else," I say.

The small staff room of the *James Bay Journal* newspaper office grows quiet as seven pair of eyes train on me. The round-table discussion is designed as an informal let's-get-to-know-you-better-session, but it's part of the competition and determines who'll make it to the final round. If I want to make the cut, I need to start talking. I know what they're waiting for. They want to hear about my philosophy of education. They're waiting for me to promote my values, to pump myself up, beat my chest, and tell them I'm the best thing that ever walked through the door of James Bay Elementary.

But I haven't got it in me. I'm still nursing a sugar hangover from last night's binge. Will I ever learn to keep my hand out of the cookie jar? Greasy popcorn and chocolate chip cookies don't mix.

Neither do dreams of basketball and romance, which came crashing to an end last night.

"Three teachers from the same elementary school making it to the semifinal round. That's never happened before." Mayor Davis looks up, nods. "Pretty impressive, if you ask me. Obviously your principal is doing something right."

They don't know the half of it. Chuck Stevens deserves his own award: Wishy-Washy Boss of the Year. He'd throw the entire teaching staff in front of a moving bus if it meant saving his own butt. And as for our three finalists? My bet is on Amy. She's out there actively promoting herself, throwing parties, donating to charities, throwing her husband's money around in hope of buying herself a ticket to the final round. It's enough to make me want to throw up. And as for Nick? I swallow down a gag.

Kent Phillips, President of our hometown bank, leans close to the Mayor. "You see that win the basketball team pulled off last night?"

Mayor Davis gives him a discreet thumbs-up. "We're talking play-offs this year."

Is that part of it? Does basketball count? But that's not fair. What does shooting hoops or winning games have to do with teaching? And for that matter, why should the way you look have anything to do with it? I tug at the ill-fitting skirt that somehow managed to hike halfway up my thigh. I knew I made the wrong choice when I plucked this suit off the hanger this morning. The skirt bunches at the waist and it's too tight through the hips. But the blue in the jacket is an exact match with the color of my eyes, which is why I bought it. Problem is, I counted on losing a few more pounds. *Not.* This morning, I thought I could get away with it. *Not*. Guaranteed my personal fashionista Priscilla would have talked me out of wearing it. *Not*.

For that to happen, she'd have to be talking to me.

Chief Dennis, James Bay Chief of Police, flips through his paperwork, frowns. "Correct me if I'm wrong, but I think there's something missing."

"I'm sorry. Could you be more specific?" The application was submitted months ago and I completed the questionnaire and wrote the paper before Christmas. I try not to squirm. I'm the last candidate being interviewed today but I already know the interview hasn't gone well. They ask a question, I mumble an answer. Why did I even bother showing up? I should have stayed home and slept in like any normal person on a Saturday morning, because there's no way in hell I'm going to win this contest. I'm a fifth-grade teacher in a too-tight skirt who can barely manage her own life, let alone a group of ten-year-olds. Whoever takes home that trophy and the one-thousand-dollar prize will be someone who makes Bay County proud. Someone photogenic, someone well known, someone with his feet planted firmly on the floor, out there in the community representing our educational system.

Someone like Nick Lamont.

My gag reflex starts again.

"There's nothing listed here about the new antibullying program at your school." Chief Dennis stares at me over his paperwork. "Weren't you the one working with the administration to develop the program?"

"Well, yes." How did he find out about that? I straighten in my seat, ignore the skirt hiking up my thighs. "But it's still in the planning stages. Plus, I'm not the only one involved."

"I understand that. But the antibully program was *your* idea, correct?"

"That's true," I admit. "It's something we just started working on this semester." Lauren and her little clique haven't let up on Tiffany since the school year started and I'm tired of them making the little girl's life a living hell. "The contest application was submitted before we started the program."

"Can you tell us a little about what's involved?" Mayor Davis asks.

"Sure." My head smacks, still on a sugar-buzz, but talking about this is a no-brainer. *Fatty Patty, out on the playground.* "According to national studies, bullying usually starts around fifth grade, so that's where we decided to focus most of our concentration. We want to teach the kids how to talk about their feelings. So many kids in schools today come from broken homes. They bop back and forth between houses and parents. Kids need stability in their lives. They need to learn how to make good choices and how not to take it out on other kids. It's our goal to work with the parents and the students so we can make a positive change. But giving the kids a voice will be the first step."

Chief Dennis nods and instantly I feel better. Maybe I have a chance in this, after all. "Today's world is different than the one we grew up in. It's no longer just about the strong kids picking on the weaker ones while they're out on the playground. Kids today have cell phones and they're on computers. Online bashing is a huge threat and cyber-bullying is just as real as playground bullying. Just watch the TV news and you'll know that. Kids need to learn how to manage their anger. They need to learn respect for themselves and for others, too… and to treat people the way they want to be treated. We're working to put a curriculum together with a program that involves role-playing and talking about feelings. Kids will make lists of things they don't like about the way people treat them. About how they feel when someone pays them a compliment. If they believe it."

Did I believe it when Sam said I was beautiful?

"If and why they say hurtful things," I add.

You're fat.

"Most of all, we need to make sure every voice is heard. Other kids need to learn to stand up and speak out. The worst thing that can happen is when someone sees or hears something and simply does nothing."

She's a mean girl, Patty.

Thank God I had Priscilla. How and why did I lose her?

Chief Dennis clears his throat. "If we get to those kids before they're too old and teach them how to work with their feelings, it could make a big difference—all the difference—in their lives. Let me know if my department can help in any way."

Lucy Carter, reporter for the *James Bay Journal*, eyes me with a thoughtful smile. "Mind if I ask you a personal question?"

"Sure, go ahead." She seems friendly enough and I have nothing to hide. I've always liked the *Journal*. It's a hometown newspaper that provides fair and accurate reporting, with stories focused on the community rather than advertising space.

"How do you do it?"

"I'm not sure I understand what you mean," I reply.

"All these commitments…" Lucy waves a hand across the paperwork. "How do you find time for a personal life?"

I bark a short laugh. Any personal life I had disappeared long ago. Sam is gone and Priscilla is barely speaking to me. As for Nick? The mere thought of facing him Monday morning makes me want to throw up. "That's easy. My kids at school *are* my life."

"Really?" A cool look settles on her face as she sits back in her chair, and I'm left with the odd feeling like I've somehow disappointed her, that she expected something else, something more from me. Then suddenly I get it. Lucy thinks I told her what I thought she'd want to hear. That I chose the easy way out. That I said what anyone would say… anyone who wants to win the contest.

But I told her the truth. Those kids are my life. They always have been. They always will be.

Mayor Davis glances around the small panel. "Anyone have any other questions?" Silence sits with us at the table. He shuffles the paperwork, closes my file. "I believe we have everything we need. We'll be in touch. Thank you for coming in today."

"Thank you for the opportunity." I grab my purse and coat as everyone stands. Low voices trail me as I head for the door to make a quick escape. There's no doubt in my mind that I blew the interview and I won't advance to the final round. My last answer, the one I gave Lucy Carter, was the clincher. *Loser, loser, big fat loser.* Five years in a row. I'll go down in school history as the Susan Lucci of the Bay County Teacher of the Year.

Footsteps follow me. "Patty?" A hand grabs my shoulder, catching me in the doorway.

I turn and face Chief Dennis. "Yes?"

"About that antibullying program… I didn't want to say anything in front of the other judges but I think you're to be commended. And everyone down at the police department feels the same. You're doing a great job." He shoots me a smile that actually puts a smidgeon of hope in my heart. Maybe I'm not such a loser after all.

"Thank you. I appreciate that."

He hesitates. "You okay?"

"Just a little nervous." I force a deep breath. "I'm glad the interview is over."

"You did fine." He nods briefly. "Go home, kick back, relax. Why worry about it? Remember, it's just a contest."

"Right," I mumble. Easy for him to say. Not like it's my life or anything. It's just a contest.

Just a contest.

## CHAPTER TWENTY

Can you OD on Cupid? Pink paper hearts and cutesy red arrows decorate the school hallways, display cases, and doors. Someone even plastered one on the janitor's broom closet. Everyone has a sweetheart but me. I shove through the door into the women's staff bathroom and smack right into Amy.

"What the hell?" Amy, in a chic silk red suit and matching heels, skitters backward. Only a quick grab for the sink prevents her from falling. She smoothes down her skirt and scowls at me. "What is your problem?"

"Sorry," I mumble. "Next time I'll be sure and knock." I head into a stall and snap the lock, sink down on the toilet fully dressed. I don't need to use the bathroom, I just need some peace and quiet. I cradle my head in my hands, close my eyes, wait for her to leave.

"And thanks to you, I snagged my nylons." Amy's voice, filled with annoyance, snakes it way under the door of the stall.

"I'm sorry." I rub my forehead and squeeze my eyes shut. Why doesn't she go away? How many times do I have to say it before she'll leave? "I'm sorry, Amy." One more time for emphasis. "Very, very sorry."

"Oh, for God's sake, Patty, quit being dramatic." She sighs. "I've got another pair in my desk. And I suppose I should forgive you. After all, it's Valentine's Day."

I shake my head, squeeze my eyes tighter. So much for finding peace and quiet in a toilet stall. Leave it to Amy to remind me what I'm trying to forget. I flush, just to save myself the grief of answering questions, and open the door. I join her at the sink, scrub my hands while she fiddles with her hair. Glittering heart-shaped earrings dangle from her ears.

She catches me watching in the mirror. "Diamonds," she says. "Hughie surprised me with them over breakfast this morning."

"Very nice," I manage to get out. Once upon a time, a man gave me a diamond to hang against my heart.

Amy preens in front of the mirror. "I love diamonds. You can dress them up or dress them down."

I rinse my hands. Compared to Amy, I look like a mouse. A very plump mouse wearing a clean white blouse and drab brown pants. At least my sweater is red, but it's not because of Valentine's Day. It was the only thing in my closet long enough to hide the elastic waistband on my pair of pants.

Amy lounges against the sink like she has all the time in the world. Why doesn't she get going? "Is this your free hour?"

"Heavens, no. I'm giving my room mothers time to clean up." She rolls her eyes. "Our party was an absolute nightmare. Cupcakes and punch all over the tables and floor. Kindergarteners can be so messy."

I yank some paper towels from the dispenser. The Amy Lynns of the world might rule the fashion industry, but they have no business in a classroom, especially with little ones. Good thing the Teacher of the Year Committee came to their senses and cut Amy in the semifinal round. Our school is down to two... Nick and me.

"Hughie is taking me out for dinner tonight. Do you have special plans?"

I shrug. I'm not about to give Amy the satisfaction of knowing I'll be alone.

"I just thought you might be doing something with Nick."

"Nick?" I look up sharply. "What does he have to do with anything?"

"Don't act so naïve." Her smile is thick, and like cake frosting so sweet you gag after the first bite. "Everyone knows you've got a crush on him."

"But I don't... I mean, we're not..." I feel the blood rush to my face. Is she being her normal mean self or is she telling me the truth? Does everyone at school think that?

"You're not what? Dating? Or maybe it's just a sex thing. I can't say I blame you. Nick is adorable. If I weren't married..." She fingers one of her diamond earrings, eyes me with a suggestive smile. "I'll bet he's great in bed."

I fight down a sudden urge to smack her. One swing is all it would take to wipe that smile off her face. I actually tried it once when we were in grade school, but Priscilla managed to stop me. But Priscilla isn't in the bathroom today. She's barely talking to me. And neither is Sam. Without the two of them cheering me on from the sidelines, the world isn't such a warm and wonderful place. Priscilla moves silently as a shadow through my life and I haven't seen or heard from Sam since New Year's Eve. I never expected to miss him so much. I ruined everything that night when I slammed the car door in his face. If only he hadn't spoiled things by bringing up the L-word.

If only I hadn't spoiled things by bringing up the F-word.

But Sam and me together? *Fatty Patty* and *Big Sam*. It sounds like something straight out of some hokey TV western from the 60's. It doesn't take much imagination to think what our kids would look like. Chubby little toddlers, round little cheeks, fat little hands begging for cookies.

How would I manage a two-year-old when I can't say no to myself?

And fighting Amy isn't worth it. Why waste my time? I shoot the crumpled paper towel at the wastebasket. It hits the rim and bounces to the floor.

She laughs. "Maybe you should ask Nick to give you private lessons on how to score."

Amy's words buzz in my brain as the door slams behind her. Is it true? Does everyone in school really think I have a crush on Nick? Maybe it was true when the school year started, but not anymore. My feelings for him ended with the final buzzer on the night of his basketball game a few weeks ago. My stomach swirls and I grip the edge of the sink for support as I think about the side of Nick I saw that night. He will do whatever it takes… flattery, flirting, lying, cheating… Nick will do anything to get what he wants.

How far would he go to win the First-Year Teacher of the Year Award?

I splash cold water on my face. Time to climb off the pity pot and get back to the classroom. The kids are busy painting the windows with tempera paint and designing Valentines for the party this afternoon. Red punch, an afternoon movie, and games galore. Cupcakes with sugary frosting. Heart-shaped cookies with pink and white icing and little candy hearts. Twenty-five fifth graders on a sugar buzz, and that goes for their teacher, too. Since Nick's basketball game, I've been on a candy binge for three straight weeks. But who cares? My kids don't care what I look like. Why should I?

I square my shoulders and head out of the bathroom. I should count myself lucky to have twenty-five Valentines in my life. For today, it's probably all I'm going to get. It will have to be enough. That, plus those cookies.

# # #

"I don't see why we have to write some stupid paper about candy." Tyler squirms in his seat and pokes one finger at the colorful little hearts covering his desk. "It's a stupid game. Why can't we just eat them?"

I hold back a sigh and explain my directions for the third time. "Use the messages you find on the candy hearts to write a one-page story. You can eat them once you finish."

Maybe Tyler's right. Maybe it is a stupid game. Ten years teaching, ten years playing the same silly Valentine's game. I'll have to come up with a new idea for next year.

"*Kiss me.*" Lauren waves one pink candy heart high with a loud snicker. "I know a good story for this one. Are we allowed to use real names?"

I rub my forehead. *Confessions of a Ten-Year-Old Vamp.* I've definitely got to think up a new game before next year.

Tiffany raises her hand. "Miss P? I need more hearts."

I head for the back row. The top of Tiffany's desk is empty and her paper is blank. "You weren't supposed to eat them until you wrote your story."

"But I didn't eat them." Her hollow eyes are dark and scared.

"Well, what happened? Everyone had the same number of hearts." I take a deep breath, try to hang on to my patience. What is it with ten-year-olds? At this age, they should be able to follow directions. "They didn't just disappear."

"Billy took them," Jenna whispers in a high voice from two rows over. "I saw him do it."

"Did not!" Billy the Kid Connolly yells from his seat. He scowls at Jenna. "Mind your own business, dork."

"Stop it!" I slap my hand on the top of his desk and candy hearts fly. My eyes narrow as I level him with a cold stare. "Did you take Tiffany's candy?"

"No." His chin juts high in the air. "Don't want any of her stupid old stuff anyway. She smells."

His words punch a hole in my stomach. Babies are born innocent and sweet. When does the meanness, the anger, the cruelty kick in?

"We don't talk about people like that in my class," I say, "or anywhere else, either." The room is deathly still except for Tiffany who sits sobbing quietly at her desk with an occasional odd hiccup. I rest a hand on the back of her chair and stare Billy down. "Do you understand me?"

His eyes hold a defiant challenge. "I guess so."

Damned if I'm going to let some bully make a little girl cry. This is my classroom and I'm in control. High time he learned it. High time they all did.

High time I learned it myself.

"You owe Tiffany an apology. I suggest you do it right now or you'll be spending the afternoon in the principal's office."

The look on his face suggests he's about to protest, then thinks the better of it. He drops his gaze, flips his pencil around the desk. "Sorry," he mutters.

"As for whether or not you took her candy, we'll discuss that later. Right now, I want you to go next door to Mr. Lamont's class and ask him for some extra hearts."

Billy drops his pencil and streaks for the door.

"Listen up, all of you." I tap my watch. "This is your first and final warning. You have exactly fifteen minutes to finish your papers or I'm canceling the party."

Heads bow as everyone grabs their pencils and candy hearts and scribbles away.

I crouch down next to Tiffany's desk. Billy is right. There is a faint foul odor about the little girl, like she needs to use more soap. Deodorant might be a good idea, too. Silently I remind myself to have a private talk with her soon. I fumble in my pocket for a clean tissue and hand it to her. "You okay?"

Tiffany swipes at her tears. "I didn't eat the candy, Miss P. You said not to, and I didn't."

"Miss P? A finger from behind taps me on my shoulder.

"Yes, Karen?" I turn to face the little girl in the desk across from Tiffany.

"What Jenna said is true. Billy did take the candy. I saw him, too."

"All right. Thank you, girls." I'll deal with Billy later. I struggle to a stand. My knees ache from squatting beside Tiffany's desk. Plus, my extra pounds aren't helping. I have got to get this dieting thing under control. I pat Tiffany on her shoulder. "You only have a few minutes left. You should start writing your story."

"But I don't have any candy." Her tears well up again. "It's too late."

"That's not something we say in my class. *It's never too late*. Start writing and as soon as Billy gets back with more candy, you can finish the story. We'll fix this, you'll see."

Tiffany's eyes hold doubt, but she picks up her pencil.

Just as I reach my desk, Billy shows up, empty-handed. "Mr. Lamont says, sorry, but he's out of candy hearts."

"Are you sure?" I frown. Nick was in the teacher's lounge this morning just before the bell rang, asking if anyone had spare candy hearts. When no one else stepped forward, I grudgingly volunteered the extra bag I bought for just-in-case.

Billy shrugs. "You want me to go ask him again?"

"No. Go back to your desk and finish your work. And share half of your candy with Tiffany," I add as he starts down the aisle.

But I can't dismiss the thought of that big sack of candy hearts I surrendered to Nick this morning. I never thought to ask but now I can't help wondering. Fifth graders are notorious for bringing in treats. Why did he need candy hearts, anyway? He should have had an ample supply of goodies to go around.

"Everyone keep working. I'll be right back."

Nick's classroom is quiet as I slip through the door and thread my way through the untidy rows to the front of the room. He stands, back to me, writing on the board. His students are busy, scribbling away, pencils in hand, candy hearts scattered on top of their desks.

Writing stories using candy hearts supplied by me.

He stole my idea. The writing-a-story-with-candy-heart-messages game is something I dreamed up on my own and I damn well know I never shared it with him. He used my idea. He used my candy. He used me.

"Mr. Lamont?" I'm steaming before he even swings around to face me.

His face scrunches in surprise. "What's up? You need something?"

"Yes. I need those candy hearts I gave you this morning."

"Didn't Billy tell you? They're all gone." He gestures at the class. "My kids are writing papers."

"I can see that." He's got some gall, standing there without the slightest hint of apology in his eyes or voice. "I need them back."

"It's a little late for that."

"I thought you wanted them for snacks." My voice shakes and I knot my hands in fists, force them behind me so I won't be tempted to slap him. What did I ever see in this man? Whatever possessed me to give him the candy this morning? I knew Nick couldn't be trusted. What would the committee for Teacher of the Year think about a candidate who cheats and steals?

"Like I said, we don't have any candy left. My kids have a paper to—"

"Do you think I'm stupid?" My voice rises as I glare at him. "I see what they're doing. And I know exactly what you did."

Loud whispering starts behind me and I quickly check myself. No matter how furious I am with Nick, I shouldn't have interrupted his classroom. I spin around. I feel the eyes of twenty-five fifth graders upon me as I thread my way through their desks to the door.

"We'll talk after school," Nick calls after me.

I don't bother answering.

# # #

"You've got to believe me. I never meant to make you mad." Nick stands in front of my desk, hands behind his back, looking exactly like one of my fifth-grade boys who knows he's in trouble with the teacher. But Nick is a man. Will he ever grow up?

"Forget it." It's taken three sugary cupcakes, two enormous heart-shaped cookies and one hour for my anger to melt into a slow simmer. What's the use in belaboring the point? Nick won't get it anyway. "It's over."

"No, it's not. I don't get it, Patty. Why are you mad? What did I do?"

If only I could clamp my hands against my ears and shut him out. If only he would leave so I wouldn't have to deal with him. If only he would stay on his own side of the wall until the end of the school year.

"Hear me out, okay? I just wanted to say…"

Sorry I'm such a jerk? That would do for starters. I bite the inside of my mouth to keep from blurting out the words.

"I just wanted to say, thank you," Nick says. "Thanks for being there and always helping out… just like you did today with those candy hearts. I don't think you realize how much that means to me, Patty. You've been great."

My stomach rolls. Nick's slick, but I'm not stupid. I am not falling for his smooth talking this time.

"Maybe I should have said something earlier. I thought you knew how I felt about you. Maybe I was wrong." His voice is soft, wounded. "You're not like other girls, you know."

Everyone knows you've got a crush on him. My cheeks burn, remembering Amy's words, how people must have laughed as they watched him play me for the fool. I've been drooling over Nick since the day we met, like he was a moist rich cookie and mine for the taking. But my appetite for Nick Lamont is gone. The only thing left I have left is a bad taste in my mouth.

I'm nothing but a joke in the teacher's lounge. *A big fat joke.*

"And as for that candy heart business today…" A ruddy flush suddenly covers his face. "I've been so busy getting ready for basketball play-offs, I didn't have time to get the party organized. I guess I sounded pretty desperate this morning. Then Ruth told me about the candy-heart game. I thought it sounded perfect; especially once she said the game was your idea."

I throw him a hard stare. Ruth was the one who told him? But she never said a word to me.

"I was only trying to buy myself some time," he continues. "I figured you wouldn't care. And basketball is nearly over. Two more weeks and we head into the play-offs. We're in first place."

I nod. I quit going to his games weeks ago, but some habits are hard to break. Despite everything, I still search out the winning scores each morning following a game. Letting go isn't easy after all these months. I've never been good at letting go of thing in my life—sugar or men.

He brings his hands from behind his back to reveal a heart-shaped box of chocolates. "I meant to give you these for Valentine's Day, but now I suppose it's more like a peace offering." He shoves the box onto my desk. "Listen, I've got to get going. I'm already late for practice and we've got a big game tomorrow night."

"Right." I stare at the chocolate. His team will be playing their archrivals.

"It would be great if you could make it. I haven't seen you at the last couple home games."

"I've been busy." Hiding out at the mall, at the library. Hiding out from Nick. From Priscilla. From Sam.

Hiding out from me.

"We can use all the cheerleaders we can get," he adds.

"I don't think so." I'm nobody's cheerleader, including my own.

"Catch you later." A quick glance at his wristwatch and he breezes out the door.

I stare at the fancy box of candy on my desk. Nick practically threw the word *fat* in my face at the basketball game, and now he's bribing me with chocolate? Is he really stupid enough to believe I'd buy into that lame excuse about him being too busy to plan a party? Teaching means more than standing in front of a class. Preparing and organizing take up valuable time, with weekly lesson plans, homework assignments, and tests to grade. Nick is too busy? We're all busy. He's got no business whining about it, especially when he's being paid extra to coach. It's time he learned to pull his own weight. Time he learned to come up with his own ideas. It will do him good. Maybe he'll actually learn a thing or two.

Mr. Lamont needs to get his lesson plans in order, and fast.

I cram the fancy box of chocolates into my overstuffed bag. Maybe Nick was right about one thing. This candy can be a peace offering. Priscilla can afford to indulge.

#

The dozen lush long-stemmed red roses on the hallway table in the cut glass vase for Priscilla are no surprise. The other dozen roses in a rich luscious pink and a card bearing my name leave me speechless.

"Why would Dr. Brown send me flowers?" I bury my face in the fragrant bouquet, inhaling the bittersweet irony. A man sends me flowers for the first time in my life, but he's not in love with me... but with my twin.

"He wanted to thank you."

"Thank me for what?"

"For sharing me with him." Priscilla dabs her eyes with a crumpled tissue. "Isn't that the sweetest thing you've ever heard? Oh, Patty, what am I going to do?" Her shoulder blades heave through the thin fabric of her blouse. "I think I'm in love with him."

I ignore the ache in my own heart and wrap my sister close. For the first time in weeks, she's finally talking to me. Thank God, thank God, whatever's wrong between us is finally crumbling. "You sound like you think being in love is a bad thing. And it's certainly nothing to cry about."

"No, you don't understand," Priscilla moans through her Kleenex. "I feel like I'm about to burst... from happiness."

"I thought that's the way you're supposed to feel when you're in love."

"How can I be happy when I know you're so miserable?"

"But I'm not miserable." I cringe slightly as the lie slides out of my mouth. Twins have a spiritual, physical, and emotional bond that can't be broken, and Priscilla's instincts are dead-on. Because I am miserable. Things aren't fine, they're horrible. And they'll stay that way until I find the courage to fix the mess I've made of my life.

"We never talk anymore, Patty." Her eyes shimmer, enormous and troubled. "That makes me sad, too."

"We're talking now," I remind her. Priscilla's not the only one who's been sad. I'm plenty sad myself, especially when I look in the mirror. Mirrors don't lie and neither does my waistband. I've quit weighing myself. I don't want to know how much I've gained. It could be two pounds, but it feels like twenty. My heart feels even heavier, holding back the truth from Priscilla. Maybe it's time I finally confessed and tell her about Nick. Tell her what happened with Sam. Admit what a fool I've been. No matter what I've done, I know she loves me. Priscilla will forgive me. She'll help me set things right.

The glare of a car's headlights pull into the driveway.

"Harold's here." She pulls back, brushes away the last of her tears with a brilliant smile. "I've probably ruined my makeup with all this crying."

"You look beautiful," I assure her softly, knowing the special moment between us is gone. Priscilla is about to walk out that door and out of my life again. And when she does, I'll be all alone.

After they leave, I climb the stairs and head for my bedroom. I kick off my shoes, slip out of my clothes, and climb into my cozy flannel nightgown. I flop on the bed, eye the alarm. I don't care if it's only seven o'clock. I'm done with Cupid, with hearts and flowers and love. No reason I can't go to bed. There's no one around offering a better suggestion. No one to tell me what time to wake up, what time to sleep. No one to care what I do, what I don't do. No one to share my triumphs with, or tell my troubles to.

No one, except...

I stare at the phone on my nightstand. Just one little phone call is all it would take. Sam left the door wide open. He told me exactly how he felt. All I have to do is pick up the phone. One phone call, one apology, and I could be in Sam's arms.

If you ever come to your senses about that guy, give me a call.

Am I ready to make that call? And what if he no longer cares? What if he's found someone else? Sam knows me better than I know myself. He saw right through me for the fool I was.

What if I call him and Sam says *no*?

I throw myself off the bed, grab my robe, jam my feet into slippers. Going to bed at seven o'clock is crazy thinking. Old-people thinking. And I am not old.

Plus, I haven't had dinner.

Dinner? Who needs dinner when there's chocolate in the house.

I'm down the stairs faster than it takes to rip the cellophane off the box. I yank off the lid and eye the assortment. I pluck out my favorite—a square dark chocolate caramel—and pop it in my mouth. Pure bliss in a one-inch square. I settle on the couch, grab the TV remote, flip through the channels, and finally end up watching a sappy romance. I'm all alone on Valentine's Day but I've still got something to comfort me, something that's never let me down.

I pop another chocolate in my mouth, savoring the love only a best friend can provide.

CHAPTER TWENTY-ONE

Billy the Kid is headed out of town.

I feel like skipping down the hall as I head for the principal's office. Billy's family is moving. A few more days and he'll be gone. Three more months and they'll all be gone for summer vacation. Three months of pure bliss. I pop into the secretary's office. "I'm here about Billy Connolly. Mr. Stevens just gave me the news."

"Such a shame we're losing him." But Mary Darcy's smile matches my own. Billy has blazed a trail back and forth between my classroom and Mary's desk all year long. The chair near her desk was like a stagecoach stop before Billy's final destination—the principal's office.

"When do you need his final grades?"

Her fingers fly over the keyboard. "I have to email his records no later than next week."

"I'll have them ready by Monday afternoon," I promise.

Billy leaving is the best news I've heard in weeks. March is a gloomy month and the gray skies and melting snowbanks have turned our playground into one big muddy mess. Exactly how I've been feeling inside the past few months: muddy and messed up. But spring is on the way. I stroll down the empty hallway to my classroom. Nick's door is open. Has he heard the news? Billy is in Nick's reading class and I'll need his grades for my record book. I hesitate in the doorway. Facing Nick gets harder every day.

I peek in his classroom. He's alone at his desk. It's now or never. I rap my knuckles against the door. "Got a minute?"

"For you? Sure, come on in." He slouches back in his chair, stretches his arms, breaks out in a big yawn. "I can use a break from this paperwork. You look good today."

I cling to the doorknob, reluctant to let go. I'm not falling for the sweet words of whipped crème coming out of his mouth. No more picking up the fork. I'm learning.

Just say no.

"I've only got a minute." I hang back from his desk. "Chuck Stevens and I just had a little talk. Did you hear about Billy Connolly?"

He nods. "Can't say I'm sorry to see him go. The kid's got an attitude."

An attitude? Nick's a fine one to talk. "I need his reading scores. Are they ready?"

"They're in here somewhere." He swipes his hand over the stack of papers. "When do you need them?"

I eye the messy pile covering his desk. Too bad the committee voting on Teacher of the Year doesn't make field trips into classrooms. They might find themselves a little surprised by one of their leading candidates' lack of organization. "No later than Monday morning. That gives you one week. Think you can manage?"

He studies me for a moment, as if he's about to say something, then suddenly his eyes narrow. "Don't worry, you'll have them in plenty of time." He tosses off the words with a confident smile. "I always get behind this time of year. I've got a lot going on with play-offs and all."

Basketball. I should have known he wouldn't be prepared. Nick will never change. He'll always have some handy excuse about why things aren't done. He'd better have those grades by Monday morning, because I'm done cutting him slack.

I head out of his classroom without another word.

#

The antique chandelier ablaze in the dining room stops me cold, as does the linen tablecloth, Mama's china and the table set for three. Dinner in the dining room? That means company, but I won't be home for dinner. Who did Priscilla invite?

I stroll into the kitchen. It's filled with the spicy aroma of homemade lasagna. Priscilla is at the sink washing lettuce leaves. I grab an apple and plop down on my scuffed wooden chair. "What's going on? Looks like you've got the dining room set up for a party."

"We're having company," she says.

"I see that. But it's Friday night, remember? I won't be home."

"How could I forget?" Her voice is tinged with remorse and regret and a tiny taste of bitterness. "Friday night. Must be a home basketball game."

I crunch into my apple, swallow a big bite of guilt over the little farce I've been playing for the past two months. I quit going to Nick's games long ago, though I never admitted it to Priscilla. But I'm tired of cruising fast food restaurants, of trekking to the mall and dining solo in the food court. I'm tired of deceiving Priscilla, of pretending to be cheering on Nick. I'm tired of the whole silly game. But it's easier than admitting the truth. Besides, basketball season is nearly over. What will one more week hurt?

I crunch a path through the apple, eating around the seeds. "So, who's coming to dinner?"

"Sam. I invited him to have dinner with Harold and me."

I pause midbite. Nearly three months have passed since New Year's Eve. Three months since I saw Sam. Does he miss me? He's never called. But then, I haven't phoned him either. I stare at the half-eaten apple in my hand. I've suddenly lost my appetite.

Priscilla drops the lettuce and turns to face me. "I didn't ask you because I didn't think you'd say yes. But I can set another place, Patty." Her face softens. "Please stay. I would love that so much. And I think Sam would, too."

I hesitate. There's such a hopeful look in her eyes. Plus, dinner smells wonderful. Priscilla's spinach lasagna, homemade salad, crusty garlic bread. But much as I hate to disappoint her, much as I miss Sam, I can't stay. I can't face him yet, especially with Priscilla and Dr. Brown around. I would have no time to talk privately with Sam. There'd be no time for me to apologize, to tell him how sorry I am for everything I said.

Plus, I don't want him seeing me like this—not after I bitched at him about how bad he looked, how he didn't take care of himself. Not when I haven't been taking care of me. I've gained three pounds and I'm heavier than I was when we first met.

I shake my head. "Sorry. Tonight's important. It's a play-off game."

"I figured it would be something like that." Priscilla sighs and turns back to preparing the salad. "You don't want to miss that."

"I'd better go get ready." I aim the apple at the garbage can. It bounces off the rim and hits the floor.

So much for being a good shot. Nick never did give me lessons. I snatch the apple off the floor and toss it in the garbage. "Tell everyone I said hello."

Priscilla doesn't answer. I shuffle into the hallway and head to retrieve my coat and purse. I hate lying to her, just as much as I hate being alone. I want her back. I want me back. Somehow I have to dig my way out of this mess.

Starting right now.

I shrug into my coat. No more fast food restaurants. No more slurping through dinner at the mall's food court. I'll grab a healthy salad at a drive-through and head back to school. There's plenty of paperwork stacked on my desk. It's Friday night and the school will be empty. I'll be able to get some work done.

And do some much-needed thinking.

# # #

The lock clicks behind me as I slip through the school door. Four hours ago this hallway was bustling with kids and staff, but now the inky blackness seems foreboding. A red exit sign glows above my head, taunting me to move forward, if I dare. The creepy feeling follows me down the hallway as I make a left turn and head into my section of the building. The corridor is dark, save for a pool of light spilling from a classroom in the center of the hall.

My classroom, I realize with an abrupt halt.

A faint hum sounds in the distance. I move a few steps closer, hear the roar of a machine. My heart rate shifts back into normal rhythm as I recognize the sound of a vacuum cleaner. Jeff the janitor must be working the night shift. I start down the hall with a light step and lighter heart. Jeff jumps in surprise as I stroll into my classroom.

"Geez, Miss P, you scared me!" He shuts down the machine and the vacuum whimpers to a halt. "What are you doing back here at school on a Friday night?"

The sight of the tall, slim man in a worn work uniform puts me immediately at ease. In the ten years I've known him, Jeff's proved honest, polite and reliable. Knowing he's around tonight eases my mind.

"I need to catch up on some paperwork."

"Well, don't let me bother you none. I'm finished in here." He unplugs the vacuum and pushes it toward the door. "Washed the desktops down, and I dusted the shelves, too, just like you asked."

"Thanks, Jeff. Nice job." Everything is neat and tidy. The clean smell of disinfectant wafts through the air.

"I'll be down the hall. Just give a holler if you need me." Jeff lugs the vacuum out the door.

I snap open my salad and drizzle nonfat dressing over a naked sliver of chicken breast resting on a bed of wilted lettuce and a few anemic tomato slices. No croutons, no bacon bits, no taste. I dig in with determination.

Ten pounds and then I call Sam.

I make quick work of the salad as I eye the paperwork stacked in neat piles around my desk. I thumb through a science quiz, then quickly dismiss the idea of scoring math sheets. It's bad enough working at school on a Friday night. Why compound the misery? Finally I settle down with a thick stack of writing assignment my kids finished this afternoon. Proofing them will gobble up time till it's safe to go home.

I settle in and the stack slowly dwindles. The distant hum of Jeff's vacuum proves more comfort than distraction. I'm never at school in the evening, save for parent-teacher conferences, and tonight feels particularly lonely. Especially since I know Sam is at our house. I check my watch as I finish the last sheet. Eight o'clock. I'll bet they've just finished dinner and Priscilla is about to serve dessert. She goes all out whenever Sam comes for dinner.

He hasn't been around in forever and all because of me. I slump forward, chin in hand, stare at the messy stack of math assignments. They'll take at least another hour to finish. Do I really want to tackle that project? Am I really that desperate? Why am I punishing myself like this, especially on a Friday night? I should be out doing something fun. I could have gone to the movies. I could have gone to the book store. I could have shopped for clothes.

Why spend money you don't have on clothes you don't need? What you really need is to lose ten pounds.

"Miss P?"

I jump in my chair. Jeff stands in the doorway.

"Sorry, I don't mean to interrupt you none. Just wanted to make sure you found that paper."

Slowly my heart rate returns to normal. "What paper?"

"I put it on your desk." Jeff's face wears a sheepish frown as he points to a small soiled sheet tucked between the piles of math and science papers. "Sorry it got dirty. My shoes messed it up. It was shoved under your door and I didn't see it when I first come in."

"Don't worry about it." I pluck it out with a tentative finger and scan the top of the grimy form showing Billy Connolly's reading scores. Well, good for Nick. For once, he actually took the initiative and turned something in on time without a reminder from me.

I flip open my record book. I finished my own grades for Billy just this afternoon. As usual, the little boy was consistent in achieving *C's* and *D's*. Now I have Nick's reading scores for Billy, I can finish the report. I smooth down the soiled paper and scan it with a quick eye, then slump back in my chair. The big fat *A* has me mesmerized and I choke out a bark of disbelief. Nick's handwritten comments, smudged with dirt from Jeff's shoes, are barely discernable, but even harder to believe. *Great kid... adds to classroom experience.* Billy adds to the classroom experience, but not in any way that could be deemed positive. Since when did Billy Connolly become a model student? Something's definitely screwed up.

No, not something. More like someone. And it wasn't Billy. I haul myself out of my chair. Someone screwed up big time but I won't find the proof in my own record book.

But I know where I can find it.

I follow the distant roar of the vacuum down to Ruth's classroom. I halt briefly at the door. Do I dare? Technically it's not illegal, but I'd rather not think about the ethics involved. How would I feel if I found out that some other teacher had sat at my desk, snooped through my papers, checked my records? I'd be mad as hell. But then, I don't have anything to prove.

Or hide.

I step into Ruth's classroom and watch as Jeff methodically works his way across the carpet. He shuts down the bulky machine when he spies me.

"Sorry to bother you, but I need a favor."

"Sure thing, Miss P."

"I need something from Mr. Lamont's room." Nothing ventured, nothing gained. And if I don't make an effort, I'll always have doubts. "Think you could unlock his room and let me in?"

"No problem." He strolls down the hallway, me tagging close behind. A large ring of keys dangles from his belt and he uses one to open Nick's room. Ten seconds later and I'm inside. "Just give me a holler when you're finished," Jeff says, "and I'll lock back up."

"Thank you." I feel guilty as hell, especially since Jeff is so eager to please. I wait as he traipses back down the long hall. Bad enough I'm reduced to sneaking around and digging through another teacher's records. The last thing I need is a witness to my crime. I don't make a move until Jeff completely disappears. I head for Nick's desk.

I paw my way frantically through the messy stacks, searching for his grade book. It's got to be here somewhere. Where would he put it? Then the answer comes, so simple, I nearly laugh. I yank open the middle desk drawer and there sits Nick's record book, ripe for the taking. I reach out to grab it, then suddenly hesitate. What if I'm wrong? What if I get caught? I've never done anything like this in my life. Granted, Jeff let me in the room, but snooping around in another teacher's files feels like breaking and entering. It goes against everything I believe in. I shouldn't be doing this.

And Billy Connolly shouldn't have gotten an *A*.

I grab the book without another thought. Flipping it open, I scan the pages, noting first and second quarter scores. I skim past blank sections, seeing pages with only names listed at the top. Where are the reading scores? They have to be here somewhere. I thumb through the remaining pages and finally locate the page with the proper dates. I blink, stare in confusion, blink again.

The page is empty.

No reading tally recorded. No scores for Billy Connolly or any other students. Just an alphabetical list of names. Six weeks into the marking period and Nick has done no grading.

I slap the book shut in disbelief. I must have read it wrong. There's no way Nick would let the assignments pile up like that. I throw a wary glance at the stacks of papers covering his desk. Some of them must be graded, at least Billy's work. Nick's report is on my desk. How did he come up with Billy's scores? What did he base his final grade on?

I grab a stack of papers, rifling through them as fast as I can. Ungraded math homework, two weeks old. I reach for another pile, unable to stop myself. Science reports from last month, with no scores. I dig deeper and finally unearth some reading papers, halting when I finally hit one with Billy's name at the top. It's dated early February. There's no red ink and no grade, either. No *A* for Billy. No *A*, *B*, *C* or *D*.

I slump back in Nick's chair and stare at the proof before my eyes. Nick hasn't kept up with his grading. He's let everything slide. He pulled Billy's *A* out of thin air. He made it up. He cheated.

A liar and a cheat.

Where have I heard those words before? The memory of a crowded bowling alley on New Year's Eve makes me cringe and I try to recall all the things Sam said that night. We were having so much fun until he brought up those allegations about Nick's past and a former teaching career. Was Sam right after all? In front of me is undeniable proof that Nick falsified Billy's reading scores. Are there other things Nick might have done? Other schools he might have taught at? Sam tried to warn me and I didn't believe him.

"Miss P?"

A polite cough from the doorway brings me straight to my feet.

"Sorry, didn't mean to scare you none." Jeff points at the clock. "It's nine o'clock and I'm fixing to leave. If you're done in here, I'll lock up."

"Yes, I'm done." *Done with him. Done for good.* I scoot out of Nick's chair and hurry out the door.

Jeff's keys jingle as he checks the lock behind us. "Find what you need?"

"Yes, thanks," I say with a feeble smile. "I found everything."

More than I ever expected.

# # #

I drive in circles through the cold dark streets pondering my options. What do I do now? I can't just charge into Chuck Steven's office and present him with what I discovered. The first thing he'll want to know is how I found out.

Oh, no problem, Mr. Stevens. Just a little breaking and entering, courtesy of Jeff.

I slam on the brakes as I nearly run a red light. I sit back, drum my fingers against the wheel, wait for the light to change. No, I don't dare approach Chuck Stevens. I can't take the chance.

Behind me a car horn blares and I floor the gas, wincing as the tires spin, then catch and squeal on pavement. I keep the car at a bare crawl the last few blocks. I've never been involved in an accident, and I don't want to start tonight. Getting worked up over something like this isn't worth it.

Nick Lamont definitely isn't worth it.

Sam was right all along. He told me I was smarter than to trust a man who was using me for a fool. Why did I waste my time gobbling up Nick's syrupy compliments? How could I have been so stupid, mooning over him all those months while my heart urged me elsewhere? Indulging in Nick Lamont was a wild romantic daydream that I'll regret for the rest of my life. It cost me dearly.

It cost me Sam.

Sam. The mere thought of him makes me want to cry. I was horrible to him on New Year's Eve, flinging that necklace in his lap. But Sam didn't speak out of jealousy or fear. He tried to warn me but I wouldn't listen. I was so captivated by the thought that someone like Nick—suave, smooth, sophisticated—could be interested in me.

The truth is devastating. Disastrous. I don't deserve someone like Nick.

I deserve someone better.

And Sam deserves someone better than me.

Home. I sit there a moment, grateful to see the driveway empty of cars. Priscilla's dinner party is over. And after what I discovered tonight, I'm not ready to face Sam. I need to figure out what to do next. Do I confront Nick personally or bide my time and wait for the perfect moment?

But how long do I wait? And what if there's never a perfect moment?

I slam the car door and head for the house. Until I figure a way through this mess, contacting Sam will have to wait.

#

Ruth's door is open. I peek inside, relieved to see her behind her desk. "Got a minute?"

She peers over her reading glasses. "Sure, come on in."

I close the door behind me, suck in a deep breath as I near her desk. If I don't handle this exactly right, she'll think I'm crazy and that is something I can't afford. I'm desperate and I need Ruth on my side. I spent all weekend locked in my room trying to figure out how to handle things. There simply is no way I can expose Nick by myself. But if I can talk Ruth into getting involved, things might be different. Ruth is his mentor. She has access to Nick's records, to files I don't.

"I need to talk to you. Privately."

Ruth frowns. "What's wrong?"

"I think we have a problem."

"What kind of problem?" She sits back in her chair and eyes me cautiously.

"Billy Connolly got an *A* in reading."

Her expression drops from concern to disbelief. "Since when? He nearly failed when I had him in class last year. He never turns his papers in."

"I know. He doesn't do any better in my classes, either."

Ruth's eyes narrow. "Doesn't he have Nick for reading?"

I have her full attention, but still I hesitate. I can't just casually mention I've gone snooping through Nick's desk. I have nothing concrete to go on save for a hunch and some things Sam told me that now make sense. I'm desperate to get a look at Nick's personnel file. That could verify the truth, if he claimed the job.

But until someone sees that file, I have nothing. Nothing except an utter belief in what Sam said.

"Ruth, I know this is going to sound crazy…"

"I'm listening."

"What if I told you that I think Nick made up Billy's grade?"

The look on her face switches from disbelief to distaste. "Why would he do that?"

"Because he didn't want to take the time to do it right." I lean in closer. "We both know there's no way Billy suddenly turned into a model student. I think Nick made up the grade. I think he's been cutting corners and not doing the work." I take a deep breath. "I think he's been giving kids grades they don't deserve."

"These are serious accusations, Patty." Her face is ashen. "I assume you have proof."

I think about the stacks of ungraded paperwork piled on Nick's desk. Ammunition that could backfire on him if anyone found it. But how do I explain my presence in Nick's classroom when I wasn't supposed to be there?

"Not exactly," I admit. "But I believe he's covering things up. And I think he's made up other things, too."

"What kind of things?"

I stop short as I read the doubt in my colleague's eyes. If I was Ruth, I probably wouldn't believe me, either. All I have are Sam's words to go by. That, and the evidence I discovered last Friday night. A messy stack of ungraded papers and an empty record book.

"Some things I've recently learned make me think that Nick hasn't been telling the truth. I don't believe he's a first-year teacher." I rush the words out before I lose my nerve.

"That's ridiculous," she says with a frown. "He's never taught before."

"How do we know that? What if he's been lying to us? How would we know? What if—"

"Patty, stop it." She throws her hands up in the air. "I cannot believe you're saying these things. Do you realize how you sound? You're talking about destroying a fellow teacher's reputation."

My heart pounds in my ears and I draw in ragged breaths. In the ten years I've known her, I've never heard Ruth speak so sharply. How can I get her to believe me? The big round clock above her desk ticking off the seconds is the only sound between us as we stare each other down.

"You say you've learned some things that make you believe this. Do you have proof?" she finally asks.

"Not exactly," I admit, "but I bet Nick's résumé would."

"Patty, you are not making sense." The sharp look on her face dissolves into the familiar Ruth I've come to know and trust. "Think about it, dear. Why would he want to lie about something like that? Nick has no reason to hide classroom experience. If he'd taught before, he'd earn more money on the pay scale."

"Exactly," I agree with a nod. "Prior experience is something you'd list on a résumé—unless you had some reason to cover it up. And I think Nick has a reason. Something happened, Ruth. Something bad. Something that got him fired."

Her face darkens. "If you know something I don't, it would be best if you told me right now."

"But that's just it. I don't know for sure. But if the two of us teamed up, I think we could come up with the truth."

Her mouth puckers in a thin, tight line. "Exactly how do you propose we do that?"

"We need to get a look at Nick's personnel file." My voice floats across the desk, barely above a whisper. "I can't do it but you could. You're his mentor, Ruth. You have access to his file."

"Out of the question." Her mouth tightens. "Not only is it highly unethical, employee records are strictly confidential. They're kept under lock and key."

"Please, Ruth?" The uneasy glimmer of fear in her eyes pushes me forward. "I know you could find a way if you try."

Records for students and teachers are stored in the filing room behind Mary Darcy's desk. Large institutional filing cabinets take up most of the room, which teachers are allowed to peruse at their leisure for as long as they like. I've thumbed through my students' records in the past. All that's required is an authorized signature.

But I'm not authorized to check out personnel files.

"What exactly do you suggest I do?" she asks testily. "Confront Mary Darcy and demand she hand over Nick's file? The first thing she'll do is ask me why I need it. And the second thing she'll do is check with Chuck Stevens. What do you suggest I tell him when questions me as to why I've taken such a sudden interest in Nick's files?"

My spirits sink as I realize I've lost her. Ruth was my one shot at clearing up the mystery. I knew it was a gamble, sharing suspicions without evidence to back it up. But I had to try.

"And just for the record," she adds, "I think you're wrong about Nick."

"If I'm wrong, I'll be the first to admit it," I softly reply. "I'm sorry to have involved you in this. Believe me, Ruth, if there was any other way, I wouldn't have asked you. But Nick's records are the only thing I can think of that might prove what I'm saying."

She picks up her red pen.

"Ruth?" I take one last shot.

She eyes me sharply.

"Just think about it… Nick gave Billy Connolly an *A* in reading. Would you have done that? Would I?"

She stares at me a long moment, then picks up her glasses and perches them on her nose. "I need to finish grading these tests."

Grading papers? *I could show you a whole desk full that need grading.*

I slip from the room and close the door behind me. I've just put ten years of friendship on the line but I had to do it. Hopefully Ruth will think about what I said. Hopefully it was enough to convince her to pay a visit to the office and check out Nick's credentials.

"There was nothing in his file."

"Are you sure?" I tuck the telephone under one ear as I strain to reach the bag of chips hidden on the highest shelf in the pantry. "Did you search the entire file?"

"I *looked* through his file," Ruth replies in a testy voice. "His résumé, his college transcript, and some letters of recommendation."

"Did you read them? Were they good?"

A heavy sigh floods the line. "Honestly, Patty, do you actually think Nick would name someone as a reference if he didn't think they'd give him a glowing report?"

As usual, Ruth is right. My fingers connect with the potato chips. I grab the bag and slump against the pantry shelf. What was I thinking? Nick's not stupid. He wouldn't list anything on his résumé that could lead to trouble.

"Patty? Are you still there?"

"Sorry, I was thinking." I puzzle for a moment. "Do you remember who those letters of reference were from?"

"Other school districts."

"So, he *has* worked at other schools." Her news confirms Sam's allegations.

"They had nothing to do with his teaching credentials. They were about his coaching experience. And almost everyone one of them was highly complimentary."

"Almost?" I catch the slight hesitation in her voice. "They weren't all filled with praise?"

"One letter did mention him being a little heavy-handed with the team. Nothing derogatory, mind you," she adds. "Just that he was young and could use a little coaching himself. And I can't say I disagree with the assessment. I've seen it myself, working with Nick this year. But it's exactly what I would expect from a first-year teacher."

"But he's not a first-year teacher, Ruth. You said there were other schools listed on his résumé."

She sighs. "I thought I made that clear. It listed his student-teaching experience, plus the years he's spent coaching. Nick has never taught before."

Sam had been insistent, but there's something else, too. I bang my fist against my thigh, trying to remember. A nagging doubt, a wisp of something skittering just beyond my reach.

"What if he did teach before, but intentionally didn't list the schools?" I suggest. "Would there by any way we could check on that?"

"Patty, dear, please listen to me." Her voice softens. "Don't take this the wrong way. I was so afraid that this would eventually happen. I know Nick is a very attractive man and it's obvious that he led you on. But no matter how badly he behaved or how much he hurt you, you simply cannot allow this... this... feeling of wanting revenge to consume your life—"

"No, Ruth, you don't understand. The thing is—"

"What I understand is that trying to get back at Nick by ruining his reputation is not the way to handle things," she interrupts. "It is not your style. You're a much better person than that. Let it go, Patty. Let him go. Take Nick for what he is and let things be."

I can't believe what I'm hearing. Does she actually think I'm wrapped up in some vain attempt to gain revenge at being dumped by Nick? If so, Ruth is sorely mistaken. Nick never dumped me. We were never dating. This whole attraction thing was completely in my head. But he did dupe us. Nick duped us all. But not anymore. Maybe Ruth didn't come up with any proof, but I know in my heart Nick's a liar and a cheat. Sam knew it, and now, so do I. Just like these potato chips, Nick Lamont is nothing but empty calories, all starch and hot air. I jam the bag of chips back in the cupboard. Feeling them crunch and crumble under my hand is immensely satisfying.

"Patty? Think about what I said."

"I'll do that." I grit my teeth. I'll do more than think. "Thanks for checking, Ruth. And thanks for the advice."

# # #

I never thought I'd be grateful to file a tax return. News of the modest refund is a pleasant surprise.

"You qualify for e-filing. Would you like to come in and sign the release form or shall we mail it?" Bill Walters' voice breezes over the phone, friendly but hurried.

"I'll stop by after school."

"Fine. I look forward to meeting you."

"I'll be there around four." My stomach tightens as I head for my classroom. I'll sign the tax return, but I'll do more than that. This is my chance to talk to Sam. I haven't seen him since New Year's Eve, more than three months ago. My heart races at the thought of seeing him again. Apologizing over the phone would be so much easier, but I owe it to Sam to say *I'm sorry* face-to-face. Swallowing my pride won't be easy but in my heart, I know it's the right thing to do.

And I'll know right away by the look in his eyes if there is any hope for the two of us. Thanks to Nick, I finally learned my lesson. Nick Lamont is a golden boy, but underneath the glitter, he is nothing but hot air. Sam might be big, but those extra pounds haven't made him flabby or weak. He's sturdy and strong with a heart forged of 24-karat gold.

Hopefully, Sam's heart still has a place for me.

# # #

Bill Walters' office is all glass and wood and situated across from the receptionist's desk. I scrawl my signature where indicated on the federal, state, and e-filing forms, desperately trying to recall the layout of the office suite from the one time I visited. If memory serves correctly, Sam's office is to the left, somewhere down the spacious carpeted hallway.

"Thanks for your help." I return Bill's pen with a smile. It's the first time I've met Sam's associate and the young accountant's professionalism and politeness come as no surprise. Sam is a savvy businessman. When it comes to investing money or hiring employees, he obviously knows what he's doing.

If only I'd listened to his advice about love.

"Give me a couple of minutes. I'll make copies for you to take with you." Bill springs to his feet and disappears from his office.

I glance through the open door. A young woman sits behind the receptionist desk, busy with paperwork. I scoot off my chair and approach the desk. "Excuse me?"

She glances up. "May I help you?"

I scan the open office area. Somewhere nearby, I hear the hum of a machine churning out copies. My tax returns aren't that long or complicated. Bill Walters will return in a few moments and there'll be no reason to prolong my stay.

Except to say I'm sorry.

"I'm looking for Sam. Is he in?"

"Mr. Curtis?"

I curse under my breath. Of course Sam is Mr. Curtis. He's head of the firm. "Yes, that's right. Mr. Curtis. Is he here today?"

"He is." The girl smiles for the first time. "Let me check and see if he's available."

My stomach bunches as she picks up the phone. Will he come bounding out to greet me like he did the last time I was here? What will he say? What will I say? My heartbeat quickens. What if he says *no*? What if…

"All set." Bill Walters strolls of the copy room and hands me a large manila envelope. "Here's a copy of both returns, as well as your original documents. We'll wait until Friday to e-file just in case you change your mind."

I cast a sidelong glance at the receptionist. She's still on the phone with her back to me. "What about your bill?" I ask him. "Do I pay now?"

"We'll send an invoice after the taxes are filed." Across the hall, his telephone rings. "Sorry, that's my conference call. I've got to take that." He sticks out his hand. "It was a pleasure meeting you, Patty. Thanks again for your business." He disappears into his office.

Turning, I zero in on the receptionist who has just hung up her own phone. One look at her face is all I need. I won't be meeting Sam today.

"I'm sorry, but Mr. Curtis is with a client." Her expression softens. "I could set up an appointment if you like, but I'm afraid it won't be anytime soon. He's fully booked through April fifteenth."

My stomach rolls as I digest the news. Sam with a client? Booked solid through next week? I might be a lot of things, but stupid isn't one of them. I can recognize a brush-off when I hear one. Sam has no desire to see me and he gave her specific instructions that she should make that quite clear.

"Never mind, it was nothing." I hug the bulky envelope of tax returns close to my chest.

"Are you sure?"

I can't stand the sight of pity in her eyes. "Thanks, I'm all set. I have everything I need." I hurry out of the office, the lie burning on my tongue. *Everything I need?*

Everything but Sam.

# # #

"You're getting married?"

"Can you believe it? He asked me this afternoon." Priscilla stares dreamily at the exquisite solitaire diamond gracing the ring finger of her left hand. Her face wears the glow of a woman in love. "I keep pinching myself so I know it's real and not just a dream. How did I get so lucky?"

I wrap my arms around her and hug her tight. "Dr. Brown's the lucky one and don't you forget it," I whisper fiercely in her ear. "The two of you were made for each other."

"We're thinking about a summer wedding," she gushes. "Just a small wedding with some friends, maybe a dinner reception." She pulls away slightly, breathless with excitement. "And naturally, I want you to be my maid of honor. Oh, please say yes, Patty. I couldn't bear it if you weren't there with me."

"Yes, yes, of course I'll be there, you silly girl." I hug her for another minute, filled with a bittersweet sadness at the thought of Priscilla walking down the aisle to meet Dr. Brown. I love her so much, and I don't begrudge her one bit of happiness. She deserves everything good life has to offer.

But what about me?

"And guess what? Harold wants to keep the house." Her eyes shine bright and luminous. "He promised me that we can live here for the rest of our lives, if that's what I want. *Whatever makes you happy*, he said. Oh, Patty, can you believe it? I won't have to move. And here's the best part: he's offered to buy you out."

My throat tightens. "What do you mean?"

"Harold will purchase your share of the house. You always said you wanted to move and now you have your chance. You'll be free to do whatever you want, whenever you want, without me around to bother you."

"Don't say that. You're not a bother. You've never been a bother." I bury my face in her shoulder. My world is crumbling fast. Snubbed by Sam, Priscilla getting married, and soon I'll be homeless. How much can one person handle? If I'd known the day would turn out like this, I never would have climbed out of bed.

"Patty, what's wrong? I thought you'd be happy."

"I am happy." I dig deep and somehow manage an enormous smile. Priscilla deserves nothing but the best. How can I deny her? "The two of you are going to be so happy. Dr. Brown is the perfect man for you."

"Is it the house?" A frown flits across her face. "You don't have to move, Patty, not if you don't want to. I just thought... I mean, you've always said—"

"Don't be silly, of course I want to move." I swipe away the last of my tears and force a laugh. "You know how I feel about this house. Now I can buy that little condo I've always wanted. Who knows? Maybe I'll even take a vacation," I add. "It's time for me to splurge. Live a little."

But with who? And for what? Life isn't much fun, going it alone.

"Harold's coming over for dinner tonight. We want to start making wedding plans. We want you to help us."

"Sorry, but I have plans tonight," I lie.

"But... but this is my wedding, Patty." Her face droops with disappointment. "Are you sure you can't break your plans? I need you."

"I'll be there through everything, I promise. Just... not tonight." I can't face this much happiness tonight.

"If it's the house—"

"It's not the house." My hand lingers on the smooth, polished railing as I climb the stairs. How many times did I slide down this banister with Priscilla standing lookout from above, watching in case Mama showed up? The two of us had so much fun together growing up in this house. It's all we've ever known. Being with Priscilla is all I've ever known. She's my other half. It's always been the two of us. But from this day forward, it will never be the same. Dr. Brown will make it three. *And three's a crowd.*

The two of them will have each other and I'll have me.

I kick off my shoes and flop on my bed, stare at the ceiling. Never in a million years would I have dreamed that my sweet fussy Priscilla, ever the hypochondriac with her box of Kleenex and allergy pump, would end up married. But her marrying Dr. Brown is the perfect solution. He'll treat her like a pampered princess. She'll have her own personal physician on call twenty-four seven. And as for me…

My gaze wanders the tiny room. In a few months, this won't be my bedroom anymore. I never thought it would be so hard, saying good-bye. No matter how much I've groused about this house, it's always been home. I swallow over the sudden lump in my throat. I am not going to cry. And I am going to move. Priscilla and Dr. Brown deserve their privacy.

She mentioned a summer wedding. Summer isn't far off.

And neither are my tears.

I sniff louder, blink harder, hug my pillow tight. Crying won't solve anything. A plan of action, that's what I need. Plus, I'll need to start house hunting soon. I need to be careful about what I buy. And if there's any leftover money, it should be invested.

The irony of it all puts a smile on my face. Invest the leftover money? As if I have any clue how to go about investing.

But someone else does.

My stomach twists as the idea tumbles around my mind. How can I call him? Sam knows I was in his office last week. He knows I asked to see him and he never bothered to call me back. It's obvious our relationship is over, and I can't say I blame him. I hurt him beyond belief. He knows I was embarrassed by how he looks. And for me to treat him so horribly? To be so rude and insensitive? To say the things I said? No wonder he doesn't want anything to do with me. I can't call him. It's too late. We haven't talked in months.

It's never too late, a little voice tugs at my heart. Isn't that what I tell my students? Teacher of the Year would never admit defeat. Teacher of the Year would find a way. *It's never too late. Never too late. Never too late.*

I sit up in bed, stare at the phone. Maybe if I beg him, Sam will at least agree to listen to what I say. That I'm sorry. That I miss him.

That I love him.

Love. Sam loved me all along but I pushed him away like kicking off the weight of a heavy blanket on a hot summer night. But tonight the truth wraps itself around me like a warm cozy comforter. There's no need to throw away these feelings. I love him. I miss him. The laughs we shared, the easy conversation, the moments we spent in each other's arms.

His soft little moustache and the way it tickled when we kissed.

Love? Yes, I love him. I've always loved him. And now I can finally admit it to myself. But admitting it to Sam is an entirely different thing. I wouldn't blame him if he doesn't take my call. Maybe his feelings have changed. Maybe they haven't.

But I will never know unless I try.

I grab the phone before I lose my nerve and punch in the number. The phone on the other end begins to ring and I empty my mind to only one thought. *Don't hang up. Don't hang up. Don't hang up.*

I hold my breath, wait through the first ring, the second and the third, only to finally hear Sam's voice. A deep rumbling hello, followed by the click of an answering machine. The message is brief but friendly, inviting the caller to leave their name and number. I rack my brain as the beeps start. I never planned on chatting with a machine. I want to talk to Sam. Maybe I should hang up.

Or maybe I should simply say *I'm sorry* and we can go from there.

The final beep sounds and I'm on.

"Hi Sam, this is Patty." I gulp a deep breath. "I'm calling because I wanted to tell you… what I mean is… well, damn, I wish you were there. I hate talking to machines."

Stupid, stupid, get on with it. I stumble forward blindly, trusting my heart to lead the way.

"You're probably wondering why I'm calling. I've thought about you so often. I wanted to call before this. I'm sorry I didn't. I'm sorry about everything, Sam. Sorry for the way I treated you. Sorry for all those horrible things I said on New Year's Eve. You were right and I was wrong, and I don't blame you if you never forgive me. God knows it's been hard enough trying to forgive myself. But I am sorry, Sam, so very very sorry. That's the reason I called. To let you know I'm sorry. And how much I miss you. And how much I—"

Beep. The machine cuts me off.

I stare at the dead phone in my hand. How much of what I said was caught on tape? Is Sam still at the office? Out on a date with someone else? Or maybe he's at home and screening his calls. Was he sitting in his living room, listening to my voice hesitate across the line? What if he simply scoffed at what I had to say? What if he already erased the message? What if he's vowed never to speak to me again?

I throw down the phone and give in to my sobs. In my heart, I know phoning Sam was the right thing but admitting *I'm sorry* hurts more than I realized. Did I think it would solve all my problems? Priscilla's dreams are coming true. She'll be able to live in the home she loves, safe in the arms of a man she adores. Priscilla gets it all. The man, the house, the kids. Maybe even a dog.

And through my tears, I start to laugh. Forget the dog. Not with Priscilla's allergies. She and Dr. Brown are both too fussy to put up with some tiny fur ball scampering around the house or some gentle giant galloping up and down the stairs. Priscilla and Dr. Brown are a perfect pair. Homebodies, made for each other.

I was made for someone, too. Someone who no longer cares.

How can I blame him after what I said? If I was Sam, I'd never speak to me again. I stopped before the three-letter F-word made it out of my mouth, but Sam got the point loud and clear. Calling him fat was cold and cruel. Even if by some miracle he forgives me, I'll never be able to forgive myself. Who am I to judge? Who am I to talk? I've gained seven pounds since the day we met. All my fat clothes are tight again. I don't deserve his friendship, much less his love. I was so careless. I took Sam for granted and now it's too late. Once upon a time I had his heart, and now it's gone for good. I have to face the truth that Sam doesn't want me. It's too late to change things.

Never too late. You're never too old to learn. Never, never, never quit. The old World War II phrase I drill into my students pounds in my brain. What kind of a teacher would I be if I let myself get away thinking like this? How can I face my class again if I let myself sink into negative thinking? I might as well surrender my teaching certificate. It's time I took my own advice. I might be a lot of things but I am NOT a quitter. What is life without hope? I can't give up because things seem too hard. No matter what, I have to keep trying. But how? It's too hard. Too much. How can I do this for the rest of my life?

Try taking it one lap at a time.

Somewhere deep in my heart, the soft sweet message floats to mind. Sam's message to me. One lap at a time. One day at a time.

I can do this. For starters, I can go back to the pool. I might not win Sam back. He might never forgive me. I've probably lost the best friend I ever had. But somehow I am going to make it through this. I have no choice.

Sliding off the bed, I jam my feet in a pair of slippers and hurry down the stairs. Soft sounds lead me to the kitchen where I find Priscilla setting the table for two. "What time is Dr. Brown supposed to be here?"

"In about an hour, after he finishes rounds at the hospital." Her forehead wrinkles. "Why?"

"Because I changed my mind, that's why." I grab some silverware from the drawer, a plate from the cupboard, and set them on the table. "And I hope you were serious about me joining you for dinner, because I'm not going anywhere. We've got a wedding to plan!"

CHAPTER TWENTY-THREE

Muddy snowbanks litter the playground and a blustery wind howls around the corners of the building. Though the calendar says spring, winter seems determined to stick around. I tuck my scarf higher around my neck, check my watch, and sigh. Three more minutes until I can ring the bell and bring them in from recess.

"Boys, stay away from there," I call as Tommy, Joseph, and David skirt closer to the plastic orange fencing roping off the construction trench near the door. Replacing the telephone system seems a waste of money, especially since our school district is supposedly pressed for funds. The budget's tight and they've axed all the extras. I'm surprised they haven't dropped the Teacher of the Year award ceremony. Probably because the prize money was put up by a service club.

And my final interview with the selection committee is set for today. Much to my surprise, despite my disastrous interview a few months ago, I've actually made it to the final round. So has Nick, though I'm doing my best not to think about his chances of winning. He can sink or swim, for all I care. I'm being interviewed during my lunch hour and I have no clue what I'll say. Hopefully they won't judge me on how I'm dressed. With today's temperatures hovering in the single digits, I'm in a thick sweater and woolen slacks. I check my watch one more time, relieved to see the hands at eleven. Less than an hour to go and I'll be out the door and on my way to the interview downtown. I clang the bell. "Line up, everyone. Single file. Inside voices."

Fifth graders crowd past me as I brace the door, shivering through my jacket. Nick shoots through the door, plants himself beside me as the last students pass. "Got a minute?"

"No. I have a reading class to teach." I seize the steel bar, struggling against the gusty wind to close the heavy door. *Damned if I'll ask him for help.*

"Reading. Right. Here, you shouldn't be doing that by yourself." He grabs the bar and yanks the door shut. "Did you see the test schedule the office posted?"

"What about it?" I scoot around him down the hall.

"You've done this testing before, right?" He follows behind me.

"We test the students every year."

"The instructions they gave us weren't very specific. Think you could spare a few minutes after school today to help me figure things out?"

He's got to be out of his mind. Just because he helped me doesn't mean I'm in the mood to help him. I shake my head as we reach my door. "Sorry."

His hand grips my shoulder. "Please, Patty?"

What a difference a few months make. Back then, that plea in his eyes would have filled me with hope... desire... purpose... but not any more. Testing isn't that hard. All he has to do is spend some time reading the instructions. But he probably can't be bothered. Nick is only willing to spend his time on the things he cares about: basketball, golf, and getting what he wants. Nick will never change. The easy way out, that's his motto. Never giving back unless it suits what he's after. He used me to get what he needed. He picked my brain, wasted my time, and nearly waltzed away with my heart. But I've taken it back. Nick Lamont was never my responsibility and I'm done being his cheerleader and coaching him from the sidelines.

It's time Mr. Lamont figured out the playbook and managed his own game.

I shoot him a blank look. "Sorry."

"But—"

"Check with Ruth. She's your mentor. Maybe she'll have some ideas."

The stunned look on Nick's face as I shut the door on him is the last thing I see.

An inbound paper airplane sails over a desktop as I hurry to the front of the classroom. I hate morning recess. The kids are revved up from being outside, and with less than an hour to go until lunch, it's hard getting them to settle down. "Take out your reading books. Who remembers where we left off?"

"Chapter twenty-two," Karen pipes up. "Can I read?"

"The girls read yesterday. It's the boys' turn today."

Joseph's hand shoots up. "Can I read, Miss P?"

I shake my head. Joseph is my best reader, with scores hovering near high school level. He doesn't need the practice. I glance around and spot the aspiring musician two rows over. Tommy's fingers drumming against his desktop are playing on my nerves. "Tommy, why don't you start us off?"

The melodic thump-thump-thump halts and the little boy drags himself to his feet. I take my seat as he flips open his book with a scowl and struggles to find his place. What is it with ten-year-old boys? Teaching them is a daily lesson in patience and tolerance. Intellectually and physically, most of them lag behind the girls. Someone should do a scientific study…

An earsplitting bell from the hallway shatters the silence.

"Hey, cool, a fire drill!" Joseph straightens in his seat.

"Do I still have to read?" Tommy's voice lifts in hope.

I slap my book shut. "Let's go."

"I don't want to go back outside again." Tyler slouches low in his seat. "It's cold out there."

"Come on, no wasting time. Everyone push in your chairs and let's go." I flash them a stern look as I push down my own annoyance. Great timing on the office's part, sandwiching a fire drill between morning recess and lunch. I haven't got time for this. My final interview with the Teacher of the Year Committee begins at noon and I have to leave early to make it in time.

"Stupid fire drills, anyway," Tyler mutters. "We just had one last week. How come we have to have another one so soon?"

His words nail my feet to the floor. Tyler's right. The kids never know when we're having a drill, but the office always alerts teachers in advance... and no one mentioned anything to me today. My heart rate takes off faster than a spark racing up the fuse of a bomb.

This is no drill.

"Everyone line up." I swallow, try to find a voice in a mouth gone dry with fear. "Come on, you know what to do." I grab my record book and press it against my chest, as if that will calm my racing heart. My feet and body don't feel connected, but somehow I manage to make it to the door. Out we all go, without hats or coats, clothed in excited, nervous chatter. I take a long whiff as we head through the hallway but it smells like it always does just before lunch. Sweaty bodies, the smell of macaroni from the school cafeteria. *No smoke*.

I herd the kids out the door and into the sunshine. Nick's reading class, along with the rest of my homeroom students, are grouped near the playground fence. A quick head count against my record book shows twenty-five fifth graders. Everyone accounted for. Everyone safe.

Tiffany tugs at my sweater. "Miss P, do you think there's really a fire?"

"I'm sure things are fine." I keep my eyes trained on Jenna, who's been assigned the task of runner and reporting to the principal that my students are all present. Hopefully we'll hear the all-clear whistle soon. The cold wind whips the playground, snatching my breath away. I stamp my feet in thin, flat shoes. For once, I wish I was wearing my thick, clunky boots. Plus my coat and mittens.

"Hey, look!" Tyler whoops. "Here come the fire trucks!"

I suck in my breath as the loud wail of sirens grows. Everyone clambers to see three yellow fire trucks lumbering around the corner, headed in our direction.

"Fire trucks! Cool!" Tyler cries. "I'll bet this is for real! The school is on fire!"

"Is the school going to burn down, Miss P?" Karen's voice rises.

"That is not going to happen." I need to douse the panic before it gains fuel and starts to spread. I point at the building. "Does anyone see smoke? Because I don't. Do you?"

Twenty-five pair of eyes anxiously scan the school. "No," Karen admits, her words echoed by several others.

"I'm cold." Joseph kicks the side of a snowbank. "I want to go back inside. How long do we have to stay out here?"

Good question. When will they let us back into the building? Chuck Stevens stands near the front door, chatting with the fire chief, and neither of them seems too concerned. None of the firemen have gone into the building. They mill about, talking among themselves. Why keep all of us outside quarantined in the cold? I glance at my watch, see the minutes ticking by. I can't miss that interview. I rub down my arms and stamp my feet. Is this an emergency or not?

"Wow, look! The TV people are here!" Tyler points at the street.

A television news truck parks near the playground perimeter. The door opens and I spot the pretty anchorwoman who does the nightly news. She's followed closely by a squat man balancing a bulky video camera on his shoulder. I suck in a deep breath. If the TV crew showed up, something's definitely wrong.

"Miss P?" A tug on my sweater and the uneasy catch in Matthew Moore's voice snags my attention. The little boy is one of the quietest students in my class and never gives me an ounce of trouble. "I don't see my brother. Michael's not here."

"What do you mean?" I crouch close beside him. Matthew's twin is in Nick's homeroom.

"He's not on the playground." His face tightens.

"Are you sure?"

"I looked and looked but I don't see him." The fear climbs in his voice as his eyes well up with tears.

"Maybe his brother's still inside. Hey, if there really is a fire, he could burn up!" Joseph aims another swift kick at the snowbank.

"You shut up!" Matthew explodes in hysterical hiccups.

"It's okay, Matthew. Everything is going to be all right." I hug him close. Staff aren't allowed to touch students, but at the moment I could care less about some stupid rule. I have a scared little boy to keep calm. I fish a Kleenex from one of my pockets. "I'm sure your brother is out here somewhere. Look, Mr. Lamont's class is right over there." Pointing, I aim Matthew's gaze at Nick's class hovering near the metal fence. "They heard the alarm and they got out."

"But Michael's not with them." His eyes wear a thick glaze of terror and he starts to shake. "What if Joseph's right? What if he's still inside?"

His horrified whisper catches in the wind. I can't just stand here and do nothing. I grab his shoulders and lock eyes with him. "Matthew, do you trust me?"

He nods.

"I want you to wait right here. I'm going to find your brother."

"Promise?"

"I promise," I say with a reassuring hug. Standing, I clamp a firm hand on Joseph's shoulder. "As for you, stop kicking that snowbank, right now." I ignore the guilty look on his face. "I'm going to go talk to Mr. Lamont. Can I trust you to be in charge?"

"Me?" Joseph's face beams with surprise. He stomps the muddy snow from his shoes and puffs up with pride. "Sure, Miss P, I'll watch the kids for you."

I head for Nick, huddled with his students near the chain link fence. I grab his arm. "We need to talk."

"About what?" He squints at me against the high noon sun.

I haul him away so we won't be overheard. "Where's Michael Moore?" I level him with a cold stare. "His brother doesn't see him and I don't, either."

"He's around here somewhere." Nick scans the playground. "I saw him a minute ago."

But his words come a little too slow. "Did you do a head count?"

"Yes, I did." His tone plays defense to the stony glare suddenly on his face. "Twenty-four kids, just like in the book."

"Then where's Michael?"

"What's it to you?" He blows out a deep breath. Icy steam fills the space between us. "That kid isn't one of your students."

That kid? "That kid might not be in my class, but he's missing. If you won't do something about it, then I will."

Nick shrugs. "Knock yourself out."

I'm tempted to knock him right off his feet. That would surely make it into the annals of playground legend... one teacher, whacking another. I stomp away before temptation gets the better of me. The hell with Nick Lamont. A little boy is missing.

Ruth stands some yards away, struggling to keep her fourth graders in order. I brush past groups of students as I head in her direction. Maybe she's seen Michael.

"I'll bet he's still in the closet," a voice sniggers, echoed by a giggling chorus.

Whirling, I spot Lauren and grab her arm. "What did you say?"

"Ouch! That hurts!" A furious scowl covers the little girl's face.

I loosen my grip but don't let go. "Tell me what you said."

Her eyes glitter like black ice. "You're not allowed to touch me."

I tighten my hold. "If you know where Michael is, I want to know right now."

"I said he's probably still in the closet," she finally mutters in a sulky tone.

"Closet?" The wind sucks away my words. "What closet?"

"The supply closet. The one near Mr. Lamont's desk." Lauren tosses her hair with a dismissive scoff. "Michael Moore is such a crybaby. He's always whining about something. Sometimes when he acts up, Mr. Lamont puts him in the closet."

"Mr. Lamont does *what?*"

"He puts him in the closet," she suddenly shouts in my face as if I've gone deaf. "To teach him a lesson."

I stagger backwards, nausea rolling in my stomach. *He left his kids alone in the classroom. He saved himself instead of them... a liar, a cheat and a coward... that's the kind of man you've been dealing with all year.*

Sam was right about Nick all along.

Lauren yanks away from me. "Just wait until my mother hears what you did. You're going to get fired."

I break rank and dart toward the principal and fire chief without answering.

Someone's going to get fired, but it won't be me.

# # #

Thirty minutes later, I finally rejoin my class with Michael Moore in tow. The firemen found him sobbing in a closet containing Nick's supplies, exactly where Lauren said he would be. Thank God the little boy wasn't hurt. Thank God the emergency wasn't worse.

353

When the telephone construction crew accidently cut the school's gas line, it put us all in danger from a potential gas leak and fatal explosion. But the gas company arrived, shut off the main line, and the threat is over. Everyone is safe, including Michael Moore, rescued by two strapping fireman in full turnout gear. I blink hard as the two brothers are reunited.

"Miss P, are you crying?" Jenna whispers.

"It's okay, Miss P," Joseph assures me. "You don't have to worry. Everybody's still here. I made sure nobody moved, just like you said."

"Thank you, Joseph." I force a smile and finger away a few tears. "You did a good job."

"No problem," he says. "You can put me in charge whenever you want. I'll take care of things."

I laugh and clap him on the shoulder. No doubt someday Joseph will run his own company, but he'll need a little more guidance before he takes on the world. All of them will. I glance around at my kids, shivering in the brisk March wind. Right now they're only ten-year-olds, barely more than babies. The years will fly and soon they'll be grown. But for now, they're still mine. There are things I still have left to teach them. I close my eyes and make a silent vow. No matter what it takes, I'm going to do my best to encourage them to expand their minds, to never, never quit, to always reach for their dreams.

A few minutes later, Chuck Stevens comes around and whispers in my ear. I break the news to the kids. "School's closing early today."

Loud cheers ring out and I put a warning finger to my lips. "Listen up. We're going back inside, but only for a few minutes. I want you to gather your coats and anything else you need."

The decision has been made by the powers that be. With the main gas valve shut off, the school has no heat. There'll be no school for the rest of the day. Maybe not even tomorrow.

But for Nick Lamont, the school year is definitely over.

CHAPTER TWENTY-FOUR

Same old school year. Same old body. Same old me.

Blue plastic floats bob on the surface of the water as I flip on my back and slowly start swimming for the other end of the pool. The lane is long and lonely, and my mind seems to be the only thing burning up calories. It races down the lane faster than I can keep up. I have to keep going.

Nothing changes if nothing changes.

I thought being back at the pool again would get me back in the swim of things. I thought doing laps and pushing my body would bring inner peace. I thought daily exercise would boost my endorphins, bring renewed energy, result in some sense of satisfaction. But I thought wrong. All I do is ache. Inside and out.

So why am I here? Why keep going? Especially since it doesn't matter anymore what I look like. I ruined my shot at Teacher of the Year when I skipped the final interview. No way was I going to abandon my kids after all the commotion with the gas leak and the trouble it caused. But I have no regrets about the way things turned out. In my heart, I know staying behind with my kids was the right thing to do. The selection committee offered to reschedule, but I decided to pass. Funny, but somewhere along the line, I lost the heart for winning. Maybe because I lost so much of me, trying to win? Some other teacher will receive the award.

But it won't be Nick Lamont.

A watered-down image of Nick splashes to mind as I touch the end of the lane, flip, and start for the other end. What a fool I was. He seemed so perfect and I craved his attention like a hot fudge sundae. But just like ice cream nuked in a microwave, Nick melted under pressure and ended up a puddle of empty calories. He didn't look so perfect that morning last week with the sweat popping in shiny beads across his forehead when confronted on the playground. He looked even uglier later that afternoon when Chuck Stevens fired him.

Pretty is as pretty does, Mama always said. What Nick did that day hadn't been pretty.

And he even hit on Priscilla.

I nearly lost it at dinner that night when Priscilla finally shared her halting tale about what had happened between them in the kitchen on Thanksgiving Day. How Nick surprised her from behind, touched and teased her though she struggled to pull away. How he told her he knew she wanted it. How he made suggestions she was too embarrassed to repeat months later, even to me.

"But why didn't you tell me?" I whispered when I finally found my voice.

"Because I didn't think you would believe me," Priscilla said haltingly. "Everything was fine until you and Ruth left us alone in the kitchen. And then Nick..." She shuddered and shook her head. "I was afraid you'd be mad."

"You bet I'd have been mad," I say through clenched teeth. "I would have killed him." The mere thought of him trying to force himself on Priscilla makes me want to grab a gun and hunt him down.

"No, you don't understand," she says softly. "I thought you would be mad at me. Nick was all you talked about. I thought you were in love with him. And I thought if you found out what had happened, that you would blame me. I didn't want you to think I encouraged him."

My eyes round in sudden understanding. "That was the night you started acting so funny. And here all this time, I thought you were mad because I broke Mama's turkey platter."

"But I was mad! I was mad at Nick—and at you, too." She hesitates. "You turned into someone different when he was around. You changed, Patty." Her voice drops. "I thought I'd lost you."

All that time wasted. All those Friday nights I pretended to be at Nick's basketball games. Brought down by my stupid, selfish pride. What a fool I've been. "I'm sorry, Priscilla. Sorry about everything. Can you ever forgive me?"

"But I'm not mad anymore, Patty, not even about Mama's turkey platter." Her eyes soften. "Someone gave me a new one, remember?"

I push away the image of Sam's face. Allowing myself to remember how I treated him leaves me with a lonely ache that might ease in time, but I doubt it will ever heal. I tried my best to put things right, but Sam never responded to my apology on his voicemail. He never acknowledged my visit to his office. I got the message, loud and clear. Sam's no longer interested. And I don't blame him. If someone treated me like that, I wouldn't be interested, either.

"I've missed you so much." Priscilla wraps me in a tight hug. "I'm so glad I have you back. At least we still have some time together before the wedding."

I fight down the tears. The private little world we've shared all our lives is disappearing. I'll be moving soon to a small, one-bedroom apartment I found close to school. It's not a condo, but it will do for now. It's time I took control of my life. Time to change what I can.

Brand new day. Brand new life. Brand new me.

Starting at the pool. And maybe this time, I'll finally get things right. It's taken me a while to figure it out, but Sam was right. *One lap at a time.* Maybe that's always been my problem. Plowing through things, never asking for help, never recognizing when I'm floundering in water over my head. The only way to the finish line is straight up the middle. One lap at a time. No skipping the in-betweens.

I kick off and start down the lane for the other end of the pool. Twenty laps yesterday and twenty-two today. I've already lost six pounds and my clothes feel looser. And I'm determined to do whatever it takes. One month and twenty pounds to go. I'm trimming down for the big event. Priscilla deserves nothing less on her wedding day.

Four laps left. I flip in the shallow end, think about the wedding and elegant reception to follow. There'll be dining, dancing, and hopefully someone to dance with. I might not have a date but I *am* the maid of honor.

A shrill blast from the lifeguard's whistle stops me. I bob upright in water over my head. The whistle shrieks again but my goggles are fogged in the warm humid air and it's hard to see. The teenage lifeguard is on his feet, pointing toward the deep end. Someone stands there, waving at me. It's a man. A man who looks like...

Sam?

No, it can't be. That person is fit and trim. It has to be these goggles. I swipe at the steamed lens, grab a better look at the man. Then I gulp and sink, sputtering a mouthful of water.

It *is* Sam.

Down I go, straight to the bottom of the pool. My feet graze the smooth tile as my mind swims with dread and delight. Sam, here at the pool! But why now? After all these months? I stay underwater as long as I dare, desperately trying to remember all the things I want to tell him. Finally my air gives out and I have no choice. I hit the surface with a prayer that my goggles are still fogged. The first thing Sam sees shouldn't be my tears. He waits, crouching beside the metal steps as I splash toward him.

"Let me help you." He offers out his hand.

I swallow hard, hesitate. How long has it been since we talked—or touched? Finally I grab hold, struggling to find my balance as I stumble up the first step, then the second. The last step is easy. Sam hauls me straight into his arms.

"No, stop!" I screech with laughter as he pulls me closer. "Are you crazy? You're getting all wet!"

"I'm crazy, all right… crazy about you." He yanks the goggles from my eyes and brushes dripping curls out of my face. "Now shut up and kiss me."

"But—"

Hungrily his mouth presses over mine and I melt into the heat of his kiss. I stand there in his arms and the tart taste of chlorine mingles on our lips as we share a deep kiss, then another and one more. The soft graze of his moustache brings rolling shivers of delight surging through my body. I missed his moustache, and everything about him. I missed this man.

This man I love.

"Cold?" His lips nuzzle against my ear.

"I'm not cold. I'm happy." But happy doesn't begin to describe how I feel being in his arms again. Finally the drought is over. I swipe some wet curls from my eyes, softly touch his face. He has new glasses and all the weight he's lost has chiseled his features into someone I barely recognize. I hug him closer, as if that can make up for all the time we lost. Months of time and all my fault. My mistake. A stupid, fat mistake.

I trace the edges of Sam's moustache with one finger. "How did you find me?"

"Priscilla." He grabs my hand, kisses the tip of my finger. "She said you'd started doing laps again at the pool."

God bless Priscilla. She brought us together at the beginning and she's led Sam back to me again. "I missed you," I confess. "I missed you so much."

"Not as much as I missed you."

His words bring a surge of hope. Maybe it's not too late to make things right.

"Sam, about those things I said..." I rush the words out. "I'm so sorry. I wouldn't blame you if you don't forgive me. God knows it's been hard enough trying to forgive myself."

"Quit beating yourself up," he replies. "A lot of what you said was true and I needed to hear it."

I bite the fleshy bottom of my lip. Typical Sam, offering me an easy way out. It would be so simple to take it. Simple and easy... but unfair to him.

"No, I was wrong. I had no business judging you or saying what I did. I've lived with the guilt for months. Besides, who am I to talk? Just look at you." I push him away, admire his new physique. "You look great, but as for me?" I shoot a rueful glance at my belly bulge and chunky thighs. "I'm still just the same old Patty. Still fat."

No more pretense, no more lies. The f-word is finally out in the open.

"You're not fat. You're beautiful." He pulls me close against him. "I love you just the way you are."

"How can you say that?" I blink hard, struggling to keep the tears from spilling down my cheeks. "How can you love me when I don't even love myself?"

"Patty, I never stopped loving you," he says. "And if you can't love yourself, then I'll love you until you do. Let me be your mirror."

"The last thing I want is to look in a mirror. I probably look like a wreck."

"Yep," he says with a grin. "But you're a beautiful wreck."

A powerful surge of happiness bubbles up inside me as Sam gives me another kiss, only to be stopped by a shrill whistle. We turn and see the lifeguard grin, give us a thumbs-up.

"Looks like someone approves," Sam chuckles. "Why don't you go get dressed?"

I search his face. I've lived so long without him. Now he's back, I don't want to let him go. "Promise you'll be here when I'm done?"

He laughs and gives me one more kiss. "I'm not going anywhere."

# # #

He loves me. He loves me not. He loves me. How can a person be deliriously happy and dreadfully scared at the same time? My stomach bunches in a tight knot as I push open the door and stumble outside, wet curls and all. What if Sam took off? What if he didn't keep his promise? I halt in the doorway, squint against the brilliant afternoon sunshine, lift my hand to shield my eyes. Is he still here?

And then I spot him, leaning against his car, and inside me it feels like a thousand firecrackers are exploding. He hasn't spotted me yet and I study him for a moment, take in how good he looks. Trim and tan in a white polo shirt and khaki pants, he's lost a lot of weight—at least forty pounds.

My heartbeat quickens as he notices me coming. It pounds in my ears as he smiles and opens his arms. It roars through my brain as I melt against him and yield to the slow sweet taste of his kiss.

"I still can't believe you're here," I say moments later when we come up for air. "It seems like a dream. I feel like pinching myself."

A slow grin spreads across his face. "If there's any pinching to be done, I'm the one who gets to do it."

"But I don't understand. Why did you come back? Why now, after all this time? It's been months since we talked." I think about New Year's Eve, how I shoved the diamond necklace in his hands, how I ranted and raved about the way he looked. Why would Sam come back? But safe in his arms, I feel brave enough to ask the question. "I thought you'd forgotten all about me."

"Never doubt it, Patty. You were always on my mind."

"I was?" I duck my head, suddenly shy.

"I almost sent you flowers for Valentine's Day. I drove to the florist and I sat there in the parking lot and thought about you." His arms tighten around me. "I sat there in the cold for half an hour until I finally talked myself out of buying you flowers."

"Priscilla got roses," I say slowly, remembering how radiant she looked as she showed me the beautiful bouquet... and how I spent Valentine's night gorging on Nick's chocolate.

"I wanted to send forget-me-nots, so you'd know that I still cared. But I knew you had to sort things out for yourself and so I decided to skip the flowers." His eyes lock on mine. "But I never stopped hoping or praying that you would change your mind."

"Wait, I'm confused." I push away slightly. "If you felt like that, then why did you snub me that day at your office?"

A frown tightens on his face. "What are you talking about?"

"That day last month when I dropped by to pick up my tax return, remember? I asked to see you but the receptionist told me you were with a client."

Sam shakes his head, looking puzzled, and I rush on. "I thought you were trying to avoid me. I thought you were still mad. And when you didn't return my call, I thought things were finished. I thought—"

"You thought wrong," he says flatly.

"But why—?"

"Patty, I had no idea you stopped by the office. No one told me you were there."

"They didn't?" I search his eyes, looking for the truth. "You're not just saying that?"

He blows out a long sigh. "Do you honestly think I could ignore you? My feelings haven't changed. I'm still in love with you."

And there they are again, the words I've longed to hear. Sam is in love with me. I shiver in delight.

"You're cold. Let's sit in the car." He opens the passenger door.

"Always the gentleman," I murmur as I brush past him and settle in the seat.

He slides behind the wheel, starts the engine, fumbles with the heater. "Where would you like to go? We'll talk over dinner."

"No, please, I'd like to stay right here. There's something I need to say and I don't want to do it over food."

His mouth tightens and my heart skips a beat. Will he hear me out? Have I made him mad without saying a word? Finally he nods. "All right."

I clench my hands together tightly in my lap. "About what I said on New Year's Eve—"

"We don't need to go into that again," he says firmly. "It's over and done with."

"Sam, please. It's important. You have to hear me out." I draw in a deep breath and gather my courage. "That night, you told me there were some things I needed to work on. Well, guess what? It turns out you were right. This was never about you, Sam. It was all about me. I was stupid and blind, and… well, I want you to know that I understand that now. And I've been trying to work on myself. To figure out who I am and what I want."

He stares at me a long moment. "And have you?"

"I think so," I say quietly. "It hasn't been easy, but I'm trying."

"What about that guy?" he finally asks.

Much as I hate to revisit what happened with Nick, Sam deserves to know the truth. In a halting tone, I tell him the story, holding back none of the details. "They fired him. I haven't seen him since," I finish soberly. I lean my head against the car seat and close my eyes. I wouldn't blame Sam for gloating. He tried to warn me about Nick and I refused to listen.

"I'm sorry things turned out the way they did," he finally says. "Not because of him, but because of what it did to you. I know he hurt you, Patty, and I'm sorry you had to go through that. But I'd be a liar if I said I felt sorry for him. I never liked the guy."

"I know." I've swallowed down the guilt and embarrassment for months, but there's no holding it back anymore. It bubbles to the surface. "I should have listened to you, Sam. You were right all along. But I guess I didn't want to hear it. Or maybe I wasn't ready to hear it. Then, after I finally began to see the truth for myself, the last thing I wanted to do was admit it—especially to you." I hang my head. "I've been so stupid. Stupid, foolish, and proud. I can't tell you how ashamed I am of myself."

"Know what I hated most? The way he treated you. He used you, Patty. It was so hard sitting there and watching him do it." Sam blows out a deep breath. "Maybe if it weren't for that damn contest, he would have left you alone."

"Maybe." I think about Nick and how proud he was to be nominated as First-Year Teacher of the Year. How proud I was to help him out. How happy I would have been, once upon a time, to hear his name pronounced the winner. "But we'll never know, will we? Besides, it doesn't matter who wins. It's just a silly contest."

"What about you?" he asks quietly. "I thought you were still in the running."

"Not any more." Briefly I fill him in on the details of that cold day in March, the gas leak that threatened our students and how I skipped the final interview.

"I'm sorry, Patty. You deserved to win." He reaches over and gently strokes my cheek. "There's always next year."

"No, I don't think so." I shake my head. "I don't need the grief."

And I don't need a Teacher of the Year Award to tell me who I am.

"Well, if you're okay with it, then so am I," he says. "I'm glad it's over."

"Me, too." In my quest for the perfect man, I came close to losing everything... Priscilla, Sam, and myself. It makes me shiver, to think how close I came.

"You're cold." He grabs my hands, rubs them briskly. "I'll turn up the heat."

"No, I'm fine." I study him for a moment. "I can't get over how good you look. Healthy and tan, like you spent lots of time in the sun." I venture a small smile. "Have you been going to a tanning salon?"

"Me?" He chuckles. "I just got back from a ten-day cruise."

His words catch me by surprise. I was half-kidding.

"I told you we shut down the office every year for two weeks once tax season ends. Usually I go to Arizona, but this year I had the urge to do something different, so I took a cruise instead. I got back today. I haven't even unpacked. When I heard your message on my answering machine, I rushed over to your house, but you weren't there."

"And Priscilla told you where to find me." My heart races as I finish his sentence with a brilliant smile.

"Here at the pool, just like the first day we met." He squeezes my fingers. "I'll never forget how you looked with those wild red curls and your pink bathing suit."

My thoughts flood back to that day last summer. Sam a few lanes over, swimming strong steady strokes while I struggled to keep my head above water in that ugly pink suit.

"By the way, whatever happened to that suit? I always liked it."

"Ugh." I winkle my nose. "I threw it away as soon as I got home that night."

His eyes widen. "You looked cute in it."

"Ha! You mean, I looked fat."

"You're not fat."

"Come on, Sam, we both know that's not true. I need to lose weight. Twenty-five pounds." Just thinking about it makes me groan. "Sometimes I wonder, what's the use? Why bother trying? I'll always be fat."

"Don't be so hard on yourself, Patty. Remember, you're talking about the woman I love."

Love. A tiny smile tugs at the corner of my mouth. Bad as I feel, Sam makes me feel good. And he looks good. I wag a finger at him. "But look at you! You look fantastic. Come on, share some of your diet secrets."

He shrugs. "There's no magic formula. Less fat, more exercise, and skip the desserts. Losing weight is hard work. A lot harder than putting it on."

"Tell me about it." I sigh. "It takes a lot of willpower."

Sam ponders for a minute. "I don't think it's willpower as much as desire," he finally says. "You have to want it for yourself. You have to want it more than anything else. More than you want to pick up the fork."

"But I want it." I grimace. "Besides, if it were that easy, I'd have lost these extra pounds years ago."

"Maybe I didn't say that right," he says carefully. "Being on a diet wasn't easy, but it was simple... once

I learned to tell myself *no*. When I finally started saying *no* to food, I lost weight. It was that simple. And that important. Nothing else mattered."

Something catches in his voice. Something that makes me pause. "But why?"

He stares at me like I'm totally dense. "Why? Because of you, Patty. You made the difference."

"Me?" My forehead wrinkles in a tight frown. "What did I do?"

"You got me to take a good hard look at myself. Until you said those things on New Year's Eve, I was content with the way I was. But you got me to thinking. And I figured if it was that important to you, maybe it should be important to me."

I'm still shamed at the memory of that bitter cold night when I cried out against him. Such cruel, spiteful words, yet somehow Sam found it in his heart to forgive me. And despite the things I said, he never stopped loving me. "You lost weight for me?"

"No, Patty. Much as I love you, I didn't do it for you. I did it for myself." He grips the steering wheel, his knuckles white against the black leather. "I've got to admit, I didn't much like the guy staring back at me in the mirror every morning. He was gaining more weight every year and I was doing my best to ignore him. But after hearing what you said, I took a good hard look at that guy. It was like seeing myself through new eyes. Your eyes. When I finally admitted the truth and accepted myself for who I am, that's when I started losing weight."

"I don't think there's much hope for me," I say with a shaky laugh, swiping away the tears streaming down my cheeks. I'm *Fatty Patty*. That chubby little girl with the bouncy curls and a craving for sweets has always been a part of me. How can I say good-bye?

"You'll never know unless you try."

"But what if it doesn't work? What if I don't lose the weight?" Sam doesn't know what he's asking.

"You still don't get it, do you?" His eyes fasten on my own. "I love you, Patty. I'll love you fat and I'll love you thin, but most of all I'll love you happy. So do us both a favor and make up your mind. I don't care. It's your choice. Either make up with the food and decide to eat, or stick with a diet and lose the weight. But this back-and-forth yo-yo thing is driving you nuts. It hurts me, watching you hurt yourself."

I suck in a deep breath. Is that what I've been doing all my life? Following diets, then giving up, breaking the rules and binging all night? No wonder I feel so crazy when I'm around food. What has chocolate ever given me except for a few moments of pleasure, followed by pounds of guilt, flabby thighs and an empty heart?

My relationship with food is a one-sided love affair.

The thought pulses through my body like a sugar rush. Is Sam right? Can it really be that simple? Can I say *no* and walk away from food?

"I've been trying to lose weight for Priscilla's wedding. I've already lost six pounds—"

"No, Patty, you can't do this for anyone but you," he says. "Not for Priscilla, not for me. Do it for yourself. Love yourself enough to do it. Put down the fork and give your heart a try."

His words bring fresh tears brimming to my eyes and I fish for a Kleenex. It takes a few minutes before I can talk again. "How did you get to be so smart?"

"Let's just say I had a great teacher." He grins. "You taught me everything I know."

"I love you, Sam Curtis," I say, watching as his face lights up with astonishment, then delight. I laugh out loud. It mirrors exactly how I feel inside. "I love you."

"Do you know how long I've waited to hear you say that?" he asks.

"Then I'll never stop saying it." I stroke his cheek. "I love you, Sam. I love you and everything about you… including your moustache. Promise you'll never shave it off?"

The beginning of a smile tugs at his mouth as he slides close and takes me in his arms. "Never is a long time."

"No, first you have to make me that promise." My body sings with a surge of desire at the thought of spending a lifetime in his arms sharing delicious kisses and more.

"Let's say I do decide to keep the moustache. What exactly do I get in return for the favor?" He wiggles his eyebrows suggestively.

"Well, there's always… me," I venture shyly. "But you'd have to be willing to bargain."

"I'm a gambling man, remember?" His lips hungrily graze my own. "I play poker every Wednesday night."

"What about the other six nights?"

"I could think of a thing or two," he whispers huskily in my ear. "Unless the teacher has other ideas."

"I'm more than willing to share a lesson plan," I say, opening my arms to him.

He pulls away some moments later as a car pulls into the pool parking lot, close to Sam's car. "We should probably go. It's getting late."

I swallow a quick smile. We've been going at it like two teenagers in the front seat of his car. I tuck my shirt into my shorts, straighten my clothes. "What about my car?"

"We can come back for it after dinner."

"Please, no place too fancy. I'm not wearing makeup, and my hair…" I lift a hand to my curls and my fingers connect with a wild frizzy mess. "Ugh."

"Relax, you look beautiful." He grins.

"And you're a liar, Sam Curtis." I grin right back.

"Got a taste for anything special?" He throws the car in reverse and carefully backs out of the space. "Just say the word, Patty. What do you want?"

What do I want? I think hard as we swing into traffic. Sam's given me license to eat as I please. He doesn't care if I'm fat or thin. The only one I need to please is myself.

And suddenly, I know exactly what I want. Not food, but Life itself… in every delicious flavor imaginable spread out before me. All I have to do is say *yes* and it's there for the taking. Life, Love, and Sam. What more could I want?

"How about it, Patty? Have you made up your mind?"

"Yes." I glance across at Sam with a brilliant smile. "Yes, I think I have."

EPILOGUE

"Stand still! Arms above your head, and don't breathe."

Madame is tiny, but her bark is mighty and I don't dare do anything but follow the dressmaker's command. I barely breathe as soft folds of shimming silk slip against my skin. The feel of such luxury makes me lightheaded, giddy, and ready to dance—but the dancing will have to wait one more week until the wedding.

"Just as I suspected." The old woman clucks impatiently as she strips her tape measure from around my waist. "We need to take in another inch. Off with the dress."

"I'll help." Priscilla bounces to her feet from a nearby chair.

"Careful," Madame warns as they free me from the delicate fabric. "I'm no miracle worker and if that necklace snags the lace, I won't be able to fix it. You should have taken it off like I told you to do," she admonishes me. "But did you listen? No! The story of my life. None of you girls listen."

I finger the diamond pendant nestled between my breasts. It's my most treasured possession and I haven't taken it off since Sam gave it back to me. I won't, either… Madame or no Madame.

"Don't you dare lose one more pound." The tiny woman wags a crooked finger at me over an armful of shimmering silk. "I'm a busy woman, you know. There's no time to take in this dress again."

"I promise." I wink at Priscilla over Madame's head.

"Like I believe you. You'll come waltzing in here next week, crying that your dress won't fit. You girls are all the same. If I had any sense, I'd retire and move to Florida." With a disdainful sniff, Madame disappears behind a curtain with my wedding gown.

"She sounds serious," Priscilla whispers.

"I don't care where she goes, as long as she doesn't take my dress with her." I smother a quick laugh. "That would give Sam quite a jolt, seeing me walk down the aisle in my slip."

"Sam wouldn't care. He thinks you're beautiful no matter what you wear." She steps back and eyes me thoughtfully. "And he's right, Patty. You are beautiful. You've always been pretty but there's something about you now that wasn't there before."

I grin. "It's called prewedding jitters."

"I don't see what you're so nervous about. Remember my wedding last month when Harold's best man couldn't find the ring? You were the only one who didn't panic."

I chuckle, remembering those tense moments at the altar a few weeks before. Everyone was flustered until I leaned over and pointed out the ring on the best man's pinky finger, exactly where he'd put it for safekeeping.

"Sam is the one I'm worried about," I confess. That man of mine has been operating in panic-mode since Priscilla and Dr. Brown strolled down the aisle a few weeks ago. "Did I tell you his latest idea? He wants to shuck the whole wedding thing and elope."

"He'll be fine," Priscilla predicts. "As for you, just remember what Madame said. Don't lose any more weight. You're perfect just the way you are."

"Think so?" I slip the colorful sheath over my head. A bit snug when I purchased it a few weeks ago, but it finally fits just right. And even though I bought it for our ten-day honeymoon cruise, I couldn't resist wearing it today. I do a happy little twirl in front of the mirror, admiring the way the orange, green, and gold colors glow against my skin.

"Very pretty, but I'm getting hungry." Priscilla pokes her head around the mirror, interrupts my twirl. "Are you ready?"

I slip on my sandals, grab my purse, and trail her out the door into the brilliant sunshine of a James Bay summer day. "Where do you want to eat?"

She points out Chuck's Bar and Grill across the street. "They make a nice chicken Caesar salad."

"Perfect." I link arms with Priscilla and we dart across the busy street. Funny, how time—and love— changes all things. Today, a salad lightly tossed with parmesan cheese, a drizzle of dressing and a side of grilled chicken sounds just right. I've grown to appreciate how good even simple foods taste. A freshly washed pear. Sweet juicy strawberries. I especially like the way they leave me feeling inside. Clean and light, not sluggish and sleepy, like after a sugar binge. If anyone had told me a year ago that I would sleep better, think clearer and feel better, all because of the food I chose to put in my mouth, I would have laughed in their face. But Sam was right. Eating healthy is simple, once you make the decision. But who would have guessed that it starts with one bite?

Just one bite saved my life.

No more worrying about trying to have it all, about trying to make my life—and my body—the way I think they should be. I've lost weight, but I'm still stuck with frizzy curls and chunky thighs. Well, so be it. I am what I am, and life is what it is. I'm dong wasting my time worrying about it. I have better things to do.

No more hiding out in bed with chocolate. No more fear that my body will betray me. No more dreading the thought of a brand new day.

No more living to eat. From now on, I'm eating to live.

Good-bye, Fatty Patty. Hello, me.

ABOUT THE AUTHOR

Kathleen Irene Paterka fell in love with writing (and food) at a very young age. By the time she graduated high school, she'd completed her first manuscript and she weighed 300 lbs. Though the extra pounds have long since disappeared, Kathleen still carries the emotional scars of being a former fatty. *FATTY PATTY* was born from the cruel teasing she endured on the school playground. Kathleen is the author of numerous novels which embrace universal themes of home, family life and love, including the Women's Fiction series, "*The James Bay Novels*". Kathleen is the resident staff writer for Castle Farms, a world renowned castle listed on the National Historic Register, and co-author of the non-fiction book *FOR THE LOVE OF A CASTLE*, published in 2012. Having lived and studied abroad, Kathleen's educational background includes a Bachelor of Arts degree from Central Michigan University. She and her husband live in the beautiful north country of Michigan's Lower Peninsula. Kathleen loves hearing from readers. You can contact her via her website at www.kathleenirenepaterka.com.

www.ingramcontent.com/pod-product-compliance
Lightning Source LLC
Chambersburg PA
CBHW020238200626
46816CB00001BA/24